STRANGE CASE OF
DR JEKYLL AND MR HYDE

broadview editions
series editor: L.W. Conolly

Robert Louis Stevenson.

STRANGE CASE OF
DR JEKYLL AND MR HYDE

Robert Louis Stevenson

third edition

edited by Martin A. Danahay

broadview editions

Library and Archives Canada Cataloguing in Publication

Stevenson, Robert Louis, 1850-1894, author
    Strange case of Dr Jekyll and Mr Hyde / Robert Louis Stevenson ; edited by Martin A. Danahay.—Third edition.

(Broadview editions)
Includes bibliographical references.
ISBN 978-1-55481-024-6 (pbk.)

    I. Danahay, Martin A., editor II. Title. III. Series: Broadview editions

PR5485.A2D36 2015   823'.8   C2015-901303-8

Broadview Editions

The Broadview Editions series represents the ever-changing canon of literature in English by bringing together texts long regarded as classics with valuable lesser-known works.

Advisory editor for this volume: Michel Pharand

Broadview Press is an independent, international publishing house, incorporated in 1985.

We welcome comments and suggestions regarding any aspect of our publications—please feel free to contact us at the addresses below or at broadview@broadviewpress.com.

North America
PO Box 1243, Peterborough, Ontario K9J 7H5, Canada
555 Riverwalk Parkway, Tonawanda, NY 14150, USA
Tel: (705) 743-8990; Fax: (705) 743-8353
email: customerservice@broadviewpress.com

UK, Europe, Central Asia, Middle East, Africa, India, and Southeast Asia
Eurospan Group, 3 Henrietta St., London WC2E 8LU, United Kingdom
Tel: 44 (0) 1767 604972; Fax: 44 (0) 1767 601640
email: eurospan@turpin-distribution.com

Australia and New Zealand
Footprint Books
1/6a Prosperity Parade, Warriewood, NSW 2102, Australia
Tel: 61 1300 260 090; Fax: 61 02 9997 3185
email: info@footprint.com.au

www.broadviewpress.com

Broadview Press acknowledges the financial support of the Government of Canada through the Canada Book Fund for our publishing activities.

Typesetting and assembly: True to Type Inc., Claremont, Canada.

PRINTED IN CANADA

Contents

Acknowledgements

My thanks to the Board of Regents of the University of Texas system and President Robert Witt and Provost George Wright of the University of Texas at Arlington for a Faculty Development Leave that enabled me to complete the research for this volume in a timely fashion. My heartfelt thanks to Professor C. Alex Pinkston who not only helped me indirectly through his article on the Richard Mansfield version of *Dr. Jekyll and Mr. Hyde*, but also provided me with a photocopy of the manuscript at a crucial point in my research. My thanks to the subscribers to the victoria listserver at Indiana University who have provided direct help with obscure references and virtual company for several years via my pc screen. Thanks also to Don LePan and the staff at Broadview Press for the opportunity to work on a text that has fascinated me for many years, and to Barbara Conolly in particular for patiently pointing out ways in which the first version of this edition could be improved. I also gratefully acknowledge the support of the Research and Graduate School of the University of Texas at Arlington, particularly Karl Petruso, for assistance with the permission fees associated with this text.

Material in Appendix E from *An Intimate Portrait of R.L.S.* by Lloyd Osbourne, copyright © 1924 by Charles Scribner's Sons, renewed 1952, is reprinted with the permission of Scribner, an imprint of Simon & Shuster Adult Publishing Group.

The Ernst Schulz studio portraits in Appendix L appear courtesy of the Darwin Collection, Cambridge University Library.

Preface to the Third Edition

The changes for this third edition are a reversion to the original title of the 1886 edition, an update of the introduction on criticism, the addition of two more letters by Robert Louis Stevenson, and a new Appendix on the Victorian gentleman. The title of this edition now reads *Strange Case of Dr Jekyll and Mr Hyde*, which is how it was originally published. Over the years many editions, including the Broadview first and second editions, have added "the" to the title, even though Stevenson regularly referred to his text as "strange case," without a definite article. While it does not affect interpretation of the text, it is more faithful to the original to follow suit and omit the definite article. A choice must often be made between common usage and the history of the text. For instance, one should really pronounce Dr. Jekyll's name "Jeekyll," rather than with the short "e" that is now common; however, adhering to this original pronunciation does not materially change interpretation of the text—although it does ruin the joke in the *Punch* parody where his name is pronounced "treacle." A number of people have questioned the wisdom of including "the" and I accede to their suggestion that I adhere to the original title in this third edition and have omitted the definite article.

One of the additional letters adds some of Stevenson's thoughts about his own "dark side" that comes out in the story, ascribing this partly to his religious upbringing as well as his views on the universality of sin, and the other documents his repudiation of reading the story in sexual terms. The appendix on the gentleman documents Victorian class divisions in terms of the body and clothing. Dr. Jekyll descends the social scale when he becomes a mere Mr., and the text reflects a dissonance between his clothing, which is that of a wealthy man, and his body, which shows signs of a lower class status. The appendix adds texts from Stevenson and others that reflect Victorian fears of the permeability of class boundaries.

As ever I am indebted to Richard Dury both as a friend and scholar for his invaluable advice over the years. I am also indebted to Michel Pharand for an incredibly thorough and helpful edit of the entire edition that uncovered some lurking typographical errors that had escaped notice for many years.

Introduction

Biographical Sketch

Robert Lewis (later changed to "Louis") Balfour Stevenson was born in Edinburgh on 13 November 1850. Stevenson may have adopted the French spelling of "Louis" rather than "Lewis" because there was a man named Lewis whom his father disliked, or because there was a tradition in the family of using the French spelling of the word. His father, Thomas Stevenson, belonged to a family of engineers who had built most of the deep-sea lighthouses around the rocky coast of Scotland. His mother, Margaret Isabella Balfour, came from a family of lawyers and church ministers. In 1857 the family moved to 17 Heriot Row, in the New Town section of Edinburgh. The New Town dated from the late eighteenth century and had wide streets and elegant houses. The poorer Old Town, by contrast, was crowded and slum-ridden. Edinburgh, like London in the nineteenth century, was divided into two distinctive areas, close to each other physically but worlds apart in terms of quality of life.

Stevenson's mother seems to have suffered from many bouts of ill health during Stevenson's formative years, and much of his education was left to the family nurse, Alison Cunningham, whom Stevenson called "Cummy." Stevenson later called Cummy "my second mother, my first wife." Deeply religious, she expounded an extreme Calvinist doctrine to the young Stevenson. She also told him many stories of body snatchers, demons, devils, and ghosts that he was to draw upon later for some of his stories, such as "Thrawn Janet" and "The Body Snatchers." As a child, Stevenson was sickly and often bedridden and also suffered from intense nightmares. Under Cummy's influence he also grew to be a very devout child.

In November 1867, aged 17, Stevenson enrolled at Edinburgh University to study engineering, with the aim of following the family tradition of lighthouse design. However, he abandoned his engineering studies and reached a compromise with his father of studying law rather than becoming a writer, which was his real ambition. Stevenson's choice of law rather than engineering and his subsequent abandonment of law for writing caused contention between father and son. A further breach was opened between them in 1873 when Thomas Stevenson discovered that his son had joined a socialist club at the university and now considered himself an agnostic.

Stevenson was called to the Scottish bar in 1875 but did not practice, since by then he knew that his one desire was to be a professional writer. As a student Stevenson had a reputation for frequenting the areas of the Old Town associated with drinking and vice, as he describes in his poem "Brasheana." He also had the reputation of being a Bohemian in his dress and manner. During summer vacations he went to France to be in the company of other young artists, both writers and painters. His first published work was an essay on travel called "Roads," and his first books were works of travel writing describing his experiences in France.

In Grez, France, in July 1876, Stevenson met Fanny Osbourne and her two children. He was 25, and she was 36. Osbourne was estranged from her husband in the United States and was in France studying art. A romance followed, with Stevenson spending more and more time in Fanny Osbourne's company when she moved to Paris and when she later accompanied him to London. In the summer of 1878 Fanny Osbourne left for the United States when her husband threatened to cut off her financial support if she did not return. She resumed living with him in San Francisco, while Stevenson stayed in London and became more and more despondent. In July 1879 Fanny Osbourne's husband left her, and she sent an urgent telegram to Stevenson informing him of the situation. Stevenson expedited plans to visit the United States and bought a cheap steamship ticket to New York. From New York he rode the railroad west to San Francisco, writing of his experiences in *Across the Plains* (1892) and *The Amateur Emigrant* (1895, posthumously).

Fanny Osbourne finalized the divorce from her husband in December 1879 and married Stevenson in May 1880. Short of money and under considerable stress, Stevenson developed several serious illnesses, one of which was the beginning of tuberculosis-like symptoms that would afflict him for the rest of his life. For their honeymoon the couple squatted in a deserted miner's shack in the Silverado Hills, an episode chronicled by Stevenson in *The Silverado Squatters* (1883).

Fanny and Stevenson returned to Scotland together, able to afford to travel first class this time because Stevenson's father had promised him an income of £250 a year. Thanks partly to Fanny's intervention, Stevenson was reconciled with his father. After a stay in Davos in Switzerland so that Stevenson could receive treatment for his diseased lungs, he and Fanny moved to different locations in southern France, finally settling in Hyères, where Stevenson spent what he said were the happiest days of his life. Becoming persuaded, however, that Hyères was unhealthy, the Stevensons moved to the Auvergne region for the summer and settled in Royat, which had hot springs and mineral waters. They later returned to Hyères. When an epidemic of cholera was reported in the region in June 1884, the Stevensons again left Hyères and reunited with Stevenson's parents in England.

The Stevensons chose to locate in Bournemouth, mainly because Lloyd, Fanny's son, was in school in the area (see Appendix E). Bournemouth at that time was a relatively new seaside resort that advertised itself as a healthy and attractive place to live because of its mild climate and surrounding pine forests. Initially the Stevensons rented "Bonallie Tower," a house in the Bransome Park area of Bournemouth. In February 1885 Stevenson's father provided the money to buy and furnish a house in the more salubrious Westbourne area of the town. It was in this house that Stevenson wrote *Strange Case of Dr. Jekyll and Mr. Hyde*. Stevenson named the house "Skerryvore" after one of the Scottish lighthouses built by his family, and had a model of the original lighthouse placed by the entrance to the house. Stevenson lived in Bournemouth for three years. While at "Skerryvore" he had frequent visits from Henry James, who had a sister living in Bournemouth, and had his portrait painted by James McNeill Whistler.

Stevenson's father died in May 1886, leaving his son a sizeable amount of money and the ability to travel wherever he wanted. The Stevensons left "Skerryvore" for New York on 21 August 1887, where Stevenson—now famous following the success of *Dr. Jekyll and Mr. Hyde*—received a warm welcome. A stage version of the story, produced by T.R. Sullivan and starring Richard Mansfield, opened in Manhattan the week after the Stevensons' arrival (see Appendix G). Stevenson did not see the play, although Fanny and her mother did go to a performance. The Stevensons subsequently went from New York to Saranac in the Adirondack mountains, the site of a sanitorium for consumptive patients, where they rented a trapper's cottage. Here Stevenson wrote *The Master of Ballantrae* (1889).

The Stevensons again abruptly decamped when in May Fanny sent an excited telegram to her husband from California saying that she had found a yacht for hire; Stevenson immediately told her to arrange for the rental. He planned to write a series of letters from the Pacific, for which he had been offered a $10,000 commission. When the yacht reached Polynesia in July 1888 Stevenson was so struck by the beauty of the islands that he decided not to return to America or England but to spend his time cruising around the Pacific islands. In 1890 he settled on Samoa, where he lived for the rest of his short life on an estate called "Vailima," containing waterfalls, precipices, ravines, and tableland. He died at age 44 on Monday, 3 December 1894, and was buried on the summit of Mount Vaea, Samoa.

The Composition of *Dr. Jekyll and Mr. Hyde*

Stevenson credits the idea for the story as emerging from his dreams, as he "saw" scenes in his sleep before writing them down. Stevenson told the *New York Herald* (8 September 1887) that "All I dreamed about Dr. Jekyll was that one man was being pressed into a cabinet, when he swallowed a drug and changed into another being. I awoke and said at once that I had found the missing link for which I had been looking so long, and before I went to sleep almost every detail of the story, as it stands, was clear to me. Of course, writing it was another thing."

Stevenson goes into more detail about the role played by dreams in the composition of *Dr. Jekyll and Mr. Hyde* in the essay "A Chapter on Dreams" (see Appendix A). Like Mary Shelley describing the composition of *Frankenstein*, he credits forces at work during his sleep for giving him images from the story that he later used as the basis of the narrative. The story shows Stevenson's persistent interest in the theme of a "double," a theme also found in *Frankenstein* and several other nineteenth-century stories. Stevenson's earliest attempt to write about such a theme was the melodrama *Deacon Brodie, or the Double Life*, which he co-wrote with W.E. Henley (see Appendix C). The central character of the play is a respected member of his community by day and a burglar by night. Like most of Stevenson's attempts at drama, this was not a commercial success. Stevenson also wrote "Markheim" (see Appendix B) about the same time as *Dr. Jekyll and Mr. Hyde*, exploring the idea of a "double" from a very different perspective in this tale of murder and repentance. The story "Olalla," written in 1885, also uses the theme of a double.

Stevenson wrote *Dr. Jekyll and Mr. Hyde* in September and October 1885. He wrote the first draft in three days, and read it aloud, as he often did, to Fanny and Lloyd Osbourne. Accounts of what happened next are conflicting, but the general course of events is clear. Fanny criticized the work, arguing that Stevenson had missed the allegory and had settled for a piece of sensational writing when it could be a masterpiece. They argued, but Stevenson eventually conceded that Fanny was right and he burned the manuscript. He then set about writing a second version, the *Dr. Jekyll and Mr. Hyde* we know today. Lloyd Osbourne gives one account of the composition of the story in his depiction of Stevenson's years in Bournemouth (see Appendix E).

Stevenson later said that the first draft of the story was the best work he had ever done, and implied that Fanny had ruined his effort. There is much speculation about why Fanny objected to the first draft, and why Stevenson destroyed it shortly afterwards. Some have suggested that the original manuscript dealt with material, perhaps sexual in nature, that a Victorian readership would have found unacceptable. Since the manuscript was destroyed and we have only oblique hints as to its content, the truth on this score will never be known.

Stevenson submitted the story to the publisher Longmans in late October or early November 1885. He had initially offered the story for serialization in *Longmans' Magazine*, but the publisher decided to publish the story as a separate book instead. Stevenson signed a contract for the book on 3 November 1885, with the agreement that he was to receive one-sixth of the retail price as a royalty on the first ten thousand copies immediately, and on all copies above that number sold through Christmas 1885 on 1 January 1886. Longmans went to press with the book right away, but by the time it was produced the bookstores had already taken in all their Christmas stock. The book was withdrawn, therefore, until January 1886. Once published, the book sold 40,000 copies in the first six months. When positive reviews started appearing in *The Times* and other newspapers, sales took off both in England and America and the book became a bestseller.

The Stage Version of *Dr. Jekyll and Mr. Hyde*[1]

The first stage adaptation of Stevenson's story followed soon after its publication in 1886. Richard Mansfield (1854–1907) was a successful American actor-manager with a keen eye for a good plot that could be adapted to the stage. After obtaining

---

1 For excerpts from the text of the play see Appendix G.

rights from Stevenson, Mansfield arranged with the young Boston author Thomas R. Sullivan to write a script for him. Between them Mansfield and Sullivan came up with a play that adds to the cast of characters in the Stevenson story by introducing a romance element, and changes the roles of some of the characters found in the original. The introduction of female characters into a story that originally took place in an almost exclusively male world has been followed in all subsequent adaptations of the story. Stevenson's story was in effect rewritten by Sullivan and Mansfield as a Victorian melodrama, with scenes of romance, secrecy, and despair not found in the original.

The play was performed for the first time at the Boston Museum in May 1887. Mansfield then moved the play to New York, and it opened there on 12 September at Madison Square Theater. Mansfield's performance was received with widespread praise, and the sudden transformation from Dr. Jekyll to Mr. Hyde, achieved through lights and special makeup, was said to provoke gasps of horror from the audience. There was less agreement among critics as to whether the adaptation of the book into a play was an overall success.

Mansfield went to London with his production of *Dr. Jekyll and Mr. Hyde*, opening it at the prestigious Lyceum on 4 August 1888. However, after a successful run of ten weeks Mansfield was forced to close down his production. The scare over the serial murders by the mysterious figure who came to be known as "Jack the Ripper" had prompted a hysteria in London in which even those who only played murderers on the stage were considered suspects. One theatregoer was so horrified by the realism of Mansfield's performance that he became convinced that Mansfield must in fact be Jack the Ripper. When Mansfield's name was mentioned in newspapers as a possible suspect in the crimes, he decided to stop the production. The English newspaper the *Daily Telegraph* claimed that "experience has taught this clever young actor that there is no taste in London for horrors on the stage. There is quite sufficient to make us shudder out of doors." The fictional murderer Mr. Hyde was thus forced off the stage by one of the first internationally famous serial killers.

The Case of "Jack the Ripper"

In the autumn of 1888 several prostitutes were murdered in the East End of London. The hideously brutal crimes were believed to have been committed by the same person. They took place in the crowded and poverty-stricken area of London known as Whitechapel, and the killer was known for a time as the "Whitechapel murderer" (see Appendix J). When one witness claimed that the murderer was wearing a leather garment such as that worn by butchers or tanners, the killer was referred to as "Leather Apron." Finally, after a boastful note was sent to a London newspaper signed by "Jack the Ripper," the killer became known in the press as "Jack the Ripper." The case was never solved.

The Jack the Ripper case is relevant here as litmus test of Victorian attitudes toward crime and such slum areas as Soho, where Mr. Hyde would go to pursue his pleasures, and Whitechapel, where the Ripper murders took place (see Appendix I). The cartoons and poems from *Punch* that were published in reaction to the murders show many of the same anxieties about crime and violence as does *Dr. Jekyll and Mr. Hyde* itself. The *Punch* cartoons and poems see crime as emerging from the slums of London, and betray a fear of crime as a reprisal by the poor and destitute living in these areas. The article from the *New York Times* shows one of the first uses of "Jekyll and Hyde" as a way of referring to a serial killer and also mentions the conjunction of the Jack the Ripper case and Mansfield's stage version of *Dr. Jekyll and Mr. Hyde*.

The case also provoked a widespread debate over the representation of violence in newspapers and fiction, raising questions about possible connections between the widespread publicity of Jack the Ripper's murders, and fictional representations of such acts, and the amount of violence and murder on the streets of London. An article in *The Times* of 10 September 1888 linked horror stories, such as those by Edgar Allan Poe, and the murders by Jack the Ripper, and the 15 September 1888 issue of *Punch* also raises the question of a link between the lurid publicity surrounding dramas such as *Dr. Jekyll and Mr. Hyde* and further crimes of violence. Other writers and cartoonists, however, pointed to other causes of violent crime: police ineptitude, criminal elements in East End London, and deplorable social conditions (see Appendix J).

Soho in the Nineteenth Century

Mr. Hyde lives in the Soho area of London. It is unclear where the name—in use since the Middle Ages—originated, but until the end of the eighteenth century Soho was a very fashionable part of the city. The character of Soho began to change when French Huguenots moved into the area, and it became associated with foreign immigrants and Bohemian artists. In the early nineteenth century the population of Soho grew extremely rapidly with further waves of immigrants, until in 1851 it was one of the most densely populated sections of London. The large houses of the previous wealthy owners were subdivided into several smaller apartments, each housing entire families. In 1854 a serious outbreak of cholera occurred in Soho and the last of the upper-class families moved out. After 1854 Soho became known as an area of cheap foreign restaurants, coffee houses, and bars. It also had a reputation for sleazy entertainment in small venues, some of them very disreputable, and for widespread prostitution.

George Augustus Sala's 1872 description of Soho (Appendix I) emphasizes the mixture of nationalities which had settled in Soho. Sala makes some disparaging references to the appearance and poor diet of the inhabitants and the amount of alcohol consumed, in a way very similar to the descriptions of Soho Stevenson gives when Mr. Utterson goes there. Arthur Ransome's account (Appendix I) is written from the perspective of one who was a poor writer and Bohemian who used to frequent the cheap restaurants and bars of the area. Interestingly, he recounts his meeting with a real-life Jekyll and Hyde, who was a banker during the day but who put on a disguise and pretended to be a Bohemian in Soho at night.

The condition of slum areas was a cause of great concern throughout the Victorian period, but in the 1880s the debate was informed by a vocabulary of "degeneration" drawn from criminologist Cesare Lombroso's texts and a reverse Darwinism that saw the inhabitants of the slums as a throwback to a more "primitive" kind of human being. J. Milner Fothergill was lecturing and writing on this topic at the same time that Stevenson was writing *Dr. Jekyll and Mr. Hyde*, and explicitly claims that a "deterioration of the race" can be seen in the biology of people in the inner-city. William Booth goes so far as to claim that the slums are part of "darkest England" and that the people who live in such areas are like "primitive" tribes inhabiting a forest. Both writers assume that white British males such as themselves are at the pinnacle of an evolutionary hierarchy. They see people living in slum areas of London as a Mr. Hyde: a violent, primitive, and amoral force that threatens mayhem and murder.

Victorian Theories of Degeneration and Crime

While the term "evolution" is well known as one of the central tenets of Charles Darwin's theories of the development of human beings, its counterpart "degeneration" is less famous but equally important. Darwin published his theories initially in *The Origin of Species* in 1859, and elaborated them over the next 13 years in various publications up until *The Descent of Man* (1871). Evolution became an established principle of biological science thanks to Darwin's efforts, but was the subject of much controversy and debate in wider Victorian society. In particular, Victorians were unsettled by the idea that humans were not separate from animals, and by the notion that they could possibly be descended from a hairy quadruped in an earlier phase of evolution. In a debate over Darwin's theories at a meeting of the British Association for the Advancement of Science at Oxford in 1860, Bishop Samuel Wilberforce asked the famous question of the scientist Thomas Henry Huxley: "was it through his grandfather or grandmother that he claimed descent from a monkey?" This question was supposed to destroy Huxley's argument by implying his family tree, far from being traceable back to the Norman Conquest (as many claimed for their lineage), was linked to the animal world. Huxley replied that he was not ashamed to have a monkey for an ancestor, but would be ashamed to be related to a man like Wilberforce, who used his intelligence and eloquence to obscure the truth.

Evolutionary theory was unsettling to the Victorians because it dissolved the boundary between the human and the animal. Contrary to popular belief, Darwin's theories did not suggest that Victorians were descended from monkeys, but that humans and monkeys, while sharing a common ancestor, had followed different evolutionary paths. Darwin's theory of evolution suggested that organisms adapted to their environment by a process of natural selection in which those that adapted best thrived while others died out. This was a process that was already familiar in the deliberate breeding of horses and dogs, and Darwin argued that a similar process was at work in nature through "natural selection."

Darwin elaborated on his theories of the common origins of species in his book *The Expression of Emotions in Man and Animals* (1872). While less famous than *The Origin of Species* this book shows a clear attempt on Darwin's part to draw direct connections between humans and animals. Darwin thought that he could detect identical expressions of emotion in both, and used photographs and drawings of different species to support his thesis. The description of violent emotions in Darwin's text parallels some of the descriptions of Mr. Hyde's emotions in *Dr. Jekyll and Mr. Hyde* (see Appendix H).

Followers of Darwin such as E. Ray Lankester, however, argued that while there was evolution, there was also a reverse process possible and that was "devolution" or "degeneration." Far from moving from simple organisms to more complex ones, Lankester suggested that organisms could "de-evolve" into simpler, less complex forms. If evolution is thought of as a form of progress, or a movement from a lower to a higher plane of existence, then Lankester's theory raised the possibility of moving from a higher to a lower form of existence.

While Lankester was arguing for this evolutionary process in reverse purely within the realm of biology, others were applying similar theories to human nature. The theory of "degeneration" also informs Bram Stoker's horror story *Dracula*.[1] An Italian doctor and early criminologist, Cesare Lombroso argued in his *Criminal Man* (1876) that criminal behaviour had a biological basis and that the brains of criminals were visibly different from those of other human beings. Lombroso further argued that criminals were more primitive than other humans, and represented a throwback to an earlier, more violent period in human development. Lombroso's argument in criminology was thus a direct counterpart to Lankester's theories of degeneration in biology. The text reproduced in Appendix H is a summary of Lombroso's theories by his daughter that makes explicit the evolutionary model at work in his theory of criminals as degenerates.

Lombroso had a profound effect on theories of crime and criminality in continental Europe, but was less of a direct influence in England. Nonetheless, theories of degeneration and the view of crime as a throwback to an earlier, more primitive and violent phase of human development were prevalent in England at the time that Stevenson wrote *Dr. Jekyll and Mr. Hyde*. Stevenson evokes theories of both evolution and degeneration in his descriptions of Mr. Hyde as a kind of monkey, and as a less developed, more primitive version of Dr. Jekyll.

The concept of "degeneration" was also used as a political category, as the excerpt from Zionist physician Max Nordau shows

---

1 See Bram Stoker, *Dracula*, ed. Glennis Byron (Peterborough, ON: Broadview Press, 1998) 468–72.

(see Appendix H). Political and cultural foes could be accused of being degenerates as a way of attacking their agendas. Implicit in Lombroso's theories, and explicit in some of his English counterparts, was the hypothesis that the lower classes were a degenerate form of life, lower on the evolutionary scale than the upper classes. In the English context this meant that some analysts described the working classes as more primitive than the upper classes, and thus more prone to violence and crime. These attitudes come across most forcefully in discussions of the degeneration of urban dwellers of slum areas such as Soho, Whitechapel, and the East End.

Dr. Jekyll and Mr. Hyde and the Critics

Henry James hailed *Dr. Jekyll and Mr. Hyde* as an artistic triumph, but expressed some ambivalence about its "popular" packaging and appeal (see Appendix F). Stevenson shared this ambivalence about the success of his narrative, telling Edmund Gosse that if he was successful he must be doing something wrong. Stevenson was generally caustic about the level of Victorian public taste. Like Mary Shelley's *Frankenstein*, *Dr. Jekyll and Mr. Hyde* has always enjoyed a wide popular readership, but has not until recently received the amount of serious critical attention it deserves. Much of this recent attention, dwelling as it has on the sexuality of the story, would not have pleased Stevenson. In a letter to John Paul Bocock in November 1887, Stevenson argued that the story was a study in hypocrisy, not sexuality, and that in any case sexuality in a story was usually only the vehicle for analysis, not the subject itself.

Most critical analyses of Stevenson's work in the early- and mid-twentieth century were disparaging of *Dr. Jekyll and Mr. Hyde*, although the story continued to be a popular success and was turned into movies, such as MGM's 1941 film version starring Spencer Tracy and Ingrid Bergman. Stevenson was not viewed as an important Victorian author until the 1970s' revival in Scottish interest in Stevenson, as shown by Jenni Calder's 1980 biography and her 1980 collection of essays, *Robert Louis Stevenson: A Critical Celebration*. Earlier developments within literary theory had also helped Stevenson to become more prominent. With the increasing influence of psychoanalysis, and the story's obvious similarities to a Freudian model of repression of the unconscious and the struggle between id and superego, analyses of *Dr. Jekyll and Mr. Hyde* as a psychological study were written by Tymms (1949), Kanzer (1951), Rogers (1970), and Schultz (1971). This strand of analysis culminates in Ronald R. Thomas's *Dreams of Authority* (1990). The psychological analysis of *Dr. Jekyll and Mr. Hyde* shaded into a widespread interest in the theme of "doubles" in nineteenth-century literature in books by Miyoshi (1969) and Miller (1985) on the "divided subject."

The most insightful analyses of the text from the perspective of sexuality have been written by Stephen Heath (1986) and Elaine Showalter (1990). Heath argues that the violence in the text is actually displaced sexuality and that "random violence replaces the sexual drive" (93–94). He also cites the connection to Freud's theories of the "ego as a facade" and his comments on the function of repression in *Civilization and Its Discontents* (97). Showalter in *Sexual Anarchy* places the text in the context of Victorian anxieties over homosexuality. Showalter sees hints of homosexuality in Stevenson himself, quoting Andrew Lang's statement that Stevenson "possessed more than any man I have ever met, the power of making other men fall in love with him" (Lang, "Recollections of Robert Louis Stevenson," 51). While conceding that Stevenson's real sexuality is not the primary issue in the text, Showalter goes on to read *Dr. Jekyll and Mr. Hyde* as a "fable of fin-de-siècle homosexual panic" in reaction to an increasingly active and vocal homosexual subculture (107).

The most important and influential re-evaluation of Stevenson in general, and of *Dr. Jekyll and Mr. Hyde* in particular, commemorated the book's one-hundredth anniversary. Edited by William Veeder and Gordon Hirsch, *Dr. Jekyll and Mr. Hyde after One Hundred Years* (1988) is a variorum edition of the text and a collection of excellent analyses of the story and of subsequent adaptations.

Dr. Jekyll and Mr. Hyde also benefited from the turn to "cultural studies" in literary criticism, which has helped erode the distinction between élite and popular texts. *Dr. Jekyll and Mr. Hyde* has become appreciated as an expression of Victorian cultural anxieties and also as an interesting barometer of the way these anxieties have changed in the different stage and screen adaptations; this is the subject of studies by Nollen (1994) and Rose (1996). C. Alex Pinkston (1996) has provided an invaluable analysis of the way in which Stevenson's tale was adapted for the stage by Richard Mansfield and T.R. Sullivan. The story has also benefited from the increased interest in nonfiction, especially in autobiography. Analyses such as those by Danahay (1993) and Thomas (1990) treat the story as an expression of anxieties about self-revelation through autobiography. *Dr. Jekyll and Mr. Hyde* ends with Dr. Jekyll's autobiographical statement in which he finally lays claim to both sides of his identity. Jekyll's autobiography, however, shows great resistance to making the "secret" world of the private individual into public knowledge through the use of the first person. Even in his last confession, Henry Jekyll says he cannot say "I" when describing Mr. Hyde's actions, he must say "he."

Stephen Arata, in *Fictions of Loss in the Victorian Fin de Siècle* (1996), cites the influence of Lombroso's "discovery" that criminals were a throwback to humanity's savage past, and sees Mr. Hyde as bearing the signs of criminal degeneracy (33). Arata places the fear of degeneracy and atavism within the discourse of "professionalism" in Victorian England and sees Hyde's vices as endemic to the upper classes and his lifestyle as that of a "monied gentleman" (35). Arata argues that the most compelling aspect of the text is "the way in which it turns the class discourses of atavism and criminality back on the bourgeoisie itself" (36). Such a reading corresponds well with Stevenson's overtly critical attitude to the Victorian bourgeoisie.

Arata also sees the story as expressing Stevenson's own anxieties on becoming a "professional" writer. Arata claims that the publication of *Dr. Jekyll and Mr. Hyde* "marked the emergence of Stevenson as a 'professional' author in the narrow sense of being able, for the first time, to support himself solely by means of his trade" (43). He quotes Stevenson as saying that when he received a lucrative commission from *Scribner's Magazine*, he was "*bourgeois* now" because of his income (letter to Edmund Gosse, 2 January 1886; see *Letters* II, 313). Arata sees the book as a criticism of the "profession" of writing motivated in large part by Stevenson's ambivalence about becoming implicated himself in the sale of popular books, which he likened to prostitution. In a letter to Edmund Gosse, Stevenson complained that "we are whores, some of us petty whores, some of us not; whores of the mind, selling to the public the amusements of our fire-side as the whore sells the pleasures of the bed" (Arata, 49).

Increasingly, the social context of Bournemouth is being recognized as a determining factor in the composition of *Dr. Jekyll and Mr. Hyde*. The years in Bournemouth undoubtedly were difficult and in many ways a time of crisis for Stevenson. As I suggest in Appendix E, Stevenson's anxieties about becoming a homeowner and member of the bourgeoisie spill over into the house symbolism in the story. Stevenson was always interested in the idea of a "double" life, as he showed by his working over several years on *Deacon Brodie* and other such tales, but while living in Bournemouth these interests took a particular form because of his environment. In part, as Arata suggests, *Dr. Jekyll and Mr. Hyde* is a criticism of the hypocrisy of Victorian "professionals," including professional writers, but it is also a criticism of the veneer of gentility that concealed so much of what was really going on in Victorian bourgeois society.

Patrick Brantlinger in *The Reading Lesson* (1998) has placed *Dr. Jekyll and Mr. Hyde* in the context of the increasing literacy of the Victorian public. Brantlinger notes that the novel "was packaged from the start to be a best-seller" and was like other lurid tales called "shilling shockers" (166). Brantlinger cites Stevenson's ambivalence about the marketplace for books and the status of his text as a "best-seller" and argues that this ambivalence was just one of the many structural splits in both the author and the text that led to his abiding interest in "double lives." Brantlinger sees in Stevenson's story a profound distrust of "criminal popularity" and reads Mr. Hyde as a figure for the debased tastes of a Victorian readership that seemed to have an insatiable appetite for shocking tales of murder. Interestingly, Brantlinger's analysis brings us full circle back to Henry James's ambivalence about the "best-seller" status of Stevenson's tale. While *Dr. Jekyll and Mr. Hyde* is now assigned in college courses as a masterpiece worthy of critical attention, it appears that its origins as popular "shilling shocker" continue to mark it as a deviant text.

Julia Reid, in *Robert Louis Stevenson, Science and the Fin de Siècle* (2006), places Stevenson within the late nineteenth-century debate over evolution and degeneration. The book ranges widely over all of Stevenson's works, but in her chapter on "Gothic Gnomes" she deals with a number of tales, including *Jekyll and Hyde*, that are "haunted" by the specter of degeneration. Reading the story in the context of late-Victorian theories of "multiplex personality" and atavism, she argues that the feelings experienced by those who see Hyde manifest the return of "primitive" instincts that are repressed in civilized Victorian society but reanimated by Jekyll's potion.

Much analysis of *Jekyll and Hyde* since 2000 has taken place in two venues: collections of essays on Robert Louis Stevenson and in the new *Journal of Stevenson Studies*, which started publishing in 2005. Collections include *Robert Louis Stevenson: Writer of Boundaries* (2006) and *European Stevenson* (2009) both edited by Richard Ambrosini and Richard Dury and based on conference proceedings, and *Robert Louis Stevenson and Joseph Conrad: Writers of Transition* edited by Linda Dryden, Stephen Arata, and Eric Massie (2009). While these collections address Stevenson's oeuvre as a whole, each contains individual articles that discuss *Jekyll and Hyde*. Other studies have used the figure of the double to link Stevenson with texts by contemporary authors, such as Nathalie Abi-Ezzi's *The Double in the Fiction of R.L. Stevenson, Wilkie Collins, and Daphne du Maurier* (2003) and Linda Dryden's *The Modern Gothic and Literary Doubles* (2003). In addition the MLA *Approaches to Teaching the Works of Robert Louis Stevenson* (2013) edited by Caroline McCracken-Flesher contains essays on the Gothic and individual studies of the tale in terms of its "strangeness" and as science fiction.

In the *Journal of Stevenson Studies* David Annwn's "'The Gnome's Lighted Scrolls': Consumerism and Pre-cinematic Visual Technologies in *The Strange Case of Dr. Jekyll and Mr. Hyde*" (2010) reads Utterson's nightmare as prefiguring later film adaptations of the story. Sara Rizzo extends analysis further into the area of graphic novels in her "Graphic visions of Dr. Jekyll" (2009). Dana Fore's "Snatching Identity: 'Passing' and Disabled Monstrosity in Stevenson's *Jekyll and Hyde* and 'The Body Snatcher'" suggests that Stevenson himself, because of his health issues, could be termed disabled and links this to the "deformity" of Mr. Hyde. The inauguration of such a journal is testament to the increasing interest in Stevenson as an innovative and influential writer of prose and poetry.

Judith Halberstam in *Skin Shows: Gothic Horror and the Technology of Monsters* (1995) has described Gothic texts like *Jekyll and Hyde* as "meaning machines available for any kind of reading" (26). In her interpretation she places the text primarily within the context of heterosexual panic and homoerotic bonds. Linking *Jekyll and Hyde* and Wilde's *Dorian Gray* she argues that in their largely male society homosexuality haunts both texts, as embodied by the ugly Hyde and the overly attractive Dorian. A large part of her analysis is based on the review by Henry James in Appendix F, and his remarks on how Stevenson achieves his literary effect without the need for women in the plot.

Halberstam's assertion that the text is a "meaning machine" has been borne out in that *Jekyll and Hyde* has continued to provoke interpretation and attempts to solve the mystery of Mr. Hyde. As Richard Dury notes in his 2004 Edinburgh edition of the text, Mr. Hyde "eludes interpretation" and "seems a signifier for everything that is feared and so hidden and excluded from consciousness" (xxix), which is what makes him such a potent cypher. Mr. Hyde can thus represent any in a long list of symptoms of cultural anxiety, and Dury enumerates them: "instinctive drives, non rational-behaviour and motivation, homosexuality, the feminine, corporeality, materiality, decay and death, annihilation and meaninglessness and also (on a sociological level) the urban poor and the criminal underclass" (xxxix). All of these interpretations of the text's significance have been proffered in the last two decades, as Mr. Hyde is adapted to the contours of each culture's most deep-seated fears and desires. Brian Rose in *Jekyll and Hyde Adapted* called *Jekyll and Hyde* a "tracer text" that could be used to diagnose the most profound anxieties of a culture, and the proliferating interpretations and adaptations of the story show that the mystery still provokes the same desire to decipher the elusive "Gothic gnome" at the heart of the story.

Robert Louis Stevenson: A Brief Chronology

1850 Robert Louis Stevenson born 13 November at 8 Howard Place, Edinburgh.

1857 Stevenson family moves to New Town section of Edinburgh.

1867 Enters Edinburgh University to study engineering.

1871 Gives up engineering for law.

1872 Passes preliminary examinations for the Scottish bar.

1875 Meets William Ernest Henley in Edinburgh Infirmary; Henley becomes close friend and literary collaborator. Visits art colonies at Grez and Fontainebleau, where he meets Fanny Osbourne. Admitted to Scottish bar.

1876 Canoe trip down the Oise River.

1878 Fanny Osbourne returns to America. Walking trip through the Cevennes. *An Inland Voyage*; *Picturesque Notes on Edinburgh*.

1879 Writes *Deacon Brodie*, a play, with Henley. Leaves for America. Spends time in Monterey, California, with Fanny Osbourne and her family. *Travels with a Donkey*. Moves to San Francisco. Married to Fanny in May; honeymoon at Silverado. Returns to England in August.

1880 *Deacon Brodie, or, The Double Life* published.

1881 Davos, Switzerland. Meets John Addington Symonds. *Virginibus Puerisque*; "Thrawn Janet."

1882 Lives in the south of France. *Familiar Studies of Men and Books*; *New Arabian Nights*.

1883 Hyères, France. *The Silverado Squatters*; *Treasure Island*.

1884 Leaves Hyères for Bournemouth. "Markheim"; "The Body Snatcher."

1885 "Skerryvore," Bournemouth. Writes more plays with Henley. Henry James visits regularly. September to October, writes *Strange Case of Dr. Jekyll and Mr. Hyde*; submits story to Longmans, Green and Company by 1 November. *A Child's Garden of Verses*; *More New Arabian Nights*; *Prince Otto*.

1886 January 9: *Dr. Jekyll and Mr. Hyde* published in England by Longman, Green and Company, and in the US by Charles Scribner's Sons; *Kidnapped*.

1887 Death of his father, Thomas Stevenson. Sails for
      America; arrives in New York City on 7 September.
      Settles at Saranac, New York. *Underwoods*; *Memories and
      Portraits*.

1888 Fanny leaves for California to find a yacht. Stevenson
      sails for the South Seas aboard the yacht *Casco*. First
      cruise to visit various islands: The Marquesas, The Pau-
      motus, The Society Islands, Hawaii.

1889 Leaves Honolulu aboard the *Equator* on second cruise.
      Purchases estate in Samoa. *The Wrong Box*; *The Master of
      Ballantrae*.

1890 Third cruise, this time aboard the ship *Janet Nicoll*.
      Settles in Samoa.

1891 *Ballads*.

1892 *Across the Plains*; *A Footnote to History*.

1893 *Island Nights' Entertainments*; *Catriona*.

1894 Stevenson dies in Samoa on 3 December. *The Ebb-Tide*.

A Note on the Text

This Broadview edition reproduces the text of the first edition of *Strange Case of Dr. Jekyll and Mr. Hyde* published by Longman, Green and Company in January 1886. While some errors of chronology in the dating of some parts of the story have been noted by later critics, these have been left uncorrected so that the text appears here as originally published.

STRANGE CASE OF DR JEKYLL AND MR HYDE

Cover of an 1897 edition of *Dr Jekyll and Mr Hyde*.

Mr. Utterson the lawyer was a man of a rugged countenance that was never lighted by a smile; cold, scanty and embarrassed in discourse; backward in sentiment; lean, long, dusty, dreary and yet somehow lovable. At friendly meetings, and when the wine was to his taste, something eminently human beaconed from his eye; something indeed which never found its way into his talk, but which spoke not only in these silent symbols of the after-dinner face, but more often and loudly in the acts of his life. He was austere with himself; drank gin when he was alone, to mortify a taste for vintages; and though he enjoyed the theatre, had not crossed the doors of one for twenty years. But he had an approved tolerance for others; sometimes wondering, almost with envy, at the high pressure of spirits involved in their misdeeds; and in any extremity inclined to help rather than to reprove. "I incline to Cain's heresy," he used to say quaintly: "I let my brother go to the devil in his own way."[1] In this character, it was frequently his fortune to be the last reputable acquaintance and the last good influence in the lives of down-going men. And to such as these, so long as they came about his chambers, he never marked a shade of change in his demeanour.

No doubt the feat was easy to Mr. Utterson; for he was undemonstrative at the best, and even his friendship seemed to be founded in a similar catholicity of good-nature. It is the mark of a modest man to accept his friendly circle ready-made from the hands of opportunity; and that was the lawyer's way. His friends were those of his own blood or those whom he had known the longest; his affections, like ivy, were the growth of time, they implied no aptness in the object. Hence, no doubt, the bond that united him to Mr. Richard Enfield, his distant kinsman, the well-known man about town. It was a nut to crack for many,[2] what these two could see in each other or what subject they could find in common. It was reported by those who encountered them in their Sunday walks, that they said nothing, looked singularly dull, and would hail with obvious relief the appearance of a friend. For all that, the two men put the greatest store by these excursions, counted them the chief jewel of each week, and not only set aside occasions of pleasure,

---

1   In Genesis 4:9 Cain refuses to accept responsibility for his brother Abel: "Am I my brother's keeper?"

2   It was difficult for people to understand.

but even resisted the calls of business, that they might enjoy them uninterrupted.

It chanced on one of these rambles that their way led them down a by-street in a busy quarter of London. The street was small and what is called quiet, but it drove a thriving trade on the week-days. The inhabitants were all doing well, it seemed, and all emulously hoping to do better still, and laying out the surplus of their gains in coquetry; so that the shop fronts stood along that thoroughfare with an air of invitation, like rows of smiling sales-women. Even on Sunday, when it veiled its more florid charms and lay comparatively empty of passage, the street shone out in contrast to its dingy neighbourhood, like a fire in a forest; and with its freshly painted shutters, well-polished brasses, and general cleanliness and gaiety of note, instantly caught and pleased the eye of the passenger.

Two doors from one corner, on the left hand going east, the line was broken by the entry of a court; and just at that point, a certain sinister block of building thrust forward its gable[1] on the street. It was two storeys high; showed no window, nothing but a door on the lower storey and a blind forehead of discoloured wall on the upper; and bore in every feature, the marks of prolonged and sordid negligence. The door, which was equipped with neither bell nor knocker, was blistered and distained. Tramps slouched into the recess and struck matches on the panels; children kept shop upon the steps; the schoolboy had tried his knife on the mouldings; and for close on a generation, no one had appeared to drive away these random visitors or to repair their ravages.

Mr. Enfield and the lawyer were on the other side of the by-street; but when they came abreast of the entry, the former lifted up his cane and pointed.

"Did you ever remark that door?" he asked; and when his companion had replied in the affirmative, "It is connected in my mind," added he, "with a very odd story."

"Indeed?" said Mr. Utterson, with a slight change of voice, "and what was that?"

"Well, it was this way," returned Mr. Enfield: "I was coming home from some place at the end of the world, about three o'clock of a black winter morning, and my way lay through a part of town where there was literally nothing to be seen but lamps. Street after street and all the folks asleep—street after street, all

---

1 The vertical side of a house that has a triangular shape at its top.

lighted up as if for a procession and all as empty as a church—till at last I got into that state of mind when a man listens and listens and begins to long for the sight of a policeman. All at once, I saw two figures: one a little man who was stumping along eastward at a good walk, and the other a girl of maybe eight or ten who was running as hard as she was able down a cross street. Well, sir, the two ran into one another naturally enough at the corner; and then came the horrible part of the thing; for the man trampled calmly over the child's body and left her screaming on the ground. It sounds nothing to hear, but it was hellish to see. It wasn't like a man; it was like some damned Juggernaut.[1] I gave a view halloa,[2] took to my heels, collared my gentleman, and brought him back to where there was already quite a group about the screaming child. He was perfectly cool and made no resistance, but gave me one look, so ugly that it brought out the sweat on me like running. The people who had turned out were the girl's own family; and pretty soon, the doctor, for whom she had been sent, put in his appearance. Well, the child was not much the worse, more frightened, according to the Sawbones;[3] and there you might have supposed would be an end to it. But there was one curious circumstance. I had taken a loathing to my gentleman at first sight. So had the child's family, which was only natural. But the doctor's case was what struck me. He was the usual cut and dry apothecary, of no particular age and colour, with a strong Edinburgh accent and about as emotional as a bagpipe. Well, sir, he was like the rest of us; every time he looked at my prisoner, I saw that Sawbones turn sick and white with desire to kill him. I knew what was in his mind, just as he knew what was in mine; and killing being out of the question, we did the next best. We told the man we could and would make such a scandal out of this as should make his name stink from one end of London to the other. If he had any friends or any credit, we undertook that he should lose them. And all the time, as we were pitching it in red hot, we were keeping the women off him as best we could for they were as wild as harpies.[4] I never saw a circle of such hateful faces; and there was the man in the middle, with a

---

1 Originally a Sanskrit term (one of the names of Krishna), in Victorian England used to denote a force that crushes people to death.
2 A hunter's cry when a fox has been sighted.
3 Slang for a doctor, especially a surgeon.
4 Figures from Greek mythology with a woman's face and body, and a bird's wings and claws, who carried out divine vengeance.

kind of black sneering coolness—frightened too, I could see that—but carrying it off, sir, really like Satan. 'If you choose to make capital out of this accident,' said he, 'I am naturally helpless. No gentleman but wishes to avoid a scene,' says he. 'Name your figure.' Well, we screwed him up to a hundred pounds for the child's family; he would have clearly liked to stick out; but there was something about the lot of us that meant mischief, and at last he struck. The next thing was to get the money; and where do you think he carried us but to that place with the door?— whipped out a key, went in, and presently came back with the matter of ten pounds in gold and a cheque for the balance on Coutts's,[1] drawn payable to bearer and signed with a name that I can't mention, though it's one of the points of my story, but it was a name at least very well known and often printed. The figure was stiff; but the signature was good for more than that if it was only genuine. I took the liberty of pointing out to my gentleman that the whole business looked apocryphal,[2] and that a man does not, in real life, walk into a cellar door at four in the morning and come out of it with another man's cheque for close upon a hundred pounds. But he was quite easy and sneering. 'Set your mind at rest,' says he, 'I will stay with you till the banks open and cash the cheque myself.' So we all set off, the doctor, and the child's father, and our friend and myself, and passed the rest of the night in my chambers; and next day, when we had breakfasted, went in a body to the bank. I gave in the cheque myself, and said I had every reason to believe it was a forgery. Not a bit of it. The cheque was genuine."

"Tut-tut," said Mr. Utterson.

"I see you feel as I do," said Mr. Enfield. "Yes, it's a bad story. For my man was a fellow that nobody could have to do with, a really damnable man; and the person that drew the cheque is the very pink of the proprieties, celebrated too, and (what makes it worse) one of your fellows who do what they call good. Black mail, I suppose; an honest man paying through the nose for some of the capers of his youth. Black Mail House is what I call the place with the door, in consequence. Though even that, you know, is far from explaining all," he added, and with the words fell into a vein of musing.

---

1   Coutts & Company private bank (founded 1692) served nobility, landed gentry, and wealthy clients in the nineteenth century.
2   Counterfeit or false.

From this he was recalled by Mr. Utterson asking rather suddenly: "And you don't know if the drawer of the cheque lives there?"

"A likely place, isn't it?" returned Mr. Enfield. "But I happen to have noticed his address; he lives in some square or other."

"And you never asked about the—place with the door?" said Mr. Utterson.

"No, sir: I had a delicacy," was the reply. "I feel very strongly about putting questions; it partakes too much of the style of the day of judgment. You start a question, and it's like starting a stone. You sit quietly on the top of a hill; and away the stone goes, starting others; and presently some bland old bird (the last you would have thought of) is knocked on the head in his own back garden and the family have to change their name. No sir, I make it a rule of mine: the more it looks like Queer Street,[1] the less I ask."

"A very good rule, too," said the lawyer.

"But I have studied the place for myself," continued Mr. Enfield. "It seems scarcely a house. There is no other door, and nobody goes in or out of that one but, once in a great while, the gentleman of my adventure. There are three windows looking on the court on the first floor; none below; the windows are always shut but they're clean. And then there is a chimney which is generally smoking; so somebody must live there. And yet it's not so sure; for the buildings are so packed together about the court, that it's hard to say where one ends and another begins."

The pair walked on again for a while in silence; and then "Enfield," said Mr. Utterson, "that's a good rule of yours."

"Yes, I think it is," returned Enfield.

"But for all that," continued the lawyer, "there's one point I want to ask: I want to ask the name of that man who walked over the child."

"Well," said Mr. Enfield, "I can't see what harm it would do. It was a man of the name of Hyde."

"Hm," said Mr. Utterson. "What sort of a man is he to see?"

"He is not easy to describe. There is something wrong with his appearance; something displeasing, something downright detestable. I never saw a man I so disliked, and yet I scarce know why. He must be deformed somewhere; he gives a strong feeling of deformity, although I couldn't specify the point. He's an extraordinary looking man, and yet I really can name nothing out

---

1 Strange or odd, also with a suggestion of sexual secrets.

of the way. No, sir; I can make no hand of it; I can't describe him. And it's not want of memory; for I declare I can see him this moment."

Mr. Utterson again walked some way in silence and obviously under a weight of consideration. "You are sure he used a key?" he inquired at last.

"My dear sir ..." began Enfield, surprised out of himself.

"Yes, I know," said Utterson; "I know it must seem strange. The fact is, if I do not ask you the name of the other party, it is because I know it already. You see, Richard, your tale has gone home. If you have been inexact in any point you had better correct it."

"I think you might have warned me," returned the other with a touch of sullenness. "But I have been pedantically exact, as you call it. The fellow had a key; and what's more, he has it still. I saw him use it not a week ago."

Mr. Utterson sighed deeply but said never a word; and the young man presently resumed. "Here is another lesson to say nothing," said he. "I am ashamed of my long tongue. Let us make a bargain never to refer to this again."

"With all my heart," said the lawyer. "I shake hands on that, Richard."

Search for Mr. Hyde

That evening Mr. Utterson came home to his bachelor house in sombre spirits and sat down to dinner without relish. It was his custom of a Sunday, when this meal was over, to sit close by the fire, a volume of some dry divinity[1] on his reading desk, until the clock of the neighbouring church rang out the hour of twelve, when he would go soberly and gratefully to bed. On this night however, as soon as the cloth was taken away, he took up a candle and went into his business room. There he opened his safe, took from the most private part of it a document endorsed on the envelope as Dr. Jekyll's Will, and sat down with a clouded brow to study its contents. The will was holograph,[2] for Mr. Utterson, though he took charge of it now that it was made, had refused to lend the least assistance in the making of it; it provided not only that, in case of the decease of Henry Jekyll, M.D., D.C.L., L.L.D.,

---

1 A dense, theological treatise.
2 Handwritten by the will maker himself.

F.R.S., etc.,[1] all his possessions were to pass into the hands of his "friend and benefactor Edward Hyde," but that in case of Dr. Jekyll's "disappearance or unexplained absence for any period exceeding three calendar months," the said Edward Hyde should step into the said Henry Jekyll's shoes without further delay and free from any burthen or obligation, beyond the payment of a few small sums to the members of the doctor's household. This document had long been the lawyer's eyesore. It offended him both as a lawyer and as a lover of the sane and customary sides of life, to whom the fanciful was the immodest. And hitherto it was his ignorance of Mr. Hyde that had swelled his indignation; now, by a sudden turn, it was his knowledge. It was already bad enough when the name was but a name of which he could learn no more. It was worse when it began to be clothed upon with detestable attributes; and out of the shifting, insubstantial mists that had so long baffled his eye, there leaped up the sudden, definite presentment of a fiend.

"I thought it was madness," he said, as he replaced the obnoxious paper in the safe, "and now I begin to fear it is disgrace."

With that he blew out his candle, put on a great-coat, and set forth in the direction of Cavendish Square, that citadel of medicine, where his friend, the great Dr. Lanyon, had his house and received his crowding patients. "If anyone knows, it will be Lanyon," he had thought.

The solemn butler knew and welcomed him; he was subjected to no stage of delay, but ushered direct from the door to the dining-room where Dr. Lanyon sat alone over his wine. This was a hearty, healthy, dapper, red-faced gentleman, with a shock of hair prematurely white, and a boisterous and decided manner. At sight of Mr. Utterson, he sprang up from his chair and welcomed him with both hands. The geniality, as was the way of the man, was somewhat theatrical to the eye; but it reposed on genuine feeling. For these two were old friends, old mates both at school and college, both thorough respecters of themselves and of each other, and, what does not always follow, men who thoroughly enjoyed each other's company.

After a little rambling talk, the lawyer led up to the subject which so disagreeably preoccupied his mind.

"I suppose, Lanyon," said he, "you and I must be the two oldest friends that Henry Jekyll has?"

---

1 Doctor of Medicine, Doctor of Civil Laws, Doctor of Laws, Fellow of the Royal Society.

"I wish the friends were younger," chuckled Dr. Lanyon. "But I suppose we are. And what of that? I see little of him now."

"Indeed?" said Utterson. "I thought you had a bond of common interest."

"We had," was the reply. "But it is more than ten years since Henry Jekyll became too fanciful for me. He began to go wrong, wrong in mind; and though of course I continue to take an interest in him for old sake's sake as they say, I see and I have seen devilish little of the man. Such unscientific balderdash," added the doctor, flushing suddenly purple, "would have estranged Damon and Pythias."[1]

This little spirit of temper was somewhat of a relief to Mr. Utterson. "They have only differed on some point of science," he thought; and being a man of no scientific passions (except in the matter of conveyancing), he even added: "It is nothing worse than that!" He gave his friend a few seconds to recover his composure, and then approached the question he had come to put. "Did you ever come across a protege of his—one Hyde?" he asked.

"Hyde?" repeated Lanyon. "No. Never heard of him. Since my time."

That was the amount of information that the lawyer carried back with him to the great, dark bed on which he tossed to and fro, until the small hours of the morning began to grow large. It was a night of little ease to his toiling mind, toiling in mere darkness and besieged by questions.

Six o'clock struck on the bells of the church that was so conveniently near to Mr. Utterson's dwelling, and still he was digging at the problem. Hitherto it had touched him on the intellectual side alone; but now his imagination also was engaged or rather enslaved; and as he lay and tossed in the gross darkness of the night and the curtained room, Mr. Enfield's tale went by before his mind in a scroll of lighted pictures. He would be aware of the great Weld of lamps of a nocturnal city; then of the Figure of a man walking swiftly; then of a child running from the doctor's; and then these met, and that human Juggernaut trod the child down and passed on regardless of her screams. Or else he would see a room in a rich house, where his friend lay asleep, dreaming and smiling at his dreams; and then the door of that room would be opened, the curtains of the bed plucked apart, the sleeper

---

1 Classical legend of two friends so devoted to each other that Damon pledged his life as bail to allow his friend Pythias to be released temporarily from jail.

recalled, and lo! there would stand by his side a Figure to whom power was given, and even at that dead hour, he must rise and do its bidding. The Figure in these two phases haunted the lawyer all night; and if at any time he dozed over, it was but to see it glide more stealthily through sleeping houses, or move the more swiftly and still the more swiftly, even to dizziness, through wider labyrinths of lamplighted city, and at every street corner crush a child and leave her screaming. And still the Figure had no face by which he might know it; even in his dreams, it had no face, or one that baffled him and melted before his eyes; and thus it was that there sprang up and grew apace in the lawyer's mind a singularly strong, almost an inordinate, curiosity to behold the features of the real Mr. Hyde. If he could but once set eyes on him, he thought the mystery would lighten and perhaps roll altogether away, as was the habit of mysterious things when well examined. He might see a reason for his friend's strange preference or bondage (call it which you please) and even for the startling clauses of the will. And at least it would be a face worth seeing: the face of a man who was without bowels of mercy: a face which had but to show itself to raise up, in the mind of the unimpressionable Enfield, a spirit of enduring hatred.

From that time forward, Mr. Utterson began to haunt the door in the by-street of shops. In the morning before office hours, at noon when business was plenty and time scarce, at night under the face of the fogged city moon, by all lights and at all hours of solitude or concourse, the lawyer was to be found on his chosen post.

"If he be Mr. Hyde," he had thought, "I shall be Mr. Seek."

And at last his patience was rewarded. It was a fine dry night; frost in the air; the streets as clean as a ballroom floor; the lamps, unshaken by any wind, drawing a regular pattern of light and shadow. By ten o'clock, when the shops were closed, the by-street was very solitary and, in spite of the low growl of London from all round, very silent. Small sounds carried far; domestic sounds out of the houses were clearly audible on either side of the roadway; and the rumour of the approach of any passenger preceded him by a long time. Mr. Utterson had been some minutes at his post, when he was aware of an odd, light footstep drawing near. In the course of his nightly patrols, he had long grown accustomed to the quaint effect with which the footfalls of a single person, while he is still a great way off, suddenly spring out distinct from the vast hum and clatter of the city. Yet his attention had never before been so sharply and decisively arrested; and it was with a strong, superstitious prevision of success that he withdrew into the entry of the court.

The steps drew swiftly nearer, and swelled out suddenly louder as they turned the end of the street. The lawyer, looking forth from the entry, could soon see what manner of man he had to deal with. He was small and very plainly dressed and the look of him, even at that distance, went somehow strongly against the watcher's inclination. But he made straight for the door, crossing the roadway to save time; and as he came, he drew a key from his pocket like one approaching home.

Mr. Utterson stepped out and touched him on the shoulder as he passed. "Mr. Hyde, I think?"

Mr. Hyde shrank back with a hissing intake of the breath. But his fear was only momentary; and though he did not look the lawyer in the face, he answered coolly enough: "That is my name. What do you want?"

"I see you are going in," returned the lawyer. "I am an old friend of Dr. Jekyll's—Mr. Utterson of Gaunt Street—you must have heard of my name; and meeting you so conveniently, I thought you might admit me."

"You will not find Dr. Jekyll; he is from home," replied Mr. Hyde, blowing in the key. And then suddenly, but still without looking up, "How did you know me?" he asked.

"On your side," said Mr. Utterson, "will you do me a favour?"

"With pleasure," replied the other. "What shall it be?"

"Will you let me see your face?" asked the lawyer.

Mr. Hyde appeared to hesitate, and then, as if upon some sudden reflection, fronted about with an air of defiance; and the pair stared at each other pretty fixedly for a few seconds. "Now I shall know you again," said Mr. Utterson. "It may be useful."

"Yes," returned Mr. Hyde, "it is as well we have met; and à propos, you should have my address." And he gave a number of a street in Soho.[1]

"Good God!" thought Mr. Utterson, "can he too have been thinking of the will?" But he kept his feelings to himself and only grunted in acknowledgment of the address.

"And now," said the other, "how did you know me?"

"By description," was the reply.

"Whose description?"

"We have common friends," said Mr. Utterson.

---

1 District in central London with a reputation for illicit activities. See Appendix I.

"Common friends?" echoed Mr. Hyde, a little hoarsely. "Who are they?"

"Jekyll, for instance," said the lawyer.

"He never told you," cried Mr. Hyde, with a flush of anger. "I did not think you would have lied."

"Come," said Mr. Utterson, "that is not fitting language."

The other snarled aloud into a savage laugh; and the next moment, with extraordinary quickness, he had unlocked the door and disappeared into the house.

The lawyer stood awhile when Mr. Hyde had left him, the picture of disquietude. Then he began slowly to mount the street, pausing every step or two and putting his hand to his brow like a man in mental perplexity. The problem he was thus debating as he walked, was one of a class that is rarely solved. Mr. Hyde was pale and dwarfish, he gave an impression of deformity without any nameable malformation, he had a displeasing smile, he had borne himself to the lawyer with a sort of murderous mixture of timidity and boldness, and he spoke with a husky, whispering and somewhat broken voice; all these were points against him, but not all of these together could explain the hitherto unknown disgust, loathing and fear with which Mr. Utterson regarded him. "There must be something else," said the perplexed gentleman. "There is something more, if I could find a name for it. God bless me, the man seems hardly human! Something troglodytic,[1] shall we say? or can it be the old story of Dr. Fell?[2] or is it the mere radiance of a foul soul that thus transpires through, and transfigures, its clay continent? The last, I think; for O my poor old Harry Jekyll, if ever I read Satan's signature upon a face, it is on that of your new friend."

Round the corner from the by-street, there was a square of ancient, handsome houses, now for the most part decayed from their high estate and let in flats and chambers to all sorts and conditions of men: map-engravers, architects, shady lawyers and the agents of obscure enterprises. One house, however, second from the corner, was still occupied entire; and at the door of this, which wore a great air of wealth and comfort, though it was now plunged in darkness except for the fanlight,[3] Mr. Utterson stopped and knocked. A well-dressed, elderly servant opened the door.

---

1 A troglodyte is a prehistoric cave dweller.

2 "Fell" means deadly or evil, and "Dr. Fell" refers to an old rhyme from the seventeenth century about a doctor with that name.

3 Semicircular window above the front door.

"Is Dr. Jekyll at home, Poole?" asked the lawyer.

"I will see, Mr. Utterson," said Poole, admitting the visitor, as he spoke, into a large, low-roofed, comfortable hall, paved with flags, warmed (after the fashion of a country house) by a bright, open fire, and furnished with costly cabinets of oak. "Will you wait here by the fire, sir? or shall I give you a light in the dining-room?"

"Here, thank you," said the lawyer, and he drew near and leaned on the tall fender. This hall, in which he was now left alone, was a pet fancy of his friend the doctor's; and Utterson himself was wont to speak of it as the pleasantest room in London. But to-night there was a shudder in his blood; the face of Hyde sat heavy on his memory; he felt (what was rare with him) a nausea and distaste of life; and in the gloom of his spirits, he seemed to read a menace in the flickering of the firelight on the polished cabinets and the uneasy starting of the shadow on the roof. He was ashamed of his relief, when Poole presently returned to announce that Dr. Jekyll was gone out.

"I saw Mr. Hyde go in by the old dissecting room door, Poole," he said. "Is that right, when Dr. Jekyll is from home?"

"Quite right, Mr. Utterson, sir," replied the servant. "Mr. Hyde has a key."

"Your master seems to repose a great deal of trust in that young man, Poole," resumed the other musingly.

"Yes, sir, he do indeed," said Poole. "We have all orders to obey him."

"I do not think I ever met Mr. Hyde?" asked Utterson.

"O, dear no, sir. He never *dines* here," replied the butler. "Indeed we see very little of him on this side of the house; he mostly comes and goes by the laboratory."

"Well, good night, Poole."

"Good night, Mr. Utterson."

And the lawyer set out homeward with a very heavy heart. "Poor Harry Jekyll," he thought, "my mind misgives me he is in deep waters! He was wild when he was young; a long while ago to be sure; but in the law of God, there is no statute of limitations. Ay, it must be that; the ghost of some old sin, the cancer of some concealed disgrace: punishment coming, *pede claudo*,[1] years after memory has forgotten and self-love condoned the fault." And the lawyer, scared by the thought, brooded awhile on his own past, groping in all the corners of memory, lest by chance some Jack-

---

1 Literally "on limping foot" (Latin), meaning slowly but inevitably.

in-the-Box of an old iniquity should leap to light there. His past was fairly blameless; few men could read the rolls[1] of their life with less apprehension; yet he was humbled to the dust by the many ill things he had done, and raised up again into a sober and fearful gratitude by the many that he had come so near to doing yet avoided. And then by a return on his former subject, he conceived a spark of hope. "This Master Hyde, if he were studied," thought he, "must have secrets of his own; black secrets, by the look of him; secrets compared to which poor Jekyll's worst would be like sunshine. Things cannot continue as they are. It turns me cold to think of this creature stealing like a thief to Harry's bedside; poor Harry, what a wakening! And the danger of it; for if this Hyde suspects the existence of the will, he may grow impatient to inherit. Ay, I must put my shoulder to the wheel—if Jekyll will but let me," he added, "if Jekyll will only let me." For once more he saw before his mind's eye, as clear as a transparency, the strange clauses of the will.

Dr. Jekyll Was Quite at Ease

A fortnight later, by excellent good fortune, the doctor gave one of his pleasant dinners to some five or six old cronies, all intelligent, reputable men and all judges of good wine; and Mr. Utterson so contrived that he remained behind after the others had departed. This was no new arrangement, but a thing that had befallen many scores of times. Where Utterson was liked, he was liked well. Hosts loved to detain the dry lawyer, when the light-hearted and loose-tongued had already their foot on the threshold; they liked to sit awhile in his unobtrusive company, practising for solitude, sobering their minds in the man's rich silence after the expense and strain of gaiety. To this rule, Dr. Jekyll was no exception; and as he now sat on the opposite side of the fire—a large, well-made, smooth-faced man of fifty, with something of a slyish cast perhaps, but every mark of capacity and kindness—you could see by his looks that he cherished for Mr. Utterson a sincere and warm affection.

"I have been wanting to speak to you, Jekyll," began the latter. "You know that will of yours?"

A close observer might have gathered that the topic was distasteful; but the doctor carried it off gaily. "My poor Utterson,"

---

1 Look back over their past actions.

said he, "you are unfortunate in such a client. I never saw a man so distressed as you were by my will; unless it were that hide-bound pedant, Lanyon, at what he called my scientific heresies. O, I know he's a good fellow—you needn't frown—an excellent fellow, and I always mean to see more of him; but a hide-bound pedant for all that; an ignorant, blatant pedant. I was never more disappointed in any man than Lanyon."

"You know I never approved of it," pursued Utterson, ruthlessly disregarding the fresh topic.

"My will? Yes, certainly, I know that," said the doctor, a trifle sharply. "You have told me so."

"Well, I tell you so again," continued the lawyer. "I have been learning something of young Hyde."

The large handsome face of Dr. Jekyll grew pale to the very lips, and there came a blackness about his eyes. "I do not care to hear more," said he. "This is a matter I thought we had agreed to drop."

"What I heard was abominable," said Utterson.

"It can make no change. You do not understand my position," returned the doctor, with a certain incoherency of manner. "I am painfully situated, Utterson; my position is a very strange—a very strange one. It is one of those affairs that cannot be mended by talking."

"Jekyll," said Utterson, "you know me: I am a man to be trusted. Make a clean breast of this in confidence; and I make no doubt I can get you out of it."

"My good Utterson," said the doctor, "this is very good of you, this is downright good of you, and I cannot find words to thank you in. I believe you fully; I would trust you before any man alive, ay, before myself, if I could make the choice; but indeed it isn't what you fancy; it is not so bad as that; and just to put your good heart at rest, I will tell you one thing: the moment I choose, I can be rid of Mr. Hyde. I give you my hand upon that; and I thank you again and again; and I will just add one little word, Utterson, that I'm sure you'll take in good part: this is a private matter, and I beg of you to let it sleep."

Utterson reflected a little, looking in the fire.

"I have no doubt you are perfectly right," he said at last, getting to his feet.

"Well, but since we have touched upon this business, and for the last time I hope," continued the doctor, "there is one point I should like you to understand. I have really a very great interest in poor Hyde. I know you have seen him; he told me so; and I fear he was rude. But I do sincerely take a great, a very great interest in that young man; and if I am taken away, Utterson, I wish you to promise me that you will bear with him and get his rights for him. I think you would, if you knew all; and it would be a weight off my mind if you would promise."

"I can't pretend that I shall ever like him," said the lawyer.

"I don't ask that," pleaded Jekyll, laying his hand upon the other's arm; "I only ask for justice; I only ask you to help him for my sake, when I am no longer here."

Utterson heaved an irrepressible sigh. "Well," said he, "I promise."

The Carew Murder Case

Nearly a year later, in the month of October, 18—, London was startled by a crime of singular ferocity and rendered all the more notable by the high position of the victim. The details were few and startling. A maid servant living alone in a house not far from the river, had gone upstairs to bed about eleven. Although a fog rolled over the city in the small hours, the early part of the night was cloudless, and the lane, which the maid's window over-looked, was brilliantly lit by the full moon. It seems she was romantically given, for she sat down upon her box, which stood immediately under the window, and fell into a dream of musing. Never (she used to say, with streaming tears, when she narrated that experience), never had she felt more at peace with all men or thought more kindly of the world. And as she so sat she became aware of an aged and beautiful gentleman with white hair, drawing near along the lane; and advancing to meet him, another and very small gentleman, to whom at first she paid less atten-tion. When they had come within speech (which was just under the maid's eyes) the older man bowed and accosted the other with a very pretty manner of politeness. It did not seem as if the subject of his address were of great importance; indeed, from his pointing, it some times appeared as if he were only inquiring his way; but the moon shone on his face as he spoke, and the girl was pleased to watch it, it seemed to breathe such an innocent and old-world kindness of disposition, yet with something high too, as of a well-founded self-content. Presently her eye wandered to the other, and she was surprised to recognise in him a certain Mr. Hyde, who had once visited her master and for whom she had conceived a dislike. He had in his hand a heavy cane, with which he was trifling; but he answered never a word, and seemed to listen with an ill-contained impatience. And then all of a sudden he broke out in a great flame of anger, stamping with his foot, brandishing the cane, and carrying on (as the maid described it) like a madman. The old gentleman took a step back, with the air of one very much surprised and a trifle hurt; and at that Mr. Hyde broke out of all bounds and clubbed him to the earth. And next moment, with ape-like fury, he was trampling his victim under foot and hailing down a storm of blows, under which the bones were audibly shattered and the body jumped upon the roadway. At the horror of these sights and sounds, the maid fainted.

It was two o'clock when she came to herself and called for the police. The murderer was gone long ago; but there lay his victim in the middle of the lane, incredibly mangled. The stick with which the deed had been done, although it was of some rare and very tough and heavy wood, had broken in the middle under the stress of this insensate cruelty; and one splintered half had rolled in the neighbouring gutter—the other, without doubt, had been carried away by the murderer. A purse and a gold watch were found upon the victim; but no cards or papers, except a sealed and stamped envelope, which he had been probably carrying to the post, and which bore the name and address of Mr. Utterson.

This was brought to the lawyer the next morning, before he was out of bed; and he had no sooner seen it and been told the circumstances, than he shot out a solemn lip. "I shall say nothing till I have seen the body," said he; "this may be very serious. Have the kindness to wait while I dress." And with the same grave countenance he hurried through his breakfast and drove to the police station, whither the body had been carried. As soon as he came into the cell, he nodded.

"Yes," said he, "I recognise him. I am sorry to say that this is Sir Danvers Carew."

"Good God, sir," exclaimed the officer, "is it possible?" And the next moment his eye lighted up with professional ambition. "This will make a deal of noise," he said. "And perhaps you can help us to the man." And he briefly narrated what the maid had seen, and showed the broken stick.

Mr. Utterson had already quailed at the name of Hyde; but when the stick was laid before him, he could doubt no longer; broken and battered as it was, he recognised it for one that he had himself presented many years before to Henry Jekyll.

"Is this Mr. Hyde a person of small stature?" he inquired.

"Particularly small and particularly wicked-looking, is what the maid calls him," said the officer.

Mr. Utterson reflected; and then, raising his head, "If you will come with me in my cab," he said, "I think I can take you to his house."

It was by this time about nine in the morning, and the first fog of the season. A great chocolate-coloured pall lowered over heaven, but the wind was continually charging and routing these embattled vapours; so that as the cab crawled from street to street, Mr. Utterson beheld a marvelous number of degrees and hues of twilight; for here it would be dark like the back-end of evening; and there would be a glow of a rich, lurid brown, like the light of some strange conflagration; and here, for a moment, the fog would be quite broken up, and a haggard shaft of daylight would glance in between the swirling wreaths. The dismal quarter of Soho seen under these changing glimpses, with its muddy ways, and slatternly passengers, and its lamps, which had never been extinguished or had been kindled afresh to combat this mournful reinvasion of darkness, seemed, in the lawyer's eyes, like a district of some city in a nightmare. The thoughts of his mind, besides, were of the gloomiest dye; and when he glanced at the companion of his drive, he was conscious of some touch of that terror of the law and the law's officers, which may at times assail the most honest.

As the cab drew up before the address indicated, the fog lifted a little and showed him a dingy street, a gin palace, a low French eating house, a shop for the retail of penny numbers[1] and twopenny salads, many ragged children huddled in the doorways, and many women of many different nationalities passing out, key in hand, to have a morning glass;[2] and the next moment the fog settled down again upon that part, as brown as umber, and cut him off from his blackguardly surroundings. This was the home of Henry Jekyll's favourite; of a man who was heir to a quarter of a million sterling.

An ivory-faced and silvery-haired old woman opened the door. She had an evil face, smoothed by hypocrisy; but her manners were excellent. Yes, she said, this was Mr. Hyde's, but he was not at home; he had been in that night very late, but had gone away again in less than an hour; there was nothing strange in that;

---

1 A reference to "penny dreadfuls," mass circulation magazines containing sensational fiction.

2 An alcoholic drink.

his habits were very irregular, and he was often absent; for instance, it was nearly two months since she had seen him till yesterday.

"Very well then, we wish to see his rooms," said the lawyer; and when the woman began to declare it was impossible, "I had better tell you who this person is," he added. "This is Inspector Newcomen of Scotland Yard."

A flash of odious joy appeared upon the woman's face. "Ah!" said she, "he is in trouble! What has he done?"

Mr. Utterson and the inspector exchanged glances. "He don't seem a very popular character," observed the latter. "And now, my good woman, just let me and this gentleman have a look about us."

In the whole extent of the house, which but for the old woman remained otherwise empty, Mr. Hyde had only used a couple of rooms; but these were furnished with luxury and good taste. A closet was filled with wine; the plate was of silver, the napery elegant; a good picture hung upon the walls, a gift (as Utterson supposed) from Henry Jekyll, who was much of a connoisseur; and the carpets were of many plies and agreeable in colour. At this moment, however, the rooms bore every mark of having been recently and hurriedly ransacked; clothes lay about the floor, with their pockets inside out; lock-fast drawers stood open; and on the hearth there lay a pile of gray ashes, as though many papers had been burned. From these embers the inspector disinterred the butt end of a green cheque book, which had resisted the action of the fire; the other half of the stick was found behind the door; and as this clinched his suspicions, the officer declared himself delighted. A visit to the bank, where several thousand pounds were found to be lying to the murderer's credit, completed his gratification.

"You may depend upon it, sir," he told Mr. Utterson: "I have him in my hand. He must have lost his head, or he never would have left the stick or, above all, burned the cheque book. Why, money's life to the man. We have nothing to do but wait for him at the bank, and get out the handbills."

This last, however, was not so easy of accomplishment; for Mr. Hyde had numbered few familiars—even the master of the servant maid had only seen him twice; his family could nowhere be traced; he had never been photographed; and the few who could describe him differed widely, as common observers will. Only on one point were they agreed; and that was the haunting sense of unexpressed deformity with which the fugitive impressed his beholders.

Incident of the Letter

It was late in the afternoon, when Mr. Utterson found his way to Dr. Jekyll's door, where he was at once admitted by Poole, and carried down by the kitchen offices and across a yard which had once been a garden, to the building which was indifferently known as the laboratory or the dissecting rooms. The doctor had bought the house from the heirs of a celebrated surgeon; and his own tastes being rather chemical than anatomical, had changed the destination of the block at the bottom of the garden. It was the first time that the lawyer had been received in that part of his friend's quarters; and he eyed the dingy, windowless structure with curiosity, and gazed round with a distasteful sense of strangeness as he crossed the theatre, once crowded with eager students and now lying gaunt and silent, the tables laden with chemical apparatus, the floor strewn with crates and littered with packing straw, and the light falling dimly through the foggy cupola. At the further end, a flight of stairs mounted to a door covered with red baize; and through this, Mr. Utterson was at last received into the doctor's cabinet.[1] It was a large room fitted round with glass presses, furnished, among other things, with a cheval glass[2] and a business table, and looking out upon the court by three dusty windows barred with iron. The fire burned in the grate; a lamp was set lighted on the chimney shelf, for even in the houses the fog began to lie thickly; and there, close up to the warmth, sat Dr. Jekyll, looking deadly sick. He did not rise to meet his visitor, but held out a cold hand and bade him welcome in a changed voice.

"And now," said Mr. Utterson, as soon as Poole had left them, "you have heard the news?"

The doctor shuddered. "They were crying it in the square,"[3] he said. "I heard them in my dining-room."

"One word," said the lawyer. "Carew was my client, but so are you, and I want to know what I am doing. You have not been mad enough to hide this fellow?"

"Utterson, I swear to God," cried the doctor, "I swear to God I will never set eyes on him again. I bind my honour to you that

---

1 Archaic term for a small office.
2 A full-length mirror mounted on a frame with hinges so that it can be titled up and down.
3 News vendors would shout out the headlines of the day to help sell their newspapers.

I am done with him in this world. It is all at an end. And indeed he does not want my help; you do not know him as I do; he is safe, he is quite safe; mark my words, he will never more be heard of."

The lawyer listened gloomily; he did not like his friend's feverish manner. "You seem pretty sure of him," said he; "and for your sake, I hope you may be right. If it came to a trial, your name might appear."

"I am quite sure of him," replied Jekyll; "I have grounds for certainty that I cannot share with any one. But there is one thing on which you may advise me. I have—I have received a letter; and I am at a loss whether I should show it to the police. I should like to leave it in your hands, Utterson; you would judge wisely, I am sure; I have so great a trust in you."

"You fear, I suppose, that it might lead to his detection?" asked the lawyer.

"No," said the other. "I cannot say that I care what becomes of Hyde; I am quite done with him. I was thinking of my own character, which this hateful business has rather exposed."

Utterson ruminated awhile; he was surprised at his friend's selfishness, and yet relieved by it. "Well," said he, at last, "let me see the letter."

The letter was written in an odd, upright hand and signed "Edward Hyde": and it signified, briefly enough, that the writer's benefactor, Dr. Jekyll, whom he had long so unworthily repaid for a thousand generosities, need labour under no alarm for his safety, as he had means of escape on which he placed a sure dependence. The lawyer liked this letter well enough; it put a better colour on the intimacy than he had looked for; and he blamed himself for some of his past suspicions.

"Have you the envelope?" he asked.

"I burned it," replied Jekyll, "before I thought what I was about. But it bore no postmark. The note was handed in."

"Shall I keep this and sleep upon it?" asked Utterson.

"I wish you to judge for me entirely," was the reply. "I have lost confidence in myself."

"Well, I shall consider," returned the lawyer. "And now one word more: it was Hyde who dictated the terms in your will about that disappearance?"

The doctor seemed seized with a qualm of faintness; he shut his mouth tight and nodded.

"I knew it," said Utterson. "He meant to murder you. You have had a fine escape."

"I have had what is far more to the purpose," returned the doctor solemnly: "I have had a lesson—O God, Utterson, what a lesson I have had!" And he covered his face for a moment with his hands.

On his way out, the lawyer stopped and had a word or two with Poole. "By the by," said he, "there was a letter handed in to-day: what was the messenger like?" But Poole was positive nothing had come except by post; "and only circulars[1] by that," he added.

This news sent off the visitor with his fears renewed. Plainly the letter had come by the laboratory door; possibly, indeed, it had been written in the cabinet; and if that were so, it must be differently judged, and handled with the more caution. The news-boys, as he went, were crying themselves hoarse along the foot-ways: "Special edition. Shocking murder of an M.P." That was the funeral oration of one friend and client; and he could not help a certain apprehension lest the good name of another should be sucked down in the eddy of the scandal. It was, at least, a ticklish decision that he had to make; and self-reliant as he was by habit, he began to cherish a longing for advice. It was not to be had directly; but perhaps, he thought, it might be fished for.

Presently after, he sat on one side of his own hearth, with Mr. Guest, his head clerk, upon the other, and midway between, at a nicely calculated distance from the fire, a bottle of a particular old wine that had long dwelt unsunned in the foundations of his house. The fog still slept on the wing above the drowned city, where the lamps glimmered like carbuncles;[2] and through the muffle and smother of these fallen clouds, the procession of the town's life was still rolling in through the great arteries with a sound as of a mighty wind. But the room was gay with firelight. In the bottle the acids were long ago resolved; the imperial dye had softened with time, as the colour grows richer in stained windows; and the glow of hot autumn afternoons on hillside vine-yards, was ready to be set free and to disperse the fogs of London. Insensibly the lawyer melted. There was no man from whom he kept fewer secrets than Mr. Guest; and he was not always sure that he kept as many as he meant. Guest had often been on business to the doctor's; he knew Poole; he could scarce have failed to hear of Mr. Hyde's familiarity about the house; he might draw conclusions: was it not as well, then, that he should see a

---

1 Short for "circular letter," a mass-produced business advertisement.
2 A red gem like a ruby; also a mythical gem supposed to emit light.

letter which put that mystery to rights? and above all since Guest, being a great student and critic of handwriting, would consider the step natural and obliging? The clerk, besides, was a man of counsel; he would scarce read so strange a document without dropping a remark; and by that remark Mr. Utterson might shape his future course.

"This is a sad business about Sir Danvers," he said.

"Yes, sir, indeed. It has elicited a great deal of public feeling," returned Guest. "The man, of course, was mad."

"I should like to hear your views on that," replied Utterson. "I have a document here in his handwriting; it is between ourselves, for I scarce know what to do about it; it is an ugly business at the best. But there it is; quite in your way: a murderer's autograph."

Guest's eyes brightened, and he sat down at once and studied it with passion. "No sir," he said: "not mad; but it is an odd hand."

"And by all accounts a very odd writer," added the lawyer.

Just then the servant entered with a note.

"Is that from Dr. Jekyll, sir?" inquired the clerk. "I thought I knew the writing. Anything private, Mr. Utterson?"

"Only an invitation to dinner. Why? Do you want to see it?"

"One moment. I thank you, sir;" and the clerk laid the two sheets of paper alongside and sedulously compared their contents. "Thank you, sir," he said at last, returning both; "it's a very interesting autograph."

There was a pause, during which Mr. Utterson struggled with himself. "Why did you compare them, Guest?" he inquired suddenly.

"Well, sir," returned the clerk, "there's a rather singular resemblance; the two hands are in many points identical: only differently sloped."

"Rather quaint," said Utterson.

"It is, as you say, rather quaint," returned Guest.

"I wouldn't speak of this note, you know," said the master.

"No, sir," said the clerk. "I understand."

But no sooner was Mr. Utterson alone that night, than he locked the note into his safe, where it reposed from that time forward. "What!" he thought. "Henry Jekyll forge for a murderer!" And his blood ran cold in his veins.

Remarkable Incident of Dr. Lanyon

Time ran on; thousands of pounds were offered in reward, for the death of Sir Danvers was resented as a public injury; but Mr. Hyde had disappeared out of the ken of the police as though he had never existed. Much of his past was unearthed, indeed, and all disreputable: tales came out of the man's cruelty, at once so callous and violent; of his vile life, of his strange associates, of the hatred that seemed to have surrounded his career; but of his present whereabouts, not a whisper. From the time he had left the house in Soho on the morning of the murder, he was simply blotted out; and gradually, as time drew on, Mr. Utterson began to recover from the hotness of his alarm, and to grow more at quiet with himself. The death of Sir Danvers was, to his way of thinking, more than paid for by the disappearance of Mr. Hyde. Now that that evil influence had been withdrawn, a new life began for Dr. Jekyll. He came out of his seclusion, renewed relations with his friends, became once more their familiar guest and entertainer; and whilst he had always been known for charities, he was now no less distinguished for religion. He was busy, he was much in the open air, he did good; his face seemed to open and brighten, as if with an inward consciousness of service; and for more than two months, the doctor was at peace.

On the 8th of January Utterson had dined at the doctor's with a small party; Lanyon had been there; and the face of the host had looked from one to the other as in the old days when the trio were inseparable friends. On the 12th, and again on the 14th, the door was shut against the lawyer. "The doctor was confined to the house," Poole said, "and saw no one." On the 15th, he tried again, and was again refused; and having now been used for the last two months to see his friend almost daily, he found this return of solitude to weigh upon his spirits. The fifth night he had in Guest to dine with him; and the sixth he betook himself to Dr. Lanyon's.

There at least he was not denied admittance; but when he came in, he was shocked at the change which had taken place in the doctor's appearance. He had his death-warrant written legibly upon his face. The rosy man had grown pale; his flesh had fallen away; he was visibly balder and older; and yet it was not so much these tokens of a swift physical decay that arrested the lawyer's notice, as a look in the eye and quality of manner that seemed to testify to some deep-seated terror of the mind. It was unlikely that the doctor should fear death; and yet that was what

Utterson was tempted to suspect. "Yes," he thought; "he is a doctor, he must know his own state and that his days are counted; and the knowledge is more than he can bear." And yet when Utterson remarked on his ill-looks, it was with an air of great firmness that Lanyon declared himself a doomed man.

"I have had a shock," he said, "and I shall never recover. It is a question of weeks. Well, life has been pleasant; I liked it; yes, sir, I used to like it. I sometimes think if we knew all, we should be more glad to get away."

"Jekyll is ill, too," observed Utterson. "Have you seen him?"

But Lanyon's face changed, and he held up a trembling hand. "I wish to see or hear no more of Dr. Jekyll," he said in a loud, unsteady voice. "I am quite done with that person; and I beg that you will spare me any allusion to one whom I regard as dead."

"Tut-tut," said Mr. Utterson; and then after a considerable pause, "Can't I do anything?" he inquired. "We are three very old friends, Lanyon; we shall not live to make others."

"Nothing can be done," returned Lanyon; "ask himself."

"He will not see me," said the lawyer.

"I am not surprised at that," was the reply. "Some day, Utterson, after I am dead, you may perhaps come to learn the right and wrong of this. I cannot tell you. And in the meantime, if you can sit and talk with me of other things, for God's sake, stay and do so; but if you cannot keep clear of this accursed topic, then, in God's name, go, for I cannot bear it."

As soon as he got home, Utterson sat down and wrote to Jekyll, complaining of his exclusion from the house, and asking the cause of this unhappy break with Lanyon; and the next day brought him a long answer, often very pathetically worded, and sometimes darkly mysterious in drift. The quarrel with Lanyon was incurable. "I do not blame our old friend," Jekyll wrote, "but I share his view that we must never meet. I mean from henceforth to lead a life of extreme seclusion; you must not be surprised, nor must you doubt my friendship, if my door is often shut even to you. You must suffer me to go my own dark way. I have brought on myself a punishment and a danger that I cannot name. If I am the chief of sinners, I am the chief of sufferers also. I could not think that this earth contained a place for sufferings and terrors so unmanning; and you can do but one thing, Utterson, to lighten this destiny, and that is to respect my silence." Utterson was amazed; the dark influence of Hyde had been withdrawn, the doctor had returned to his old tasks and amities; a week ago, the prospect had smiled with every promise of a cheerful and an honoured age; and now in a moment, friendship, and peace of mind, and the whole tenor of his life were wrecked. So great and unprepared a change pointed to madness; but in view of Lanyon's manner and words, there must lie for it some deeper ground.

A week afterwards Dr. Lanyon took to his bed, and in something less than a fortnight he was dead. The night after the funeral, at which he had been sadly affected, Utterson locked the door of his business room, and sitting there by the light of a melancholy candle, drew out and set before him an envelope addressed by the hand and sealed with the seal of his dead friend. "Private: for the hands of J.G. Utterson alone, and in case of his predecease *to be destroyed unread*," so it was emphatically superscribed; and the lawyer dreaded to behold the contents. "I have buried one friend to-day," he thought: "what if this should cost me another?" And then he condemned the fear as a disloyalty, and broke the seal. Within there was another enclosure, likewise sealed, and marked upon the cover as "not to be opened till the death or disappearance of Dr. Henry Jekyll." Utterson could not trust his eyes. Yes, it was disappearance; here again, as in the mad will which he had long ago restored to its author, here again were the idea of a disappearance and the name of Henry Jekyll bracketed. But in the will, that idea had sprung from the sinister suggestion of the man Hyde; it was set there with a purpose all too plain and horrible. Written by the hand of Lanyon, what should it mean? A great curiosity came on the trustee, to disregard the prohibition and dive at once to the bottom of these mysteries; but professional honour and faith to his dead friend were stringent obligations; and the packet slept in the inmost corner of his private safe.

It is one thing to mortify curiosity, another to conquer it; and it may be doubted if, from that day forth, Utterson desired the society of his surviving friend with the same eagerness. He thought of him kindly; but his thoughts were disquieted and fearful. He went to call indeed; but he was perhaps relieved to be denied admittance; perhaps, in his heart, he preferred to speak with Poole upon the doorstep and surrounded by the air and sounds of the open city, rather than to be admitted into that house of voluntary bondage, and to sit and speak with its inscrutable recluse. Poole had, indeed, no very pleasant news to communicate. The doctor, it appeared, now more than ever confined himself to the cabinet over the laboratory, where he would sometimes even sleep; he was out of spirits, he had grown very silent, he did not read; it seemed as if he had something on his mind. Utterson became so used to the unvarying character of these reports, that he fell off little by little in the frequency of his visits.

Incident at the Window

It chanced on Sunday, when Mr. Utterson was on his usual walk with Mr. Enfield, that their way lay once again through the by-street; and that when they came in front of the door, both stopped to gaze on it.

"Well," said Enfield, "that story's at an end at least. We shall never see more of Mr. Hyde."

"I hope not," said Utterson. "Did I ever tell you that I once saw him, and shared your feeling of repulsion?"

"It was impossible to do the one without the other," returned Enfield. "And by the way what an ass you must have thought me, not to know that this was a back way to Dr. Jekyll's! It was partly your own fault that I found it out, even when I did."

"So you found it out, did you?" said Utterson. "But if that be so, we may step into the court and take a look at the windows. To tell you the truth, I am uneasy about poor Jekyll; and even outside, I feel as if the presence of a friend might do him good."

The court was very cool and a little damp, and full of premature twilight, although the sky, high up overhead, was still bright with sunset. The middle one of the three windows was halfway open; and sitting close beside it, taking the air with an infinite sadness of mien, like some disconsolate prisoner, Utterson saw Dr. Jekyll.

"What! Jekyll!" he cried. "I trust you are better."

"I am very low, Utterson," replied the doctor drearily, "very low. It will not last long, thank God."

"You stay too much indoors," said the lawyer. "You should be out, whipping up the circulation like Mr. Enfield and me. (This is my cousin—Mr. Enfield—Dr. Jekyll.) Come now; get your hat and take a quick turn with us."

"You are very good," sighed the other. "I should like to very much; but no, no, no, it is quite impossible; I dare not. But indeed, Utterson, I am very glad to see you; this is really a great pleasure; I would ask you and Mr. Enfield up, but the place is really not fit."

"Why then," said the lawyer, good-naturedly, "the best thing we can do is to stay down here and speak with you from where we are."

"That is just what I was about to venture to propose," returned the doctor with a smile. But the words were hardly uttered, before the smile was struck out of his face and succeeded by an expression of such abject terror and despair, as froze the very blood of the two gentlemen below. They saw it but for a glimpse, for the window was instantly thrust down; but that glimpse had been sufficient, and they turned and left the court without a word. In silence, too, they traversed the by-street; and it was not until they had come into a neighbouring thoroughfare, where even upon a Sunday there were still some stirrings of life, that Mr. Utterson at last turned and looked at his companion. They were both pale; and there was an answering horror in their eyes.

"God forgive us, God forgive us," said Mr. Utterson.

But Mr. Enfield only nodded his head very seriously, and walked on once more in silence.

The Last Night

Mr. Utterson was sitting by his fireside one evening after dinner, when he was surprised to receive a visit from Poole.

"Bless me, Poole, what brings you here?" he cried; and then taking a second look at him, "What ails you?" he added; "is the doctor ill?"

"Mr. Utterson," said the man, "there is something wrong."

"Take a seat, and here is a glass of wine for you," said the lawyer. "Now, take your time, and tell me plainly what you want."

"You know the doctor's ways, sir," replied Poole, "and how he shuts himself up. Well, he's shut up again in the cabinet; and I don't like it, sir—I wish I may die if I like it. Mr. Utterson, sir, I'm afraid."

"Now, my good man," said the lawyer, "be explicit. What are you afraid of?"

"I've been afraid for about a week," returned Poole, doggedly disregarding the question, "and I can bear it no more."

The man's appearance amply bore out his words; his manner was altered for the worse; and except for the moment when he had first announced his terror, he had not once looked the lawyer in the face. Even now, he sat with the glass of wine untasted on his knee, and his eyes directed to a corner of the floor. "I can bear it no more," he repeated.

"Come," said the lawyer, "I see you have some good reason, Poole; I see there is something seriously amiss. Try to tell me what it is."

"I think there's been foul play," said Poole, hoarsely.

"Foul play!" cried the lawyer, a good deal frightened and rather inclined to be irritated in consequence. "What foul play? What does the man mean?"

"I daren't say, sir," was the answer; "but will you come along with me and see for yourself?"

Mr. Utterson's only answer was to rise and get his hat and greatcoat; but he observed with wonder the greatness of the relief that appeared upon the butler's face, and perhaps with no less, that the wine was still untasted when he set it down to follow.

It was a wild, cold, seasonable night of March, with a pale moon, lying on her back as though the wind had tilted her, and a flying wrack of the most diaphanous and lawny texture. The wind made talking difficult, and flecked the blood into the face. It seemed to have swept the streets unusually bare of passengers, besides; for Mr. Utterson thought he had never seen that part of London so deserted. He could have wished it otherwise; never in his life had he been conscious of so sharp a wish to see and touch his fellow-creatures; for struggle as he might, there was borne in upon his mind a crushing anticipation of calamity. The square, when they got there, was all full of wind and dust, and the thin trees in the garden were lashing themselves along the railing. Poole, who had kept all the way a pace or two ahead, now pulled up in the middle of the pavement, and in spite of the biting weather, took off his hat and mopped his brow with a red pocket-handkerchief. But for all the hurry of his coming, these were not the dews of exertion that he wiped away, but the moisture of some strangling anguish; for his face was white and his voice, when he spoke, harsh and broken.

"Well, sir," he said, "here we are, and God grant there be nothing wrong."

"Amen, Poole," said the lawyer.

Thereupon the servant knocked in a very guarded manner; the door was opened on the chain; and a voice asked from within, "Is that you, Poole?"

"It's all right," said Poole. "Open the door."

The hall, when they entered it, was brightly lighted up; the fire was built high; and about the hearth the whole of the servants, men and women, stood huddled together like a flock of sheep. At the sight of Mr. Utterson, the housemaid broke into hysterical whimpering; and the cook, crying out "Bless God! it's Mr. Utterson," ran forward as if to take him in her arms.

"What, what? Are you all here?" said the lawyer peevishly. "Very irregular, very unseemly; your master would be far from pleased."

"They're all afraid," said Poole.

Blank silence followed, no one protesting; only the maid lifted up her voice and now wept loudly.

"Hold your tongue!" Poole said to her, with a ferocity of accent that testified to his own jangled nerves; and indeed, when the girl had so suddenly raised the note of her lamentation, they had all started and turned towards the inner door with faces of dreadful expectation. "And now," continued the butler, addressing the knife-boy, "reach me a candle, and we'll get this through hands[1] at once." And then he begged Mr. Utterson to follow him, and led the way to the back garden.

"Now, sir," said he, "you come as gently as you can. I want you to hear, and I don't want you to be heard. And see here, sir, if by any chance he was to ask you in, don't go."

Mr. Utterson's nerves, at this unlooked-for termination, gave a jerk that nearly threw him from his balance; but he recollected his courage and followed the butler into the laboratory building through the surgical theatre, with its lumber of crates and bottles, to the foot of the stair. Here Poole motioned him to stand on one side and listen; while he himself, setting down the candle and making a great and obvious call on his resolution, mounted the steps and knocked with a somewhat uncertain hand on the red baize of the cabinet door.

"Mr. Utterson, sir, asking to see you," he called; and even as he did so, once more violently signed to the lawyer to give ear.

A voice answered from within: "Tell him I cannot see anyone," it said complainingly.

"Thank you, sir," said Poole, with a note of something like triumph in his voice; and taking up his candle, he led Mr. Utterson back across the yard and into the great kitchen, where the fire was out and the beetles were leaping on the floor.

"Sir," he said, looking Mr. Utterson in the eyes, "was that my master's voice?"

"It seems much changed," replied the lawyer, very pale, but giving look for look.

---

1 Dealt with.

"Changed? Well, yes, I think so," said the butler. "Have I been twenty years in this man's house, to be deceived about his voice? No, sir; master's made away with; he was made away with eight days ago, when we heard him cry out upon the name of God; and *who's* in there instead of him, and *why* it stays there, is a thing that cries to Heaven, Mr. Utterson!"

"This is a very strange tale, Poole; this is rather a wild tale, my man," said Mr. Utterson, biting his finger. "Suppose it were as you suppose, supposing Dr. Jekyll to have been—well, murdered, what could induce the murderer to stay? That won't hold water; it doesn't commend itself to reason."

"Well, Mr. Utterson, you are a hard man to satisfy, but I'll do it yet," said Poole. "All this last week (you must know) him, or it, or whatever it is that lives in that cabinet, has been crying night and day for some sort of medicine and cannot get it to his mind. It was sometimes his way—the master's, that is—to write his orders on a sheet of paper and throw it on the stair. We've had nothing else this week back; nothing but papers, and a closed door, and the very meals left there to be smuggled in when nobody was looking. Well, sir, every day, ay, and twice and thrice in the same day, there have been orders and complaints, and I have been sent flying to all the wholesale chemists in town. Every time I brought the stuff back, there would be another paper telling me to return it, because it was not pure, and another order to a different form. This drug is wanted bitter bad, sir, whatever for."

"Have you any of these papers?" asked Mr. Utterson.

Poole felt in his pocket and handed out a crumpled note, which the lawyer, bending nearer to the candle, carefully examined. Its contents ran thus: "Dr. Jekyll presents his compliments to Messrs. Maw. He assures them that their last sample is impure and quite useless for his present purpose. In the year 18—, Dr. J. purchased a somewhat large quantity from Messrs. M. He now begs them to search with the most sedulous care, and should any of the same quality be left, to forward it to him at once. Expense is no consideration. The importance of this to Dr. J. can hardly be exaggerated." So far the letter had run composedly enough, but here with a sudden splutter of the pen, the writer's emotion had broken loose. "For God's sake," he had added, "Find me some of the old."

"This is a strange note," said Mr. Utterson; and then sharply, "How do you come to have it open?"

"The man at Maw's was main angry, sir, and he threw it back to me like so much dirt," returned Poole.

"This is unquestionably the doctor's hand, do you know?" resumed the lawyer.

"I thought it looked like it," said the servant rather sulkily; and then, with another voice, "But what matters hand of write?" he said. "I've seen him!"

"Seen him?" repeated Mr. Utterson. "Well?"

"That's it!" said Poole. "It was this way. I came suddenly into the theatre[1] from the garden. It seems he had slipped out to look for this drug or whatever it is; for the cabinet door was open, and there he was at the far end of the room digging among the crates. He looked up when I came in, gave a kind of cry, and whipped upstairs into the cabinet. It was but for one minute that I saw him, but the hair stood upon my head like quills. Sir, if that was my master, why had he a mask upon his face? If it was my master, why did he cry out like a rat, and run from me? I have served him long enough. And then ..." The man paused and passed his hand over his face.

"These are all very strange circumstances," said Mr. Utterson, "but I think I begin to see daylight. Your master, Poole, is plainly seized with one of those maladies that both torture and deform the sufferer; hence, for aught I know, the alteration of his voice; hence the mask and his avoidance of his friends; hence his eagerness to find this drug, by means of which the poor soul retains some hope of ultimate recovery—God grant that he be not deceived! There is my explanation; it is sad enough, Poole, ay, and appalling to consider; but it is plain and natural, hangs well together, and delivers us from all exorbitant alarms."

"Sir," said the butler, turning to a sort of mottled pallor, "that thing was not my master, and there's the truth. My master"—here he looked round him and began to whisper—"is a tall, fine build of a man, and this was more of a dwarf." Utterson attempted to protest. "O, sir," cried Poole, "do you think I do not know my master after twenty years? Do you think I do not know where his head comes to in the cabinet door, where I saw him every morning of my life? No, sir, that thing in the mask was never Dr. Jekyll—God knows what it was, but it was never Dr. Jekyll; and it is the belief of my heart that there was murder done."

"Poole," replied the lawyer, "if you say that, it will become my duty to make certain. Much as I desire to spare your master's feelings, much as I am puzzled by this note which seems to prove

---

1 A lecture theatre built for tutorials in medicine.

him to be still alive, I shall consider it my duty to break in that door."

"Ah, Mr. Utterson, that's talking!" cried the butler.

"And now comes the second question," resumed Utterson: "Who is going to do it?"

"Why, you and me, sir," was the undaunted reply.

"That is very well said," returned the lawyer; "and whatever comes of it, I shall make it my business to see you are no loser."

"There is an axe in the theatre," continued Poole; "and you might take the kitchen poker for yourself."

The lawyer took that rude but weighty instrument into his hand, and balanced it. "Do you know, Poole," he said, looking up, "that you and I are about to place ourselves in a position of some peril?"

"You may say so, sir, indeed," returned the butler.

"It is well, then, that we should be frank," said the other. "We both think more than we have said; let us make a clean breast. This masked figure that you saw, did you recognise it?"

"Well, sir, it went so quick, and the creature was so doubled up, that I could hardly swear to that," was the answer. "But if you mean, was it Mr. Hyde?—why, yes, I think it was! You see, it was much of the same bigness; and it had the same quick light way with it; and then who else could have got in by the laboratory door? You have not forgot, sir, that at the time of the murder he had still the key with him? But that's not all. I don't know, Mr. Utterson, if ever you met this Mr. Hyde?"

"Yes," said the lawyer, "I once spoke with him."

"Then you must know as well as the rest of us that there was something queer about that gentleman—something that gave a man a turn—I don't know rightly how to say it, sir, beyond this: that you felt it in your marrow kind of cold and thin."

"I own I felt something of what you describe," said Mr. Utterson.

"Quite so, sir," returned Poole. "Well, when that masked thing like a monkey jumped from among the chemicals and whipped into the cabinet, it went down my spine like ice. O, I know it's not evidence, Mr. Utterson; I'm book-learned enough for that; but a man has his feelings, and I give you my bible-word it was Mr. Hyde!"

"Ay, ay," said the lawyer. "My fears incline to the same point. Evil, I fear, founded—evil was sure to come—of that connection. Ay truly, I believe you; I believe poor Harry is killed; and I believe his murderer (for what purpose, God alone can tell) is still lurking in his victim's room. Well, let our name be vengeance. Call Bradshaw."

The footman came at the summons, very white and nervous.

"Pull yourself together, Bradshaw," said the lawyer. "This suspense, I know, is telling upon all of you; but it is now our intention to make an end of it. Poole, here, and I are going to force our way into the cabinet. If all is well, my shoulders are broad enough to bear the blame. Meanwhile, lest anything should really be amiss, or any malefactor seek to escape by the back, you and the boy must go round the corner with a pair of good sticks, and take your post at the laboratory door. We give you ten minutes, to get to your stations."

As Bradshaw left, the lawyer looked at his watch. "And now, Poole, let us get to ours," he said; and taking the poker under his arm, led the way into the yard. The scud[1] had banked over the moon, and it was now quite dark. The wind, which only broke in puffs and draughts into that deep well of building, tossed the light of the candle to and fro about their steps, until they came into the shelter of the theatre, where they sat down silently to wait. London hummed solemnly all around; but nearer at hand, the stillness was only broken by the sound of a footfall moving to and fro along the cabinet floor.

"So it will walk all day, sir," whispered Poole; "ay, and the better part of the night. Only when a new sample comes from the chemist, there's a bit of a break. Ah, it's an ill conscience that's such an enemy to rest! Ah, sir, there's blood foully shed in every step of it! But hark again, a little closer—put your heart in your ears, Mr. Utterson, and tell me, is that the doctor's foot?"

The steps fell lightly and oddly, with a certain swing, for all they went so slowly; it was different indeed from the heavy creaking tread of Henry Jekyll. Utterson sighed. "Is there never anything else?" he asked.

Poole nodded. "Once," he said. "Once I heard it weeping!"

"Weeping? how that?" said the lawyer, conscious of a sudden chill of horror.

"Weeping like a woman or a lost soul," said the butler. "I came away with that upon my heart, that I could have wept too."

But now the ten minutes drew to an end. Poole disinterred the axe from under a stack of packing straw; the candle was set upon the nearest table to light them to the attack; and they drew near with bated breath to where that patient foot was still going up and

---

1 Light clouds moving rapidly across the sky.

down, up and down, in the quiet of the night. "Jekyll," cried Utterson, with a loud voice, "I demand to see you." He paused a moment, but there came no reply. "I give you fair warning, our suspicions are aroused, and I must and shall see you," he resumed; "if not by fair means, then by foul—if not of your consent, then by brute force!"

"Utterson," said the voice, "for God's sake, have mercy!"

"Ah, that's not Jekyll's voice—it's Hyde's!" cried Utterson. "Down with the door, Poole!"

Poole swung the axe over his shoulder; the blow shook the building, and the red baize door leaped against the lock and hinges. A dismal screech, as of mere animal terror, rang from the cabinet. Up went the axe again, and again the panels crashed and the frame bounded; four times the blow fell; but the wood was tough and the fittings were of excellent workmanship; and it was not until the fifth, that the lock burst in sunder and the wreck of the door fell inwards on the carpet.

The besiegers, appalled by their own riot and the stillness that had succeeded, stood back a little and peered in. There lay the cabinet before their eyes in the quiet lamplight, a good fire glowing and chattering on the hearth, the kettle singing its thin strain, a drawer or two open, papers neatly set forth on the business table, and nearer the fire, the things laid out for tea; the quietest room, you would have said, and, but for the glazed presses full of chemicals, the most commonplace that night in London.

Right in the midst there lay the body of a man sorely contorted and still twitching. They drew near on tiptoe, turned it on its back and beheld the face of Edward Hyde. He was dressed in clothes far too large for him, clothes of the doctor's bigness; the cords of his face still moved with a semblance of life, but life was quite gone; and by the crushed phial in the hand and the strong smell of kernels that hung upon the air, Utterson knew that he was looking on the body of a self-destroyer.

"We have come too late," he said sternly, "whether to save or punish. Hyde is gone to his account; and it only remains for us to find the body of your master."

The far greater proportion of the building was occupied by the theatre, which filled almost the whole ground storey and was lighted from above, and by the cabinet, which formed an upper storey at one end and looked upon the court. A corridor joined the theatre to the door on the by-street; and with this the cabinet communicated separately by a second flight of stairs. There were besides a few dark closets and a spacious cellar. All these they now thoroughly examined. Each closet needed but a glance, for all were empty, and all, by the dust that fell from their doors, had stood long unopened. The cellar, indeed, was filled with crazy lumber, mostly dating from the times of the surgeon who was Jekyll's predecessor; but even as they opened the door, they were advertised of the uselessness of further search, by the fall of a perfect mat of cobweb which had for years sealed up the entrance. Nowhere was there any trace of Henry Jekyll, dead or alive.

Poole stamped on the flags of the corridor. "He must be buried here," he said, hearkening to the sound.

"Or he may have fled," said Utterson, and he turned to examine the door in the by-street. It was locked; and lying near by on the flags, they found the key, already stained with rust.

"This does not look like use," observed the lawyer.

"Use!" echoed Poole. "Do you not see, sir, it is broken? much as if a man had stamped on it."

"Ay," continued Utterson, "and the fractures, too, are rusty." The two men looked at each other with a scare. "This is beyond me, Poole," said the lawyer. "Let us go back to the cabinet."

They mounted the stair in silence, and still with an occasional awestruck glance at the dead body, proceeded more thoroughly to examine the contents of the cabinet. At one table, there were traces of chemical work, various measured heaps of some white salt being laid on glass saucers, as though for an experiment in which the unhappy man had been prevented.

"That is the same drug that I was always bringing him," said Poole; and even as he spoke, the kettle with a startling noise boiled over.

This brought them to the fireside, where the easy-chair was drawn cosily up, and the tea things stood ready to the sitter's elbow, the very sugar in the cup. There were several books on a shelf; one lay beside the tea things open, and Utterson was amazed to find it a copy of a pious work, for which Jekyll had several times expressed a great esteem, annotated, in his own hand, with startling blasphemies.

Next, in the course of their review of the chamber, the searchers came to the cheval glass, into whose depths they look-ed with an involuntary horror. But it was so turned as to show them nothing but the rosy glow playing on the roof, the fire sparkling in a hundred repetitions along the glazed front of the presses, and their own pale and fearful countenances stooping to look in.

"This glass has seen some strange things, sir," whispered Poole.

"And surely none stranger than itself," echoed the lawyer in the same tones. "For what did Jekyll"—he caught himself up at the word with a start, and then conquering the weakness—"what could Jekyll want with it?" he said.

"You may say that!" said Poole.

Next they turned to the business table. On the desk among the neat array of papers, a large envelope was uppermost, and bore, in the doctor's hand, the name of Mr. Utterson. The lawyer unsealed it, and several enclosures fell to the floor. The first was a will, drawn in the same eccentric terms as the one which he had returned six months before, to serve as a testament in case of death and as a deed of gift in case of disappearance; but in place of the name of Edward Hyde, the lawyer, with indescribable amazement, read the name of Gabriel John Utterson. He looked at Poole, and then back at the paper, and last of all at the dead malefactor stretched upon the carpet.

"My head goes round," he said. "He has been all these days in possession; he had no cause to like me; he must have raged to see himself displaced; and he has not destroyed this document."

He caught up the next paper; it was a brief note in the doctor's hand and dated at the top. "O Poole!" the lawyer cried, "he was alive and here this day. He cannot have been disposed of in so short a space; he must be still alive, he must have fled! And then, why fled? and how? and in that case, can we venture to declare this suicide? O, we must be careful. I foresee that we may yet involve your master in some dire catastrophe."

"Why don't you read it, sir?" asked Poole.

"Because I fear," replied the lawyer solemnly. "God grant I have no cause for it!" And with that he brought the paper to his eyes and read as follows:

"My dear Utterson,—When this shall fall into your hands, I shall have disappeared, under what circumstances I have not the penetration to foresee, but my instinct and all the circumstances of my nameless situation tell me that the end is sure and must be early. Go then, and first read the narrative which Lanyon warned me he was to place in your hands; and if you care to hear more, turn to the confession of

"Your unworthy and unhappy friend,

"HENRY JEKYLL."

"There was a third enclosure?" asked Utterson.

"Here, sir," said Poole, and gave into his hands a considerable packet sealed in several places.

The lawyer put it in his pocket. "I would say nothing of this paper. If your master has fled or is dead, we may at least save his credit. It is now ten; I must go home and read these documents in quiet; but I shall be back before midnight, when we shall send for the police."

They went out, locking the door of the theatre behind them; and Utterson, once more leaving the servants gathered about the fire in the hall, trudged back to his office to read the two narratives in which this mystery was now to be explained.

Dr. Lanyon's Narrative

On the ninth of January, now four days ago, I received by the evening delivery a registered envelope, addressed in the hand of my colleague and old school companion, Henry Jekyll. I was a good deal surprised by this; for we were by no means in the habit of correspondence; I had seen the man, dined with him, indeed, the night before; and I could imagine nothing in our intercourse that should justify the formality of registration. The contents increased my wonder; for this is how the letter ran:

"10th December, 18—.

"Dear Lanyon,—You are one of my oldest friends; and although we may have differed at times on scientific questions, I cannot remember, at least on my side, any break in our affection. There was never a day when, if you had said to me, 'Jekyll, my life, my honour, my reason, depend upon you,' I would not have sacrificed my fortune or my left hand to help you. Lanyon, my life, my honour, my reason, are all at your mercy; if you fail me to-night, I am lost. You might suppose, after this preface, that I am going to ask you for something dishonourable to grant. Judge for yourself.

"I want you to postpone all other engagements for to-night— ay, even if you were summoned to the bedside of an emperor; to take a cab, unless your carriage should be actually at the door; and with this letter in your hand for consultation, to drive straight to my house. Poole, my butler, has his orders; you will find him waiting your arrival with a locksmith. The door of my cabinet is then to be forced; and you are to go in alone; to open the glazed press (letter E) on the left hand, breaking the lock if it be shut; and to draw out, with all its contents as they stand, the fourth drawer from the top or (which is the same thing) the third from the bottom. In my extreme distress of mind, I have a morbid fear of misdirecting you; but even if I am in error, you may know the right drawer by its contents: some powders, a phial and a paper book. This drawer I beg of you to carry back with you to Cavendish Square exactly as it stands.

"That is the first part of the service: now for the second. You should be back, if you set out at once on the receipt of this, long before midnight; but I will leave you that amount of margin, not only in the fear of one of those obstacles that can neither be prevented nor foreseen, but because an hour when your servants are in bed is to be preferred for what will then remain to do. At midnight, then, I have to ask you to be alone in your consulting room, to admit with your own hand into the house a man who will present himself in my name, and to place in his hands the drawer that you will have brought with you from my cabinet. Then you will have played your part and earned my gratitude completely. Five minutes afterwards, if you insist upon an explanation, you will have understood that these arrangements are of capital importance; and that by the neglect of one of them, fantastic as they must appear, you might have charged your conscience with my death or the shipwreck of my reason.

"Confident as I am that you will not trifle with this appeal, my heart sinks and my hand trembles at the bare thought of such a possibility. Think of me at this hour, in a strange place, labouring under a blackness of distress that no fancy can exaggerate, and yet well aware that, if you will but punctually serve me, my troubles will roll away like a story that is told. Serve me, my dear Lanyon, and save

Your friend,

H.J."

"P.S. I had already sealed this up when a fresh terror struck upon my soul. It is possible that the post office may fail me, and this letter not come into your hands until to-morrow morning. In that case, dear Lanyon, do my errand when it shall be most convenient for you in the course of the day; and once more expect my messenger at midnight. It may then already be too late; and if that night passes without event, you will know that you have seen the last of Henry Jekyll."

Upon the reading of this letter, I made sure my colleague was insane; but till that was proved beyond the possibility of doubt, I felt bound to do as he requested. The less I understood of this farrago,[1] the less I was in a position to judge of its importance; and an appeal so worded could not be set aside without a grave responsibility. I rose accordingly from table, got into a hansom, and drove straight to Jekyll's house. The butler was awaiting my arrival; he had received by the same post as mine a registered letter of instruction, and had sent at once for a locksmith and a carpenter. The tradesmen came while we were yet speaking; and we moved in a body to old Dr. Denman's surgical theatre, from which (as you are doubtless aware) Jekyll's private cabinet is most conveniently entered. The door was very strong, the lock excellent; the carpenter avowed he would have great trouble and have to do much damage, if force were to be used; and the locksmith was near despair. But this last was a handy fellow, and after two hour's work, the door stood open. The press marked E was unlocked; and I took out the drawer, had it filled up with straw and tied in a sheet, and returned with it to Cavendish Square.

Here I proceeded to examine its contents. The powders were neatly enough made up, but not with the nicety of the dispensing chemist; so that it was plain they were of Jekyll's private manufacture; and when I opened one of the wrappers I found what seemed to me a simple crystalline salt of a white colour. The phial, to which I next turned my attention, might have been about half-full of a blood-red liquor, which was highly pungent to the sense of smell and seemed to me to contain phosphorus and some volatile ether. At the other ingredients, I could make no guess. The book was an ordinary version book[2] and contained little but a series of dates. These covered a period of many years, but I observed that the entries ceased nearly a year ago and quite abruptly. Here and there a brief remark was appended to a date, usually no more than a single word: "double" occurring perhaps six times in a total of several hundred entries; and once very early in the list and followed by several marks of exclamation, "total failure!!!" All this, though it whetted my curiosity, told me little that was definite. Here were a phial of some tincture, a paper of some salt, and the record of a series of experiments that had led (like too many of Jekyll's investigations) to no end of practical usefulness. How could the presence of these articles in my house

1 Confused mixture, mess.
2 A book with plain pages.

affect either the honour, the sanity, or the life of my flighty colleague? If his messenger could go to one place, why could he not go to another? And even granting some impediment, why was this gentleman to be received by me in secret? The more I reflected, the more convinced I grew that I was dealing with a case of cerebral disease; and though I dismissed my servants to bed, I loaded an old revolver, that I might be found in some posture of self-defence.

Twelve o'clock had scarce rung out over London, ere the knocker sounded very gently on the door. I went myself at the summons, and found a small man crouching against the pillars of the portico.

"Are you come from Dr. Jekyll?" I asked.

He told me "yes" by a constrained gesture; and when I had bidden him enter, he did not obey me without a searching backward glance into the darkness of the square. There was a policeman not far off, advancing with his bull's eye open;[1] and at the sight, I thought my visitor started and made greater haste.

These particulars struck me, I confess, disagreeably; and as I followed him into the bright light of the consulting room, I kept my hand ready on my weapon. Here, at last, I had a chance of clearly seeing him. I had never set eyes on him before, so much was certain. He was small, as I have said; I was struck besides with the shocking expression of his face, with his remarkable combination of great muscular activity and great apparent debility of constitution, and—last but not least—with the odd, subjective disturbance caused by his neighbourhood. This bore some resemblance to incipient rigor,[2] and was accompanied by a marked sinking of the pulse. At the time, I set it down to some idiosyncratic, personal distaste, and merely wondered at the acuteness of the symptoms; but I have since had reason to believe the cause to lie much deeper in the nature of man, and to turn on some nobler hinge than the principle of hatred.

This person (who had thus, from the first moment of his entrance, struck in me what I can only describe as a disgustful curiosity) was dressed in a fashion that would have made an ordinary person laughable; his clothes, that is to say, although they were of rich and sober fabric, were enormously too large for him in every measurement—the trousers hanging on his legs and rolled up to keep them from the ground, the waist of the coat

---

1 A kind of lantern that can be used like a flashlight.
2 Goosebumps.

below his haunches, and the collar sprawling wide upon his shoulders. Strange to relate, this ludicrous accoutrement was far from moving me to laughter. Rather, as there was something abnormal and misbegotten in the very essence of the creature that now faced me—something seizing, surprising and revolting—this fresh disparity seemed but to fit in with and to reinforce it; so that to my interest in the man's nature and character, there was added a curiosity as to his origin, his life, his fortune and status in the world.

These observations, though they have taken so great a space to be set down in, were yet the work of a few seconds. My visitor was, indeed, on fire with sombre excitement.

"Have you got it?" he cried. "Have you got it?" And so lively was his impatience that he even laid his hand upon my arm and sought to shake me.

I put him back, conscious at his touch of a certain icy pang along my blood. "Come, sir," said I. "You forget that I have not yet the pleasure of your acquaintance. Be seated, if you please." And I showed him an example, and sat down myself in my customary seat and with as fair an imitation of my ordinary manner to a patient, as the lateness of the hour, the nature of my preoccupations, and the horror I had of my visitor, would suffer me to muster.

"I beg your pardon, Dr. Lanyon," he replied civilly enough. "What you say is very well founded; and my impatience has shown its heels to my politeness. I come here at the instance of your colleague, Dr. Henry Jekyll, on a piece of business of some moment; and I understood ..." He paused and put his hand to his throat, and I could see, in spite of his collected manner, that he was wrestling against the approaches of the hysteria—"I understood, a drawer ..."

But here I took pity on my visitor's suspense, and some perhaps on my own growing curiosity.

"There it is, sir," said I, pointing to the drawer, where it lay on the floor behind a table and still covered with the sheet.

He sprang to it, and then paused, and laid his hand upon his heart; I could hear his teeth grate with the convulsive action of his jaws; and his face was so ghastly to see that I grew alarmed both for his life and reason.

"Compose yourself," said I.

He turned a dreadful smile to me, and as if with the decision of despair, plucked away the sheet. At sight of the contents, he uttered one loud sob of such immense relief that I sat petrified.

And the next moment, in a voice that was already fairly well under control, "Have you a graduated glass?"[1] he asked.

I rose from my place with something of an effort and gave him what he asked.

He thanked me with a smiling nod, measured out a few minims of the red tincture and added one of the powders. The mixture, which was at first of a reddish hue, began, in proportion as the crystals melted, to brighten in colour, to effervesce audibly, and to throw off small fumes of vapour. Suddenly and at the same moment, the ebullition[2] ceased and the compound changed to a dark purple, which faded again more slowly to a watery green. My visitor, who had watched these metamorphoses with a keen eye, smiled, set down the glass upon the table, and then turned and looked upon me with an air of scrutiny.

"And now," said he, "to settle what remains. Will you be wise? will you be guided? will you suffer me to take this glass in my hand and to go forth from your house without further parley? or has the greed of curiosity too much command of you? Think before you answer, for it shall be done as you decide. As you decide, you shall be left as you were before, and neither richer nor wiser, unless the sense of service rendered to a man in mortal distress may be counted as a kind of riches of the soul. Or, if you shall so prefer to choose, a new province of knowledge and new avenues to fame and power shall be laid open to you, here, in this room, upon the instant; and your sight shall be blasted by a prodigy to stagger the unbelief of Satan."

"Sir," said I, affecting a coolness that I was far from truly possessing, "you speak enigmas, and you will perhaps not wonder that I hear you with no very strong impression of belief. But I have gone too far in the way of inexplicable services to pause before I see the end."

"It is well," replied my visitor. "Lanyon, you remember your vows: what follows is under the seal of our profession. And now, you who have so long been bound to the most narrow and material views, you who have denied the virtue of transcendental medicine, you who have derided your superiors—behold!"

He put the glass to his lips and drank at one gulp. A cry followed; he reeled, staggered, clutched at the table and held on, staring with injected[3] eyes, gasping with open mouth; and as I

---

1 Glass container marked with lines indicating quantity.
2 Boiling or bubbling.
3 Distended or swollen.

looked there came, I thought, a change—he seemed to swell—his face became suddenly black and the features seemed to melt and alter—and the next moment, I had sprung to my feet and leaped back against the wall, my arm raised to shield me from that prodigy, my mind submerged in terror.

"O God!" I screamed, and "O God!" again and again; for there before my eyes—pale and shaken, and half fainting, and groping before him with his hands, like a man restored from death—there stood Henry Jekyll!

What he told me in the next hour, I cannot bring my mind to set on paper. I saw what I saw, I heard what I heard, and my soul sickened at it; and yet now when that sight has faded from my eyes, I ask myself if I believe it, and I cannot answer. My life is shaken to its roots; sleep has left me; the deadliest terror sits by me at all hours of the day and night; I feel that my days are numbered, and that I must die; and yet I shall die incredulous. As for the moral turpitude that man unveiled to me, even with tears of penitence, I cannot, even in memory, dwell on it without a start of horror. I will say but one thing, Utterson, and that (if you can bring your mind to credit it) will be more than enough. The creature who crept into my house that night was, on Jekyll's own confession, known by the name of Hyde and hunted for in every corner of the land as the murderer of Carew.

HASTIE LANYON

Henry Jekyll's Full Statement of the Case

I was born in the year 18— to a large fortune, endowed besides with excellent parts, inclined by nature to industry, fond of the respect of the wise and good among my fellow-men, and thus, as might have been supposed, with every guarantee of an honourable and distinguished future. And indeed the worst of my faults was a certain impatient gaiety[1] of disposition, such as has made the happiness of many, but such as I found it hard to reconcile with my imperious desire to carry my head high, and wear a more than commonly grave countenance before the public. Hence it came about that I concealed my pleasures; and that when I reached years of reflection, and began to look round me

---

1 "Gay" in the 1880s could simply mean happy, but could also mean loose or immoral, especially if applied to women, when it would imply prostitution.

and take stock of my progress and position in the world, I stood already committed to a profound duplicity of life. Many a man would have even blazoned[1] such irregularities as I was guilty of; but from the high views that I had set before me, I regarded and hid them with an almost morbid sense of shame. It was thus rather the exacting nature of my aspirations than any particular degradation in my faults, that made me what I was, and, with even a deeper trench than in the majority of men, severed in me those provinces of good and ill which divide and compound man's dual nature. In this case, I was driven to reflect deeply and inveterately on that hard law of life, which lies at the root of religion and is one of the most plentiful springs of distress. Though so profound a double-dealer, I was in no sense a hypocrite; both sides of me were in dead earnest; I was no more myself when I laid aside restraint and plunged in shame, than when I laboured, in the eye of day, at the furtherance of knowledge or the relief of sorrow and suffering. And it chanced that the direction of my scientific studies, which led wholly towards the mystic and the transcendental, reacted and shed a strong light on this consciousness of the perennial war among my members.[2] With every day, and from both sides of my intelligence, the moral and the intellectual, I thus drew steadily nearer to that truth, by whose partial discovery I have been doomed to such a dreadful shipwreck: that man is not truly one, but truly two. I say two, because the state of my own knowledge does not pass beyond that point. Others will follow, others will outstrip me on the same lines; and I hazard the guess that man will be ultimately known for a mere polity of multifarious, incongruous[3] and independent denizens. I for my part, from the nature of my life, advanced infallibly in one direction and in one direction only. It was on the moral side, and in my own person, that I learned to recognise the thorough and primitive duality of man; I saw that, of the two natures that contended in the Weld of my consciousness, even if I could rightly be said to be either, it was only because I was radically both; and from an early date, even before the course of my scientific discoveries had begun to suggest the most naked possibility of such a miracle, I had learned to dwell with pleasure, as a beloved daydream, on the thought of the separation of these elements. If each, I told myself,

---

1 To "blazon" is to publish or boast of a deed.
2 Parts of the body.
3 A polity is an organized society or government, but adjectives such as multifarious and incongruous suggest disorganization and conflict.

could but be housed in separate identities, life would be relieved of all that was unbearable; the unjust might go his way, delivered from the aspirations and remorse of his more upright twin; and the just could walk steadfastly and securely on his upward path, doing the good things in which he found his pleasure, and no longer exposed to disgrace and penitence by the hands of this extraneous evil. It was the curse of mankind that these incongruous faggots[1] were thus bound together—that in the agonised womb of consciousness, these polar twins should be continuously struggling. How, then, were they dissociated?

I was so far in my reflections when, as I have said, a side light began to shine upon the subject from the laboratory table. I began to perceive more deeply than it has ever yet been stated, the trembling immateriality, the mist-like transience, of this seemingly so solid body in which we walk attired. Certain agents I found to have the power to shake and to pluck back that freshly vestment, even as a wind might toss the curtains of a pavilion. For two good reasons, I will not enter deeply into this scientific branch of my confession. First, because I have been made to learn that the doom and burthen of our life is bound for ever on man's shoulders, and when the attempt is made to cast it off, it but returns upon us with more unfamiliar and more awful pressure. Second, because, as my narrative will make alas! too evident, my discoveries were incomplete. Enough, then, that I not only recognised my natural body for the mere aura and effulgence of certain of the powers that made up my spirit, but managed to compound a drug by which these powers should be dethroned from their supremacy, and a second form and countenance substituted, none the less natural to me because they were the expression, and bore the stamp, of lower elements in my soul.

I hesitated long before I put this theory to the test of practice. I knew well that I risked death; for any drug that so potently controlled and shook the very fortress of identity, might by the least scruple[2] of an overdose or at the least inopportunity in the moment of exhibition, utterly blot out that immaterial tabernacle which I looked to it to change. But the temptation of a discovery so singular and profound, at last overcame the suggestions of alarm. I had long since prepared my tincture; I purchased at once, from a firm of wholesale chemists, a large quantity of a particular salt which I knew, from my experiments, to be the last

---

1 A bundle of sticks tied together.
2 A small unit of weight.

ingredient required; and late one accursed night, I compounded the elements, watched them boil and smoke together in the glass, and when the ebullition had subsided, with a strong glow of courage, drank off the potion.

The most racking pangs succeeded: a grinding in the bones, deadly nausea, and a horror of the spirit that cannot be exceeded at the hour of birth or death. Then these agonies began swiftly to subside, and I came to myself as if out of a great sickness. There was something strange in my sensations, something indescribably new and, from its very novelty, incredibly sweet. I felt younger, lighter, happier in body; within I was conscious of a heady reck-lessness, a current of disordered sensual images running like a mill race in my fancy, a solution of the bonds of obligation, an unknown but not an innocent freedom of the soul. I knew myself, at the first breath of this new life, to be more wicked, tenfold more wicked, sold a slave to my original evil; and the thought, in that moment, braced and delighted me like wine. I stretched out my hands, exulting in the freshness of these sensations; and in the act, I was suddenly aware that I had lost in stature.

There was no mirror, at that date, in my room; that which stands beside me as I write, was brought there later on and for the very purpose of these transformations. The night, however, was far gone into the morning—the morning, black as it was, was nearly ripe for the conception of the day—the inmates of my house were locked in the most rigorous hours of slumber; and I determined, flushed as I was with hope and triumph, to venture in my new shape as far as to my bedroom. I crossed the yard, wherein the constellations looked down upon me, I could have thought, with wonder, the first creature of that sort that their unsleeping vigilance had yet disclosed to them; I stole through the corridors, a stranger in my own house; and coming to my room, I saw for the first time the appearance of Edward Hyde.

I must here speak by theory alone, saying not that which I know, but that which I suppose to be most probable. The evil side of my nature, to which I had now transferred the stamping effi-cacy, was less robust and less developed than the good which I had just deposed. Again, in the course of my life, which had been, after all, nine tenths a life of effort, virtue and control, it had been much less exercised and much less exhausted. And hence, as I think, it came about that Edward Hyde was so much smaller, slighter and younger than Henry Jekyll. Even as good shone upon the countenance of the one, evil was written broadly and plainly on the face of the other. Evil besides (which I must still believe to be the lethal side of man) had left on that body an imprint of deformity and decay. And yet when I looked upon that ugly idol in the glass, I was conscious of no repugnance, rather of a leap of welcome. This, too, was myself. It seemed natural and human. In my eyes it bore a livelier image of the spirit, it seemed more express and single, than the imperfect and divided countenance I had been hitherto accustomed to call mine. And in so far I was doubtless right. I have observed that when I wore the semblance of Edward Hyde, none could come near to me at first without a visible misgiving of the flesh. This, as I take it, was because all human beings, as we meet them, are commingled out of good and evil: and Edward Hyde, alone in the ranks of mankind, was pure evil.

I lingered but a moment at the mirror: the second and conclusive experiment had yet to be attempted; it yet remained to be seen if I had lost my identity beyond redemption and must flee before daylight from a house that was no longer mine; and hurrying back to my cabinet, I once more prepared and drank the cup, once more suffered the pangs of dissolution, and came to myself once more with the character, the stature and the face of Henry Jekyll. That night I had come to the fatal crossroads. Had I approached my discovery in a more noble spirit, had I risked the experiment while under the empire of generous or pious aspirations, all must have been otherwise, and from these agonies of death and birth, I had come forth an angel instead of a fiend. The drug had no discriminating action; it was neither diabolical nor divine; it but shook the doors of the prisonhouse of my disposition; and like the captives of Philippi,[1] that which stood within ran forth. At that time my virtue slumbered; my evil, kept awake by ambition, was alert and swift to seize the occasion; and the thing that was projected was Edward Hyde. Hence, although I had now two characters as well as two appearances, one was wholly evil, and the other was still the old Henry Jekyll, that incongruous compound of whose reformation and improvement I had already learned to despair. The movement was thus wholly toward the worse.

Even at that time, I had not yet conquered my aversions to the dryness of a life of study. I would still be merrily disposed at times; and as my pleasures were (to say the least) undignified, and I was not only well known and highly considered, but growing towards the elderly man, this incoherency of my life was

---

1 Prisoners miraculously freed by an earthquake (Acts 16:26).

daily growing more unwelcome. It was on this side that my new power tempted me until I fell in slavery. I had but to drink the cup, to doff at once the body of the noted professor, and to assume, like a thick cloak, that of Edward Hyde. I smiled at the notion; it seemed to me at the time to be humorous; and I made my preparations with the most studious care. I took and furnished that house in Soho, to which Hyde was tracked by the police; and engaged as a housekeeper a creature whom I knew well to be silent and unscrupulous. On the other side, I announced to my servants that a Mr. Hyde (whom I described) was to have full liberty and power about my house in the square; and to parry mishaps, I even called and made myself a familiar object, in my second character. I next drew up that will to which you so much objected; so that if anything befell me in the person of Dr. Jekyll, I could enter on that of Edward Hyde without pecuniary loss. And thus fortified, as I supposed, on every side, I began to profit by the strange immunities of my position.

Men have before hired bravos[1] to transact their crimes, while their own person and reputation sat under shelter. I was the first that ever did so for his pleasures. I was the first that could thus plod in the public eye with a load of genial respectability, and in a moment, like a schoolboy, strip off these lendings and spring headlong into the sea of liberty. But for me, in my impenetrable mantle, the safety was complete. Think of it—I did not even exist! Let me but escape into my laboratory door, give me but a second or two to mix and swallow the draught that I had always standing ready; and whatever he had done, Edward Hyde would pass away like the stain of breath upon a mirror; and there in his stead, quietly at home, trimming the midnight lamp in his study, a man who could afford to laugh at suspicion, would be Henry Jekyll.

The pleasures which I made haste to seek in my disguise were, as I have said, undignified; I would scarce use a harder term. But in the hands of Edward Hyde, they soon began to turn toward the monstrous. When I would come back from these excursions, I was often plunged into a kind of wonder at my vicarious depravity. This familiar[2] that I called out of my own soul, and sent forth alone to do his good pleasure, was a being inherently malign and villainous; his every act and thought centred on self; drinking pleasure with bestial avidity from any degree of torture to

---

1   Criminals paid to perform illegal acts, including murder.
2   Either a member of one's family or close friend, or, in witchcraft, an evil spirit that carries out one's commands.

another; relentless like a man of stone. Henry Jekyll stood at times aghast before the acts of Edward Hyde; but the situation was apart from ordinary laws, and insidiously relaxed the grasp of conscience. It was Hyde, after all, and Hyde alone, that was guilty. Jekyll was no worse; he woke again to his good qualities seemingly unimpaired; he would even make haste, where it was possible, to undo the evil done by Hyde. And thus his conscience slumbered.

Into the details of the infamy at which I thus connived (for even now I can scarce grant that I committed it) I have no design of entering; I mean but to point out the warnings and the successive steps with which my chastisement approached. I met with one accident which, as it brought on no consequence, I shall no more than mention. An act of cruelty to a child aroused against me the anger of a passerby, whom I recognised the other day in the person of your kinsman; the doctor and the child's family joined him; there were moments when I feared for my life; and at last, in order to pacify their too just resentment, Edward Hyde had to bring them to the door, and pay them in a cheque drawn in the name of Henry Jekyll. But this danger was easily eliminated from the future, by opening an account at another bank in the name of Edward Hyde himself; and when, by sloping my own hand backward, I had supplied my double with a signature, I thought I sat beyond the reach of fate.

Some two months before the murder of Sir Danvers, I had been out for one of my adventures, had returned at a late hour, and woke the next day in bed with somewhat odd sensations. It was in vain I looked about me; in vain I saw the decent furniture and tall proportions of my room in the square; in vain that I recognised the pattern of the bed curtains and the design of the mahogany frame; something still kept insisting that I was not where I was, that I had not wakened where I seemed to be, but in the little room in Soho where I was accustomed to sleep in the body of Edward Hyde. I smiled to myself, and, in my psychological way, began lazily to inquire into the elements of this illusion, occasionally, even as I did so, dropping back into a comfortable morning doze. I was still so engaged when, in one of my more wakeful moments, my eye fell upon my hand. Now the hand of Henry Jekyll (as you have often remarked) was professional in shape and size: it was large, firm, white and comely.[1] But the hand which I now saw, clearly enough, in the yellow light of a

---

1   Pretty, beautiful, delicate.

mid-London morning, lying half shut on the bed clothes, was lean, corded, knuckly, of a dusky pallor and thickly shaded with a swart[1] growth of hair. It was the hand of Edward Hyde.

I must have stared upon it for near half a minute, sunk as I was in the mere stupidity of wonder, before terror woke up in my breast as sudden and startling as the crash of cymbals; and bounding from my bed, I rushed to the mirror. At the sight that met my eyes, my blood was changed into something exquisitely thin and icy. Yes, I had gone to bed Henry Jekyll, I had awakened Edward Hyde. How was this to be explained? I asked myself; and then, with another bound of terror—how was it to be remedied? It was well on in the morning; the servants were up; all my drugs were in the cabinet—a long journey, down two pair of stairs, through the back passage, across the open court and through the anatomical theatre, from where I was then standing horror-struck. It might indeed be possible to cover my face; but of what use was that, when I was unable to conceal the alteration in my stature? And then with an overpowering sweetness of relief, it came back upon my mind that the servants were already used to the coming and going of my second self. I had soon dressed, as well as I was able, in clothes of my own size: had soon passed through the house, where Bradshaw stared and drew back at seeing Mr. Hyde at such an hour and in such a strange array; and ten minutes later, Dr. Jekyll had returned to his own shape and was sitting down, with a darkened brow, to make a feint of break-fasting.

Small indeed was my appetite. This inexplicable incident, this reversal of my previous experience, seemed, like the Babylonian finger on the wall,[2] to be spelling out the letters of my judgment; and I began to reflect more seriously than ever before on the issues and possibilities of my double existence. That part of me which I had the power of projecting, had lately been much exercised and nourished; it had seemed to me of late as though the body of Edward Hyde had grown in stature, as though (when I wore that form) I were conscious of a more generous tide of blood; and I began to spy a danger that, if this were much pro-longed, the balance of my nature might be permanently over-thrown, the power of voluntary change be forfeited, and the char-acter of Edward Hyde become irrevocably mine. The power of

---

1 Dark, swarthy; also suggests evil.
2 A magical finger that wrote a prophesy of doom at Belshazzar's feast (Daniel 5:24).

the drug had not been always equally displayed. Once, very early in my career, it had totally failed me; since then I had been obliged on more than one occasion to double, and once, with infinite risk of death, to treble the amount; and these rare uncertainties had cast hitherto the sole shadow on my contentment. Now, however, and in the light of that morning's accident, I was led to remark that whereas, in the beginning, the difficulty had been to throw off the body of Jekyll, it had of late, gradually but decidedly transferred itself to the other side. All things therefore seemed to point to this: that I was slowly losing hold of my original and better self, and becoming slowly incorporated with my second and worse.

Between these two, I now felt I had to choose. My two natures had memory in common, but all other faculties were most unequally shared between them. Jekyll (who was composite) now with the most sensitive apprehensions, now with a greedy gusto, projected and shared in the pleasures and adventures of Hyde; but Hyde was indifferent to Jekyll, or but remembered him as the mountain bandit remembers the cavern in which he conceals himself from pursuit. Jekyll had more than a father's interest; Hyde had more than a son's indifference. To cast in my lot with Jekyll, was to die to those appetites which I had long secretly indulged and had of late begun to pamper. To cast it in with Hyde, was to die to a thousand interests and aspirations, and to become, at a blow and forever, despised and friendless. The bargain might appear unequal; but there was still another consideration in the scales; for while Jekyll would suffer smartingly in the fires of abstinence, Hyde would be not even conscious of all that he had lost. Strange as my circumstances were, the terms of this debate are as old and commonplace as man; much the same inducements and alarms cast the die for any tempted and trembling sinner; and it fell out with me, as it falls with so vast a majority of my fellows, that I chose the better part and was found wanting in the strength to keep to it.

Yes, I preferred the elderly and discontented doctor, surrounded by friends and cherishing honest hopes; and bade a resolute farewell to the liberty, the comparative youth, the light step, leaping pulses and secret pleasures, that I had enjoyed in the disguise of Hyde. I made this choice perhaps with some unconscious reservation, for I neither gave up the house in Soho, nor destroyed the clothes of Edward Hyde, which still lay ready in my cabinet. For two months, however, I was true to my determination; for two months, I led a life of such severity as I had never before attained to, and enjoyed the compensations of an approving conscience. But time began at last to obliterate the freshness of my alarm; the praises of conscience began to grow into a thing of course; I began to be tortured with throes and longings, as of Hyde struggling after freedom; and at last, in an hour of moral weakness, I once again compounded and swallowed the transforming draught.

I do not suppose that, when a drunkard reasons with himself upon his vice, he is once out of five hundred times affected by the dangers that he runs through his brutish, physical insensibility; neither had I, long as I had considered my position, made enough allowance for the complete moral insensibility and insensate readiness to evil, which were the leading characters of Edward Hyde. Yet it was by these that I was punished. My devil had been long caged, he came out roaring. I was conscious, even when I took the draught, of a more unbridled, a more furious propensity to ill. It must have been this, I suppose, that stirred in my soul that tempest of impatience with which I listened to the civilities of my unhappy victim; I declare at least, before God, no man morally sane could have been guilty of that crime upon so pitiful a provocation; and that I struck in no more reasonable spirit than that in which a sick child may break a plaything. But I had voluntarily stripped myself of all those balancing instincts, by which even the worst of us continues to walk with some degree of steadiness among temptations; and in my case, to be tempted, however slightly, was to fall.

Instantly the spirit of hell awoke in me and raged. With a transport of glee, I mauled the unresisting body, tasting delight from every blow; and it was not till weariness had begun to succeed, that I was suddenly, in the top fit of my delirium, struck through the heart by a cold thrill of terror. A mist dispersed; I saw my life to be forfeit; and fled from the scene of these excesses, at once glorying and trembling, my lust of evil gratified and stimulated, my love of life screwed to the topmost peg. I ran to the house in Soho, and (to make assurance doubly sure) destroyed my papers; thence I set out through the lamplit streets, in the same divided ecstasy of mind, gloating on my crime, light-headedly devising others in the future, and yet still hastening and still hearkening in my wake for the steps of the avenger. Hyde had a song upon his lips as he compounded the draught, and as he drank it, pledged the dead man. The pangs of transformation had not done tearing him, before Henry Jekyll, with streaming tears of gratitude and remorse, had fallen upon his knees and lifted his clasped hands to God. The veil of self-indulgence was rent from head to foot. I saw my life as a whole: I followed it up from the days of childhood, when I had walked with my father's hand, and through the self-denying toils of my professional life, to arrive again and again, with the same sense of unreality, at the damned horrors of the evening. I could have screamed aloud; I sought with tears and prayers to smother down the crowd of hideous images and sounds with which my memory swarmed against me; and still, between the petitions, the ugly face of my iniquity stared into my soul. As the acuteness of this remorse began to die away, it was succeeded by a sense of joy. The problem of my conduct was solved. Hyde was thenceforth impossible; whether I would or not, I was now confined to the better part of my existence; and O, how I rejoiced to think of it! with what willing humility, I embraced anew the restrictions of natural life! with what sincere renunciation, I locked the door by which I had so often gone and come, and ground the key under my heel!

The next day, came the news that the murder had been overlooked,[1] that the guilt of Hyde was patent to the world, and that the victim was a man high in public estimation. It was not only a crime, it had been a tragic folly. I think I was glad to know it; I think I was glad to have my better impulses thus buttressed and guarded by the terrors of the scaffold. Jekyll was now my city of refuge; let but Hyde peep out an instant, and the hands of all men would be raised to take and slay him.

I resolved in my future conduct to redeem the past; and I can say with honesty that my resolve was fruitful of some good. You know yourself how earnestly in the last months of the last year, I laboured to relieve suffering; you know that much was done for others, and that the days passed quietly, almost happily for myself. Nor can I truly say that I wearied of this beneficent and innocent life; I think instead that I daily enjoyed it more completely; but I was still cursed with my duality of purpose; and as the first edge of my penitence wore off, the lower side of me, so long indulged, so recently chained down, began to growl for license. Not that I dreamed of resuscitating Hyde; the bare idea of that would startle me to frenzy: no, it was in my own person that I was once more tempted to trifle with my conscience; and it was as an ordinary secret sinner that I at last fell before the assaults of temptation.

---

1 Witnessed.

There comes an end to all things; the most capacious measure is filled at last; and this brief condescension to my evil finally destroyed the balance of my soul. And yet I was not alarmed; the fall seemed natural, like a return to the old days before I had made my discovery. It was a fine, clear, January day, wet under foot where the frost had melted, but cloudless overhead; and the Regent's park[1] was full of winter chirruppings and sweet with spring odours. I sat in the sun on a bench; the animal within me licking the chops of memory; the spiritual side a little drowsed, promising subsequent penitence, but not yet moved to begin. After all, I reflected, I was like my neighbours; and then I smiled, comparing myself with other men, comparing my active goodwill with the lazy cruelty of their neglect. And at the very moment of that vainglorious thought, a qualm came over me, a horrid nausea and the most deadly shuddering. These passed away, and left me faint; and then as in its turn the faintness subsided, I began to be aware of a change in the temper of my thoughts, a greater boldness, a contempt of danger, a solution of the bonds of obligation. I looked down; my clothes hung formlessly on my shrunken limbs; the hand that lay on my knee was corded and hairy. I was once more Edward Hyde. A moment before I had been safe of all men's respect, wealthy, beloved—the cloth laying for me in the diningroom at home; and now I was the common quarry of mankind, hunted, houseless, a known murderer, thrall to the gallows.

My reason wavered, but it did not fail me utterly. I have more than once observed that, in my second character, my faculties seemed sharpened to a point and my spirits more tensely elastic; thus it came about that, where Jekyll perhaps might have succumbed, Hyde rose to the importance of the moment. My drugs were in one of the presses of my cabinet; how was I to reach them? That was the problem that (crushing my temples in my hands) I set myself to solve. The laboratory door I had closed. If I sought to enter by the house, my own servants would consign me to the gallows. I saw I must employ another hand, and thought of Lanyon. How was he to be reached? how persuaded? Supposing that I escaped capture in the streets, how was I to make my way into his presence? and how should I, an unknown and displeasing visitor, prevail on the famous physician to rifle the study of his colleague, Dr. Jekyll? Then I remembered that of

---

1 One of London's Royal Parks, designed by architect John Nash (1752–1835) under commission by the Prince Regent (later George IV) and opened to the public in 1835.

my original character, one part remained to me: I could write my own hand; and once I had conceived that kindling spark, the way that I must follow became lighted up from end to end. Thereupon, I arranged my clothes as best I could, and summoning a passing hansom, drove to an hotel in Portland street, the name of which I chanced to remember. At my appearance (which was indeed comical enough, however tragic a fate these garments covered) the driver could not conceal his mirth. I gnashed my teeth upon him with a gust of devilish fury; and the smile withered from his face—happily for him—yet more happily for myself, for in another instant I had certainly dragged him from his perch. At the inn, as I entered, I looked about me with so black a countenance as made the attendants tremble; not a look did they exchange in my presence; but obsequiously took my orders, led me to a private room, and brought me wherewithal to write. Hyde in danger of his life was a creature new to me: shaken with inordinate anger, strung to the pitch of murder, lusting to inflict pain. Yet the creature was astute; mastered his fury with a great effort of the will; composed his two important letters, one to Lanyon and one to Poole; and that he might receive actual evidence of their being posted, sent them out with directions that they should be registered.

Thenceforward, he sat all day over the fire in the private room, gnawing his nails; there he dined, sitting alone with his fears, the waiter visibly quailing before his eye; and thence, when the night was fully come, he set forth in the corner of a closed cab, and was driven to and fro about the streets of the city. He, I say—I cannot say, I. That child of Hell had nothing human; nothing lived in him but fear and hatred. And when at last, thinking the driver had begun to grow suspicious, he discharged the cab and ventured on foot, attired in his misfitting clothes, an object marked out for observation, into the midst of the nocturnal passengers, these two base passions raged within him like a tempest. He walked fast, hunted by his fears, chattering to himself, skulking through the less frequented thoroughfares, counting the minutes that still divided him from midnight. Once a woman spoke to him, offering, I think, a box of lights. He smote her in the face, and she fled.

When I came to myself at Lanyon's, the horror of my old friend perhaps affected me somewhat: I do not know; it was at least but a drop in the sea to the abhorrence with which I looked back upon these hours. A change had come over me. It was no longer the fear of the gallows, it was the horror of being Hyde that racked me. I received Lanyon's condemnation partly in a dream;

it was partly in a dream that I came home to my own house and got into bed. I slept after the prostration of the day, with a stringent and profound slumber which not even the nightmares that wrung me could avail to break. I awoke in the morning shaken, weakened, but refreshed. I still hated and feared the thought of the brute that slept within me, and I had not of course forgotten the appalling dangers of the day before; but I was once more at home, in my own house and close to my drugs; and gratitude for my escape shone so strong in my soul that it almost rivalled the brightness of hope.

I was stepping leisurely across the court after breakfast, drinking the chill of the air with pleasure, when I was seized again with those indescribable sensations that heralded the change; and I had but the time to gain the shelter of my cabinet, before I was once again raging and freezing with the passions of Hyde. It took on this occasion a double dose to recall me to myself; and alas, six hours after, as I sat looking sadly in the fire, the pangs returned, and the drug had to be re-administered. In short, from that day forth it seemed only by a great effort as of gymnastics, and only under the immediate stimulation of the drug, that I was able to wear the countenance of Jekyll. At all hours of the day and night, I would be taken with the premonitory shudder; above all, if I slept, or even dozed for a moment in my chair, it was always as Hyde that I awakened. Under the strain of this continually impending doom and by the sleeplessness to which I now condemned myself, ay, even beyond what I had thought possible to man, I became, in my own person, a creature eaten up and emptied by fever, languidly weak both in body and mind, and solely occupied by one thought: the horror of my other self. But when I slept, or when the virtue of the medicine wore off, I would leap almost without transition (for the pangs of transformation grew daily less marked) into the possession of a fancy brimming with images of terror, a soul boiling with causeless hatreds, and a body that seemed not strong enough to contain the raging energies of life. The powers of Hyde seemed to have grown with the sickliness of Jekyll. And certainly the hate that now divided them was equal on each side. With Jekyll, it was a thing of vital instinct. He had now seen the full deformity of that creature that shared with him some of the phenomena of consciousness, and was co-heir with him to death: and beyond these links of community, which in themselves made the most poignant part of his distress, he thought of Hyde, for all his energy of life, as of something not only hellish but inorganic. This was the shocking thing; that the slime of the pit seemed to utter cries and voices; that the amorphous dust gesticulated and sinned; that what was dead, and had no shape, should usurp the offices of life. And this again, that that insurgent horror was knit to him closer than a wife, closer than an eye; lay caged in his flesh, where he heard it mutter and felt it struggle to be born; and at every hour of weakness, and in the confidence of slumber, prevailed against him, and deposed him out of life. The hatred of Hyde for Jekyll was of a different order. His terror of the gallows drove him continually to commit temporary suicide, and return to his subordinate station of a part instead of a person; but he loathed the necessity, he loathed the despondency into which Jekyll was now fallen, and he resented the dislike with which he was himself regarded. Hence the apelike tricks that he would play me, scrawling in my own hand blasphemies on the pages of my books, burning the letters and destroying the portrait of my father; and indeed, had it not been for his fear of death, he would long ago have ruined himself in order to involve me in the ruin. But his love of life is wonderful; I go further: I, who sicken and freeze at the mere thought of him, when I recall the abjection and passion of this attachment, and when I know how he fears my power to cut him off by suicide, I find it in my heart to pity him.

It is useless, and the time awfully fails me, to prolong this description; no one has ever suffered such torments, let that suffice; and yet even to these, habit brought—no, not alleviation—but a certain callousness of soul, a certain acquiescence of despair; and my punishment might have gone on for years, but for the last calamity which has now fallen, and which has finally severed me from my own face and nature. My provision of the salt, which had never been renewed since the date of the first experiment, began to run low. I sent out for a fresh supply, and mixed the draught; the ebullition followed, and the first change of colour, not the second; I drank it and it was without efficiency. You will learn from Poole how I have had London ransacked; it was in vain; and I am now persuaded that my first supply was impure, and that it was that unknown impurity which lent efficacy to the draught.

About a week has passed, and I am now finishing this statement under the influence of the last of the old powders. This, then, is the last time, short of a miracle, that Henry Jekyll can think his own thoughts or see his own face (now how sadly altered!) in the glass. Nor must I delay too long to bring my writing to an end; for if my narrative has hitherto escaped destruction, it has been by a combination of great prudence and great good luck. Should the throes of change take me in the act of writing it, Hyde will tear it in pieces; but if some time shall have elapsed after I have laid it by, his wonderful selfishness and circumscription to the moment will probably save it once again from the action of his apelike spite. And indeed the doom that is closing on us both has already changed and crushed him. Half an hour from now, when I shall again and forever reindue that hated personality, I know how I shall sit shuddering and weeping in my chair, or continue, with the most strained and fearstruck ecstasy of listening, to pace up and down this room (my last earthly refuge) and give ear to every sound of menace. Will Hyde die upon the scaffold? or will he find the courage to release himself at the last moment? God knows; I am careless; this is my true hour of death, and what is to follow concerns another than myself. Here then, as I lay down the pen and proceed to seal up my confession, I bring the life of that unhappy Henry Jekyll to an end.

Appendix A: Stevenson's "A Chapter on Dreams" (1888)

[Stevenson's "A Chapter on Dreams" was first published in *Scribner's Magazine*, 3 January 1888. Written during October 1887, the essay closely resembles an interview given to the *New York Herald*, 8 September 1887. While the essay is autobiographical, Stevenson coyly writes as if it is about someone else, and then reveals that he himself is the subject. In a small way Stevenson thus duplicates the uncertainties about identity found in the tale of *Dr. Jekyll and Mr. Hyde*. The essay is here reprinted from *The Complete Works of Robert Louis Stevenson*, vol. 12 (New York: Scribner's, 1921).]

"A Chapter on Dreams"

The past is all of one texture—whether feigned or suffered—whether acted out in three dimensions, or only witnessed in that small theatre of the brain which we keep brightly lighted all night long, after the jets are down[1] and darkness and sleep reign undisturbed in the remainder of the body. There is no distinction on the face of our experiences; one is vivid indeed, and one dull, and one pleasant, and another agonising to remember; but which of them is what we call true, and which a dream, there is not one hair to prove. The past stands on a precarious footing; another straw split in the Weld of metaphysic, and behold us robbed of it. There is scarce a family that can count four generations but lays a claim to some dormant title or some castle and estate: a claim not prosecutable in any court of law, but flattering to the fancy and a great alleviation of idle hours. A man's claim to his own past is yet less valid. A paper might turn up (in proper story-book fashion) in the secret drawer of an old ebony secretary,[2] and restore your family to its ancient honours, and reinstate mine in a certain West Indian islet (not far from St. Kitt's,[3] as beloved tradition hummed in my young ears) which was once ours, and is now unjustly some one else's, and for that matter (in the state of the sugar trade) is not worth anything to anybody. I do not say that these revolutions are likely; only no man can deny that they are possible; and the past, on the other hand, is lost

---

1 Flames from gas lighting, turned down low at night.
2 A desk, especially one that is primarily a surface for writing.
3 An island in the West Indies, now an independent nation, but during Stevenson's time a part of the British Empire.

for ever: our old days and deeds, our old selves, too, and the very world in which these scenes were acted, all brought down to the same faint residuum as a last night's dream, to some incontinuous images, and an echo in the chambers of the brain. Not an hour, not a mood, not a glance of the eye, can we revoke; it is all gone, past conjuring.[1] And yet conceive us robbed of it, conceive that little thread of memory that we trail behind us broken at the pocket's edge; and in what naked nullity should we be left! For we only guide ourselves, and only know ourselves, by these airpainted pictures of the past.

Upon these grounds, there are some among us who claim to have lived longer and more richly than their neighbours; when they lay asleep they claim they were still active; and among the treasures of memory that all men review for their amusement, these count in no second place the harvests of their dreams. There is one of this kind whom I have in my eye, and whose case is perhaps unusual enough to be described. He was from a child an ardent and uncomfortable dreamer. When he had a touch of fever at night, and the room swelled and shrank, and his clothes, hanging on a nail, now loomed up instant to the bigness of a church, and now drew away into a horror of infinite distance and infinite littleness, the poor soul was very well aware of what must follow, and struggled hard against the approaches of that slumber which was the beginning of sorrows. But his struggles were in vain; sooner or later the night-hag would have him by the throat, and pluck him, strangling and screaming, from his sleep. His dreams were at times commonplace enough, at times very strange: at times they were almost formless, he would be haunted, for instance, by nothing more definite than a certain hue of brown, which he did not mind in the least while he was awake, but feared and loathed while he was dreaming; at times, again, they took on every detail of circumstance, as when once he supposed he must swallow the populous world, and awoke screaming with the horror of the thought. The two chief troubles of his very narrow existence—the practical and everyday trouble of school tasks and the ultimate and airy one of hell and judgment—were often confounded together into one appalling nightmare. He seemed to himself to stand before the Great White Throne; he was called on, poor little devil, to recite some form of words, on which his destiny depended; his tongue stuck, his memory was blank, hell gasped for him; and he would awake, clinging to the curtain-rod with his knees to his chin.

These were extremely poor experiences, on the whole; and at that time of life my dreamer would have very willingly parted with his

---

1 No longer accessible to memory.

power of dreams. But presently, in the course of his growth, the cries and physical contortions passed away, seemingly for ever; his visions were still for the most part miserable, but they were more constantly supported; and he would awake with no more extreme symptom than a flying heart, a freezing scalp, cold sweats, and the speechless midnight fear. His dreams, too, as befitted a mind better stocked with particulars, became more circumstantial, and had more the air and continuity of life. The look of the world beginning to take hold on his attention, scenery came to play a part in his sleeping as well as in his waking thoughts, so that he would take long, uneventful journeys and see strange towns and beautiful places as he lay in bed. And, what is more significant, an odd taste that he had for the Georgian[1] costume and for stories laid in that period of English history, began to rule the features of his dreams; so that he masqueraded there in a three-cornered hat, and was much engaged with Jacobite[2] conspiracy between the hour for bed and that for breakfast. About the same time, he began to read in his dreams—tales, for the most part, and for the most part after the manner of G.P.R. James,[3] but so incredibly more vivid and moving than any printed book, that he has ever since been malcontent with literature.

And then, while he was yet a student, there came to him a dream-adventure which he has no anxiety to repeat; he began, that is to say, to dream in sequence and thus to lead a double life—one of the day, one of the night—one that he had every reason to believe was the true one, another that he had no means of proving to be false. I should have said he studied, or was by way of studying, at Edinburgh college, which (it may be supposed) was how I came to know him. Well, in his dream-life, he passed along the day in the surgical theatre, his heart in his mouth, his teeth on edge, seeing monstrous malformations and the abhorred dexterity of surgeons. In a heavy, rainy, foggy evening he came forth into the South Bridge, turned up the High Street, and entered the door of a tall *land*,[4] at the top of which he supposed

---

1 The period during which four different Georges reigned as King of England, covering most of the eighteenth century.

2 A conspiracy by the supporters of the Scottish Stuart pretenders to the throne, known as "Jacobites," who tried unsuccessfully to gain control of England.

3 George Payne Rainsford James (1799–1860), a doctor by profession and former naval officer, who wrote numerous successful adventure novels, including *Henry Masterton* (1832) and *Ticonderoga* (1854).

4 Scottish word meaning a multi-storey house subdivided into apartments.

himself to lodge. All night long, in his wet clothes, he climbed the stairs, stair after stair in endless series, and at every second flight a flaring lamp with a reflector. All night long, he brushed by single persons passing downward—beggarly women of the street, great, weary, muddy labourers, poor scarecrows of men, pale parodies of women—but all drowsy and weary like himself, and all single, and all brushing against him as they passed. In the end, out of a northern window, he would see day beginning to whiten over the Firth,[1] give up the ascent, turn to descend, and in a breath be back again upon the streets, in his wet clothes, in the wet, haggard dawn, trudging to another day of monstrosities and operations. Time went quicker in the life of dreams, some seven hours (as near as he can guess) to one; and it went, besides, more intensely, so that the gloom of these fancied experiences clouded the day, and he had not shaken off their shadow ere it was time to lie down and to renew them. I cannot tell how long it was that he endured this discipline; but it was long enough to leave a great black blot upon his memory, long enough to send him, trembling for his reason, to the doors of a certain doctor; whereupon with a simple draught he was restored to the common lot of man.

The poor gentleman has since been troubled by nothing of the sort; indeed, his nights were for some while like other men's, now blank, now chequered with dreams, and these sometimes charming, sometimes appalling, but except for an occasional vividness, of no extraordinary kind. I will just note one of these occasions, ere I pass on to what makes my dreamer truly interesting. It seemed to him that he was in the first floor of a rough hill-farm. The room showed some poor efforts at gentility, a carpet on the floor, a piano, I think, against the wall; but, for all these refinements, there was no mistaking he was in a moorland place, among hillside people, and set in miles of heather. He looked down from the window upon a bare farmyard, that seemed to have been long disused. A great, uneasy stillness lay upon the world. There was no sign of the farm-folk or of any live-stock, save for an old, brown, curly dog of the retriever breed, who sat close in against the wall of the house and seemed to be dozing. Something about this dog disquieted the dreamer; it was quite a nameless feeling, for the beast looked right enough—indeed, he was so old and dull and dusty and broken down, that he should rather have awakened pity; and yet the conviction came and grew upon the dreamer that this was no proper dog at all, but something hellish. A great many dozing summer flies hummed about the yard; and presently the dog thrust forth his paw, caught a fly in his open palm, carried it to his mouth like an ape, and

---

1 Scottish word for a long, narrow inlet, in this instance the Firth of Forth.

looking suddenly up at the dreamer in the window, winked to him with one eye. The dream went on, it matters not how it went; it was a good dream as dreams go; but there was nothing in the sequel worthy of that devilish brown dog. And the point of interest for me lies partly in that very fact: that having found so singular an incident, my imperfect dreamer should prove unable to carry the tale to a fit end and fall back on indescribable noises and indiscriminate horrors. It would be different now; he knows his business better!

For, to approach at last the point: This honest fellow had long been in the custom of setting himself to sleep with tales, and so had his father before him; but these were irresponsible inventions, told for the teller's pleasure, with no eye to the crass public or the thwart[1] reviewer: tales where a thread might be dropped, or one adventure quitted for another, on fancy's least suggestion. So that the little people who manage man's internal theatre had not as yet received a very rigorous training; and played upon their stage like children who should have slipped into the house and found it empty, rather than like drilled actors performing a set piece to a huge hall of faces. But presently my dreamer began to turn his former amusement of story-telling to (what is called) account; by which I mean that he began to write and sell his tales. Here was he, and here were the little people who did that part of his business, in quite new conditions. The stories must now be trimmed and pared and set upon all fours, they must run from a beginning to an end and fit (after a manner) with the laws of life; the pleasure, in one word, had become a business; and that not only for the dreamer, but for the little people of his theatre. These understood the change as well as he. When he lay down to prepare himself for sleep, he no longer sought amusement, but printable and profitable tales; and after he had dozed off in his boxseat, his little people continued their evolutions with the same mercantile designs. All other forms of dream deserted him but two: he still occasionally reads the most delightful books, he still visits at times the most delightful places; and it is perhaps worthy of note that to these same places, and to one in particular, he returns at intervals of months and years, finding new Weld-paths, visiting new neighbours, beholding that happy valley under new effects of noon and dawn and sunset. But all the rest of the family of visions is quite lost to him: the common, mangled version of yesterday's affairs, the raw-head-and-bloody-bones nightmare, rumoured to be the child of toasted cheese—these and their like are gone; and, for the most part, whether awake or asleep, he is simply occupied—he or his little people—in consciously

1 Obstructive.

making stories for the market. This dreamer (like many other persons) has encountered some trifling vicissitudes of fortune. When the bank begins to send letters and the butcher to linger at the back gate, he sets to belabouring his brains after a story, for that is his readiest money-winner; and, behold! at once the little people begin to bestir themselves in the same quest, and labour all night long, and all night long set before him truncheons of tales upon their lighted theatre. No fear of his being frightened now; the flying heart and the frozen scalp are things by-gone; applause, growing applause, growing interest, growing exultation in his own cleverness (for he takes all the credit), and at last a jubilant leap to wakefulness, with the cry, "I have it, that'll do!" upon his lips: with such and similar emotions he sits at these nocturnal dramas, with such outbreaks, like Claudius in the play,[1] he scatters the performance in the midst. Often enough the waking is a disappointment: he has been too deep asleep, as I explain the thing; drowsiness has gained his little people, they have gone stumbling and maundering through their parts; and the play, to the awakened mind, is seen to be a tissue of absurdities. And yet how often have these sleepless Brownies[2] done him honest service, and given him, as he sat idly taking his pleasure in the boxes, better tales than he could fashion for himself.

Here is one, exactly as it came to him. It seemed he was the son of a very rich and wicked man, the owner of broad acres and a most damnable temper. The dreamer (and that was the son) had lived much abroad, on purpose to avoid his parent; and when at length he returned to England, it was to find him married again to a young wife, who was supposed to suffer cruelly and to loathe her yoke. Because of this marriage (as the dreamer indistinctly understood) it was desirable for father and son to have a meeting; and yet both being proud and both angry, neither would condescend upon a visit. Meet they did accordingly, in a desolate, sandy country by the sea; and there they quarreled, and the son, stung by some intolerable insult, struck down the father dead. No suspicion was aroused; the dead man was found and buried, and the dreamer succeeded to the broad estates, and found himself installed under the same roof with his father's widow, for whom no provision had been made. These two lived very much alone, as people may after a bereavement, sat down to table together, shared the long evenings, and grew daily better friends; until it seemed to him of a sudden that she was prying about dangerous matters, that she had conceived a notion of his guilt, that she watched him and tried

---

1 King Claudius in Shakespeare's *Hamlet*.

2 In folklore, goblin-like creatures who live in the home and help with household tasks.

him with questions. He drew back from her company as men draw back from a precipice suddenly discovered; and yet so strong was the attraction that he would drift again and again into the old intimacy, and again and again be startled back by some suggestive question or some inexplicable meaning in her eye. So they lived at cross purposes, a life full of broken dialogue, challenging glances, and suppressed passion; until, one day, he saw the woman slipping from the house in a veil, followed her to the station, followed her in the train to the sea-side country, and out over the sand-hills to the very place where the murder was done. There she began to grope among the bents,[1] he watching her, flat upon his face; and presently she had something in her hand—I cannot remember what it was, but it was deadly evidence against the dreamer—and as she held it up to look at it, perhaps from the shock of the discovery, her foot slipped, and she hung at some peril on the brink of the tall sand-wreaths. He had no thought but to spring up and rescue her; and there they stood face to face, she with that deadly matter openly in her hand—his very presence on the spot another link of proof. It was plain she was about to speak, but this was more than he could bear—he could bear to be lost, but not to talk of it with his destroyer; and he cut her short with trivial conversation. Arm in arm, they returned together to the train, talking he knew not what, made the journey back in the same carriage, sat down to dinner, and passed the evening in the drawing room as in the past. But suspense and fear drummed in the dreamer's bosom. "She has not denounced me yet"—so his thoughts ran—"when will she denounce me? Will it be to-morrow?" And it was not to-morrow, nor the next; and their life settled back on the old terms, only that she seemed kinder than before, and that, as for him, the burthen of his suspense and wonder grew daily more unbearable, so that he wasted away like a man with a disease. Once, indeed, he broke all bounds of decency, seized an occasion when she was abroad, ransacked her room, and at last, hidden away among her jewels, found the damning evidence. There he stood, holding this thing, which was his life, in the hollow of his hand, and marvelling at her inconsequent behaviour, that she should seek, and keep, and yet not use it, and then the door opened, and behold herself. So, once more, they stood, eye to eye, with the evidence between them; and once more she raised to him a face brimming with some communication; and once more he shied away from speech and cut her off. But before he left the room, which he had turned upside down, he laid back his death-warrant where he had found it; and at that, her face lighted up. The next thing he heard, she

---

1 Reedy grass.

was explaining to her maid, with some ingenious falsehood, the disorder of her things. Flesh and blood could bear the strain no longer; and I think it was the next morning (although chronology is always hazy in the theatre of the mind) that he burst from his reserve. They had been breakfasting together in one corner of a great, parqueted, sparely furnished room of many windows; all the time of the meal she had tortured him with sly allusions; and no sooner were the servants gone and these two protagonists alone together, than he leaped to his feet. She too sprang up, with a pale face; with a pale face, she heard him as he raved out his complaint: Why did she torture him so? she knew all, she knew he was no enemy to her; why did she not denounce him at once? what signified her whole behaviour? why did she torture him? and yet again, why did she torture him? and when he had done, she fell upon her knees, and with outstretched hands: "Do you not understand?" she cried. "I love you!"

Hereupon, with a pang of wonder and mercantile delight, the dreamer awoke. His mercantile delight was not of long endurance; for it soon became plain that in this spirited tale there were unmarketable elements; which is just the reason why you have it here so briefly told. But his wonder has still kept growing; and I think the reader's will also, if he consider it ripely. For now he sees why I speak of the little people as of substantive inventors and performers. To the end they had kept their secret. I will go bail for the dreamer (having excellent grounds for valuing this candour) that he had no guess whatever at the motive of the woman—the hinge of the whole well-invented plot—until the instant of that highly dramatic declaration. It was not his tale; it was the little people's! And observe: not only was the secret kept, the story was told with really guileful craftsmanship. The conduct of both actors is (in the cant phrase) psychologically correct, and the emotion aptly graduated up to the surprising climax. I am awake now, and I know this trade; and yet I cannot better it. I am awake, and I live by this business; and yet I could not outdo—could not perhaps equal—that craft artifice (as of some old, experienced carpenter of plays, some Dennery[1] or Sardou[2]) by which the same situation is twice presented and the two actors twice brought face to face over the evidence, only once it is in her hand, once in his—and these in their due order, the least dramatic first. The more I think of it, the more I am moved to press upon the world my question: Who are the Little People? They are near connections of the dreamer's, beyond doubt; they share in his financial worries and have an eye to the bank-book; they share plainly

---

1 Adolphe Dennery (1811–99), French playwright.
2 Victorien Sardou (1831–1908), French playwright.

in his training; they have plainly learned like him to build the scheme of a considerate story and to arrange emotion in progressive order; only I think they have more talent; and one thing is beyond doubt, they can tell him a story piece by piece, like a serial, and keep him all the while in ignorance of where they aim. Who are they, then? And who is the dreamer?

Well, as regards the dreamer, I can answer that, for he is no less a person than myself;—as I might have told you from the beginning, only that the critics murmur over my consistent egotism;—and as I am positively forced to tell you now, or I could advance but little farther with my story. And for the Little People, what shall I say they are but just my Brownies, God bless them! Who do one-half my work for me while I am fast asleep, and in all human likelihood, do the rest for me as well, when I am wide awake and fondly suppose I do it for myself. That part which is done while I am wide awake and fondly suppose I do it for myself. That part which is done while I am sleeping is the Brownies' part beyond contention; but that which is done when I am up and about is by no means necessarily mine, since all goes to show the Brownies have a hand in it even then. Here is a doubt that much concerns my conscience. For myself—what I call I, my conscience, ego, the denizen of the pineal gland[1] unless he has changed his residence since Descartes,[2] the man with the conscience and the variable bank-account, the man with the hat and the boots, and the privilege of voting and not carrying his candidate at the general elections—I am sometimes tempted to suppose he is no story-teller at all, but a creature as matter of fact as any cheesemonger or any cheese, and a realist bemired up to the ears in actuality; so that, by that account, the whole of my published fiction should be the single-handed product of some Brownie, some Familiar,[3] some unseen collaborator, whom I keep locked in a back garret, while I get all the praise and he but a share (which I cannot prevent him getting) of the pudding. I am an excellent adviser, something like Molière's[4] servant; I pull back and I cut down; and I dress the whole in the best words and sentences that I can find and make; I hold the pen, too; and I do the sitting at the table, which is about the worst of it; and when all is done, I make up the manuscript and pay for the registration; so that, on the whole, I have some claim to share, though not so largely as I do, in the profits of our common enterprise.

---

1 A gland in the brain.

2 René Descartes (1596–1650), French philosopher.

3 A demon in the shape of an animal under the control of a witch or wizard.

4 Jean-Baptiste Poquelin (1622–73), known by his stage name Molière, one of the most accomplished and famous writers of comedy for the French stage.

I can but give an instance or so of what part is done sleeping and what part awake, and leave the reader to share what laurels there are, at his own nod, between myself and my collaborators; and to do this I will take a book that a number of persons have been polite enough to read, the *Strange Case of Dr. Jekyll and Mr. Hyde*. I had long been trying to write a story on this subject, to find a body, a vehicle, for that strong sense of man's double being which must at times come in upon and overwhelm the mind of every thinking creature. I had even written one, *The Travelling Companion*, which was returned by an editor on the plea that it was a work of genius and indecent, and which I burned the other day on the ground that it was not a work of genius, and that *Jekyll* had supplanted it. Then came one of those financial fluctuations to which (with an elegant modesty) I have hitherto referred in the third person. For two days I went about racking my brains for a plot of any sort; and on the second night I dreamed the scene at the window, and a scene afterwards split in two, in which Hyde, pursued for some crime, took the powder and underwent the change in the presence of his pursuers. All the rest was made awake, and consciously, although I think I can trace in much of it the manner of my Brownies. The meaning of the tale is therefore mine, and had long pre-existed in my garden of Adonis,[1] and tried one body after another in vain; indeed, I do most of the morality, worse luck! and my Brownies have not a rudiment of what we call a conscience. Mine, too, is the setting, mine the characters. All that was given me was the matter of three scenes, and the central idea of a voluntary change becoming involuntary. Will it be thought ungenerous, after I have been so liberally ladling out praise to my unseen collaborators, if I here toss them over, bound hand and foot, into the arena of the critics? For the business of the powders, which so many have censured, is, I am relieved to say, not mine at all but the Brownies'. Of another tale, in case the reader should have glanced at it, I may say a word: the not very defensible story of *Olalla*.[2] Here the court, the mother, the mother's niche, Olalla, Olalla's chamber, the meetings on the stair, the broken window, the ugly scene of the bite, were all given me in bulk and detail as I have tried to write them; to this I added only the external scenery (for in my dream I never was beyond the court), the portrait, the characters of Felipe and the priest, the moral, such as it is, and the last

---

1   A beautiful young man loved by Aphrodite, and often used generally as a synonym for male beauty.

2   Stevenson's "Olalla" was first published in the *Court and Society Review* (Christmas 1885) and reprinted in *The Merry Men and Other Fables* (1887). Stevenson was never satisfied with this tale of a "double" and felt it rang false where "Markheim" rang true.

pages, such as, alas! they are. And I may even say that in this case the moral itself was given me; for it arose immediately on a comparison of the mother and the daughter, and from the hideous trick of atavism in the first. Sometimes a parabolic sense is still more undeniably present in a dream; sometimes I cannot but suppose my Brownies have been aping Bunyan,[1] and yet in no case with what would possibly be called a moral in a tract; never with the ethical narrowness; conveying hints instead of life's larger limitations and that sort of sense which we seem to perceive in the arabesque of time and space.

For the most part, it will be seen, my Brownies are somewhat fantastic, like their stories hot and hot, full of passion and the picturesque, alive with animating incident; and they have no prejudice against the supernatural. But the other day they gave me a surprise, entertaining me with a love-story, a little April comedy, which I ought certainly to hand over to the author of *A Chance Acquaintance*, for he could write it as it should be written, and I am sure (although I mean to try) that I cannot.—But who would have supposed that a Brownie of mine should invent a tale for Mr. Howells?[2]

---

1 John Bunyan (1628–88), author of the spiritual autobiography *Pilgrim's Progress* (1678).

2 Noted American literary critic William Dean Howells (1837–1920), editor-in-chief of the *Atlantic Monthly*. His novel *A Chance Acquaintance* was published in 1873. His best-selling novels included *The Rise of Silas Lapham* (1885).

Appendix B: Stevenson's "Markheim" (1884)

[Stevenson wrote "Markheim" in late November 1884. A revised version was published in *The Merry Men and Other Tales and Fables* (1887). In the story, Stevenson explores the idea of a "double" character, as he does in *Dr. Jekyll and Mr. Hyde*, but from a very different perspective. The essay is here reprinted from *The Complete Works of Robert Louis Stevenson*, vol. 11 (New York: Scribner's, 1921).]

"Yes," said the dealer, "our windfalls are of various kinds. Some customers are ignorant, and then I touch a dividend of my superior knowledge. Some are dishonest," and here he held up the candle, so that the light fell strongly on his visitor, "and in that case," he continued, "I profit by my virtue."

Markheim had but just entered from the day-light streets, and his eyes had not yet grown familiar with the mingled shine and darkness in the shop. At these pointed words, and before the near presence of the flame, he blinked painfully and looked aside.

The dealer chuckled. "You come to me on Christmas Day," he resumed, "when you know that I am alone in my house, put up my shutters, and make a point of refusing business. Well, you will have to pay for that; you will have to pay for my loss of time, when I should be balancing my books; you will have to pay, besides, for a kind of manner that I remark in you to-day very strongly. I am the essence of discretion, and ask no awkward questions; but when a customer cannot look me in the eye, he has to pay for it." The dealer once more chuckled; and then, changing to his usual business voice, though still with a note of irony, "You can give, as usual, a clear account of how you came into the possession of the object?" he continued. "Still your uncle's cabinet? A remarkable collector, sir!"

And the little pale, round-shouldered dealer stood almost on tiptoe, looking over the top of his gold spectacles, and nodding his head with every mark of disbelief. Markheim returned his gaze with one of infinite pity, and a touch of horror.

"This time," said he, "you are in error. I have not come to sell, but to buy. I have no curios to dispose of; my uncle's cabinet is bare to the wainscot; even were it still intact, I have done well on the Stock Exchange, and should more likely add to it than otherwise, and my errand to-day is simplicity itself. I seek a Christmas present for a lady," he continued, waxing more fluent as he struck into the speech he had prepared; "and certainly I owe you every excuse for thus disturbing you upon so small a matter. But the thing was neglected yesterday; I must produce my little compliment at dinner; and, as you very well know, a rich marriage is not a thing to be neglected."

There followed a pause, during which the dealer seemed to weigh this statement incredulously. The ticking of many clocks among the curious lumber of the shop, and the faint rushing of the cabs in a near thoroughfare, filled up the interval of silence.

"Well, sir," said the dealer, "be it so. You are an old customer after all; and if, as you say, you have the chance of a good marriage, far be it from me to be an obstacle.—Here is a nice thing for a lady now," he went on, "this hand glass[1]—fifteenth century, warranted; comes from a good collection, too; but I reserve the name, in the interests of my customer, who was just like yourself, my dear sir, the nephew and sole heir of a remarkable collector."

The dealer, while he thus ran on in his dry and biting voice, had stooped to take the object from its place; and, as he had done so, a shock had passed through Markheim, a start both of hand and foot, a sudden leap of many tumultuous passions to the face. It passed as swiftly as it came, and left no trace beyond a certain trembling of the hand that now received the glass. "A glass," he said hoarsely, and then paused, and repeated it more clearly. "A glass? For Christmas? Surely not?"

"And why not?" cried the dealer. "Why not a glass?"

Markheim was looking upon him with an indefinable expression. "You ask me why not?" he said. "Why, look here—look in it—look at yourself! Do you like to see it? No! nor I—nor any man."

The little man had jumped back when Markheim had so suddenly confronted him with the mirror; but now, perceiving there was nothing worse on hand, he chuckled. "Your future lady, sir, must be pretty hard-favoured," said he.

"I ask you," said Markheim, "for a Christmas present, and you give me this—this damned reminder of years, and sins and follies—this handconscience! Did you mean it? Had you a thought in your mind? Tell me. It will be better for you if you do. Come, tell me about yourself. I hazard a guess now, that you are in secret a very charitable man?"

The dealer looked closely at his companion. It was very odd, Markheim did not appear to be laughing; there was something in his face like an eager sparkle of hope, but nothing of mirth.

"What are you driving at?" the dealer asked.

---

1 Hand-held mirror.

"Not charitable?" returned the other, gloomily. "Not charitable; not pious; not scrupulous; unloving, unbeloved; a hand to get money, a safe to keep it. Is that all? Dear God, man, is that all?"

"I will tell you what it is," began the dealer, with some sharpness, and then broke off again into a chuckle. "But I see this is a love-match of yours, and you have been drinking the lady's health."

"Ah!" cried Markheim, with a strange curiosity. "Ah, have you been in love? Tell me about that." "I," cried the dealer. "I in love! I never had the time, nor have I the time to-day for all this nonsense. Will you take the glass?"

"Where is the hurry?" returned Markheim. "It is very pleasant to stand here talking; and life is so short and insecure that I would not hurry away from any pleasure—no, not even from so mild a one as this. We should rather cling, cling to what little we can get, like a man at a cliff's edge. Every second is a cliff, if you think upon it—a cliff a mile high—high enough, if we fall, to dash us out of every feature of humanity. Hence it is best to talk pleasantly. Let us talk of each other; why should we wear this mask? Let us be confidential. Who knows we might become friends?"

"I have just one word to say to you," said the dealer. "Either make your purchase, or walk out of my shop."

"True, true," said Markheim. "Enough fooling. To business. Show me something else." The dealer stooped once more, this time to replace the glass upon the shelf, his thin blond hair falling over his eyes as he did so. Markheim moved a little nearer, with one hand in the pocket of his great-coat; he drew himself up and filled his lungs; at the same time many different emotions were depicted together on his face—terror, horror, and resolve, fascination and a physical repulsion; and through a haggard lift of his upper lip, his teeth looked out. "This, perhaps, may suit," observed the dealer; and then, as he began to re-arise, Markheim bounded from behind upon his victim. The long, skewer-like dagger flashed and fell. The dealer struggled like a hen, striking his temple on the shelf, and then tumbled on the floor in a heap.

Time had some score of small voices in that shop,[1] some stately and slow as was becoming to their great age; others garrulous and hurried. All these told out the seconds in an intricate chorus of tickings. Then the passage of a lad's feet, heavily running on the pavement, broke in upon these smaller voices and startled Markheim into the consciousness of his surroundings. He looked about him awfully. The candle stood on the counter, its flame solemnly wagging in a draught; and by

---

1 I.e., the shop was filled with clocks.

that inconsiderable movement, the whole room was filled with noise-less bustle and kept heaving like a sea: the tall shadows nodding, the gross blots of darkness swelling and dwindling as with respiration, the faces of the portraits and the china gods changing and wavering like images in water. The inner door stood ajar, and peered into that leaguer of shadows with a long slit of daylight like a pointing finger.

From these fear-stricken rovings, Markheim's eyes returned to the body of his victim, where it lay both humped and sprawling, incredibly small and strangely meaner than in life. In these poor, miserly clothes, in that ungainly attitude, the dealer lay like so much sawdust. Markheim had feared to see it, and, lo! it was nothing. And yet, as he gazed, this bundle of old clothes and pool of blood began to find eloquent voices. There it must lie; there was none to work the cunning hinges or direct the miracle of locomotion—there it must lie till it was found. Found! ay, and then? Then would this dead flesh lift up a cry that would ring over England, and gill the world with the echoes of pursuit. Ay, dead or not, this was still the enemy. "Time was that when the brains were out," he thought; and the first word struck into his mind. Time, now that the deed was accomplished—time, which had closed for the victim, had become instant and momentous for the slayer.

The thought was yet in his mind, when, first one and then another, with every variety of pace and voice—one deep as the bell from a cathedral turret, another ringing on its treble notes the prelude of a waltz—the clocks began to strike the hour of three in the afternoon.

The sudden outbreak of so many tongues in that dumb chamber staggered him. He began to bestir himself, going to and fro with the candle, beleaguered by moving shadows, and startled to the soul by chance resections. In many rich mirrors, some of home designs, some from Venice or Amsterdam, he saw his face repeated and repeated, as it were an army of spies; his own eyes met and detected him; and the sound of his own steps, lightly as they fell, vexed the surrounding quiet. And still as he continued to fill his pockets, his mind accused him, with a sickening iteration, of the thousand faults of his design. He should have chosen a more quiet hour; he should have prepared an alibi; he should not have used a knife; he should have been more cautious, and only bound and gagged the dealer, and not killed him; he should have been more bold, and killed the servant also; he should have done all things otherwise; poignant regrets, weary, incessant toiling of the mind to change what was unchangeable, to plan what was now useless, to be the architect of the irrevocable past. Meanwhile, and behind all this activity, brute terrors, like the scurrying of rats in a deserted attic, filled the more remote chambers of his brain with riot; the hand of the constable would fall heavy on his shoulder, and his nerves would jerk like a hooked fish; or he beheld, in galloping defile,[1] the dock, the prison, the gallows, and the black coffin.

Terror of the people in the street sat down before his mind like a besieging army. It was impossible, he thought, but that some rumour of the struggle must have reached their ears and set on edge their curiosity; and now, in all the neighbouring houses, he divined them sitting motionless and with uplifted ear—solitary people, condemned to spend Christmas dwelling alone on memories of the past, and now startlingly recalled from that tender exercise; happy family parties, struck into silence round the table, the mother still with raised finger: every degree and age and humour, but all, by their own hearts, prying and hearkening and weaving the rope that was to hang him. Sometimes it seemed to him he could not move too softly; the clink of the tall Bohemian goblets rang out loudly like a bell; and alarmed by the bigness of the ticking, he was tempted to stop the clocks. And then, again, with a swift transition of his terrors, the very silence of the place appeared a source of peril, and a thing to strike and freeze the passerby; and he would step more boldly, and bustle aloud among the contents of the shop, and imitate, elaborate bravado, the movements of a busy man at ease in his own house.

But he was now so pulled about by different alarms that, while one portion of his mind was still alert and cunning, another trembled on the brink of lunacy. One hallucination in particular took a strong hold on his credulity. The neighbour hearkening with white face beside his window, the passer-by arrested by a horrible surmise on the pavement—these could at worst suspect, they could not know; through the brick walls and shuttered windows only sounds could penetrate. But here, within the house, was he alone? He knew he was; he had watched the servant set forth sweethearting,[2] in her poor best, "out for the day" written in every ribbon and smile. Yes, he was alone, of course; and yet, in the bulk of empty house above him, he could surely hear a stir of delicate footing—he was surely conscious, inexplicably conscious of some presence. Ay, surely; to every room and corner of the house his imagination followed it; and now it was a faceless thing, and yet had eyes to see with; and again it was a shadow of himself; and yet again behold the image of the dead dealer, reinspired with cunning and hatred.

At times, with a strong effort, he would glance at the open door which still seemed to repel his eyes. The house was tall, the skylight small and dirty, the day blind with fog; and the light that filtered down

---

1 The verb *défiler* (French) means to march or gallop in single file; a *défilé* is a parade.

2 I.e., to meet her boyfriend.

to the ground story was exceedingly faint, and showed dimly on the threshold of the shop. And yet, in that strip of doubtful brightness, did there not hang wavering a shadow?

Suddenly, from the street outside, a very jovial gentleman began to beat with a staff on the shop door, accompanying his blows with shouts and railleries in which the dealer was continually called upon by name. Markheim, smitten into ice, glanced at the dead man. But no! he lay quite still; he was fled away far beyond ear-shot of these blows and shootings; he was sunk beneath seas of silence; and his name, which would once have caught his notice above the howling of a storm, had become an empty sound. And presently the jovial gentleman desisted from his knocking and departed.

Here was a broad hint to hurry what remained to be done, to get forth from this accusing neighbourhood, to plunge into a bath of London multitudes, and to reach, on the other side of day, that haven of safety and apparent innocence—his bed. One visitor had come: at any moment another might follow and be more obstinate. To have done the deed, and yet not to reap the profit would be too abhorrent a failure. The money, that was now Markheim's concern; and as a means to that, the keys.

He glanced over his shoulder at the open door, where the shadow was still lingering and shivering; and with no conscious repugnance of the mind, yet with a tremor of the belly, he drew near the body of his victim. The human character had quite departed. Like a suit half stuffed with bran, the limbs lay scattered, the trunk doubled, on the floor; and yet the thing repelled him. Although so dingy and inconsiderable to the eye, he feared it might have more significance to the touch. He took the body by the shoulders, and turned it on its back. It was strangely light and supple, and the limbs, as if they had been broken, fell into the oddest postures. The face was robbed of all expression; but it was as pale as wax, and shockingly smeared with blood about one temple. That was, for Markheim, the one displeasing circumstance. It carried him back, upon the instant, to a certain fair day[1] in a fishers' village: a grey day, a piping wind, a crowd upon the street, the blare of brasses, the booming of drums, the nasal voice of a ballad-singer; and a boy going to and fro, buried over head in the crowd and divided between interest and fear, until, coming out upon the chief place of concourse, he beheld a booth and a great screen with pictures, dismally designed, garishly coloured: Brownrigg with her apprentice; the Mannings with their murdered guest; Weare in the

---

1 Local festival.

death-grip of Thurtell;[1] and a score besides of famous crimes. The thing was as clear as an illusion; he was once again that little boy; he was looking once again, and with the same sense of physical revolt, at these vile pictures; he was still stunned by the thumping of the drums. A bar of that day's music returned upon his memory; and at that, for the first time, a qualm came over him, a breath of nausea, a sudden weakness of the joints, which he must instantly resist and conquer.

He judged it more prudent to confront than to flee from these considerations; looking the more hardily in the dead face, bending his mind to realise the nature and greatness of his crime. So little a while ago that face had moved with every change of sentiment, that pale mouth had spoken, that body had been all on fire with governable energies; and now, and by his act, that piece of life had been arrested, as the horologist,[2] with interjected finger, arrests the beating of the clock. So he reasoned in vain; he could rise to no more remorseful consciousness; the same heart which had shuddered before the painted effigies of crime looked on its reality unmoved. At best, he felt a gleam of pity for one who had been endowed in vain with all those faculties that can make the world a garden of enchantment, one who had never lived and who was now dead. But of penitence, no, not a tremor.

With that, shaking himself clear of these considerations, he found the keys and advanced towards the open door of the shop. Outside, it had begun to rain smartly; and the sound of the shower upon the roof had banished silence. Like some dripping cavern, the chambers of the house were haunted by an incessant echoing, which filled the ear and mingled with the ticking of the clocks. And, as Markheim approached the door, he seemed to hear, in answer to his own cautious tread, the steps of another foot withdrawing up the stair. The shadow still palpitated loosely on the threshold. He threw a ton's weight of resolve upon his muscles, and drew back the door.

The faint, foggy daylight glimmered dimly on the bare floor and stairs; on the bright suit of armour posted, halbert[3] in hand, upon the landing; and on the dark wood-carvings and framed pictures that hung

---

1 Elizabeth Brownrigg was the most hated of female criminals of the eighteenth
   century. In 1767 she beat to death one of her girl apprentices. In 1849 the
   Mannings murdered their friend, Patrick O'Connor, and buried his body in
   quicklime under their kitchen floor. In October 1823 Thurtell bludgeoned
   Weare to death with his gun when it failed to go off during his initial attempt
   at murder.
2 Maker of or dealer in clocks and watches.
3 A combination spear and battle axe; also spelled halberd.

against the yellow panels of the wainscot. So loud was the beating of the rain through all the house that, in Markheim's ears, it began to be distinguished into many different sounds. Footsteps and sighs, the tread of regiments marching in the distance, the chink of money in the counting, and the creaking of doors held stealthily ajar, appeared to mingle with the patter of the drops upon the cupola and the gushing of the water in the pipes. The sense that he was not alone grew upon him to the verge of madness. On every side he was haunted and begirt by presences. He heard them moving in the upper chambers; from the shop, he heard the dead man getting to his legs; and as he began with a great effort to mount the stairs, feet fled quietly before him and followed stealthily behind. If he were but deaf, he thought, how tranquilly he would possess his soul! And then again, and hearkening with ever fresh attention, he blessed himself for that unresting sense which held the outposts and stood a trusty sentinel upon his life. His head turned continually on his neck; his eyes, which seemed starting from their orbits, scouted on every side, and on every side were half rewarded as with the tail of something nameless vanishing. The four-and-twenty steps to the first floor were four-and-twenty agonies.

On that first story, the doors stood ajar, three of them like three ambushes, shaking his nerves like the throats of cannon. He could never again, he felt, be sufficiently immured and fortified from men's observing eyes; he longed to be home, girt in by walls, buried among bedclothes, and invisible to all but God. And at that thought he wondered a little, recollecting tales of other murderers and the fear they were said to entertain of heavenly avengers. It was not so, at least, with him. He feared the laws of nature, lest, in their callous and immutable procedure, they should preserve some damning evidence of his crime. He feared tenfold more, with a slavish, superstitious terror, some scission[1] in the continuity of man's experience, some wilful illegality of nature. He played a game of skill, depending on the rules, calculating consequence from cause; and what if nature, as the defeated tyrant overthrew the chess-board, should break the mould of their succession? The like had befallen Napoleon (so writers said) when the winter changed the time of its appearance.[2] The like might befall Markheim: the solid walls might become transparent and reveal his doings like those of bees in a glass hive; the stout planks might yield under his foot like quicksands and detain him in their clutch; ay, and there were soberer accidents that might destroy him: if, for instance, the house should fall and imprison him beside the body of his victim; or the

---

1 A sharp cut or divide.

2 Napoleon's invasion of Russia in 1812 supposedly was thwarted by the early arrival of one of the most brutal winters of the nineteenth century.

house next door should fly on fire, and the firemen invade him from all sides. These things he feared; and, in a sense, these things might be called the hands of God reached forth against sin. But about God himself he was at ease; his act was doubtless exceptional, but so were his excuses, which God knew; it was there, and not among men, that he felt sure of justice.

When he had got safe into the drawing-room, and shut the door behind him, he was aware of a respite from alarms. The room was quite dismantled, uncarpeted besides, and strewn with packing-cases and incongruous furniture; several great pier-glasses,[1] in which he beheld himself at various angles, like an actor on a stage; many pictures, framed and unframed, standing, with their faces to the wall; a fine Sheraton[2] sideboard, a cabinet of marquetry,[3] and a great old bed, with tapestry hangings. The windows opened to the floor; but by great good-fortune the lower part of the shutters had been closed, and this concealed him from the neighbours. Here, then, Markheim drew in a packing-case before the cabinet, and began to search among the keys. It was a long business, for there were many; and it was irksome, besides; for, after all, there might be nothing in the cabinet, and time was on the wing. But the closeness of the occupation sobered him. With the tail of his eye he saw the door—even glanced at it from time to time directly, like a besieged commander pleased to verify the good state of his defences. But in truth he was at peace. The rain falling in the street sounded natural and pleasant. Presently, on the other side, the notes of a piano were wakened to the music of a hymn, and the voices of many children took up the air and words. How stately, how comfortable was the melody! How fresh the youthful voices! Markheim gave ear to it smilingly, as he sorted out the keys; and his mind was thronged with answerable ideas and images; church-going children and the pealing of the high organ; children afield, bathers by the brookside, ramblers on the brambly common, kite-fliers in the windy and cloud-navigated sky; and then, at another cadence of the hymn, back again to church, and the somnolence of summer Sundays, and the high genteel voice of the parson (which he smiled a little to recall) and the painted Jacobean tombs, and the dim lettering of the Ten Commandments in the chancel.

And as he sat thus, at once busy and absent, he was startled to his feet. A flash of ice, a flash of fire, a bursting gush of blood, went over him, and then he stood transfixed and thrilling. A step mounted the

---

1 Large, tall mirrors.

2 Thomas Sheraton (1751–1806), British cabinet maker.

3 Inlaid decoration on furniture.

stair slowly and steadily, and presently a hand was laid upon the knob, and the lock clicked, and the door opened.

Fear held Markheim in a vice. What to expect he knew not, whether the dead man walking, or the official ministers of human justice, or some chance witness blindly stumbling in to consign him to the gallows. But when a face was thrust into the aperture, glanced round the room, looked at him, nodded and smiled as if in friendly recognition, and then withdrew again, and the door closed behind it, his fear broke loose from his control in a hoarse cry. At the sound of this the visitant returned.

"Did you call me?" he asked, pleasantly, and with that he entered the room and closed the door behind him.

Markheim stood and gazed at him with all his eyes. Perhaps there was a film upon his sight, but the outlines of the new-comer seemed to change and waver like those of the idols in the wavering candle-light of the shop; and at times he thought he knew him; and at times he thought he bore a likeness to himself; and always, like a lump of living terror, there lay in his bosom the conviction that this thing was not of the earth and not of God.

And yet the creature had a strange air of the commonplace, as he stood looking on Markheim with a smile; and when he added: "You are looking for the money, I believe?" it was in the tones of every-day politeness.

Markheim made no answer.

"I should warn you," resumed the other, "that the maid has left her sweetheart earlier than usual and will soon be here. If Mr. Markheim be found in this house, I need not describe to him the consequences."

"You know me?" cried the murderer.

The visitor smiled. "You have long been a favourite of mine," he said; "and I have long observed and often sought to help you."

"What are you?" cried Markheim, "the devil?"

"What I may be," returned the other, "cannot affect the service I propose to render you."

"It can," cried Markheim; "it does! Be helped by you? No, never; not by you! You do not know me yet; thank God, you do not know me!"

"I know you," replied the visitant, with a sort of kind severity or rather firmness. "I know you to the soul."

"Know me!" cried Markheim. "Who can do so? My life is but a travesty and slander on myself. I have lived to belie my nature. All men do; all men are better than this disguise that grows about and stifles them. You see each dragged away by life, like one whom bravos[1] have

---

1 Criminals paid to perform illegal acts, including murder.

seized and muffled in a cloak. If they had their own control—if you could see their faces, they would be altogether different, they would shine out for heroes and saints! I am worse than most; my self is more overlaid; my excuse is known to me and God. But, had I the time, I could disclose myself."

"To me?" inquired the visitant.

"To you before all," returned the murderer. "I supposed you were intelligent. I thought—since you exist—you would prove a reader of the heart. And yet you would propose to judge me by my acts! Think of it; my acts! I was born and I have lived in a land of giants; giants have dragged me by the wrists since I was born out of my mother— the giants of circumstance. And you would judge me by my acts! But can you not look within? Can you not understand that evil is hateful to me? Can you not see within me the clear writing of conscience, never blurred by any wilful sophistry, although too often disregarded? Can you not read me for a thing that surely must be common as humanity—the unwilling sinner?"

"All this is very feelingly expressed," was the reply, "but it regards me not. These points of consistency are beyond my province, and I care not in the least by what compulsion you may have been dragged away, so as you are but carried in the right direction. But time flies; the servant delays, looking in the faces of the crowd and at the pictures on the hoardings, but still she keeps moving nearer; and remember, it is as if the gallows itself was striding towards you through the Christmas streets! Shall I help you; I, who know all? Shall I tell you where to find the money?"

"For what price?" asked Markheim.

"I offer you the service for a Christmas gift," returned the other.

Markheim could not refrain from smiling with a kind of bitter triumph. "No," said he, "I will take nothing at your hands; if I were dying of thirst, and it was your hand that put the pitcher to my lips, I should find the courage to refuse. It may be credulous, but I will do nothing to commit myself to evil."

"I have no objection to a death-bed repentance," observed the visitant.

"Because you disbelieve their efficacy!" Markheim cried. "I do not say so," returned the other; "but I look on these things from a different side, and when the life is done my interest falls. The man has lived to serve me, to spread black looks under colour of religion, or to sow tares[1] in the wheatfield, as you do, in a course of weak compliance with desire. Now that he draws so near to his deliverance, he can add

---

1 Weeds; Matthew 13:25: "But while men slept, his enemy came and sowed tares among the wheat, and went his way."

but one act of service—to repent, to die smiling, and thus to build up in confidence and hope the more timorous of my surviving followers. I am not so hard a master. Try me. Accept my help. Please yourself in life as you have done hitherto; please yourself more amply, spread your elbows at the board; and when the night begins to fall and the curtains to be drawn, I tell you, for your greater comfort, that you will find it even easy to compound your quarrel with your conscience, and to make a truckling[1] peace with God. I came but now from such a death-bed, and the room was full of sincere mourners, listening to the man's last words: and when I looked into that face, which had been set as a flint against mercy, I found it smiling with hope."

"And do you, then, suppose me such a creature?" asked Markheim. "Do you think I have no more generous aspirations than to sin, and sin, and sin, and, at last, sneak into heaven? My heart rises at the thought. Is this, then, your experience of mankind? or is it because you find me with red hands that you presume such baseness? and is this crime of murder indeed so impious as to dry up the very springs of good?"

"Murder is to me no special category," replied the other. "All sins are murder, even as all life is war. I behold your race, like starving mariners on a raft, plucking crusts out of the hands of famine and feeding on each other's lives. I follow sins beyond the moment of their acting; I find in all that the last consequence is death; and to my eyes, the pretty maid who thwarts her mother with such taking graces on a question of a ball, drips no less visibly with human gore than such a murderer as yourself. Do I say that I follow sins? I follow virtues also; they differ not by the thickness of a nail, they are both scythes for the reaping angel of Death. Evil, for which I live, consists not in action but in character. The bad man is dear to me; not the bad act, whose fruits, if we could follow them far enough down the hurtling cataract of the ages, might yet be found more blessed than those of the rarest virtues. And it is not because you have killed a dealer, but because you are Markheim, that I offered to forward your escape."

"I will lay my heart open to you," answered Markheim. "This crime on which you find me is my last. On my way to it I have learned many lessons; itself is a lesson, a momentous lesson. Hitherto I have been driven with revolt to what I would not; I was a bond-slave to poverty, driven and scourged. There are robust virtues that can stand in these temptations; mine was not so: I had a thirst of pleasure. But today, and out of this deed, I pluck both warning and riches—both the power and a fresh resolve to be myself. I become in all things a free actor in the

---

1 Submissive, servile.

world; I begin to see myself all changed, these hands the agents of good, this heart at peace. Something comes over me out of the past; something of what I have dreamed on Sabbath evenings to the sound of the church organ, of what I forecast when I shed tears over noble books, or talked, an innocent child, with my mother. There lies my life; I have wandered a few years, but now I see once more my city of destination."

"You are to use this money on the Stock Exchange, I think?" remarked the visitor; "and there, if I mistake not, you have already lost some thousands?"

"Ah," said Markheim, "but this time I have a sure thing."

"This time, again, you will lose," replied the visitor quietly.

"Ah, but I keep back the half!" cried Markheim.

"That also you will lose," said the other.

The sweat started upon Markheim's brow.

"Well, then, what matter?" he exclaimed. "Say it be lost, say I am plunged again in poverty, shall one part of me, and that the worst, continue until the end to over-ride the better? Evil and good run strong in me, haling[1] me both ways. I do not love the one thing, I love all. I can conceive great deeds, renunciations, martyrdoms; and though I be fallen to such a crime as murder, pity is no stranger to my thoughts. I pity the poor; who knows their trials better than myself? I pity and help them; I prize love, I love honest laughter; there is no good thing nor true thing on earth but I love it from my heart. And are my vices only to direct my life, and my virtues to lie without effect, like some passive lumber of the mind? Not so; good, also, is a spring of acts."

But the visitant raised his finger. "For six-and-thirty years that you have been in this world," said he, "through many changes of fortune and varieties of humour, I have watched you steadily fall. Fifteen years ago you would have started at a theft. Three years back you would have blenched at the name of murder. Is there any crime, is there any cruelty or meanness, from which you still recoil?—five years from now I shall detect you in the fact! Downward, downward, lies your way; nor can anything but death avail to stop you."

"It is true," Markheim said huskily, "I have in some degree complied with evil. But it is so with all: the very saints, in the mere exercise of living, grow less dainty and take on the tone of their surroundings."

"I will propound to you one simple question," said the other; "and as you answer, I shall read to you your moral horoscope. You have grown in many things more lax; possibly you do right to be so; and at

---

1 Pulling, hauling.

any account, it is the same with all men. But granting that, are you in any one particular, however trifling, more difficult to please with your own conduct, or do you go in all things with a looser rein?"

"In any one?" repeated Markheim, with an anguish of consideration. "No," he added, with despair, "in none! I have gone down in all."

"Then," said the visitor, "content yourself with what you are, for you will never change; and the words of your part on this stage are irrevocably written down."

Markheim stood for a long while silent, and indeed it was the visitor who first broke the silence. "That being so," he said, "shall I show you the money?"

"And grace?" cried Markheim.

"Have you not tried it?" returned the other. "Two or three years ago, did I not see you on the platform of revival meetings, and was not your voice the loudest in the hymn?"

"It is true," said Markheim; "and I see clearly what remains for me by way of duty. I thank you for these lessons from my soul; my eyes are opened, and I behold myself at last for what I am."

At this moment, the sharp note of the doorbell rang through the house; and the visitant, as though this were some concerted signal for which he had been waiting, changed at once in his demeanour. "The maid!" he cried. "She has returned, as I forewarned you, and there is now before you one more difficult passage. Her master, you must say, is in; you must let her in, with an assured but rather serious countenance—no smiles, no over-acting, and I promise you success! Once the girl within, and the door closed, the same dexterity that has already rid you of the dealer will relieve you of this last danger in your path. Thenceforward you have the whole evening—the whole night, if needful—to ransack the treasures of the house and to make good your safety. This is help that comes to you with the mask of danger. Up!" he cried: "up, friend; your life hangs trembling in the scales: up, and act!"

Markheim steadily regarded his counsellor. "If I be condemned to evil acts," he said, "there is still one door of freedom open—I can cease from action. If my life be an ill thing, I can lay it down. Though I be, as you say truly, at the beck of every small temptation, I can yet, by one decisive gesture, place myself beyond the reach of all. My love of good is damned to barrenness; it may, and let it be! But I have still my hatred of evil; and from that, to your galling disappointment, you shall see that I can draw both energy and courage."

The features of the visitor began to undergo a wonderful and lovely change: they brightened and softened with a tender triumph; and, even as they brightened, faded and dislimned.[1] But Markheim did not pause to watch or understand the transformation. He opened the door and went down-stairs very slowly, thinking to himself. His past went soberly before him; he beheld it as it was, ugly and strenuous like a dream, random as chance-medley—a scene of defeat. Life, as he thus reviewed it, tempted him no longer; but on the further side he perceived a quiet haven for his bark.[2] He paused in the passage, and looked into the shop, where the candle still burned by the dead body. It was strangely silent. Thoughts of the dealer swarmed into his mind, as he stood gazing. And then the bell once more broke out into impatient clamour.

He confronted the maid upon the threshold with something like a smile.

"You had better go for the police," said he: "I have killed your master."

---

1 Disappeared.
2 Small boat.

Appendix C: Stevenson's Deacon Brodie (1879)

[Stevenson wrote *Deacon Brodie* in collaboration with W.E. Henley. First drafts by Stevenson have been dated from as early as 1864. Henley and Stevenson worked most intensively on the play between October 1878 and January 1880. The copyright edition of the play was published as *Deacon Brodie, or the Double Life: A Melodrama, Founded on Facts, in Four Acts and Ten Tableaux* by T. and A. Constable, Edinburgh, December 1879. Corrected copies of the edition were used for performances in 1882, 1883, 1884, and 1887. In the brief soliloquy below, from Act I, Scene ix, Deacon Brodie resolves to commit one more night-time burglary to raise the money his sister needs in order to marry, vowing that this is the last time he will commit such a crime. As usual, he uses a clothes press to make it look as if he is sleeping in his bed when he is in fact prowling around the city at night, leading the nocturnal half of his divided existence. The parallels with the divided Dr. Jekyll's night-time activities as Mr. Hyde are striking. The soliloquy is reprinted from *The Complete Works of Robert Louis Stevenson*, vol. 12 (New York: Scribner's, 1921).]

([Brodie] closes, locks, and double-bolts both doors.)

BRODIE. Now for one of the Deacon's headaches! Rogues all, rogues all (goes to clothes-press, and proceeds to change his coat). On with the new coat and into the new life! Down with the Deacon and up with the robber! (Changing neck-band and ruffles.) Eh God! how still the house is! There's something in hypocrisy after all. If we were as good as we seem, what would the world be? The city has its vizard[1] on, and we—at night we are our naked selves. Trysts are keeping, bottles cracking, knives are stripping; and here is Deacon Brodie flaming forth the man of men he is!—How still it is! ... My father and Mary— Well! the day for them, the night for me; the grimy cynical night that makes all cats grey, and all honesties of one complexion. Shall a man not have *half* a life of his own?—not eight hours out of twentyfour? Eight shall he have should he dare the pit of Tophet.[2] (Takes out money.) Where's the blunt?[3] I must be cool to-night, or steady,

---

1   Mask or disguise.
2   A shrine, south of ancient Jerusalem, where human sacrifices were believed to have been performed; also used as a synonym for hell.
3   Money.

Deacon, you must win; damn you, you must! You must win back the dowry that you've stolen, and marry your sister and pay your debts, and gull the world a little longer! (As he blows out the lights.) The Deacon's going to bed—the poor sick Deacon! *Allons!* (Throws up the window, and looks out.) Only the stars to see me! (Addressing the bed.) Lie there, Deacon! sleep and be well to-morrow. As for me, I'm a man once more till morning. (Gets out of the window.)

Appendix D: Letters, 1885-87

[After consulting with doctors upon his return to England from the continent in July 1884, Stevenson moved to Bournemouth because of its supposedly beneficial climate. The climate does not seem to have had its desired effect because Stevenson was in ill health for most of his time there. For the first two months Stevenson and Fanny lived in a lodging house called Wensleydale. Stevenson wrote frequently to his parents, complaining about his health and asking for money. By this time Stevenson was living in "Skerryvore," the house purchased for him by his father. Unless otherwise noted, letters reprinted here have been selected from Project Gutenberg e-text #637 of *The Letters of Robert Louis Stevenson*, ed. Sidney Colvin (NewYork: Scribner's, 1921) at www.gutenberg.org/cache/epub/637/pg637.txt]

Skerryvore, Bournemouth, December 26th, 1885

MY DEAR LOW,[1]—
... A photograph will be taken of my ugly mug and sent to you for ulterior purposes: I have another thing coming out,[2] which I did not put in the way of the Scribners, I can scarce tell how; but I was sick and penniless and rather back on the world, and mismanaged it. I trust they will forgive me....

[In this next letter Stevenson expresses his enduring affection for his cousin, Katharine de Mattos, dedicating *Dr. Jekyll and Mr. Hyde* to her and composing a poem about their childhood years in Scotland.]

Skerryvore, Bournemouth, January 1st, 1886

DEAREST KATHARINE,—Here, on a very little book and accompanied with lame verses, I have put your name. Our kindness is now getting well on in years; it must be nearly of age; and it gets more valuable to me with every time I see you. It is not possible to express any sentiment, and it is not necessary to try, at least between us. You know very well that I love you dearly, and that I always will. I only wish the verses

---

1 Will H. Low (1853–1932) was an American artist who lived in Europe and was a lifelong friend of Stevenson.
2 *Dr. Jekyll and Mr. Hyde.*

were better, but at least you like the story; and it is sent to you by the one that loves you—Jekyll, and not Hyde.

R.L.S.

[The copy of an edition of Keats's *Lamia*, illustrated by William Low, for which Stevenson had been waiting had finally arrived and Stevenson writes an appreciation of the book. He then goes on to make intriguing remarks about the applicability of that tale to himself and Low.]

Skerryvore, Bournemouth, January 2nd, 1886

MY DEAR LOW,—

... I send you herewith a Gothic gnome for your Greek nymph;[1] but the gnome is interesting, I think, as he came out of a deep mine, where he guards the fountain of tears. It is not always the time to rejoice,—yours ever

R.L.S.

P.S. The gnome's name is *Jekyll & Hyde*; I believe you will find he likewise quite willing to answer to the name Low or Stevenson.

[Edmund Gosse (1849–1928), the well-known Victorian author and literary critic, was another frequent correspondent of Stevenson's. In this letter Stevenson admits to ambivalence on being the successful author of a popular work like *Dr. Jekyll and Mr. Hyde*. His opinion of bourgeois Victorian taste was not high, and so he feels that success may in some way be a mark of failure on his part to convey a critical enough message. The letter is a striking example of Stevenson's divided attitudes to his public and his growing fame.]

Skerryvore, Bournemouth, January 2nd, 1886

MY DEAR GOSSE,—Thank you for your letter, so interesting to my vanity. There is a review in the *St. James's*, which, as it seems to hold somewhat of your opinions, and is besides written with a pen and not a poker, we think may possibly be yours.[2] The *Prince* has done fairly

---

1   The subject of Keats's poem, Lamia was a nymph, originally a snake, who assumed the form of a woman.

2   Stevenson thought that an anonymous review of his novel *Prince Otto* had been written by Gosse, erroneously as it turned out.

well in spite of the reviews, which have been bad; he was, as you doubtless saw, well slated in the *Saturday*; one paper received it as a child's story; another (picture my agony) described it as a "Gilbert comedy."[1] It was amusing to see the race between me and Justin M'Carthy:[2] The Milesian has won by a length.

That is the hard part of literature. You aim high, and you take longer over your work, and it will not be so successful as if you had aimed low and rushed it. What the public likes is work (of any kind) a little loosely executed; so long as it is a little wordy, a little slack, a little dim and knotless, the dear public likes it; it should (if possible) be a little dull into the bargain. I know that good work sometimes hits; but, with my hand on my heart, I think it is by an accident. And I know also that good work must succeed at last; but that is not the doing of the public; they are only shamed into silence or affectation. I do not write for the public; I do write for money, a nobler deity; and most of all for myself, not perhaps any more noble, but both more intelligent and nearer home.

Let us tell each other sad stories of the bestiality of the beast whom we feed. What he likes is the newspaper; and to me the press is the mouth of a sewer, where lying is professed as from an university chair, and everything prurient, and ignoble, and essentially dull, finds its abode and pulpit. I do not like mankind; but men, and not all of these—and fewer women. As for respecting the race, and, above all, that fatuous rabble of burgesses called "the public," God save me from such irreligion!—that way lies disgrace and dishonour. There must be something wrong in me, or I would not be popular.

This is perhaps a trifle stronger than my sedate and permanent opinion. Not much, I think. As for the art that we practice, I have never been able to see why its professors should be respected. They chose the primrose path; when they found it was not all primroses, but some of it brambly, and much of it uphill, they began to think and to speak of themselves as holy martyrs. But a man is never martyred in any honest sense in the pursuit of his pleasure; and *delirium tremens* has more of the honour of the cross. We were full of the pride of life, and chose, like prostitutes, to live by a pleasure. We should be paid if we give the pleasure we pretend to give; but why should we be honoured?

R.L.S.

---

1 A reference to the comic operas of Gilbert and Sullivan.
2 Justin M'Carthy (1830–1912), author of the recently published novel *Camiola* (1886).

[Responding to a review of his works by Edward Sheridan Purcell (1824–99), Stevenson, in the extract below, links *Jekyll and Hyde* to his own ethical doubts. The next letter is reproduced from *The Letters of Robert Louis Stevenson*, vol. 5, ed. Bradford A. Booth and Ernest Mehew (New Haven, Yale UP, 1995).]

Skerryvore, Bournemouth February 27th 1886
(*Letters*, vol. 5, pp. 212–13)

[...] Second. What you say about the confusion of my ethics, I own to be all too true. It is, as you say, where I fall and fall almost consciously. I have the old Scotch Presbyterian preoccupation about these problems; itself morbid; I have alongside that a second, perhaps more— possibly less—morbid element—the dazzled incapacity to choose, of an age of transition. The categorical imperative is ever with me, but utters dark oracles. This is a ground almost of pity. The Scotch side came out plain in Dr. Jekyll; the XIXth century side probably baffled me even there, and in most other places baffles me entirely. Ethics are my veiled mistress; I love them, but I know not what they are. Is it my fault? Partly, of course, it is; because I love my sins like other people. Partly my merit, because I do not take, and rest contented in, the first subterfuge.

[John Addington Symonds (1840–93), a successful poet and literary critic, was a friend of Stevenson's until his marriage to Fanny. Fanny and Symonds did not get along, and the two saw each other infrequently thereafter. In this letter Stevenson expresses regret at some of the material included in *Dr. Jekyll and Mr. Hyde*, and then goes on to give a glowing opinion of the writings of Fyodor Dostoyevsky.]

Skerryvore, Bournemouth [Spring 1886]

MY DEAR SYMONDS,—If we have lost touch, it is (I think) only in a material sense; a question of letters, not hearts. You will find a warm welcome at Skerryvore from both the lightkeepers; and, indeed, we never tell ourselves one of our financial fairy tales, but a run to Davos[1] is a prime feature. I am not changeable in friendship; and I think I can promise you have a pair of trusty well-wishers and friends in Bournemouth: whether they write or not is but a small thing; the flag may not be waved, but it is there.

---

1 The Swiss town where Stevenson had lived before moving to Bournemouth.

Jekyll is a dreadful thing, I own; but the only thing I feel dreadful about is that damned old business of the war in the members.[1] This time it came out; hope it will stay in, in future.

Raskolnikoff[2] is easily the greatest book I have read in ten years; I am glad you took to it. Many find it dull: Henry James could not finish it: all I can say is, it nearly finished me. It was like having an illness. James did not care for it because the character of Raskolnikoff was not objective; and at that I divined a great gulf between us, and, on further reflection, the existence of a certain impotence in many minds of to-day, which prevents them from living in a book or a character, and keeps them standing afar off, spectators of a puppet show. To such I suppose the book may seem empty in the centre; to the others it is a room, a house of life, into which they themselves enter, and are tortured and purified. The Juge d'Instruction I thought a wonderful, weird, touching, ingenious creation: the drunken father, and Sonia, and the student friend, and the uncircumscribed, protoplasmic humanity of Raskolnikoff, all upon a level that filled me with wonder: the execution also, superb in places. Another has been translated *Humiliés et Offensés*—. It is even more incoherent than *Le Crime et le Châtiment*, but breathes much of the same lovelygoodness, and has passages of power. Dostoieffsky is a devil of a swell,[3] to be sure. Have you heard that he became a stout, imperialist conservative? It is interesting to know. To something of that side, the balance leans with me also in view of the incoherency and incapacity of all. The old boyish idea of the march on Paradise being now out of season, and all plans and ideas that I hear debated being built on a superb indifference to the first principles of human character, a helpless desire to acquiesce in anything of which I know the worst assails me. Fundamental errors in human nature of two sorts stand on the skyline of all this modern world of aspirations. First, that it is happiness that men want; and second, that happiness consists of anything but an internal harmony. Men do not want, and I do not think they would accept, happiness; what they live for is rivalry, effort, success—the elements our friends wish to eliminate. And, on the other hand, happiness is a question of morality—or of immorality, there is no difference—and conviction. Gordon was happy in Khartoum,[4] in his worst hours of danger and

---

1 James 4:1: "... your lusts that war in your members."
2 The protagonist of Dostoyevsky's *Crime and Punishment* (1866).
3 A stylishly dressed gentleman.
4 A reference to the siege of Khartoum (13 March 1884–26 January 1885), in the Sudan, in which General Gordon and all his troops were killed.

fatigue; Marat[1] was happy, I suppose, in his ugliest frenzy; Marcus Aurelius[2] was happy in the detested camp; Pepys[3] was pretty happy, and I am pretty happy on the whole, because we both somewhat crowingly accepted a via media, both liked to attend to our affairs, and both had some success in managing the same. It is quite an open question whether Pepys and I ought to be happy; on the other hand, there is no doubt that Marat had better be unhappy. He was right (if he said it) that he was la misère humaine, cureless misery—unless perhaps by the gallows. Death is a great and gentle solvent; it has never had justice done it, no, not by Whitman.[4]

As for those crockery chimney-piece ornaments, the bourgeois (*quorum pars*),[5] and their cowardly dislike of dying and killing, it is merely one symptom of a thousand how utterly they have got out of touch of life. Their dislike of capital punishment and their treatment of their domestic servants are for me the two daunting emblems of their hollowness.

God knows where I am driving to. But here comes my lunch.

Which interruption, happily for you, seems to have stayed the issue. I have now nothing to say, that had formerly such a pressure of twaddle. Pray don't fail to come this summer. It will be a great disappointment, now it has been spoken of, if you do.—Yours ever,

ROBERT LOUIS STEVENSON

[F.W.H. Myers (1843–1901) sent Stevenson a very long and detailed critique of *Dr. Jekyll and Mr. Hyde*. This is Stevenson's reply.]

Skerryvore, Bournemouth, March 1st, 1886

MY DEAR SIR,—I know not how to thank you: this is as handsome as it is clever. With almost every word I agree—much of it I even knew before—much of it, I must confess, would never have been, if I had been able to do what I like, and lay the thing by for the matter of a year. But the wheels of Byles the Butcher[6] drive exceeding swiftly, and

---

1 Jean-Paul Marat (1743–93), a leader of a radical faction during the French Revolution, was assassinated while taking a bath.
2 Marcus Aurelius Claudius Quintillius, a Roman emperor in 270 CE, died or was killed a few weeks after being proclaimed emperor.
3 Samuel Pepys (1633–1703), famous British diarist who was for a period in disgrace when he fell out of political favour.
4 Walt Whitman (1819–92), perhaps the most famous American poet of his day.
5 For the most part (Latin).
6 A tradesman trying to collect a debt.

Jekyll was conceived, written, re-written, re-rewritten, and printed inside ten weeks. Nothing but this white-hot haste would explain the gross error of Hyde's speech at Lanyon's. Your point about the specialised Wend is more subtle, but not less just: I had not seen it.— About the picture, I rather meant that Hyde had brought it himself; and Utterson's hypothesis of the gift an error.—The tidiness of the room, I thought, but I dare say my psychology is here too ingenious to be sound, was due to the dread weariness and horror of the imprisonment. Something has to be done: he would tidy the room. But I dare say it is false.

I shall keep your paper; and if ever my works come to be collected, I will put my back into these suggestions. In the meanwhile, I do truly lack words in which to express my sense of gratitude for the trouble you have taken. The receipt of such a paper is more than a reward for my labours. I have read it with pleasure, and as I say, I hope to use it with profit.—Believe me, your most obliged,

ROBERT LOUIS STEVENSON

[Stevenson never saw Richard Mansfield's production of *Jekyll and Hyde*, though his wife and her mother did when they were in New York. Stevenson is responding to a review of Mansfield's performance in his letter to the critic, journalist, and editor John Paul Bocock. The next letter is reproduced from *The Letters of Robert Louis Stevenson*, vol. 6, ed. Bradford A. Booth and Ernest Mehew (New Haven: Yale UP, 1995).]

Saranac Lake, New York, Mid-November, 1887

Your prominent drama critic, writing like a journalist, has written like a braying ass; what he meant is probably quite different and true enough—that the book is ugly and the allegory like the usual pulpit fudge and not just enough to the modesty of facts. You are right as to Mansfield: Hyde was the younger of the two. He was not good looking however; and not, Great Gods! a mere voluptuary. There is no harm in a voluptuary; and none, with my hand on my heart and in the sight of God, none—no harm whatever—in what prurient fools call "immorality." The harm was in Jekyll, because he was a hypocrite—not because he was fond of women; he says so himself; but people are so filled of folly and inverted lust, that they can think of nothing but sexuality. The hypocrite let out his beast Hyde—who is no more sexual than another, but who is the essence of cruelty and malice, and selfishness and cowardice: and these are diabolical in man—not this poor wish to have a woman, that they make such a cry about. I know, and I dare to say, you know as well as I, that bad and good, even to our human eyes, has no more connection with what is called dissipation than it has with flying kites. But the sexual field and the business field are perhaps the two best fitted for the display of cruelty and cowardice and selfishness. That is what people see; and these they confound.

Appendix E: Stevenson in Bournemouth, 1884–87

[Stevenson liked to think of himself as a "Bohemian" artist when younger, and being established in Bournemouth, where Stevenson lived from 1884 to 1887 and where *Dr. Jekyll and Mr. Hyde* was written, seems to have contradicted his image of himself as a free spirit who led a vagabond life. In the comic adventure story he co-authored with Lloyd Osbourne, *The Wrong Box* (1889), Bournemouth and Victorian society are satirized for their mindless conformity, and Bournemouth was in many ways the epitome of the "genteel" Victorian town created specifically for the growing middle class. The emphasis on Dr. Jekyll's "respectable" yet humdrum bourgeois life may have some personal force for Stevenson, who was chaffing at the domestic routines of life in Bournemouth and disliked being a "beastly householder." Mr. Hyde's flat in Soho, given Soho's reputation (see Appendix I), may reflect a nostalgia for Stevenson's own Bohemian student days and a desire to escape the responsibilities of respectable middle age. The relationship between Jekyll and Hyde is also characterized as almost a father and son relationship, and reflects further ambivalence on Stevenson's part towards living in a house purchased for him by his father, in addition to his mixed feelings of gratitude for his generosity and frustration at being still dependent on his father.

The following passages from *An Intimate Portrait of R.L.S.* (New York: Scribner's, 1924) by Stevenson's stepson, Lloyd Osbourne (1868-1947), depict both the ennui and the energy created for Stevenson by "Skerryvore," his home in Bournemouth, and a compelling account of the composition of *Dr. Jekyll and Mr. Hyde*.]

"Skerryvore" was an unusually attractive suburban house, set in an acre and a half of ground; and its previous owner—a retired naval captain—had been at no little expense to improve and add to it. Somehow it was typical of an old sailor; it was so trim, so well arranged, so much thought had been given to its many conveniences. One felt it was a dream-come true of long years passed at sea—even to the natty little stable, the miniature coachhouse, and the faultlessly bricked court, faultlessly slanted to the central drain. Of course it had a pigeon-cote; what old seaman would be happy ashore without one? And through all my memories of "Skerryvore" run that melodious cooing and the flutter of wings on the lawn.

The house and five hundred pounds toward furnishing it were a wedding present to my mother from RLS's parents. The wanderers were now anchored; over their heads was their own roof-tree; they paid rates and taxes, and were called on by the vicar; Stevenson, in the word he hated most of all, had become the "burgess" of his former jeers. Respectability, dulness, and similar villas encompassed him for miles in every direction.

In his heart I doubt if he really ever liked "Skerryvore"; he never spoke of it with regret; left it with no apparent pang. The Victorianism it exemplified was jarring to every feeling he possessed, though with his habitual philosophy he not only endured it, but even persuaded himself that he liked it. But so far as he had any snobbishness it was his conviction—which was really somewhat naive—that artists were instinctive aristocrats, who never could be content in the middle class. I suppose when he said "artists" he meant himself, and certainly of all men he was the least fitted for ordinary English suburban life. Not that he saw much of it; he was virtually a prisoner in that house the whole time he lived in it; for him those years in "Skerryvore" were gray, indeed.

His health throughout was at its lowest ebb; never was he so spectral, so emaciated, so unkempt and tragic a figure. His long hair, his eyes, so abnormally brilliant in his wasted face, his sick-room garb, picked up at random and to which he gave no thought—all are ineffaceably pictured in my mind; and with the picture is an ineffable pity. Once at sunset I remember him entering the dining-room, and with his cloak already about him, mutely interrogating my mother for permission to stroll in the garden. It had rained for several days and this was his first opportunity for a breath of outside air.

"Oh, Louis, you mustn't get your feet wet," she said in an imploring voice.

He made no protest; he was prepared for the denial; but such a look of despair crossed his face that it remains with me yet. Then still silent he glanced again toward the lawn with an inexpressible longing.

Afterward in Samoa I reminded him of that little scene at a moment when his exile was weighing most heavily on him. We were both on horseback and had stopped for a cigarette; the palms were rustling in the breeze, and the lovely shores of Upolu far below were spread out before us in the setting sun. He gave a little shudder at the recollection I had evoked, and after a moody pause exclaimed: "And all for five minutes in a damned back yard! No, no, no, I would be a fool ever to leave Samoa!" And, as though to emphasize the contrast, dug the spurs into his horse and started off at a headlong gallop.

Of course his health varied. There were periods when he was comparatively well, when he would go to London to spend a few days. Once he even got as far as Paris; once he went to Dorchester to see Thomas Hardy, and continuing on to Exeter was overtaken by an illness that lasted three weeks and brought him to death's door. But in general he was a prisoner in his own house and saw nothing of Bournemouth save his own little garden. There could be no pretense he was not an invalid and a very sick man. He had horrifying hemorrhages, long spells when he was doomed to lie motionless on his bed lest the slightest movement should restart the flow, when he would speak in whispers, and one sat beside him and tried to be entertaining—in that room he was only too likely to leave in his coffin.

How thus handicapped he wrote his books is one of the marvels of literature—books so robustly and aboundingly alive that it is incredible they came out of a sick-room; and such well-sustained books with no slowing down of their original impetus, nor the least suggestion of those intermissions when their author lay at the point of death. Those years in "Skerryvore" were exceedingly productive. The "Strange Case of Dr. Jekyll and Mr. Hyde" was written here; so was "Kidnapped"; so was "Markheim," and any number of his best short stories; so too, was the "Life of Fleeming Jenkin."

One day he came down to luncheon in a very preoccupied frame of mind, hurried through his meal—an unheard-of thing for him to do—and on leaving said he was working with extraordinary success on a new story that had come to him in a dream, and that he was not to be interrupted or disturbed even if the house caught fire.

For three days a sort of hush descended on "Skerryvore"; we all went about, servants and everybody, in a tiptoeing silence; passing Stevenson's door I would see him sitting up in bed, filling page after page, and apparently never pausing for a moment. At the end of three days the mysterious task was finished, and he read aloud to my mother and myself the first draft of "The Strange Case of Dr. Jekyll and Mr. Hyde."

I listened to it spellbound. Stevenson, who had a voice the greatest actor might have envied, read it with an intensity that made shivers run up and down my spine. When he came to the end, gazing at us in triumphant expectancy and keyed to a pitch of indescribable self-satisfaction—as he waited, and I waited, for my mother's outburst of enthusiasm—I was thunderstruck at her backwardness. Her praise was constrained; the words seemed to come with difficulty; and then all at once she broke out with criticism. He had missed the point, she said; had missed the allegory; had made it merely a story—a magnificent bit of sensationalism—when it should have been a masterpiece.

Stevenson was beside himself with anger. He trembled; his hand shook on the manuscript; he was intolerably chagrined. His voice, bitter and challenging, overrode my mother's in a fury of resentment. Never had I seen him so impassioned, so outraged, and the scene became so painful that I went away, unable to bear it any longer. It was with a sense of tragedy that I listened to their voices from the adjoining room, the words lost but fraught with an emotion that struck at my heart.

When I came back my mother was alone. She was sitting, pale and desolate before the fire, and staring into it. Neither of us spoke. Had I done so it would have been to reproach her, for I thought she had been cruelly wrong. Then we heard Louis descending the stairs, and we both quailed as he burst in as though to continue the argument even more violently than before. But all he said was: "You are right I have absolutely missed the allegory, which, after all, is the whole point of it—the very essence of it." And with that, as though enjoying my mother's discomfiture and her ineffectual start to prevent him, he threw the manuscript into the fire! Imagine my feelings—my mother's feelings—as we saw it blazing up; as we saw those precious pages wrinkling and blackening and turning into flame.

My first impression was that he had done it out of pique. But it was not. He really had been convinced, and this was his dramatic amend. When my mother and I both cried out at the folly of destroying the manuscript he justified himself vehemently. "It was all wrong," he said. "In trying to save some of it I should have got hopelessly off the track. The only way was to put temptation beyond my reach."

Then ensued another three days of feverish industry on his part, and of a hushed, anxious, and tiptoeing anticipation on ours; of meals where he scarcely spoke; of evenings unenlivened by his presence; of awed glimpses of him, sitting up in bed, writing, writing, writing, with the counterpane littered with his sheets. The culmination was the "Jekyll and Hyde" that every one knows; that, translated into every European tongue and many Oriental, has given a new phrase to the world.

The writing of it was an astounding feat from whatever aspect it may be regarded. Sixty-four thousand words in six days; more than ten thousand words a day. To those who know little of such things I may explain that a thousand words a day is a fair average for any writer of fiction. Anthony Trollope set himself this quota;[1] it was Jack London's;[2] it is—and has been—a sort of standard of daily literary accomplishment. Stevenson multiplied it by ten; and on top of that copied out the whole in another two days, and had it in the post on the third!

It was a stupendous achievement; and the strange thing was that, instead of showing lassitude afterward, he seemed positively refreshed and revitalized; went about with a happy air; was as uplifted as though he had come into a fortune; looked better than he had in months.

---

1 Anthony Trollope (1815–82), British novelist known for his self-disciplined approach to writing and consequent prolific output.

2 Jack London (1876–1916), American novelist best known for *The Call of the Wild* (1903).

Appendix F: Reviews of Dr. Jekyll and Mr. Hyde

[From its first publication *Dr. Jekyll and Mr. Hyde* has been viewed as a literary success, although as Henry James's[1] ambivalent comments suggest, it was at first too popular a work to be comfortably called a masterpiece. The story was quoted widely in sermons shortly after its publication, usually cited as an example of the dangers of sin and vice. The reviews selected here show a more nuanced appreciation of the story, and a level of insight that sets them apart from many of the early reviews. Selections are from *Robert Louis Stevenson: The Critical Heritage*, ed. Paul Robert Maixner (London: Routledge & Kegan Paul, 1981).]

1. Unsigned, *The Times* (25 January 1886)

Nothing Mr. Stevenson has written as yet has so strongly impressed us with the versatility of his very original genius as this sparsely-printed little shilling volume. From the business point of view we can only marvel in these practical days at the lavish waste of admirable material, and what strikes us as a disproportionate expenditure on brain-power, in relation to the tangible results. Of two things, one. Either the story was a flash of intuitive psychological research, dashed off in a burst of inspiration; or else it is the product of the most elaborate forethought, fitting together all the parts of an intricate and inscrutable puzzle. The proof is that every connoisseur who reads the story once, must certainly read it twice. He will read it the first time, passing from surprise to surprise, in a curiosity that keeps growing, because it is never satisfied. For the life of us, we cannot make out how such and such an incident can possibly be explained on grounds that are intelligible or in any way plausible. Yet all the time the seriousness of the tone assures us that explanations are forthcoming. In our impatience we are hurried towards the denouement, which accounts for everything upon strictly scientific grounds, though the science be the science of problematical futurity. Then, having drawn a sigh of relief at having found even a fantastically speculative issue from our embarrassments, we begin reflectively to call to mind how systematically the writer has been working towards it. Never for a moment, in the most

---

1   American novelist (1843–1916) resident of England and friends with Stevenson and many other contemporary literary figures.

startling situations, has he lost his grasp of the grand ground-facts of a wonderful and supernatural problem. Each apparently incredible or insignificant detail has been thoughtfully subordinated to his purpose. And if we say, after all, on a calm retrospect, that the strange case is absurdly and insanely improbable, Mr. Stevenson might answer in the words of Hamlet, that there are more things in heaven and in earth than are dreamed of in our philosophy.[1] For we are still groping by doubtful lights on the dim limits of boundless investigation; and it is always possible that we may be on the brink of a new revelation as to the unforeseen resources of the medical art. And at all events, the answer should suffice for the purposes of Mr. Stevenson's sensational *tour d'esprit*.

The "Strange Case of Dr. Jekyll" is sensational enough in all conscience, and yet we do not promise it the wide popularity of "Called Back." The *brochure* that brought fame and profit to the late Mr. Fargus[2] was pitched in a more commonplace key, and consequently appealed to more vulgar circles. But, for ourselves, we should many times sooner have the credit of "Dr. Jekyll," which appeals irresistibly to the most cultivated minds, and must be appreciated by the most competent critics. Naturally, we compare it with the sombre masterpieces of Poe, and we may say at once that Mr. Stevenson has gone far deeper. Poe embroidered richly in the gloomy grandeur of his imagination upon themes that were but too material, and not very novel—on the sinister destiny overshadowing a doomed family, on a living and breathing man kept prisoner in a coffin or vault, on the wild whirling of a human waif in the boiling eddies of the Maelstrom—while Mr. Stevenson evolves the ideas of his story from the world that is unseen, enveloping everything in weird mystery, till at last it pleases him to give us the password. We are not going to tell his strange story, though we might well do so, and only excite the curiosity of our readers. We shall only say that we are shown the shrewdest of lawyers hopelessly puzzled by the inexplicable conduct of a familiar friend. All the antecedents of a life of virtue and honour seem to be belied by the discreditable intimacy that has been formed with one of the most callous and atrocious of criminals. A crime committed under the eyes of a witness goes unavenged, though the notorious criminal has been identified, for he disappears as absolutely as if the earth had swallowed him. He reappears in due time where we should least expect to see him, and for some miserable days he leads a charmed life, while he excites the superstitious terrors of all about him. Indeed, the strongest nerves are

---

1   William Shakespeare, *Hamlet* (I.v.167–68): "There are more things in heaven and earth, Horatio, Than are dreamt of in your philosophy."

2   Frederick John Fargus's (1847–85) novel *Called Back* was published in 1885.

shaken by stress of sinister circumstances, as well they may be, for the worthy Dr. Jekyll—the benevolent physician—has likewise vanished amid events that are enveloped in impalpable mysteries; nor can any one surmise what has become of him. So with overwrought feelings and conflicting anticipations we are brought to the end, where all is accounted for, more or less credibly.

Nor is it the mere charm of the story, strange as it is, which fascinates and thrills us. Mr. Stevenson is known for a master of style, and never has he shown his resources more remarkably than on this occasion. We do not mean that the book is written in excellent English— that must be a matter of course; but he has weighed his words and turned his sentences so as to sustain and excite throughout the sense of mystery and of horror. The mere artful use of an "it" for a "he" may go far in that respect, and Mr. Stevenson has carefully chosen his language and missed no opportunity. And if his style is good, his motive is better, and shows a higher order of genius. Slight as is the story, and supremely sensational, we remember nothing better since George Eliot's "Romola"[1] than this delineation of a feeble but kindly nature steadily and inevitably succumbing to the sinister influences of besetting weaknesses. With no formal preaching and with out a touch of Pharisaism, he works out the essential power of Evil, which, with its malignant patience and unwearying perseverance, gains ground with each casual yielding to temptation, till the once well-meaning man may actually become a Wend, or at least wear the reflection of the Wend's image. But we have said enough to show our opinion of the book, which should be read as a finished study in the art of fantastic literature.

2. Julia Wedgewood, *Contemporary Review* (April 1886), xlix, 594–95

By far the most remarkable work we have to notice this time is "The Strange Case of Dr. Jekyll and Mr. Hyde," a shilling story, which the reader devours in an hour, but to which he may return again and again, to study a profound allegory and admire a model of style. It is a perfectly original production; it recalls, indeed, the work of Hawthorne,[2] but this is by kindred power, not by imitative workmanship. We will not do so much injustice to any possible reader of this

---

1 George Eliot's (1819–80) novel *Romola* was written in 1862–63 and published serially.

2 Nathaniel Hawthorne (1804–64), whose short story "The Marble Faun" (1859), published in England as "Transformations," concerns a murder and its effects on two American art students.

weird tale as to describe its motif, but we blunt no curiosity in saying that its motto might have been the sentence of a Latin father—"Omnis anima et rea et testis est."[1] Mr. Stevenson has set before himself the psychical problem of Hawthorne's "Transformations," viewed from a different and perhaps an opposite point of view, and has dealt with it with more vigour if with less grace. Here it is not the child of Nature who becomes manly by experience of sin, but a fully-developed man who goes through a different form of the process, and if the delineation is less associated with beautiful imagery, the parable is deeper, and, we would venture to add, truer. Mr. Stevenson represents the individualizing influence of modern democracy in its more concentrated form. Whereas most fiction deals with the relation between man and woman (and the very fact that its scope is so much narrowed is a sign of the atomic character of our modern thought), the author of this strange tale takes an even narrower range, and sets himself to investigate the meaning of the word *self*. No woman's name occurs in the book, no romance is even suggested in it; it depends on the interest of an idea; but so powerfully is this interest worked out that the reader feels that the same material might have been spun out to cover double the space, and still have struck him as condensed and close-knit workmanship. It is one of those rare fictions which make one understand the value of temperance in art. If this tribute appears exaggerated, it is at least the estimate of one who began Mr. Stevenson's story with a prejudice against it, arising from a recent perusal of its predecessor, his strangely dull and tasteless "Prince Otto." It is a psychological curiosity that the same man should have written both, and if they were bound up together, the volume would form the most striking illustration of a warning necessary for others besides the critic—the warning to judge no man by any single utterance, how complete soever.

3. From Henry James, *Partial Portraits* (London: Macmillan, 1894), 169–71

Is *Doctor Jekyll and Mr. Hyde* a work of high philosophic intention, or simply the most ingenious and irresponsible of fictions? It has the stamp of a really imaginative production, that we may take it in different ways; but I suppose it would generally be called the most serious of the author's tales. It deals with the relation of the baser parts of man to his nobler, of the capacity for evil that exists in the most generous natures; and it expresses these things in a fable which is a wonderfully happy invention. The subject is endlessly interesting, and rich in all

---

1 Every soul is guilty and a witness (Latin).

sorts of provocation, and Mr. Stevenson is to be congratulated on having touched the core of it. I may do him injustice, but it is, however, here, not the profundity of the idea which strikes me so much as the art of the presentation—the extremely successful form. There is a genuine feeling for the perpetual moral question, a fresh sense of the difficulty of being good and the brutishness of being bad; but what there is above all is a singular ability in holding the interest. I confess that that, to my sense, is the most edifying thing in the short, rapid, concentrated story, which is really a masterpiece of concision. There is some thing almost impertinent in the way, as I have noticed, in which Mr. Stevenson achieves his best effects without the aid of the ladies, and *Doctor Jekyll* is a capital example of his heartless independence. It is usually supposed that a truly poignant impression cannot be made without them, but in the drama of Mr. Hyde's fatal ascendancy they remain altogether in the wing. It is very obvious—I do not say it cynically—that they must have played an important part in his development. The gruesome tone of the tale is, no doubt, deepened by their absence: it is like the late afternoon light of a foggy winter Sunday, when even inanimate objects have a kind of wicked look. I remember few situations in the pages of mystifying fiction more to the purpose than the episode of Mr. Utterson's going to Doctor Jekyll's to confer with the butler when the Doctor is locked up in his laboratory, and the old servant, whose sagacity has hitherto encountered successfully the problems of the sideboard and the pantry, confesses that this time he is utterly baffled. The way the two men, at the door of the laboratory, discuss the identity of the mysterious personage inside, who has revealed himself in two or three inhuman glimpses to Poole, has those touches of which irresistible shudders are made. The butler's theory is that his master has been murdered, and that the murderer is in the room, personating him with a sort of clumsy diabolism. "Well, when that masked thing like a monkey jumped from among the chemicals and whipped into the cabinet, it went down my spine like ice." That is the effect upon the reader of most of the story. I say of most rather than of all, because the ice rather melts in the sequel, and I have some difficulty in accepting the business of the powders, which seems to me too explicit and explanatory. The powders constitute the machinery of the transformation, and it will probably have struck many readers that this uncanny process would be more conceivable (so far as one may speak of the conceivable in such a case), if the author had not made it so definite.

4. John Addington Symonds to Robert Louis Stevenson, 3 March 1886, *The Letters of John Addington Symonds*, **vol. 3, ed. Herbert M. Schueller and Robert L. Peters (Detroit: Wayne State UP, 1967–69), 120–21**

3 March 1886

My dear Louis

At last I have read *Dr. Jekyll*. It makes me wonder whether a man has the right so to scrutinize "the abysmal deeps of personality." It is indeed a dreadful book, most dreadful because of a certain moral callousness, a want of sympathy, a shutting out of hope. The art is burning and intense. The "Peau de Chagrin"[1] disappears; Poe[2] is as water. As a piece of literary work, this seems to me the finest you have done—in all that regards style, invention, psychological analysis, exquisite fitting of parts, and admirable employment of motives to realize the abnormal. But it has left such a deeply painful impression on my heart that I do not know how I am ever to turn to it again.

The fact is that, viewed as an allegory, it touches one too closely. Most of us at some epoch of our lives have been upon the verge of developing a Mr. Hyde.

Physical and biological Science on a hundred lines is reducing individual freedom to zero, and weakening the sense of responsibility. I doubt whether the artist should lend his genius to this grim argument. Your Dr. Jekyll seems to me capable of loosening the last threads of self-control in one who should read it while wavering between his better and worse self. It is like the Cave of Despair in the "Faery Queen."[3]

I had the great biologist Lauder Brunton[4] with me a fortnight back. He was talking about Dr. Jekyll and a book by W.O. Holmes[5] in which atavism is played with. I could see that, though a Christian, he held

---

1 A novel by Honoré de Balzac (1799–1850), translated into English as *The Wild Ass's Skin.*

2 Edgar Allan Poe (1809–49), American writer whose stories mixed horror and fantasy. The parallels between Poe's *Murders in the Rue Morgue* (1841) and *Dr. Jekyll and Mr. Hyde* are frequently noted in contemporary reviews of Stevenson's work.

3 An epic poem by Edmund Spenser (1552–99) celebrating Elizabeth I (1533–1603).

4 Sir Thomas Lauder Brunton (1844–1916), Scottish physician who played a major role in establishing pharmacology as a rigorous science.

5 Oliver Wendell Holmes (1809–94), American doctor and writer, whose psychological story "Elsie Venner" (1861) expressed controversial religious views.

very feebly to the theory of human liberty; and these two works of fiction interested him, as Dr. Jekyll does me, upon that point at issue.

I understand now thoroughly how much a sprite you are. Really there is something not quite human in your genius!

The denouement would have been finer, I think, if Dr. Jekyll by a last supreme effort of his lucid self had given Mr. Hyde up to justice— which might have been arranged after the scene in Lanyon's study. Did you ever read Raskolnikow?[1] How fine is that ending! Had you made your hero act thus, you would at least have saved the sense of human dignity. The doors of Broadmoor[2] would have closed on Mr. Hyde.

Goodbye. I seem quite to have lost you. But if I come to England I shall try to see you.

Love to your wife.

Ever yrs

J A Symonds

5. *Punch* 90 (6 February 1886): 64

[This *Punch* parody pokes fun at *Dr. Jekyll and Mr. Hyde*, but also makes some astute observations. Mr. Utterson is seen as a "bore," and attention is drawn to the way in which Stevenson withholds crucial information from the reader to create suspense.]

THE STRANGE CASE OF DR. T. AND MR. H.
Or Two Single Gentlemen rolled into one.

CHAPTER I.—Story of the Bore.

Mr. STUTTERSON, the lawyer, was a man of a rugged countenance, that was never lighted by a smile, not even when he saw a little old creature in clothes much too large for him, come round the corner of a street and trample a small boy nearly to death. The little old creature would have rushed away, when an angry crowd surrounded him, and tried to kill him. But he suddenly disappeared into a house that did not belong to him, and gave the crowd a cheque with a name upon it that cannot be divulged until the very last chapter of this interesting narrative. Then the crowd allowed the little old creature to go away.

"Let us never refer to the subject again," said Mr. Stutterson.

---

1 See p. 125, note 2.
2 A famous English prison.

"With all my heart," replied the entire human race, escaping from his button-holding propensities.

CHAPTER II.—Mr. Hidanseek is found in the
Vague Murder Case.

Mr. STUTTERSON thought he would look up his medical friends. He was not only a bore, but a stingy one. He called upon the Surgeons when they were dining, and generally managed to obtain an entrance with the soup. "You here!" cried Dr. ONION, chuckling. "Don't speak to me about TREKYL—he is a fool, an ass, a dolt, a humbug, and my oldest friend."

"You think he is too scientific, and makes very many extraordinary experiments," said STUTTERSON, disposing of the fish, two entrees and the joint.

"Precisely," replied ONION, chuckling more than ever—"as you will find out in the last Chapter. And now, as you have cleared the table, hadn't you better go?"

"Certainly," returned the Lawyer, departing (by the way, *not* returning), and he went to visit Mr. HIDANSEEK. He found that individual, and asked to see his face.

"Why not?" answered the little old creature in the baggy clothes, defiantly. "Don't you recognize me?"

"Mr. R.L. STEVENSON says I mustn't," was the wary response; "for, if I did, I should spoil the last chapter."

Shortly after this Mr. HIDANSEEK, being asked the way by a Baronet out for a midnight stroll, immediately hacked his interrogator to pieces with a heavy umbrella. Mr. STUTTERSON therefore called upon Dr. TREKYL, to ask for an explanation.

"Wait a moment," said that eminent physician, retiring to an inner apartment, where he wrote the following note:—

"Please, Sir, I didn't do it."

"TREKYL forge for a murderer!" exclaimed STUTTERSON; and his blood ran cold in his veins.

CHAPTER III.—And any quantity of Chapters to make
your flesh creep.

And so it turned out that TREKYL made a will, which contained a strange provision that, if he disappeared, HIDANSEEK was to have all his property. Then Dr. ONION went mad with terror, because, after some whiskey-and-water, he fancied that his old friend TREKYL had turned into the tracked and hunted murderer, HIDANSEEK.

"Was it the whiskey?" asked STUTTERSON.

"Wait until the end!" cried the poor medical man, and, with a loud shriek, he slipped out of his coat, leaving the button-hole in the bore's hand, and died!

CHAPTER THE LAST.—The wind-up.

I am writing this—I, TREKYL, the man who signed the cheque for HIDANSEEK in Chapter I., and wrote the forged letter a little later on. I hope you are all puzzled. I had no fixed idea how it would end when I began, and I trust you will see your way clearer through the mystery than I do, when you have come to the imprint.

As you may have gathered from ONION's calling me "a humbug, &c., &c.," I was very fond of scientific experiments. I was. And I found one day, that I, TREKYL, had a great deal of sugar in my composition. By using powdered acidulated drops[1] I discovered that I could change myself into somebody else. It was very sweet!

So I divided myself into two, and thought of a number of things. I thought how pleasant it would be to have no conscience, and be a regular bad one, or, as the vulgar call it, bad 'un. I swallowed the acidulated drops, and in a moment I became a little old creature, with an acquired taste for trampling out children's brains, and hacking to death (with an umbrella) midnight Baronets who had lost their way. I had a grand time of it! It was all the grander, because I found that by substituting sugar for the drops I could again become the famous doctor, whose chief employment was to give Mr. STUTTERSON all my dinner. So much bad had been divided into the acidulated HIDANSEEK that I hadn't enough left in the sugary TREKYL to protest against the bore's importunities.

Well, that acidulated fool HIDANSEEK got into serious trouble, and I wanted to cut him. But I couldn't; when I had divided myself into him one day, I found it impossible to get the right sort of sugar to bring me back again. For the right sort of sugar was adulterated, and adulterated sugar cannot be obtained in London!

And now, after piecing all this together, if you can't see the whole thing at a glance, I am very sorry for you, and can help you no further. The fact is, I have got to the end of my "141 pages for a shilling." I might have made myself into four or five people instead of two,—who are quite enough for the money.

---

1 Sour candies made sweet on the outside by a sugar coating.

Trick photograph of Richard Mansfield as Jekyll/Hyde in the stage adaptation of *Dr. Jekyll and Mr. Hyde*. Courtesy Library of Congress.

Appendix G: The Stage Version of Dr. Jekyll and Mr. Hyde

[The excerpts here are transcribed from an unpublished prompt book held in the Richard Mansfield collection of the Smithsonian Institution, Washington, DC, and are published courtesy of the Smithsonian Institution. See the Introduction, pp. 15-16, for a brief discussion of the genesis, performance, and impact of the play.]

DR. JEKYLL AND MR. HYDE,
adapted for the stage by Richard Mansfield and T.R. Sullivan

ACT ONE, SCENE ONE: SLAVE AND MASTER

(Enter Jekyll, through garden)

Jekyll: It must not be. I can never marry her with this hideous secret, this new danger threatening me at every step. My duty is clear. I must see her no more.

Utterson: Jekyll.

Jekyll: Ah. Oh, Utterson—is that you? I—

Utterson: What is it? You're not ill?

Jekyll: Ill? No; you startled me, that's all. I was never better; never, in my life.

Utterson: Um. Well I'm glad to hear it. You come most opportunely. I was writing you a letter. There's no need of it now. If you'll give me a moment.

Jekyll: Business, eh? Well?

Utterson: Sit down. It's about that will of yours. (Jekyll looks about anxiously) Oh, we are quite alone. Jekyll, I don't like it.

Jekyll: My poor Utterson you are unfortunate in your client. I never knew a man so distressed as you were by my will; except, perhaps that pedant Lanyon at my scientific heresies. No man ever disappointed me as Lanyon has.

Utterson: You know I refused to draw up the will. I never approved of it.

Jekyll: Yes, yes I know. You have told me so.

Utterson: Well I tell you so again. To one clause in it I object particularly.

Jekyll: To what clause?

Utterson: You make a large bequest to your "friend and benefactor Edward Hyde." So far, so good. But you add, that in case of your disappearance or unexplained absence, for a period exceeding three calendar months, the said Hyde shall inherit without further delay, without further question.

Jekyll: Well?

Utterson: As your old friend and legal adviser, I protest against that revision. It is dangerous—unheard of—monstrously unjust.

Jekyll: Unjust?

Utterson: To Miss Carew, your future wife, yes ... (a pause)

Jekyll: Well, have you done?

Utterson: No, I have not done; to-day I have learned something of this man Hyde.

Jekyll: I do not care to listen longer. We must agree to drop this matter.

Utterson: What I heard was abominable.

Jekyll: It can make no change. You do not understand my position (after a pause, more calmly). I am painfully situated, Utterson; this case is a very strange one—very strange. Talking will not mend it.

Utterson: (Follows him and puts hand on his shoulder) Harry, you know me thoroughly. I am to be trusted. I will get you out of this. Make a clean breast of it in confidence, I beg you.

Jekyll: (Putting hand on Utterson's shoulder) My dear fellow this is downright good of you. I would trust you before any man alive, before myself, had I the choice. But it is not what you fancy. The moment I please I can be rid Hyde. There I give you my hand upon it—(takes his hand)—and thank you again and again. But this is a private matter; pray let it sleep.

Utterson: As you please. Are you going up-stairs?

Jekyll: In a moment yes. One word more. I have really a great interest in poor Hyde—a very great interest. If I am taken away, promise me to bear with him, and to get him his rights. You would, if you knew all.

Utterson: I hope I may never see the man.

Jekyll: It would take a weight off my mind if you would promise.

Utterson: You don't want me to like him, do you?

Jekyll: (Laying his hand on Utterson's arm) No, only do him justice for my sake, when I am gone.

Utterson: (After pause, sighing) Well I promise (They shake hands going, aside) Much good that interview did either of us. (exit)

Jekyll: Poor humankind. Bound by laws as rigid as the sheepskin covers of the book that holds them. And I, who have toiled for freedom doomed to eternal wretchedness, the possessor of a secret I dare not even whisper. Heaven help me, Heaven help me. (Stands at fire)

Agnes: Harry.

Jekyll: (At table, not hearing her, aside) In the power of the monster, I myself created. In its power. What if it should present itself here— before them—what if....

Agnes (aside): What does he say? Harry.

Jekyll: Agnes. (shrinking from her) Is that you?

Agnes: Yes, there is something wrong. I have seen it in your face for days. What is it Harry? You must let me share in this. How else am I to help you?

Jekyll: You cannot help me. There is no help for me on earth.

Agnes: Harry.

Jekyll: We are at the cross-roads—we must part before it is too late. I must go on alone.

Agnes: Part?

Jekyll: Yes.

Agnes: Are you out of your senses? Do you know me? I have promised to be your wife—I love you. Look, this is I—Agnes Carew.

Jekyll: It is you who do not know me. I am unfit to live upon the good earth with you. You do not know me, I tell you.

Agnes: Are you not Henry Jekyll?

Jekyll: The philanthropist, the man of science, the distinguished person—before the world, yes. How if it were all a lie? If I were like one possessed of a Wend—wearing at times, another shape, vile, monstrous, hideous beyond belief?

Agnes: Oh, be silent. (Hiding face in hands)

Jekyll: Yes, a Wend without conscience, and without remorse—inventing crimes and longing only to commit them.

Agnes: This is horrible. Who accuses you. You are ill and tired—you are not yourself.

Jekyll: That is true. I am but half myself—the other half is—

Agnes: Mine. You have no right to accuse it falsely.

Jekyll: You will not believe—if I dared tell you—

Agnes: You shall tell me nothing.

Jekyll: You are right. It is best to part so.

Agnes: Part? How little you know me. If you have sins to conquer, I have mine. Who is there without sin in all the world? We are born into it to help one another. And when you need me most, am I to give you up—to leave you.

Jekyll: You can say these things. You ask me nothing.

Agnes: No, you have won my love—you must accept it.

Jekyll: But if you knew—

Agnes: (Drawing nearer, tenderly) How much I might confess to you. You would not listen.

Jekyll: Darling, I—no I cannot tell her that, never that.

Agnes: Who ever lived that was not tempted by the Wend. To be tempted is not to yield. We will resist.

Jekyll: (Embracing her) You are an angel.

Agnes: (In his arms) Harry, do you remember, where I met you first?

Jekyll: In the ward of the hospital—yes.

Agnes: Where you watched by my poor old nurse who was dying. You were there night and day, with all that human skill could do, with more than human patience and devotion. I tried to thank you for your kind looks—your gentle words. I could not speak.

Jekyll: But your eyes said it all. And then I loved you. It was a strange courtship.

Agnes: That is the man I know. There is no other. Drive away these morbid fancies—for my sake—for my sake.

Jekyll: (Kissing her. Rises) For your sake, yes. You shall teach me to control myself. It will take courage.

Agnes: To me you are without fear—without reproach.

Jekyll: To you at my best always. See. The stars are coming out. Which among them all is ours?

Agnes: The brightest. (Exeunt through window into garden)

[later in the same scene]

Agnes: I do believe that papa has fallen asleep. (Sees Hyde and draws back with low cry) Ah.

Sir Danvers: (Waking) How cold it is. Ha. (Seeing Hyde and rising) What's this? (Draws back with a shudder)

Agnes: (Shrinking back) Papa, papa.

Sir Danvers: (Pushing her off) Leave the room Agnes.

Agnes: Papa, papa.

Sir Danvers: (After a pause, more gently) Do as I bid you child. (Exit Agnes silently) Now sir what business brings you to my house?

Hyde: Agnes. Why did you send her away?

Sir Danvers: My daughter's name. Why? What's that to you?

Hyde: Call her back I say. I saw her face through the window, I like it.

Sir Danvers: Scoundrel, leave my house.

Hyde: (Laughs defiantly) Eh. That's good.

Sir Danvers: Monster, who and what are you? Go or—

Hyde: Go? I? Why I will make the house mine; the girl mine if I choose.

Sir Danvers: Infernal villain, I'll—(Steps towards him)

Hyde: Hands off, or it will be your death, I warn you.

Sir Danvers: By Heaven, I'll—(Grapples with him)
                    (Hyde throttles him)
                    (Hyde up to window)

                (Curtain as Hyde leaves Sir Danvers)

Act Two: Hide and Seek

Scene 1. Mr. Hyde's Chambers in Soho

Hyde: Still as death. Not a sound. I thought some one tracked my footsteps in the street. I saw the shadow. (Seeing his own shadow on wall of landing) It was my own. Shut it out; shut it out. (Closes door and laughs) Who's there? (Trembles and then laughs, indicating himself) Why it is this, this that I love. Who would suspect me of this. That this could kill—and kill—and kill, for mere sport of killing. Why no one. My own self is sanctuary. I need not fear. But no more shadows—no more shadows (Lights candles on table). Fool, she has forgotten the brandy.

(Enter Rebecca with decanter and glasses)

Hyde: Oh, you're there are you. The brandy.

(Puts wine down)

Rebecca: Here.
Hyde: You have something to tell me.
Rebecca: A man has asked for you.
Hyde: (Starting) A man. When?
Rebecca: An hour ago.
Hyde: What did he want?
Rebecca: You.
Hyde: What was he like?
Rebecca: A man like any other.
Hyde: Like me?
Rebecca: No. Thank Heaven.
Hyde: (Sneering) Heaven. Choose your words better.
Rebecca: The other place then.
Hyde: Curse your tongue. Go. (Rebecca starts to go) Stop. (Rebecca returns) What's their gossip on the street corner?
Rebecca: What should they talk of? The murder.
Hyde: Murder? What murder?
Rebecca: The old man—the rich general.
Hyde: And they say?—
Rebecca: That the murderer is discovered.
Hyde: (Trembling) Discovered? (Recovering himself) What's that to me. I don't know him. I don't know him.
Rebecca: Nor I. If I did—
Hyde: Well?

Rebecca: It would be worth money to me.

Hyde: What could you do with money?

Rebecca: Count it, and keep it—to count again.

Hyde: (Throwing coins on the floor) There's money for you. (Laughing at her as she springs forward) Hark ye. If I am asked for again, say I'm gone.

Rebecca: (Busy with coins) Gone?

Hyde: (Fiercely) Gone way. Do you hear? (Rising and threatening)

Rebecca: Aye. I have ears.

Hyde: Use them, and spare your tongue. Now go. (Rebecca shrinks up to door and exit)

Hyde: (Alone at table) I must destroy all clues and begone. First to lock the door. (Locks and bolts door) (Stops. Listening) Hark. (Growling at his own fear) Why should I tremble so? Sir Danvers Carew is in his grave. No, curse it; up there—or down there. (Fills glass) The ghost—(Doors open wide)—of Sir Danvers Carew. (Hyde up and starts) You're there are you. This is a merry meeting. Your hand (as if shaking it). A little nearer to the fire; the evening air is chilly. Your health sir, and a warm grave to you in the morning. (Door closes) (Drinks and puts glass down)

(Rebecca and Newcomen heard outside in discussion)

Rebecca: He is gone away, I tell you.

Newcomen: I tell you, I must come in.

Hyde: Hark. (Exit)

Newcomen: (Forcing his way in at door) I say I must come in. Aha. Snug quarters. Very snug. And the lodger?

Rebecca: He is not here.

Newcomen: And if a friendly gentleman should come to call upon him, you wouldn't for the life of him recollect his name—

Rebecca: I don't know his name.

Newcomen: You don't? Don't know his name. Dear, dear. That's a good un, so it is.

Rebecca: I have many lodgers. I ask no questions and am well paid for it.

Newcomen: (Takes out pocket book) I am Inspector Newcomen from Scotland Yard.

Rebecca: (Drawing nearer to him, eagerly) He's in trouble. What has he done? What has he done?

Newcomen: (Pushing her off) Gently now, gently. (Counting bank notes and watching her at the sight of them) Now these are bank notes—notes—money, you see?

Rebecca: Yes, yes. I see.

Newcomen: Five, ten, fifteen, twenty—they are yours. (Gives notes to Rebecca)

Rebecca: Mine. Mine. (Snatching notes and counting them) Why this is twenty pounds, twenty pounds.

Newcomen: All yours—and much more—if you will help me to a few words with this gentleman. He's a very popular character, don't you see?

Rebecca: (Putting up money) I hate him.

Newcomen: Hate him. Dear me, dear me. Come, that's business. Oh, we're getting on.

Rebecca: Hush, hush. Speak lower. There are mice in the walls.

Newcomen: Mice in the walls; dear me, dear me. Ay, and out on 'em too. (Aside) The old she devil.

Rebecca: (After looking cautiously about, whispers) His name is—

Newcomen: His name is—

Rebecca: Hyde. (Scratching on wall outside)

Newcomen: Dear, dear me. Hyde, and he's here?

Rebecca: No. But he will come back. Go to the street door and watch. When the right man comes, I will hold the light in his face—so. (Picks up candle, and holds it in Newcomen's face)

Newcomen: You're a hangel—of light. (Rebecca laughs and re-places candle) A real out-and-houter. Blest if you haint.

Rebecca: And the money, the money.

Newcomen: Wages paid weekly—reg'lar—when earned.

Rebecca: Not so loud. Go. (Points to door toward which Newcomen goes. She runs after and detains him) Twenty pound, eh. Twenty pound, eh.

Newcomen: Easy now, easy. Dear me, dear me. No love making. Dear, dear me. I'm a married man; wife and children. Dear, dear me. (Exit)

Rebecca: (In front of table, takes out money) Five, ten, fifteen—(Enter Hyde creeping down softly) Twenty. Twenty pound. (Hyde snatches notes. Rebecca recoils in horror)

Hyde: What did you whisper there?

Rebecca: The money; give me the money. (Hyde tears notes into bits and throws them down. Rebecca drops, and fumbles for them wailing. He catches her by the throat.)

Hyde: You sold me, did you?

Rebecca: (Freeing herself) No, no.

Hyde: (Catching her again and shaking her) What did you tell him? Eh?

Rebecca: (gasping) Nothing, nothing.

Hyde: (About to strangle her) That's a lie. (Throwing her from him) Another and I'll kill you. Now, go. (Rebecca to door and exit sobbing) I must be gone. (Burning papers in fire) But I'll leave no trace, no trace but ashes. (Footsteps outside) Hark. (extinguishes candle. Exit) Too late; too late. (Rebecca and Newcomen enter with lighted candle)

CURTAIN

ACT FOUR: THE LAST NIGHT

Scene: Dr. Jekyll's Cabinet

(Jekyll discovered alone at window.
He holds in his hand a glass into which
he drops liquor from a phial)

Jekyll: (Putting phial on table at window, and holding glass up to the light) It will not do. Experiment is fruitless. Failure succeeds failure. The salt is not the same. A curse on the science that can reveal half truths and then betray us. Without this tincture I am doomed. I were better in my grave. (Clock strikes six) Six o'clock. So late,—and still Lanyon does not come. It is foolish to wait longer. I know already the answer that he brings. My hope is but the merest thread, and on that depends my life. I am like the condemned wretch who has taken his last look at earth, yet, still hopes for reprieve. (Knock at door) He is there; no, that is not his knock. What then? (The knock is repeated) Who's there?

Poole: Only me sir, Poole.

Jekyll: (Aside) I dare not see him. He half suspects my secret. (Aloud) You have the answer from the chemist?

Poole: Yes sir, a written message.

Jekyll: Very good, pass it to me quick. (Draws paper from aside the door) (Reads) "Mr. Whitelock regrets that he can only fill Dr. Jekyll's order with a sample like the last." (Tears paper to pieces angrily) Useless, useless; and Lanyon's word will still be the same. Why wait to hear it; rather let me die now in my own shape, which even as I speak may be taken from me. (Shuddering) Ah, anything but that. Let the dead man's face they look upon be that of Henry Jekyll—not the face of Hyde. I laid the poison ready for the time when it should come. It has come now. (Shudders) That shudder again. Is it the warning? have we changed places already? (Waits a moment not daring to look in the glass. Looks with a cry of joy) No, thank Heaven my own self still. (Supports himself panting by table) But what horrors incredible this glass has seen and known. With what wild joy I first looked upon the face I now hate and loathe believing my discovery a blessing to mankind, alas. It was terrible in its incompleteness. Stay. What if Lanyon has found the last ingredient, that will give me the power to conquer this fiendish transformation. I might live, be happy—marry, as I promised. (Covers his face with his hands) Coward; what right have I even to think of her? No right. (Takes up poison) Now. (About to drink) (Knock at door) Lanyon's knock. Can Heaven be merciful? (Unlocks door) Come in, come in. (Enter Lanyon)

Lanyon: Henry.

Jekyll: Come in. (Locking door and looking eagerly at Lanyon's face) You have brought? (Lanyon shakes his head) I saw it in your face; sit down my poor Lanyon; you are trembling.

Lanyon: (Sitting) It is nothing. I have not been myself since—since—

Jekyll: (Sits in armchair) I understand. You saw the chemists?

Lanyon: Yes, they remembered your first purchase of the salt, but assured me that the old supply was long ago exhausted. That furnished you lately was from a fresh invoice.

Jekyll: And it is useless like all the others. With Poole's help I have ransacked every chemist's shop in London. This last interview of yours was my forlorn hope. Did you beg them to search their cellars.

Lanyon: More than that. I searched with them. Praying to find some crate that had been overlooked. But in vain.

Jekyll: Then all is over. The first supply was impure. I am persuaded that unknown impurity gave the drug its powers. We cannot reproduce it, Lanyon; I am a dead man.

Lanyon: (Rises and crosses to him) Courage, what you fear may never take place after all.

Jekyll: Do not believe it. I have trifled too long with my conscience. I have destroyed the balance of my soul. The evil power within me has mastery. It is Hyde now that controls Jekyll. Not Jekyll Hyde.

Lanyon: What do you mean? (Clings to table) (Jekyll fainting) (Jekyll sits in arm chair. Lanyon sits on front of table)

Jekyll: Three days ago I dropped asleep in this chair where I am sitting now. How long I slept, I do not know, but waking, my eyes fell upon my hand as it lay there. Not this that I now hold up to you, but a distorted hand of a dusky pallor. I turned, and saw in the glass, not my face, but his, the Monster's, Hyde's, there—there.

Lanyon: You were transformed without the drug then?

Jekyll: Yes, as often, of late, I have slowly lost the hold upon my original, my better self. To restore it at first was the work of a moment. I had only to mix the draught and drink it. But for that I used the last of the old powders. Once transformed again, death alone can save me. (Rises) (Lanyon sits in chair. Jekyll crosses to Lanyon)

Lanyon: My poor Harry.

Jekyll: To prolong my own agony I have destroyed your peace of mind. Forgive me, Lanyon. The nightmare that has haunted you will soon be over. Soon I shall trouble you no more.

Lanyon: (Rises) No, no. It can't be. This awful presence is gone; it will not return again. The end has come. Have you not suffered already, as no man ever did. You must seek a place of safety. Here new dangers threaten.

Jekyll: What new danger have I to fear.

Lanyon: Utterson has found a clue.

Jekyll: The forged letter—I had forgotten that.

Lanyon: He believes you to be Hyde's accomplice. At any moment the police may search the house. You must leave it at once and go with me.

Jekyll: To whom do you say this? To Dr. Jekyll or Mr. Hyde?

Lanyon: Harry, I entreat you. (Steps forward)

Jekyll: To force you to compound a felony, and make that monster your companion. Why? To what end? He is proscribed and branded. He would not be safe one hour. No, leave him to escape them in his own time; in his own way.

Lanyon: But here you cannot escape from yourself. There is danger for you even in the sight of these surroundings.

Jekyll: That is true. There is not an instant to be lost. Lanyon, I have one last request. If you were ever my friend you will hear and grant it.

Lanyon: Speak, what must I do?

Jekyll: It concerns one whose name I hardly dare to breathe. You have guessed it.

Lanyon: Agnes.

Jekyll: Do not fear. While I live, I would not have her know my story. I dare not speak with her—I might betray myself. It is not that, but I must see her, Lanyon—once, only once, while I'm still myself.

Lanyon: But how?

Jekyll: I have found the way. From that window, I could see her face. The court is narrow—we are high above it. Bring her there upon some pretense. No matter what—she will never see me; never know. But I may look upon her once; only once—before—

Lanyon: I understand, and I will do it; but on one condition. Give me your promise first.

Jekyll: What condition?

Lanyon: That until this change you fear has come, you will make no attempt upon your life.

Jekyll: (Turns away) I promise. (Gives his hand) There's my hand upon it. Once more I promise.

Lanyon: (Holding his hand—other on shoulder) Meantime, have faith. Do not give way. Do not despair.

Jekyll: Goodbye, old friend. Whatever happens, pity me—and forgive me if you can.

Lanyon: Whatever happens, my place is here with you.

Jekyll: (Unbolting door) Yes. first bring her here, and come to me afterward alone. I will watch for your signal.

Lanyon: Courage, courage. (Exit)

Jekyll: (Bolting doors behind him) And so farewell. For we shall never meet again—I know it. I am left to face death alone. Ah, were death all. It is the other nameless terror that racks me. Terror of myself now we are one. (Shivers and supports himself by chair) Again that shudder of the grave. Have we changed places already? (Looks in glass) No. Not yet, not yet. (Kneels at chair and bursts into tears) Fool, to waste time like a woman in tears. My papers, now, make the minutes last. (Sits and takes papers from drawer) This is my full confession. (Looking over it) I have not spared myself. (Writing) For Gabriel Utterson, let him deal with it as he pleases, and this my last will revoking the other which he holds. (Laughing bitterly) He will like this better. It cancels my bequest to Hyde. Hyde! What could Hyde do with money? Poor, hunted wretch. The wealth of London would not save him now. (Writing) This too, for Gabriel Utterson. (Rises shuddering) The devil's hand is at my throat. No, it is past. Agnes, where is Agnes? He promised that I should see her. (Up to window which he opens) She must come quickly—or I shall be gone. Night is closing in. The stars are coming out. How often together, Agnes and I, have wondered at them. And now, for me, no dawn, no twilight—Only the outer blackness of the grave. Will they never come? (Looks out and draws back hastily) The Inspector of police. Well, and why not? Dr. Jekyll surely may take a breath of air, unchallenged. I am like a child and start at nothing. He is gone again. All is still, only the roar of London. Hark, voices. Lanyon has kept his promise. She is there. She is there. They pass—she knows nothing. I will not have it thus. I must speak with her, if only one word. Agnes, Agnes, look, it is I Henry Jekyll. She has seen me. She will come. Thank Heaven, she will come. (Falls into chair) She only once before—I shall see her face—I shall hear her voice. (He has slowly turned into Hyde, and now sees himself in the glass, and rises with a shriek) (Murmur of voices, swelling louder, until all on stage) (Jekyll crouches trembling) (Loud knocking at the door)

Utterson: Jekyll. Jekyll.

Hyde: (Aside, in terror) Utterson, the police. (Knock repeated)

Utterson: Jekyll. I demand to see you. If not of your consent, then brute force.

Hyde: (On floor) Utterson, for God's sake, have mercy.

Utterson: That's not his voice. Down with the door. (Heavy blows on door)

Hyde: (Aside) Poison, here. (Up to table, takes up phial)

(Doors broken down and Utterson enters, followed by Poole, Lanyon)

Hyde: (Drinks and throws away phial, coughs and falls)

Utterson: (To front of table. All others in doorway) Murderer, what have you done with Jekyll?

Hyde: Gone. Gone. (Dies) (Lanyon advances, Poole to back of table)

Agnes: (Outside) Henry, where is he? (Enters) What is there?

CURTAIN (Lights up quickly as soon as curtain falls)

Appendix H: Degeneration and Crime

1. From Charles Darwin, *The Expression of the Emotions in Man and Animals* (London: John Murray, 1872), chapter 10, "Anger"

[Charles Darwin's (1809–82) *The Expression of the Emotions in Man and Animals* was first published in 1872, and a second edition appeared in 1889, seven years after Darwin's death. The selection given here is taken from the first edition. The extract shows Darwin's belief that there existed a one-to-one correspondence of emotions in humans and animals, and that the expression of emotions such as anger represented the human inheritance from a violent progenitor. Similarities between Darwin's descriptions and Mr. Hyde's behaviour are striking.]

Shakespeare sums up the chief characteristics of rage as follows:—

> In peace there's nothing so becomes a man
> As modest stillness and humility;
> But when the blast of war blows in our ears,
> Then imitate the action of the tiger:
> Stiffen the sinews, summon up the blood,
> Then lend the eye a terrible aspect;
> Now set the teeth, and stretch the nostril wide,
> Hold hard the breath, and bend up every spirit
> To his full height! On, on, you noblest English.
> *Henry V*, act iii. sc. 1.

The lips are sometimes protruded during rage in a manner, the meaning of which I do not understand, unless it depends on our descent from some ape-like animal. Instances have been observed, not only with Europeans, but with the Australians and Hindoos. The lips, however, are much more commonly retracted, the grinning or clenched teeth being thus exposed. This has been noticed by almost every one who has written on expression. The appearance is as if the teeth were uncovered, ready for seizing or tearing an enemy, though there may be no intention of acting in this manner. Mr. Dyson Lacy has seen this grinning expression with the Australians, when quarrelling, and so has Gaika with the Kafirs of South America. Dickens, in speaking of an atrocious murderer who had just been caught, and was surrounded by a furious mob, describes "the people as jumping up one behind another, snarling with their teeth, and making at him like wild beasts" (*Oliver Twist*, vol iii, p. 245).[1]

Every one who has had much to do with young children must have seen how naturally they take to biting, when in a passion. It seems as instinctive in them as in young crocodiles, who snap their little jaws as soon as they emerge from the egg.

A grinning expression and the protrusion of the lips appear sometimes to go together. A close observer says that he has seen many instances of intense hatred (which can hardly be distinguished from rage, more or less suppressed) in Orientals, and once in an elderly English woman. In all these cases there "was a grin, not a scowl—the lips lengthening, the cheeks settling downwards, the eyes half-closed, whilst the brow remained perfectly calm...."

Dr. Maudsley, after detailing various strange animal-like traits in idiots, asks whether these are not due to the reappearance of primitive instincts—"a faint echo from a far-distant past, testifying to a kinship which man has almost outgrown." He adds, that as every human brain passes, in the course of its development, through the same stages as those occurring in the lower vertebrate animals, and as the brain of an idiot is in an arrested condition, we may presume that it "will manifest its most primitive functions, and no higher functions." Dr. Maudsley thinks that the same view may be extended to the brain in its degenerated condition in some insane patients; and asks, whence come "the savage snarl, the destructive disposition, the obscene language, the wild howl, the offensive habits, displayed by some of the insane? Why should a human being, deprived of his reason, ever become so brutal in character, as some do, unless he has the brute nature within him?" This question must, as it would appear, be answered in the affirmative....

Sneering, Defiance: Uncovering the canine tooth on one side.—The expression which I wish here to consider differs but little from that already described, when the lips are retracted and the grinning teeth exposed. The difference consists solely in the upper lip being retracted in such a manner that the canine tooth on one side of the face alone is shown; the face itself being generally a little upturned and half averted from the person causing offense. The other signs of rage are not necessarily present. This expression may occasionally be observed in a person who sneers at or defies another, though there may be no real anger; as when any one is playfully accused of some fault, and answers, "I scorn the imputation." The expression is not a common one, but I have seen it exhibited with perfect distinctness by a lady

---

1   Charles Dickens (1812–70) published *Oliver Twist* in 1837–39.

who was being quizzed by another person. It was described by Parsons as long ago as 1746, with an engraving, showing the uncovered canine on one side. Mr. Rejlander, without my having made any allusion to the subject, asked me whether I had ever noticed this expression, as he had been much struck by it. He has photographed for me a lady, who sometimes unintentionally displays the canine on one side, and who can do so voluntarily with unusual distinctness.

The expression of a half-playful sneer graduates into one of great ferocity when, together with a heavily frowning brow and fierce eye, the canine tooth is exposed. A Bengalee boy was accused before Mr. Scott of some misdeed. The delinquent did not dare to give vent to his wrath in words, but it was plainly shown on his countenance, sometimes by a defiant frown, and sometimes "by a thoroughly canine snarl." When this was exhibited, "the corner of the lip over the eye-tooth, which happened in this case to be large and projecting, was raised on the side of his accuser, a strong frown being still retained on the brow." Sir C. Bell states that the actor Cooke could express the most determined hate "when with the oblique cast of his eyes he drew up the outer part of the upper lip, and discovered a sharp angular tooth...."

The expression here considered, whether that of a playful sneer or ferocious snarl, is one of the most curious which occurs in man. It reveals his animal descent; for no one, even if rolling on the ground in a deadly grapple with an enemy, and attempting to bite him, would try to use his canine teeth more than his other teeth.

We may readily believe from our affinity to the anthropomorphous apes that our male semi-human progenitors possessed great canine teeth, and men are now occasionally born having them of unusually large size, with interspaces in the opposite jaw for their receptions. We may further suspect, notwithstanding that we have no support from analogy, that our semi-human progenitors uncovered their canine teeth when prepared for battle, as we still do when feeling ferocious, or when merely sneering at or defying some one, without any intention of making a real attack with our teeth.

2. From Gina Lombroso Ferrero, *Criminal Man According to the Classification of Cesare Lombroso* (New York: G.P. Putnam's Sons, 1911)

[Cesare Lombroso (1835–1909) was an Italian doctor who, while on the faculty of the University of Turin, grew interested in what he viewed as the physiological basis of crime. Lombroso became convinced that the brains of criminals were different from those of other people and first published his theories in *Criminal Man* (*L'Uomo Delin-*

quente) in 1876. The study was widely distributed and republished, and went through five editions, becoming longer and more comprehensive each time. Lombroso's daughters, Paola and Gina, worked closely with their father and promoted his ideas after his death. Lombroso was a founding figure in what came to be called "criminal anthropology" in England, and in its modern form is now known as criminology. In *Criminal Man* Lombroso defines criminality as innate and biologically determined. Criminals, he says, are "atavisms," throwbacks to an earlier form of humanity, and are instinctively violent. Lombroso and his followers discount all environmental factors, and rely heavily on stereotypes of behaviour to define "criminals." *Criminal Man* was an extremely influential book, and at least indirectly shaped the portrayal of Mr. Hyde as an atavistic criminal. The selection given here is taken from a summary of his theories by his daughter Gina.]

CHAPTER I
ORIGIN AND CAUSES OF CRIME

In order to determine the origin of actions which we call criminal, we shall be forced to hark back to a very remote period in the history of the human race. In all the epochs of which records exist, we find traces of criminal actions. In fact, if we study minutely the customs of savage peoples, past and present, we find that many acts that are now considered criminal by civilised nations were legitimate in former times, and are today reputed such among primitive races.

CRIMINALITY OF CHILDREN

The criminal instincts common to primitive savages would be found proportionally in nearly all children, if they were not influenced by moral training and example. This does not mean that without educative restraints, all children would develop into criminals. According to the observations made by Prof. Mario Carrara at Cagliari, the bands of neglected children who run wild in the streets of the Sardinian capital and are addicted to thievish practices and more serious vices, spontaneously correct themselves of these habits as soon as they have arrived at puberty.

This fact, that the germs of moral insanity and criminality are found normally in mankind in the first stages of his existence, in the same way as forms considered monstrous when exhibited by adults frequently exist in the foetus, is such a simple and common phenomenon that it eluded notice until it was demonstrated clearly by observers like Moreau, Perez, and Bain. The child, like certain adults, whose abnormality consists in a lack of moral sense, represents what is known to alienists as a morally insane being and to criminologists as a born criminal, and it certainly resembles these types in its impetuous violence.

Perez (*Psychologie de l'enfant*, 2d ed., 1882) remarks on the frequency and precocity of anger in children:

> During the first two months, it manifests by movements of the eyebrows and hands undoubted fits of temper when undergoing any distasteful process, such as washing or when deprived of any object it takes a fancy to. At the age of one, it goes to the length of striking those who incur its displeasure, of breaking plates or throwing them at persons it dislikes, exactly like savages.

Moreau (*De l'Homicide chez les enfants*, 1882) cites numerous cases of children who fly into a passion if their wishes are not complied with immediately. In one instance observed by him a very intelligent child of eight, when reproved, even in the mildest manner by his parents or strangers, would give way to violent anger, snatching up the nearest weapon, or if he found himself unable to take revenge, would break anything he could lay his hands on.

A baby girl showed an extremely violent temper, but became of gentle disposition after she had reached the age of two (Perez). Another, observed by the same author, when only eleven months old, flew into a towering rage, because she was unable to pull off her grandfather's nose. Yet another, at the age of two, tried to bite another child who had a doll like her own, and she was so much affected by her anger that she was ill for three days afterwards.

Nino Bixio, when a boy of seven (*Vita*, Guerzoni, 1880) on seeing his teacher laugh because he had written his exercise on office letter-paper, threw the inkstand at the man's face. This boy was literally the terror of the school, on account of the violence he displayed at the slightest offense. Infants of seven or eight months have been known to scratch at any attempt to withdraw the breast from them, and to retaliate when slapped.

A backward and slightly hydrocephalous boy whom my father had under observation, began at the age of six to show violent irritation at the slightest reproof or correction. If he was able to strike the person who had annoyed him, his rage cooled immediately; if not, he would scream incessantly and bite his hands with gestures similar to those often witnessed in caged bears who have been teased and cannot retaliate.

The above cases show that the desire for revenge is extremely common and precocious in children. Anger is an elementary instinct innate in human beings. It should be guided and restrained, but can never be extirpated....

The criminal is an atavistic being, a relic of a vanished race. This is by no means an uncommon occurrence in nature. Atavism, the reversion to a former state, is the first feeble indication of the reaction opposed by nature to the perturbing causes which seek to alter her delicate mechanism. Under certain unfavourable conditions, cold or poor soil, the common oak will develop characteristics of the oak of the Quaternary period. The dog left to run wild in the forest will in a few generations revert to the type of his original wolf-like progenitor, and the cultivated garden roses when neglected show a tendency to reassume the form of the original dog-rose. Under special conditions produced by alcohol, chloroform, heat, or injuries, ants, dogs and pigeons become irritable and savage like their wild ancestors.

This tendency to alter under special conditions is common to human beings, in whom hunger, syphilis, trauma, and, still more frequently, morbid conditions inherited from insane, criminal or diseased progenitors, or the abuse of nerve poisons, such as alcohol, tobacco, or morphine, cause various alterations, of which criminality—that is, a return to the characteristics peculiar to primitive savages—is in reality the least serious, because it represents a less advanced stage than other forms of cerebral alteration....

The atavistic origin of crime is certainly one of the most important discoveries of criminal anthropology, but it is important only theoretically, since it merely explains the phenomenon. Anthropologists soon realised how necessary it was to supplement this discovery by that of the origin, or causes which call forth in certain individuals these atavistic or criminal instincts, for it is the immediate causes that constitute the practical nucleus of the problem and it is their removal that renders possible the cure of the disease.

These causes are divided into organic and external factors of crime: the former remote and deeply rooted, the latter momentary but frequently determining the criminal act, and both closely related and fused together.

Heredity is the principal organic cause of criminal tendencies. It may be divided into two classes: indirect heredity from a generically degenerate family with frequent cases of insanity, deafness, syphilis, epilepsy, and alcoholism among its members; direct heredity from criminal parentage.

Indirect Heredity. Almost all forms of chronic, constitutional diseases, especially those of a nervous character: chorea, sciatica, hysteria, insanity, and above all, epilepsy, may give rise to criminality in the descendants....

Direct Heredity. The effects of direct heredity are still more serious, for they are aggravated by environment and education. Official statistics show that 20% of juvenile offenders belong to families of doubtful reputation and 26% to those whose reputation is thoroughly bad. The criminal Galletto, a native of Marseilles, was the nephew of the equally ferocious anthropophagous violator of women, Orsolano. Dumollar was the son of a murderer; Patetot's grandfather and great-grandfather were in prison, as were the grandfathers and fathers of Papa, Crocco, Serravalle and Cavallante, Comptois and Lempave; the parents of the celebrated female thief Bans Refus, were both thieves.

Race. This is of great importance in view of the atavistic origin of crime. There exist whole tribes and races more or less given to crime, such as the tribe Zakka Khel in India. In all regions of Italy, whole villages constitute hot-beds of crime, owing, no doubt, to ethnical causes: Artena in the province of Rome, Carde and San Giorgio Canavese in Piedmont, Pergola in Tuscany, San Severo in Apulia, San Mauro and Nicosia in Sicily. The frequency of homicide in Calabria, Sicily, and Sardinia is fundamentally due to African and Oriental elements.

In the gipsies we have an entire race of criminals with all the passions and vices common to delinquent types: idleness, ignorance, impetuous fury, vanity, love of orgies, and ferocity. Murder is often committed for some trifling gain. The women are skilled thieves and train their children in dishonest practices. On the contrary, the percentage of crimes among Jews is always lower than that of the surrounding population; although there is a prevalence of certain specific forms of offenses, often hereditary, such as fraud, forgery, libel, and chief of all, traffic in prostitution; murder is extremely rare....

There is one disease that without other causes—either inherited degeneracy or vices resulting from a bad education and environment—is capable of transforming a healthy individual into a vicious, hopelessly evil being. That disease is alcoholism, which has been discussed in a previous chapter, but to which I must refer briefly again, because it is such an important factor of criminality.

Temporary drunkenness alone will give rise to crime, since it inflames the passions, obscures the mental and moral faculties, and destroys all sense of decency, causing men to commit offenses in a state of automatism or a species of somnambulism. Sometimes drunkenness produces kleptomania. A slight excess in drinking will cause men of absolute honesty to appropriate any objects they can lay their hands upon. When the effects of drink have worn off they feel shame and remorse and hasten to restore the stolen goods. Alcohol, however, more often causes violence. An officer known to my father, when drunk, twice attempted to run his sword through his friends and his own attendant.

But besides the crimes of violence committed during a drunken fit, the prolonged abuse of alcohol, opium, morphia, coca, and other nervines may give rise to chronic perturbation of the mind, and without other causes, congenital or educative, will transform an honest, well-bred, and industrious man into an idle, violent, and apathetic fellow,—into an ignoble being, capable of any depraved action, even when he is not directly under the influence of the drug....

Meteoric Causes are frequently the determining factor of the ultimate impulsive act, which converts the latent criminal into an effective one. Excessively high temperature and rapid barometric changes, while predisposing epileptics to convulsive seizures and the insane to uneasiness, restlessness, and noisy outbreaks, encourage quarrels, brawls, and stabbing affrays. To the same reason may be ascribed the prevalence during the hot months, of rape, homicide, insurrections, and revolts. In comparing statistics of criminality in France with those of the variations in temperature, Ferri noted an increase in crimes of violence during the warmer years. An examination of European and American statistics shows that the number of homicides decreases as we pass from hot to cooler climates. Holzendorf calculates that the number of murders committed in the Southern States of North America is fifteen times greater than those committed in the Northern States. A low temperature, on the contrary, has the effect of increasing the number of crimes against property, due to increased need, and both in Italy and America the proportion of thefts increases the farther north we go.

Density of Population. The agglomeration of persons in a large town is a certain incentive to crimes against property. Robbery, frauds, and criminal associations increase, while there is a decrease in crimes against the person, due to the restraints imposed by mutual supervision.

He who has studied mankind, or, better still, himself [writes my father], must have remarked how often an individual, who is respectable and self-controlled in the bosom of his family, becomes indecent and even immoral when he finds himself in the company of a number of his fellows, to whatever class they may belong. The primitive instincts of theft, homicide, and lust, the germs of which lie dormant in each individual as long as he is alone, particularly if kept in check by sound moral training, awaken and develop suddenly into gigantic proportions when he comes into contact with others, the increase being greater in those who already possess such criminal tendencies in a marked degree.

In all large cities, low lodging-houses form the favourite haunts of crime.

Imitation. The detailed accounts of crimes circulated in large towns by newspapers, have an extremely pernicious influence, because example is a powerful agent for evil as well as for good.

Immigration. The agglomeration of population produced by immigration is a strong incentive to crime, especially that of an associated nature, due to increased want, lessened supervision and the consequent ease with which offenders avoid detection. In New York the largest contingent of criminality is furnished by the immigrant population....

Education. Contrary to general belief, the influence of education on crime is very slight.

Professions. The trades and professions which encourage inebriety in those who follow them (cooks, confectioners, and inn-keepers), those which bring the poor (servants of all kinds, especially footmen, coachmen, and chauffeurs) into contact with wealth, or which provide means for committing crimes (bricklayers, blacksmiths, etc.) furnish a remarkable share of criminality. Still more so is this the case with the professions of notary, usher of the courts, attorneys, and military men.

It should be observed, however; that the characteristic idleness of criminals makes them disinclined to adopt any profession, and when they do, their extreme fickleness prompts them to change continually.

Economic Conditions. Poverty is often a direct incentive to theft, when the miserable victims of economic conditions find themselves and their families face to face with starvation, and it acts further indirectly through certain diseases: pellagra, alcoholism, scrofula and scurvy, which are the outcome of misery and produce criminal degeneration; its influence has nonetheless been exaggerated. If thieves are generally penniless, it is because of their extreme idleness and astonishing extravagance, which makes them run through huge sums with greatest of ease, not because poverty has driven them to theft....

3. From Max Nordau, *Degeneration* (1892; New York: D. Appleton & Co., 1895)

[While Max Nordau (1849–1923) pays homage to Lombroso in this extract, he can be seen to be stretching Lombroso's ideas to include any behaviour of which he disapproves. Nordau applies the concept of "degeneration" to artists and writers, accusing those of whom he disapproves of exhibiting signs of devolution or degeneration, and thus of incipient insanity and criminality (which are synonymous terms for him). Stevenson in his Bohemian phase would have been classified by Nordau as a "degenerate," and Nordau's book is a clear attempt to use the concept of degeneration to further a conservative political agenda. While Stevenson also draws upon the concept of "degeneration" in *Dr. Jekyll and Mr. Hyde,* his politics are substantially different from those of Nordau.]

PROFESSOR CAESAR LOMBROSO,
TURIN
DEAR AND HONOURED MASTER,

I dedicate this book to you, in open and joyful recognition of the fact
that without your labours it could never have been written.

The notion of degeneracy, first introduced into science by Morel,[1]
and developed with so much genius by yourself, has in your hands
already shown itself extremely fertile in the most diverse directions.
On numerous obscure points of psychiatry, criminal law, politics, and
sociology, you have poured a veritable flood of light, which those alone
have not perceived who obdurately close their eyes, or who are too
short-sighted to derive benefit from any enlightenment whatsoever.

But there is a vast and important domain into which neither you
nor your disciples have hitherto borne the torch of your method—the
domain of art and literature.

Degenerates are not always criminals, prostitutes, anarchists, and
pronounced lunatics; they are often authors and artists. These,
however, manifest the same mental characteristics, and for the most
part the same somatic features, as the members of the above-men-
tioned anthropological family, who satisfy their unhealthy impulses
with the knife of the assassin or the bomb of the dynamiter, instead of
with pen and pencil.

Some among these degenerates in literature, music, and painting
have in recent years come into extraordinary prominence, and are
revered by numerous admirers as creators of a new art, and heralds of
the coming centuries.

This phenomenon is not to be disregarded. Books and works of art
exercise a powerful suggestion to the masses. It is from these productions that an age derives its ideals of morality and beauty. If they are
absurd and anti-social, they exert a disturbing and corrupting influence on the views of a whole generation. Hence the latter, especially
the impressionable youth, easily excited to enthusiasm for all that is
strange and seemingly new, must be warned and enlightened as to the
real nature of the creations so blindly admired. This warning the ordinary critic does not give. Exclusively literary and aesthetic culture is,
moreover, the worst preparation conceivable for a true knowledge of
the pathological character of the works of degenerates. The verbose
rhetorician exposes with more or less grace, or cleverness, the subjec-

---

1   Bénédict Morel (1809–73), French psychiatrist and author of the influential
    treatise on degeneration, *Traité des Dégénérescences* (1857).

tive impressions received from the works he criticises, but is incapable of judging if these works are the productions of a shattered brain, and also the nature of the mental disturbance expressing itself by them.

Now I have undertaken the work of investigating (as much as possible after your method) the tendencies of the fashions in art and literature; of proving that they have their source in the degeneracy of their authors, and that the enthusiasm of their admirers is for manifestations of more or less pronounced moral insanity, imbecility, and dementia. Thus, this book is an attempt at a really scientific criticism, which does not base its Judgment of a book upon the purely accidental, capricious, and variable emotions it awakens—emotions depending on the temperament and mood of the individual reader—but upon the psycho-physiological elements from which it sprang. At the same time it ventures to fill a void still existing in your powerful system.

I have no doubt as to the consequences to myself of my initiative. There is at the present day no danger in attacking the Church, for it no longer has the stake at its disposal. To write against rulers and governments is likewise nothing venturesome, for at the worst nothing more than imprisonment could follow, with compensating glory of martyrdom. But grievous is the fate of him who has the audacity to characterize aesthetic fashions as forms of mental decay. The author or artist attacked never pardons a man for recognising in him a lunatic or a charlatan; the subjectively garrulous critics are furious when it is pointed out how shallow and incompetent they are, or how cowardly when swimming with the stream; and even the public is angered when forced to see that it has been running after fools, quack dentists, and mountebanks, as so many prophets. Now, the graphomaniacs and their critical body-guard dominate nearly the entire press, and in the latter possess an instrument of torture by which, in Indian fashion, they can rack the troublesome spoiler of sport, to his life's end.

The danger, however, to which he exposes himself cannot deter a man from doing that which he regards as his duty. When a scientific truth has been discovered, he owes it to humanity, and has no right to withhold it. Moreover, it is as little possible to do this as for a woman voluntarily to prevent the birth of the mature fruit of her womb.

Without aspiring to the most distant comparison of myself with you, one of the loftiest mental phenomena of the century, I may yet take for my example the smiling serenity with which you pursue your own way, indifferent to ingratitude, insult, and misunderstanding. Pray remain, dear and honoured master, ever favourably disposed towards your gratefully devoted
MAX NORDAU.

Appendix I: London in the 1880s

1. From George Augustus Sala, *Gaslight and Daylight with Some London Scenes They Shine Upon* (London: Tinsley Brothers, 1872)

[George Augustus Sala (1829–95) was a journalist and novelist who first made his mark as a regular contributor to Charles Dickens's *Household Words*. He published books of "travel writing" in which he would roam the streets of London and report on the sights and events of London, especially night-time London. In this selection he describes the area in and around Soho and characterizes the inhabitants in ways that echo Stevenson's description of Soho as seen by Mr. Utterson.]

"Perfidious Patmos"[1]

The Patmos of London I may describe as an island bounded by four squares; on the north by that of Soho, on the south by that of Leicester, on the east by the quadrangle of Lincoln's Inn Fields (for the purlieus of Long Acre and Seven Dials are all Patmos), and on the west by Golden Square.

The trapezium of streets enclosed within this boundary are not, by any means, of an aristocratic description. A maze of sorry thoroughfares, a second-rate butcher's meat and vegetable market, two model lodging-houses, a dingy parish church, and some 'brick barns' of dissent are within its boundaries. No lords or squires of high degree live in this political Alsatia.[2] The houses are distinguished by a plurality of bell-pulls inserted in the door-jambs, and by a plurality of little brass name-plates, bearing the names of in-dwelling artisans. Everybody (of nubile age and English extraction) seems to be married, and to have a great many children, whose education appears to be conducted chiefly on the out door principle.

As an uninterested stranger, and without a guide, you might, perambulating these shabby streets, see in them nothing which would peculiarly distinguish them from that class of London veins known

---

1 The island where St. John the Apostle fled to write the *Book of Revelations*. Sala is here suggesting that this area of London is an island of safety for refugees from across Europe.

2 A region, now part of France, that has changed hands several times and thus has a mix of languages and cultures.

inelegantly, but expressively, as 'back slums.' At the first glance you see nothing but dingy houses teeming with that sallow, cabbage-stalk and fried dish sort of population, indigenous to back slums. The pinafored children are squabbling or playing in the gutters; while from distant courts come faintly and fitfully threats of Jane to tell Ann's mother; together with that unmeaning monotonous chant or dirge which street-children sing, why, or with what object, I know not. Grave dogs sit on door-steps—their heads patiently cocked on one side, waiting for the door to be opened, as—in this region of perpetual beer-fetching—they know must soon be the case. The beer itself, in vases of strangely-diversified patterns, and borne by Hebes[1] of as diversified appearance, is incessantly threading the needle through narrow courts and alleys. The public-house doors are always on the swing; the bakers' shops (they mostly sell 'seconds') are always full; so are the cookshops, so are the coffee-shops: step into one, and you shall have a phase of Patmos before you incontinent.

2. From Arthur Ransome, *Bohemia in London* (London: S. Swift, 1912)

[Arthur Ransome (1884–1967) was a journalist and writer who lived a penniless, Bohemian existence for 12 years before becoming an established author. His book *Bohemia in London* is an autobiographical account of his early days in the poorer sections of London. In his descriptions of the bars and cafés of Soho he provides the following anecdote of his encounter with a man leading a "double life."]

There is always a strange crowd at this place, dancers and singers from the music halls, sad women pretending to be merry, coarse women pretending to be refined, and men of all types grimacing and clinking glasses with the women. And then there are the small groups indifferent to everything but the jollity and swing of the place, thumping their beer mugs on the table over some mighty point of philosophy or criticism, and ready to crack each others' heads for joy in the arguments of Socialism or Universal Peace.

I was seated at a table here one night, admiring the picture in which a gnome pours some hot liquid on another gnome who lies shrieking in a vat, when I noticed a party of four men sitting at a table opposite. Three were obviously hangers-on of one or other of the arts, the sort of men who are proud of knowing an actor or two to speak to, and are ready to talk with importance of their editorial duties on the *Draper's*

---

1 Hebe was the Greek goddess of youth, here used ironically.

Shop in Macclesfield Street, Soho, 1883. Courtesy the Museum of London.

Compendium or the *Toyshop Times*. The fourth was different. A huge felt hat banged freely down over a wealth of thick black hair, bright blue eyes, an enormous black beard, a magnificent manner (now and again he would rise and bow profoundly, with his hat upon his heart, to some girls on the other side of the room), a way of throwing his head back when he drank, of thrusting it forward when he spoke, an air of complete abandon to the moment and the moment's thought; he took me tremendously. He seemed to be delighting his friends with impromptu poetry. I did a mean but justifiable thing, and carried my pot of beer to a table just beside him, where I could see him better, and also hear his conversation. It was twaddle, but such downright, spirited, splendid twaddle, flung out from the heart of him in a grand, careless way that made me think of largesse royally scattered on a mob. His blue twinkling eyes decided me. When, a minute or two later, he went out, I followed, and found him vociferating to his gang upon the pavement. I pushed in, so as to exclude them, and asked him:

"Are you prose or verse?"

"I write verse, but I dabble in the other thing." It was the answer I had expected.

"Very good. Will you come to my place to-morrow night at eight? Tobacco. Beer. Talk."

"I love beer. I adore tobacco. Talking is my life. I will come."

"Here is my card. Eight o'clock tomorrow. Good-night." And so I left him.

He came, and it turned out that he worked in a bank from ten to four every day, and played the wild Bohemian every night. His beard was a disguise. He spent his evenings seeking for adventure, he said, and apologised to me for earning an honest living. He was really delightful. So are our friendships made; there is no difficulty about them, no diffidence; you try a man as you would a brand of tobacco; if you agree, then you are friends; if not, why then you are but two blind cockchafers who have collided with each other in a summer night, and boom away again each in his own direction.

3. From J. Milner Fothergill, *The Town Dweller: His Needs and Wants* (London, 1889)

[Milner Fothergill (1841–88) was a medical writer and member of the College of Physicians in London. Fothergill delivered a lecture on the subject of the "town dweller" in the same year as the publication of *Dr. Jekyll and Mr. Hyde.* In the book based on this lecture, published in 1889, Fothergill elaborates on his thesis that the inhabitants of inner-city London are a separate species from upper-class Londoners.]

Assuming the Norse to be the highest type of mankind, we find the town dweller to be a reversion to an earlier and lowlier ethnic form. While the rustic remains an Anglo-Dane, his cousin in London is smaller and darker, showing a return to the Celto-Iberian race. This is readily seen by a visit to Madame Tussaud's[1] in winter. The figures in effigy are large blonde beings with blue eyes and fair hair. Massive and substantial, weighing half as much again as a rule as the living beings present (a few comparatively recent additions excepted). The living crowd are smaller, lighter and darker; the contrast being very marked. It is well to repeat the visit in summer, when the persons visiting the exhibition are largely excursionists from the country. They resemble the persons in effigy; and no deterioration of the race is perceptible. A few visits to the waxworks carry with them instructive lessons.

Nor is this reversion confined to the Celto-Iberian. In the true bred cockney of the East End, the most degenerate cockney, we can see a

---

1 Famous London wax museum that opened in 1835.

return to an earlier archaic type of man. Mr. Cantlie made careful observations and measurements of several cockneys. He says of one, "height five feet, three inches; his jaws are misshapen; he cannot bring his front teeth within half an inch of each other; his upper jaw is pointed, and falls within the arch of the lower." And this cockney with "undershot" jaw is a matter of my own personal observation. Now let us contrast with this what Dr. Beddoe, F.R.S., says, of a pre-Aryan race, which were dispossessed by the wave of Celto-Iberian conquest. Among their characteristics were "forward projecting jaws," while "the average height of this variety is five feet, three inches." It would seem that the cockney, reared under unfavourable circumstances, manifests a decided reversion to an earlier and lowlier ethnic form. In appearance, the East-ender, to the mind of the writer, bears a strong resemblance as to figure and feature, to the small and ugly Erse who are raised in the poorer districts of Ireland. This tendency in town dwellers to degenerate on the lines of reversion to older racial types, has an interest of its own for the anthropologist. While the deterioration, both physical and mental of town bred organisms, is a matter not meant for the philanthropist, but for the social economist. As towns grow larger and more numerous, the Cymri are going to have their own again—though not exactly in the manner prophesied by the old Welsh bards.

4. From William Booth, *In Darkest England and the Way Out* (New York: Funk & Wagnall, 1890)

[The term "Darkest England" was a shorthand for inner-city poverty, and was also applied to the capital in the phrase "Darkest London." In *In Darkest England and the Way Out* (1890) William Booth (1829–1919), the founder of the Salvation Army, claims that the inner cities of England are a territory comparable in size and unhealthiness to parts of recently explored Africa. Booth quotes Stanley's description of an African forest, then maps this onto the British Isles. The text manages to disparage simultaneously Africans and the British working classes. The hysterical tone of the book comes from W.T. Stead, the crusading editor of the *Pall Mall Gazette* and author of *The Maiden Tribute of Modern Babylon* (1885), who collaborated with Booth on *In Darkest England*. The text is an extreme example of the way in which the inner city poor were demonized and turned into foreign and inexplicable figures who could, like Mr. Hyde, erupt into irrational violence at any moment.]

This summer the attention of the civilised world has been arrested by the story which Mr. Stanley[1] has told of 'Darkest Africa', and his journeyings across the heart of the Lost Continent. In all that spirited narrative of heroic endeavour, nothing has so much impressed the imagination as his description of the immense forest, which offered an almost impenetrable barrier to his advance. The intrepid explorer, in his own phrase, 'marched, tore, ploughed, and cut his way for one hundred and sixty days through this inner womb of the true tropical forest.' The mind of man with difficulty endeavours to realise this immensity of wooded wilderness, covering a territory half as large again as the whole of France, where the rays of the sun never penetrate, where in the dark, dank air, filled with the steam of the heated morass, human beings dwarfed into pygmies and brutalized into cannibals lurk and live and die. Mr. Stanley vainly endeavours to bring home to us the full horror of that awful gloom. He says:

Take a thick Scottish copse dripping with rain; imagine this to be a mere undergrowth nourished under the impenetrable shade of ancient trees ranging from 100 to 180 feet high; briars and thorns abundant; lazy creeks meandering through the depths of the jungle, and sometimes a deep affluent of a great river. Imagine this forest and jungle in all stages of decay and growth, rain pattering on you every other day of the year; an impure atmosphere with its dread consequences, fever and dysentery; gloom throughout the day and darkness almost palpable throughout the night; and then if you can imagine such a forest extending the entire distance from Plymouth to Peterhead,[2] you will have a fair idea of some of the inconveniences endured by us in the Congo forest....

It is a terrible picture, and one that has engraved itself deep on the heart of civilization. But while brooding over the awful presentation of life as it exists in the vast African forest, it seemed to me only too vivid a picture of many parts of our own land. As there is a darkest Africa is there not also a darkest England? Civilisation, which can breed its own barbarians, does it not also breed its own pygmies? May we not find a parallel at our own doors, and discover within a stone's throw of our cathedrals and palaces similar horrors to those which Stanley has found existing in the great Equatorial forest?

The more the mind dwells upon the subject, the closer the analogy appears. The ivory raiders who brutally traffic in the unfortunate

---

1 Sir Henry Morton Stanley (1841–1904), explorer of Africa, famous for locating the Scottish explorer and missionary David Livingstone. In November 1874 Stanley left for Zanzibar to explore the Congo. His travels were widely chronicled in British and American newspapers.

2 Plymouth is a town on the south coast of England; Peterhead is the most easterly coastal town in Scotland.

denizens of the forest glades, what are they but the publicans who flourish on the weakness of our poor? The two tribes of savages, the human baboon and the handsome dwarf, who will not speak lest it impede him in his task, may be accepted as the two varieties who are continually present with us—the vicious, lazy lout, and the toiling slave. They, too, have lost all faith of life being other than it is and has been. As in Africa, it is all trees, trees, trees with no other world conceivable; so is it here—it is all vice and poverty and crime. To many the world is all slum, with the Workhouse as an intermediate purgatory before the grave. And just as Mr. Stanley's Zanzibaris lost faith, and could only be induced to plod on in brooding sullenness of dull despair, so the most of our social reformers, no matter how cheerily they may have started off soon become depressed and despairing. Who can battle against the ten thousand million trees? Who can hope to make headway against the innumerable adverse conditions which doom the dweller in Darkest England to eternal and immutable misery? What wonder is it that many of the warmest hearts and enthusiastic workers feel disposed to repeat the lament of the old English chronicler, who, speaking of the evil days which fell upon our forefathers in the reign of Stephen, said, "It seemed to them as if God and his Saints were dead."

An analogy is as good as a suggestion; it becomes wearisome when it is pressed too far. But before leaving it, think for a moment how close the parallel is, and how strange it is that so much interest should be excited by a narrative of human squalor and human heroism in a distant continent, while greater squalor and heroism not less magnificent may be observed at our very doors.

The Equatorial Forest traversed by Stanley resembles that Darkest England of which I have to speak, alike in its vast extent—both stretch, in Stanley's phrase, "as far as from Plymouth to Peterhead"; its monotonous darkness, its malaria and its gloom, its dwarfish dehumanized inhabitants, the slavery to which they are subjected, their privations and their misery. That which sickens the stoutest heart, and causes many of our bravest and best to fold their hands in despair, is the apparent impossibility of doing more than merely to peck at the outside of the endless tangle of monotonous undergrowth; to let light into it, to make a road clear through it, that shall not be immediately choked up by the ooze of the morass and the luxuriant parasitical growth of the forest—who dare hope for that? At present, alas, it would seem as though no one dares even to hope! It is the great Slough of Despond[1] of our time.

---

1   From John Bunyan's *Pilgrim's Progress* (1678), an allegorical bog into which the central character sinks under the weight of his sins.

And what a slough it is no man can gauge who has not waded therein, as some of us have done, up to the very neck for long years. Talk about Dante's Hell,[1] and all the horrors and cruelties of the torture-chamber of the lost! The man who walks with open eyes and with bleeding heart through the shambles of our civilization needs no such fantastic images of the poet to teach him horror. Often and often, when I have seen the young and the poor and the helpless go down before my eyes into the morass, trampled underfoot by beasts of prey in human shape that haunt these regions, it seemed as if God were no longer in His world, but that in His stead reigned a Wend, merciless as Hell, ruthless as the grave. Hard it is, no doubt, to read in Stanley's pages of the slave-traders coldly arranging for the surprise of a village, the capture of the inhabitants, the massacre of those who resist, and the violation of all the women; but the stony streets of London, if they could but speak, would tell of tragedies as awful, of ruin as complete, of ravishments as horrible, as if we were in Central Africa; only the ghastly devastation is covered, corpselike, with the artificialities and hypocrisies of modern civilization.

The lot of a Negress in the Equatorial Forest is not, perhaps, a very happy one, but is it so very much worse than that of many a pretty orphan girl in our Christian capital? We talk about the brutalities of the Dark Ages, and we profess to shudder as we read in books of the shameful exaction of the rights of feudal superior. And yet here, beneath our very eyes, in our theatres, in our restaurants, and in many other places, unspeakable though it be but to name it, the same hideous abuse flourishes unchecked. A young penniless girl, if she be pretty, is often hunted from pillar to post by her employers, confronted always by the alternative—Starve or Sin. And when once the poor girl has consented to buy the right to earn her living by the sacrifice of her virtue, then she is treated as a slave and an outcast by the very men who have ruined her. Her word becomes unbelievable, her life an ignominy, and she is swept downward, ever downward, into the bottomless perdition of prostitution. But there, even in the lowest depths, excommunicated by Humanity and outcast from God, she is far nearer the pitying heart of the One true Saviour than all the men who forced her down, aye, and than all the Pharisees and Scribes[2] who stand silently by while these fiendish wrongs are perpetrated before their very eyes.

The blood boils with impotent rage at the sight of these enormities, callously inflicted, and silently borne by these miserable victims. Nor

---

1 Dante's *Inferno* (from his *Divine Comedy* [1321]) gives a vivid description of Hell.

2 Two groups reprimanded by Jesus, according to biblical sources.

is it only women who are the victims, although their fate is the most tragic. Those firms which reduce sweating to a fine art, who systematically and deliberately defraud the workman of his pay, who grind the faces of the poor, and who rob the widow and the orphan, and who for a presence make great professions of public-spirit and philanthropy, these men nowadays are sent to Parliament to make laws for the people. The old prophets sent them to Hell—but we have changed all that. They send their victims to Hell, and are rewarded by all that wealth can do to make their lives comfortable. Read the House of Lords' Report on the Sweating System,[1] and ask if any African slave system, making due allowance for the superior civilisation, and therefore sensitiveness, of the victims, reveals more misery.

Darkest England, like Darkest Africa, reeks with malaria. The foul and fetid breath of our slums is almost as poisonous as that of the African swamp. Fever is almost as chronic there as on the Equator. Every year thousands of children are killed off by what is called defects of our sanitary system. They are in reality starved and poisoned, and all that can be said is that, in many cases, it is better for them that they were taken away from the trouble to come.

Just as in Darkest Africa it is only a part of the evil and misery that comes from the superior race who invade the forest to enslave and massacre its miserable inhabitants, so with us, much of the misery of those whose lot we are considering arises from their own habits. Drunkenness and all manner of uncleanness, moral and physical, abound. Have you ever watched by the bedside of a man in delirium tremens? Multiply the sufferings of that one drunkard by the hundred thousand, and you have some idea of what scenes are being witnessed in all our great cities at this moment. As in Africa streams intersect the forest in every direction, so the gin-shop stands at every corner with its River of the Water of Death flowing seventeen hours out of the twenty-four for the destruction of the people. A population sodden with drink, steeped in vice, eaten up by every social and physical malady, these are the denizens of Darkest England amidst whom my life has been spent, and to whose rescue I would now summon all that is best in the manhood and womanhood of our land.

---

1 One of the numerous government investigations into the appalling working conditions in British factories, particularly the "sweat shops" of the textile industry.

Shops in London's West End (Regent's Quadrant), c. 1880. Courtesy the Museum of London.

Appendix J: "Jack the Ripper"

1. New York Times (9 September 1888)

[This article from the *New York Times* relates incidents from the Whitechapel murders and the hunt for "Leather Apron" as "Jack the Ripper" was called then. The article also uses "Jekyll and Hyde" as a catchphrase, and refers to the Richard Mansfield production of *Dr. Jekyll and Mr. Hyde* then playing at the Lyceum.]

"Whitechapel Startled by a Fourth Murder"
from our own correspondent.

London, Sept. 8.—Not even during the riots and fog of February, 1886, have I seen London so thoroughly excited as it is to-night. The Whitechapel fiend murdered his fourth victim this morning and still continues undetected, unseen, and unknown. There is a panic in Whitechapel which will instantly extend to other districts should he change his locality, as the four murders are in everybody's mouth. The papers are full of them, and nothing else is talked of. The latest murder is exactly like its predecessor. The victim was a woman street walker of the lowest class. She had no money, having been refused lodgings shortly before because she lacked 8d. Her throat was cut so completely that everything but the spine was severed, and the body was ripped up, all the viscera being scattered about. The murder in all its details was inhuman to the last degree, and, like the others, could have been the work only of a bloodthirsty beast in human shape. It was committed in the most daring manner possible. The victim was found in the back yard of a house in Hanbury-street at 6 o'clock. At 5:15 the yard was empty. To get there the murderer must have led her through a passageway in the house full of sleeping people, and murdered her within a few yards of several people sleeping by open windows. To get away, covered with blood as he must have been, he had to go back through the passageway and into a street filled with early market people, Spitalfields[1] being close by. Nevertheless, not a sound was heard and no trace of the murderer exists.

All day long Whitechapel has been wild with excitement. The four murders have been committed within a gunshot of each other, but the detectives have no clue. The London police and detective force is

---

1 In the East End of London, an area famous for its markets and overcrowded conditions in the Victorian period.

probably the stupidest in the world. The man called "Leather Apron," of whom I cabled you, is still at large. He is well known, but they have not been able to arrest him, and he will doubtless do another murder in a day or so. One clue discovered this morning by a reporter may develop into something. An hour and a half after the murder a man with bloody hands, torn shirt, and a wild look entered a public house half a mile from the scene of the murder. The police have a good description of him and are trying to trace it. The assassin, however, is as cunning as he is daring. Both in this and in the last murder he took but a few minutes to murder his victim in a spot which had been examined but a quarter of an hour before. Both the character of the deed and the cool cunning alike exhibit the qualities of a monomaniac.

Such a series of murders has not been known in London for a hundred years. There is a bare possibility that it may turn out to be something like a case of Jekyll and Hyde, as Joseph Taylor, a perfectly reliable man, who saw the suspected person this morning in a shabby dress, swears that he has seen the same man coming out of a lodging house in Wilton street very differently dressed. However that may be, the murders are certainly the most ghastly and mysterious known to English police history. What adds to the weird effect they exert on the London mind is the fact that they occur while everybody is talking about Mansfield's "Jekyll and Hyde" at the Lyceum.

2. *The Times* (10 September 1888)

[The London *Times* in the following editorial asks if the Whitechapel murders are not connected to fictional representations of murder and horror stories, and mentions De Quincey and Poe as examples. *Dr. Jekyll and Mr. Hyde* is not mentioned, but it obviously falls within the same category as works by De Quincey and Poe.]

The series of shocking crimes perpetrated in Whitechapel, which on Saturday culminated in the murder of the woman CHAPMAN, is something so distinctly outside the ordinary range of human experience that it has created a kind of stupor extending far beyond the district where the murders were committed. One may search the ghastliest efforts of fiction and fail to find anything to surpass these crimes in diabolical audacity. The mind travels back to the pages of DE QUINCEY for an equal display of scientific delight in the details of butchery; or EDGAR ALLAN POE's "Murders in the Rue Morgue" recur in the endeavour to conjure up some parallel for this murderer's brutish savagery. But, so far as we know, nothing in fact or fiction equals these outrages at once in their horrible nature and in the effect which they have produced upon the popular imagination. The circumstances that the murders seem to be the work of one individual, that his blows fall exclusively upon wretched wanderers of the night, and that each successive crime has gained something in atrocity upon, and has followed closer on the heels of, its predecessor—these things mark out the Whitechapel murders, even before their true history is unravelled, as unique in the annals of crime. All ordinary experiences of motive leave us at a loss to comprehend the fury which has prompted the cruel slaughter of at least three, and possibly four, women, each unconnected with the other by any tie except that of their miserable mode of livelihood. Human nature would not be itself if these shocking occurrences, all taking place within a short distance of one another, and all bearing a ghastly resemblance, had not thrown the inhabitants into a state of panic—a panic, it must be feared, as favourable to the escape of the assassin as it is dangerous to innocent persons whose appearance or conduct is sufficiently irregular to excite suspicion.

3. *Punch* (15 September 1888)

[The cartoon and poems here selected from *Punch* magazine are reactions to the series of murders attributed to the mysterious figure known as "Jack the Ripper." The short article entitled "A Serious Question" asks if lurid advertising for sensational dramatizations of murder are not causing crimes such as the "Whitechapel Murders," as they were known then. "Blind-Man's Buff" accompanied a cartoon sharply critical of the inability of the London police to apprehend the perpetrator of the serial murders. The "Nemesis of Neglect" cartoon and poem respond overtly to a letter to the *Times* of London that blamed the terrible living conditions in inner city London for the rash of murders in Whitechapel. The poem and the cartoon portray murder as a direct result of the treatment of the inner-city poor, but also represent areas of London such as Soho and Whitechapel as swamps and jungles. Finally, "Horrible London: or, The Pandemonium of Posters" satirizes the lurid posters advertising mysterious murders that saturated London.]

A SERIOUS QUESTION.

Is it not within the bounds of probability that to the highly-coloured pictorial advertisements to be seen on almost all the hoardings in London, vividly representing sensational scenes of murder, exhibited as "the great attractions" of certain dramas, the public may be to a certain extent indebted for the horrible crimes in Whitechapel? We say it most seriously;—imagine the effect of these gigantic pictures of violence and assassination by knife and pistol on the morbid imagination of unbalanced minds. These hideous picture-posters are a blot on our civilisation, and a disgrace to the Drama.

4. *Punch* (22 September 1888)

BLIND-MAN'S BUFF.

A STRANGE mad game to play in such a place!
The monster City's maze, whose paths to trace
Might tax another Theseus,[1] the resort
Of worse than Minotaurs, for blindful sport
Would seem the most unfitting of all scenes;
What is it there such solemn fooling means?

Means? Ask purblind Municipal Muddledom
The true significance of the City Slum.
Ask, but expect no answer more exact
Than blundering palterers[2] with truth and fact
Range in their pigeon-holes in order neat,
The awkward questionings of sense to meet,
And, meeting, blandly baffle. Lurking crime
Haunts from of old these dens of darksome slime.
There, where well-armed Authority fears to tread,
Murder and outrage rear audacious head,
Unscanned, untracked. As the swift-sliding snake
Slips to the covert of the swamp's foul brake,
Fearless of following where no foot may find
Firm resting, where the foetid fumes that blind,
The reeking mists that palsy, guard its lair;
So Crime sneaks to the Slum's seclusion. There
Revealing light, the foe of all things ill,
With no intrusive ray floods in to fill
Those hideous alleys, and those noisome nooks,
With health and safety. Flush with limpid brooks
The slime-fouled gutters of the Ghetto, drive
Plinlimmon's[3] breeze through Labour's choking hive,
But let not light into the loathsome den
Where hags called women, ghouls in guise of men

---

1 Hero of Greek legend who killed the Cretan Minotaur, a bull-headed man fed with human flesh living in the centre of a labyrinth.
2 People who speak insincerely.
3 A river in South Wales; its "Devil's Bridge" crosses a particularly wild and forbidding gorge.

Live on death-dealing, feed a loathly life,
On the chance profits of the furtive knife.
The robber's mountain haunt, the outlaw's cave,
Guarded by rocks or sheltered by the wave
From feet intrusive, furnish no such lair
For desperate villany or dull dispair,
As this obscene Alsatia[1] of the slums.
Town's carrion-hordes flock hither; hither comes
The haggard harpy[2] of the pavement, she
The victim's victim, whose delirious glee
Makes mirth a crackling horror; hither slink
The waifs of passion and the wrecks of drink.
Multiform wretchedness in rags and grime,
Hopeless of good and ripe for every crime;
A seething mass of misery and vice,
These grim but secret-guarding haunts entice.
Look at these walls; they reek with dirt and damp,
But in their shadows crouched the homeless tramp
May huddle undisturbed the black night through.
Those narrow winding courts—in thought—pursue.
No light there breaks upon the bludgeoned wife,
No flash of day arrests the lifted knife,
There shrieks arouse not, nor do groans affright.
These are but normal noises of the night
In this obscure Gehenna.[3] Must it be
That the black slum shall furnish sanctuary
To all light-shunning creatures of the slime,
Vermine of vice, carnivora of crime?
Must it be here that Mammon[4] finds its tilth,
And harvests gold from haunts of festering filth?
How long? The voice of sense seems stricken dumb,
What time the sordid Spectre of the Slum,
Ruthless red-handed Murder sways the scene,
Mocking of glance, and merciless of mien.

---

1 A frequently disputed area between France and Germany; a place where confusion reigns.
2 Mythical Greek monster, half woman, half bird, sent by the gods to punish
   mortals.
3 Hell.
4 Material wealth as opposed to spiritual values. Matthew 6:24: "No man can
   serve two masters: for either he will hate the one, and love the other; or else
   he will hold to the one, and despise the other. Ye cannot serve God and
   mammon."

Mocking? Ah, yes! At Law the ghoul may laugh,
The sword is here as harmless as the staff
Of crippled age; its sleuthhounds are at fault,
Justice appears not only blind but halt.
It seems to play a merely blinkered game,
Blundering about without a settled aim.
Like boys at Blind-Man's Buff. A pretty sport
For Law's sworn guards in rascaldom's resort!
The bland official formula to-day
Seems borrowed from the tag of Nursery play,
"Turn round three times," upon no settled plan,
Flounder and fumble, and "catch whom you can!"

5. *Punch* (29 September 1888)

THE NEMESIS OF NEGLECT.

"Just as long as the dwellings of this race continue in their present condition, their whole surroundings a sort of warren of foul alleys garnished with the flaring lamps of the gin-shops, and offering to all sorts of lodgers, for all conceivable wicked purposes, every possible accommodation to further brutalise, we shall have still to go on—affecting astonishment that in such a state of things we have outbreaks, from time to time, of the horrors of the present day." "S.G.O.," in *The Times* 18 September 1888, in a letter entitled, "At Last."

THERE is no light along those winding ways
Other than lurid gleams like marsh-fires fleeting;
Thither the sunniest of summer days
Sends scarce one golden shaft of gladsome greeting.
June noonday has no power upon its gloom
More than the murky fog-flare of December;
A Stygian[1] darkness seems its settled doom;
Life, like a flickering ember,
There smoulders dimly on in deathly wise,
Like sleep-dulled glitter in a serpent's eyes.
Yet as that sullen sinister cold gleam
At sight of prey to a fierce flame shall quicken,
So the dull life that lurks in this dread scene.
By the sharp goad of greed or hatred stricken,

---

1 From the river Styx, a dark place that in Greek myth divides the land of the
   dead from the land of the living.

Flares into hideous force and fierceness foul,
Swift as the snake to spring and strong to capture.
Here the sole joys are those of the man-ghoul.
Thirst-thrill and ravin-rapture.
Held DANTE's Circles[1] such a dwelling-place?
Did primal sludge e'er harbour such a race?
It is not Hades,[2] nor that world of slime
Where dragons tare and man-shaped monsters fought.
Civilisation's festering heart of crime
Is here, and here some loathly glimpse is caught
Of its barbaric beating, pulsing through
Fair limbs and flaunting garb wherewith 'tis hidden.
Mere human sewage? True, O Sage! most true!
Society's kitchen-midden![3]
But hither crowd the ills which are our bane:
And thence in viler shape creep forth again.
Whence? Foulness filters here from honest homes
And thievish dens, town-rookery, rural village.
Vice to be nursed to violence hither comes,
Nurture unnatural, abhorrent tillage!
What sin soever amidst luxury springs,
Here amidst poverty finds full fruition.
There is no name for the unsexed foul things
Plunged to their last perdition
In this dark Malebolge,[4] ours—which yet
We build, and populate, and then—forget!
It will not be forgotten; it will find
A voice, like the volcano, and will scatter
Such hideous wreck among us, deaf and blind,
As all our sheltering shams shall rend and shatter.
The den is dark, secluded, it may yield
To Belial[5] a haunt, to Mammon profit;
But we shall reap the tillage of that Weld
In harvest meet for Tophet.[6]
Slum-farming knaves suck shameful wealth from sin,

---

1 In Dante's epic poem *Inferno*, there are nine circles of suffering through which
   the narrator must pass.
2 The lower world (hell) of Greek myth.
3 Garbage heap.
4 The eighth circle of hell in Dante's *Inferno*.
5 The biblical name for the devil or one of his minions.
6 A shrine, south of ancient Jerusalem, where human sacrifices were believed to
   have been performed; also used as a synonym for hell.

PUNCH, OR THE LONDON CHARIVARI.—September 29, 1888.

THE NEMESIS OF NEGLECT.

"THERE FLOATS A PHANTOM ON THE SLUM'S FOUL AIR,
SHAPING, TO EYES WHICH HAVE THE GIFT OF SEEING,
INTO THE SPECTRE OF THAT LOATHLY LAIR.
FACE IT—FOR VAIN IS FLEEING!
RED-HANDED, RUTHLESS, FURTIVE, UNERECT,
'TIS MURDEROUS CRIME—THE NEMESIS OF NEGLECT!"

But a dread Nemesis[1] abides therein.
Dank roofs, dark entries, closely-clustered walls,
Murder-inviting nooks, death-reeking gutters,
A boding voice from your foul chaos calls,

---

1 An unbeatable opponent; an irresistible force; Greek goddess of revenge.

When will men heed the warning that it utters?
There floats a phantom on the slum's foul air,
Shaping, to eyes which have the gift of seeing,
Into the Spectre of that loathly lair.
Face it—for vain is fleeing!
Red-handed, ruthless, furtive, unerect,
'Tis murderous Crime—the Nemesis of Neglect!

6. *Punch* (13 October 1888)

HORRIBLE LONDON: OR, THE PANDEMONIUM OF POSTERS.

THE Demon set forth in novel disguise
(All methods of mischief the master-Wend tries)
Quoth he, "There's much ill to be wrought through the eyes.
I think, without being a boaster,
I can give their most 'cute Advertisers a start,
And beat them all round at the Bill-sticker's art.
I will set up in business in Babylon's mart,
As the new Pandemonium Poster!"
So he roved the huge city with wallet at waist,
With a brush, and a stick, and a pot full of paste,
And there wasn't a wall or a hoarding,
A space in a slum, or a blank on a fence,
A spare square of brick in a neighbourhood dense,
Or a bit of unoccupied boarding,
But there the new poster, who didn't much care
For the menacing legend, "Bill-stickers beware!"
Right soon was tremendously busy
With placards portentous in purple and blue,
Of horrible subject and hideous hue,
Enough to bemuddle an aeronaut's view,
And turn the best steeple-Jack dizzy.
Oh, the flamboyant flare of those fiendish designs,
With their sanguine paint-splashes and sinister lines!
Gehenna seemed visibly glaring
In paint from those villainous daubs. There were men
At murderous work in malodorous den,
And ghoul-woman gruesomely staring.
The whole sordid drama of murder and guilt,
The steel that strikes home, and the blood that is spilt,
Was pictured in realist colours,
With emphasis strong on the black and the red,
The fear of the stricken, the glare of the dead;

All dreads and disasters and dolours
That haunt poor Humanity's dismallest state,
The horrors of crime and the terrors of fate,
As conceived by the crudest of fancies,
Were limned on these posters in terrible tints,
In the style of the vilest sensational prints
Or the vulgarest penny romances.

That Bill-sticker paused in his work with a look
Which betrayed the dark demon, and gleesomely shook
His sides in a spasm of laughter.
Quoth he, with a sinister wag of his head,
"By my horns, the good artist has lavished the red!
His home of coarse horror—this house of the dead
Looks crimson from basement to rafter.
How strange that a civilised City—ho! ho!
'Tis their fatuous dream to consider it so!—
Which is nothing too lovely at best, should bestow
Such a liberal license on spoilers!
These mural monstrosities, reeking of crime,
Flaring horridly forth amidst squalor and grime,
Must have an effect which will tell in good time
Upon legions of dull-witted toilers.
Taken in through the eyes such suggestions of sin
A sympathy morbid and monstrous must win
From the grovelling victims of gloom and bad gin,
Who gapingly gaze on them daily;
A fine picture-gallery this for the People!
Oh, while this endures, spite of School Board and Steeple,
My work must be going on gaily!"

7. From D.G. Halsted, *Doctor in the Nineties* (London: Christopher Jones, 1959)

[D.G. Halsted (b. 1865) gives a fascinating account of what it was like to be a doctor in the East End of London during the "Jack the Ripper" scare. As a doctor he was viewed with suspicion by patrolling policemen because of speculation that the murderer may have had a medical degree. He describes his discomfort walking around the streets of London at night feeling that he was being watched. He also mentions the *Punch* theory that the murders may have been incited by lurid representations of violence, and various other theories current at the time as to the identity of "Jack the Ripper."]

It was during my time at the London Hospital, just before I went off to Durham, that the East End, and indeed the whole of the country, was shaken to its core by a series of the most foul, brutal and inhuman murders ever committed in the long annals of crime. The reader may already have guessed that I am referring to the multiple outrages attributed to the so called "Jack the Ripper," who held Whitechapel in the grip of an unknown terror all through the later part of 1888. For all their frantic efforts, house-to-house searches and cross-questioning, of suspects in their hundreds, the Metropolitan Police were baffled then, and to this very day the mystery remains unsolved.

I must be one of the few surviving inhabitants of Whitechapel to remember those dark days of Jack the Ripper. With what seemed a depressing regularity, the mangled corpses of the Ripper's unfortunate victims were brought round to the London Hospital, to await the skilled examination of the best medical brains at the disposal of Scotland Yard. Owing to the extraordinary knowledge of anatomy displayed by the murderer, no medical man, however high his character or reputation, could be entirely exempted from suspicion, and naturally those of us at the London Hospital, right in the heart of Whitechapel, were in the limelight. The East End was alive with plain-clothes men. They were lurking in every alleyway, ready to pounce at the slightest breath of suspicion, and this more than anything gave us a sinister feeling when walking through the streets of these tumble-down haunts of pilfering and pauperism where we lived and worked....

Speculation abounded as to the identity of the murderer. The obvious suggestion was made by many people that Jack the Ripper was a butcher by trade, and was simply applying his knowledge of the anatomy of cows, pigs and sheep to the human body. The proximity of the Aldgate shambles[1] to the scene of the two murders lent some credence to this theory, and for a time the spotlight of police investigation was turned on to the professional slaughtermen, but once again it failed to illuminate anything whatsoever.

A certain section of medical opinion, on the other hand, dismissed the rather prosaic suggestion that the murderer belonged to one of these humble trades involving skill with the knife, and was inclined to believe, from the perverted cunning with which the killer had repeatedly evaded justice, that he was a member of the upper classes, which would certainly account for his being completely unknown among the habitually criminal section of society. Some doctors thought, furthermore, that they could clearly detect the work of a homicidal maniac, in spite of the fact that homicidal maniacs are not generally in a con-

---

1 Area of London with a large meat market and many butcher shops.

dition to take elaborate evasive measures against the police hue and cry. But, anyway, it was suggested that all supposedly 'cured' homicidal maniacs who had at any time in the past been released from institutions should be rounded up once more and closely questioned. The suggestion was not acted upon, and I remember that *The Lancet*[1] came out against the homicidal maniac theory.

A theory familiar to modern ears was put forward by *Punch*. Always ready with some bright idea, the irrepressible Mr. Punch maintained that the lurid posters which even in those days were put up to advertise murder mysteries on the stage, had an evil and corrupting influence on those who were daily confronted with them in the streets, and that the murderer might well have been tempted into excess by seeing these horrible crimes of the imagination so realistically displayed....

Then a bombshell burst on us medical men at the London Hospital. The Coroner at the inquest on Annie Chapman gave it as his considered opinion, that while a slaughterman could have been responsible for the murder, it could equally well have been executed with an instrument such as medical men used for post-mortem purposes. Suspicion immediately turned upon my colleagues and myself, and I often had the feeling, especially when I was walking home late at night, that the inhabitants were shunning me and that the plain-clothes men were following my movements....

---

1 British medical journal (founded 1823), one of the oldest and best known in the world.

Appendix K: Victorian Psychology

1. From Thomas Carlyle, "The Age of Romance," *Fraser's Magazine* 85-135 (1837): vols. 1-4

[Thomas Carlyle (1795–1881), one of the "sages" of the Victorian era, was a historian, philosopher, political commentator, and satirist. He is not usually thought of as a "psychologist," but in his essay "The Age of Romance" he discusses desire and its repression in his time; his portrait of a typical Victorian man sounds much like Dr. Jekyll before he releases Mr. Hyde. When Carlyle uses the term "romance" he means a story of adventure and passion that contrasts with humdrum everyday existence.]

The Age of Romance has not ceased; it never ceases; it does not, if we will think of it, so much as very sensibly decline. "The passions are repressed by social forms; great passions no longer show themselves?" Why, there are passions still great enough to replenish Bedlam,[1] for it never wants tenants; to suspend men from bedposts, from improved-drops at the west end of Newgate.[2] A passion that explosively shivers asunder the Life it took rise in, ought to be regarded as considerable: more no passion, in the highest heyday of Romance, yet did. The passions, by grace of the Supernal and also of the Infernal Powers (for both have a hand in it), can never fail us.

And then, as to "social forms," be it granted that they are of the most buckram[3] quality, and bind men up into the pitifulest straitlaced commonplace existence,—you ask, Where is the Romance? In the Scotch way one answers. Where is it not? That very spectacle of an Immortal Nature, with faculties and destiny extending through Eternity, hampered and bandaged up, by nurses, pedagogues, posturemasters, and the tongues of innumerable old women (named "force of public opinion"); by prejudice, custom, want of knowledge, want of money, want of strength, into, say, the meagre Pattern-Figure that, in

---

1 In 1676 the Hospital of St. Mary of Bethlehem was opened in London as an insane asylum; over the centuries it became known as "Bedlam." By the nineteenth century "Bedlam" was used generically to denote any insane asylum.

2 The name originally referred to Newgate prison in London, which was one of the most notorious prisons in the country. There has been a Newgate prison in London since 1188, and its name has become synonymous with crime and punishment generally.

3 Stiff cotton cloth.

these days, meets you in all thoroughfares: a "god-created Man," all
but abnegating the character of Man; forced to exist, automatised,
mummy-wise (scarcely in rare moments audible or visible from amid
his wrappages and cerements), as Gentleman or Gigman;[1] and so
selling his birthright of Eternity for the three daily meals, poor at best,
which Time yields:—is not this spectacle itself highly romantic, tragi-
cal, if we had eyes to look at it? The high-born (highest-born for he
came out of Heaven) lies drowning in the despicablest puddles; the
priceless gift of Life, which he can have but *once*, for he waited a whole
Eternity to be born, and now has a whole Eternity waiting to see what
he will do when born,—*this* priceless gift we see strangled slowly out
of him by innumerable packthreads; and there remains of the glorious
Possibility, which we fondly named Man, nothing but an inanimate
mass of foul loss and disappointment, which we wrap in shrouds and
bury underground,—surely with well-merited tears. To the Thinker
here lies Tragedy enough; the epitome and marrow of all Tragedy
whatsoever.

2. From Henry Maudsley, "The Double Brain," *Mind* 54 (April 1889): 161–87

[Henry Maudsley (1835–1918) was one of the most influential psychologists of his generation. He was born near Settle in Yorkshire in
1835 and graduated at age 21 with a medical degree from the University of London. Two years later he was appointed the Medical
Superintendent of the Manchester Royal Lunatic Asylum and later
Physician to the West London Hospital and Physician of Medical
Jurisprudence at University College. He also became editor of the
Journal of Mental Science and exerted a profound influence on fellow
"alienists" (the term for "psychiatrist" in the Victorian period). Maud-
sley was much influenced by the work of Charles Darwin, Cesare
Lombroso, and Benedict Augustine Morel on "degeneration" (see
Appendix H). He became widely respected for his publications on
insanity and psychology. His publications included *The Physiology and
Pathology of Mind* (1867), *Body and Mind* (1870), *Responsibility in
Mental Disease* (1874), and innumerable influential articles in the
Journal of Mental Science on the development of the brain, cognition,
and insanity. Maudsley believed that the mind could only be under-
stood from a physiological point of view and believed insanity to be
rooted in disordered bodily functions. He used his brand of "physio-

---

1 A "gig" was a kind of carriage; Carlyle is using it here as a synonym for
respectability.

logical psychology" to link degeneration, madness, and theories of evolution. He especially believed that "vice" of any kind was linked to degeneration and that the signs of degeneration were passed on by heredity. His essay on "The Double Brain" shows the Victorians' belief that the mind was divided into antagonist halves at the physical level.]

Is the brain, which is notably double in structure, a double organ, "seeming parted, but yet a union in partition"? Or is it a seeming whole made up actually of two organs? Have we, in fact, two brains as we have two eyes, two lungs, two kidneys? Or have we one brain as we have one body, built of two similar halves...?

We have now reached the point where appears plainly the full answer to the previously put question—to wit, how comes it to pass that the hemispheres of the brain, when dictating different movements, yet have an understanding in common and work together to a common end. They are organs of *one* body—two like structures moulded on one stem—in the organic life of which their basic unity lies; nowise supereminent and independent organs apart, that govern the body from the platform of a higher life, but organs of the body, living in it and by it and for it; and their functions are not, like those of the limbs, functions of the animal life only or mainly, but functions in which the *whole* life, animal and organic, is represented. It is from the life of the whole body that the constituents of the mental life are derived, and inasmuch as the cerebral hemispheres are organs ministering to this life, they must necessarily have its fundamental unity. Superpose on this basal[1] unity of being the effects of education of the hemispheres in joint working, begun with the first movements of life and continued throughout it, and we have a sufficient explanation of their communion of function in thoughts, feelings and acts....

I pass on now to a rapid survey of some of the leading phenomena of mental disorder in order to see how they stand in relation to the foregoing conclusions. The two main types of mental disorder, mania and melancholia, notably present very different and almost opposite features: in the former there is great exaltation of self with answering lively display thereof in thought, feeling and conduct—phenomena witnessing to a generally brisk and easy reflex action; in the latter, great depression of self with answering sluggish expression of thought, feeling and conduct—phenomena witnessing to dull, slow and inert reflex function.... Consider the typical features of the two states: on the one hand, exaggerated self-confidence and exultant feeling of well-being, quick and acute perception, extraordinary memory, overflowing

---

1 Forming or belonging to a bottom layer or base.

rush of ideas, multitudinous projects, extreme susceptibility, voluble talk, unresting activity, an absence of all sense of effort, boastful self-assertion, delusions of greatness and power; on the other band, loss of self-confidence and great self-distrust, no relish for or interest in or hold on the affairs of life, incapacity of attention, sluggish and inefficient memory, deadness of feeling and dulness of thought, inability or aversion to will and act, sense of infinite effort in order to make the least exertion, despairing self-depreciation, delusions of ruin or damnation, or of possession or persecution by devil or other malignant power. The maniac never feels the least doubt that he is himself, when actually he is not himself but alienated from his true self; the melancholic feels and laments that he is not himself, that he and things around him are changed and unreal, that he is another self or in subjection to another self, when his main affliction is a loss of faith in self. The question is then whether it is right to look on this deep sense of the want of unity of being, this mental inability to realise self and its correlative loss of hold on the not-self, as being due to the failure of the organic driving force. That is the present contention: there is in fact the weakness resulting from the incomplete union or actual disunion, a self divided against itself by a commencing or completed disruption, and there are in consequence the dual and confusing suggestions of self coming from the weak and, almost independent action of the disunited halves....

The phenomena of dreaming may be cited in further illustration and confirmation of the position here taken up. During sleep the organic life does not cease, like the animal life, but goes on at a lower rate of activity; the consequence being that the hemispheres, lacking the force necessary to full unity of action and yet taking up the organic impressions from the body, as well as any chance-impressions from without, manufacture from them the most incongruous dream-images and events....

Having pointed out thus far how exaltation and abasement of the Ego or self answer respectively to *excess* and *defect* of the fund of organic energy in the brain, I go on now to note briefly that great *perversion* of this energy is followed by complete disintegration of the Ego or self. For this purpose I may fitly call in evidence certain cases of the deepest and most distracting nervous distress in which, without any known structural disease, a strange, disquieting, indescribable sensation is felt suddenly at the epigastrium[1] or in its neighbourhood, diffuses itself vaguely through the body or mounts towards the head, and occasions instantly a distracting and overwhelming apprehension of

---

1　The region just over the stomach and below the sternum.

impending dissolution of self: not a definite apprehension of death, nothing which can be grasped definitely in thought and feeling, but a vague, vast, indescribable feeling of impending horror, an unspeakable anguish. The impetuous and overpowering feeling is accompanied, perhaps, by the sense of a vehement rush of something, not blood, to the head, and may issue in scarcely resistible or actually irresistible impulse to an act of desperation, suicidal or homicidal, which is then, so to speak, the psychomotor convulsive outcome of it: in itself it is probably the pathological parallel on the sensory side of what convulsion is on the motor side. The sufferer who, after the attack is over, quietly recognises that his fears were groundless, and during it even remembers that he has had similar seizures before, cannot at the time of agony hold his intellectual ground at all; his power of thinking is abolished, his intellectual and moral unity dissolved, in face of the rushing mighty sensation of deranged organic unity.

In order to facilitate conception of the discordant action of the hemispheres and of its probable effects in thought, feeling and conduct, let us consider a person's movements when from deranged action of the dual organs of animal life there is no longer that unity of function which belongs to them in a state of health, and thereupon endeavour to imagine what the effect would be of a similar unity-destroying action upon the mental functions. Suppose a person to be afflicted with similar spasmodic or convulsive movements of the limbs of both sides, but not of such intensity as to incapacitate him from walking of a stumbling, rickety sort; imagine next his motions to be, like his thoughts, self-conscious; what would be the revelation of themselves that they would make? Most likely an exultation and pride in their new activity, of the convulsive nature of which, being equally and similarly affected, they would be unaware. Let the supposition be of such a convulsive action of the limbs of one side only; what would be the revelation then? Of a self bound to another self which was hindering and opposing it—of a self divided against itself, a distracted or double self. Both in movements and in mental functions the full unity of function is the unity of a double organisation; wherefore, if there be duality, instead of unity, of the latter, we cannot fail to have phenomena marking the disintegration of self, cannot have phenomena that consist only with its integrity....

As regards perception, it is obvious that a person whose hemispheres were at variance because of disorder of one of them must perceive a real object with the one hemisphere and an unreal object with the other, and perceive them both as equally real when equally vivid; his life, therefore, must needs be a succession of incoherent relations to the external world according as the one or the other was in the ascendant; at one time he would attend to and act in relation to his wrong perception, at another time he would attend to and act, in relation to the true perception. In like manner his memory will be a memory of two selves, and oftentimes of two incompatible selves: he will speak quite correctly of actual events and his doings in them, so that there seems no fault in him, but immediately afterwards must speak with equal certitude of unreal events and his supposed doings in them, so that there will seem no health in him. Judgment and will must necessarily be equally lamed and deranged, since the same division runs through them, and they must display the same sort of incoherent function. The individual will not only think double and perhaps act double, but the ideas of his double thinking and doing will be inconsistent and incompatible—he will be literally *distracted*.

Such are the effects which might theoretically be looked for from a dual and discordant action of the hemispheres. A survey of the phenomena of mental derangement discloses many facts that might be adduced in support of the theory. Take for first illustration the mode of coming-on and going-off of the attack in some cases of insanity: there is notable a brief period at the outset when the sound hemisphere appears to hold the lead and to repress or ignore the suggestions of the unsound hemisphere, whereas after a time of struggle and uncertainty the unsound hemisphere may be thought to gain the entire lead and to draw the other with it in such servitude that it does not rebel nor even suggest a doubt; and in like manner when the disease is passing off there are intruding intimations of doubt of the unsound thought which, little regarded at first, return in greater force by degrees and eventually grow to certainties that overcome and suppress its delusions. More striking still is the example of the person who is possessed by alternate voices, the one profane and blasphemous, the other reverent and devout; or of one who is to all intents and purposes two selves at the same time, his real self having his natural feelings and seeing things in their true light, and his morbid self with unnatural feelings and perverted notions, the two engaged perpetually in an inconclusive conflict which drives him to the deepest despair and perhaps even to suicide; or of one who, having extravagantly insane delusions on some subject concerning which he talks such absurd and incoherent nonsense as would seem incompatible with the persistence of any sense in the conduct of life, nevertheless exhibits such sound reason and good judgment on all other subjects as render it marvelous that he cannot correct his false bearings and put himself right with the world. Do not such facts as these suit well with the theory of a dual and inconsistent action of the hemispheres?

3. From F.H. Myers, "Multiplex Personality," *The Nineteenth Century* (November 1886): 648–66

[After reading *Strange Case of Dr. Jekyll and Mr. Hyde*, Frederic William Henry Myers (1843–1901) sent a copy of his essay "Multiplex Personality" to Stevenson, pointing out what he felt was a strong common interest in both pieces of writing. Myers was Professor of Classics at Cambridge University in England. He published volumes of poetry and studies of Classical literature in *Essays Classical and Modern* (2 vols., 1883). In 1882 Myers helped found the Society for Psychical Research, which pursued a scientific approach to studying such phenomena as telepathy and séances. He devoted most of his energies to studying the evidence for life after death, publishing the results of a lifetime of research and speculation in *Human Personality and Its Survival of Bodily Death* (2 vols., 1903). "Multiplex Personality" shows its author's erudition in Classical scholarship and his interest in such issues as mesmerism and multiple personality disorder. It also shows his acceptance of both Darwinian evolution and degeneration theory. While Myers entitles his essay "Multiplex Personality," he is actually interested, like Maudsley, in the "double" brain and examines cases that seem to reveal the duality of identity.]

As their bodies changed, so their thoughts changed as well.
Empedocles [translation of original Greek text][1]

I purpose in this paper briefly to suggest certain topics for reflection, topics which will need to be more fully worked out elsewhere. My theme is the multiplex and mutable character of that which we know as the Personality of man, and the practical advantage which we may gain by discerning and working upon this as yet unrecognized modifiability. I shall begin by citing a few examples of hysterical transfer, of morbid disintegration; I shall then show that these spontaneous readjustments of man's being are not all of them pathological or retrogressive; nay, that the familiar changes of sleep and waking contain the hint of further alternations which may be beneficially acquired. And, lastly, I shall point out that we can already by artificial means induce and regulate some central nervous changes which effect physical and moral good; changes which may be more restorative than sleep, more rapid than education. Here, I shall urge, is an avenue open at once to

---

1 Greek philosopher Empedocles (490–430 BCE) is discussing the influence that human daytime experience has on our dreams at night and underlining the connection between body and dreams.

scientific and to philanthropic endeavour, a hope which hangs neither on fable nor on fancy, but is based on actual experience and consists with rational conceptions of the genesis and evolution of man....

[Myers now gives the example of a young male patient named "Louis V," in a French asylum, who would have unaccountable episodes during which he "would preach with a monkey-like rather than with reasoned clearness, radicalism in politics and atheism in religion."]

Is there, then, the reader may ask, any assignable law which governs these strange revolutions? Any reason why Louis V should at one moment seem a mere lunatic or savage, at another moment should rise into decorous manhood, at another should recover his physical soundness, but sink backward in mind into the child? Briefly, and with many reserves and technicalities perforce omitted, the view of the doctors who have watched him is somewhat as follows: A sudden shock, falling on an unstable organization, has effected in this boy a profounder severance between the functions of the right and left hemispheres of the brain than has perhaps ever been observed before. We are accustomed, of course, to see the right side of the body paralysed and insensible in consequence of injury to the left hemisphere, which governs it, and *vice versa*. And we are accustomed in hysterical cases where there is no actual traceable injuring to either hemisphere to see the defects in sensation and motility shift, rapidly shift, as I may say, at a touch from one side of the body to the other. But we cannot usually trace any corresponding change in the mode of functioning of what we assume as the "highest centres," the centres which determine those manifestations of intelligence, character, memory, on which our *identity* mainly depends. Yet in some cases of *aphasia* and of other forms of *asemia* (the loss of power over *signs*, spoken or written words and the like) phenomena have occurred which have somewhat prepared us to find that the loss of power to use the left which certainly is in some ways the more developed hemisphere may bring with it a retrogression in the higher characteristics of human life.... Those who have followed these lines of observation may be somewhat prepared to think it possible that in Louis V's case the alternate predominance of right or left hemisphere affects memory and character as well as motor and sensory innervation. Inhibit his left brain (and right side) and he becomes, as one may say, not only left-handed but *sinister*; he manifests himself through nervous arrangements which have reached a lower degree of evolution. And he can represent in memory those periods only when his personality had assumed the same attitude, when he had crystallized about the same point. Inhibit his right brain, and the higher qualities of character is modesty; there is the sense of duty the qualities which man has developed as he has risen from the savage level. But nevertheless he is only half himself....

For even if these profoundest spontaneous changes are beyond the reach of imitation, there are smaller changes, long familiar to us, which we now see in a new light, as imitatable in a manner which shall reproduce their advantages without their drawbacks. There is the painless trance which sometimes supervenes in hysteria; there is the action of alcohol; there is especially the action of opium, which from the first commended itself by its psychical effect, by the emotional tranquility which it induces. Such at least seems to be the inference from the well-known passage, where the wifely Helen determines to give her husband and his friends the chance of talking comfortably, without interrupting themselves by perpetual tears and lamentations....

> Then heaven-born Helen in their cups would throw
> Nepenthes, woeless banisher of woe:
> This whoso drank daylong no tear should shed
> No, though he gazed on sire and mother dead;
> No, though his own son on that dreamy day
> Before his own eyes raging foes should slay.[1]

[There follows a long discussion of the therapeutic uses of hypnotism.]

Looking at that growing class of civilized persons who suffer from neuralgia, indigestion, and other annoying but not dangerous forms of malaise, let us consider whether we cannot induce in those of them who are fortunate enough to be readily hypnotisable a third condition of life, which shall be as waking but without its uneasiness and as sleep without the blankness of its repose, a state in which the mind may go serenely onward and the body have no power to distract her energy or to dispute her sway.

Is there anything in nature to render this ideal impossible? Let us consider the history of pain. Pain, it may be plausibly suggested, is an advantage acquired by our ancestors in the course of their struggle for existence. It would be useless to the fortunate animalcule, which, if you chop it in two, is simply two animalcules instead of one. But as soon as the organism is complex enough to suffer partial injury, and active enough to check or avoid such injury before it has gone far, the pain becomes a useful warning, and the sense of pain is thus one of

---

1 In Book IV of Homer's *The Odyssey* Helen puts the drug Nepenthe into the Greeks' wine to make them forget their sorrow over the loss of their comrades.

the first and most generalized of the perceptive faculties which place living creatures in relation with the external world. And to the human infant it is necessary still. The burnt child must have some reason to dread the fire, or he will go on poking it with his fingers. But, serviceable though pain may still be to the child and the savage, civilised men and women have now a good deal more of it than they can find any use for. Some kinds of pain, indeed (like neuralgia, which prevents the needed rest), are wholly detrimental to the organism and have arisen by mere correlation with other susceptibilities which are in themselves beneficial. Now if this correlation were inevitable if it were impossible to have acute sense-perceptions, vivid emotional development, without these concomitant nervous pains we should have to accept the annoyance without more ado. But certain spontaneously occurring facts, and certain experimental facts, have shown us that the correlation is not inevitable; that the sense of pain can be abolished, while other sensibilities are retained, to an extent far beyond what the common experience of life would have led us to suppose possible....

These speculations, especially where they point to moral progress as attainable by physiological artifice, will seem to many of my readers venturesome and unreal. And in these days of conflicting dogmas and impracticable utopias Science, better aware than either priest or demagogue of how little man can truly know, is tempted to confine herself to his material benefit, which can be made certain, and to let his moral progress which is a speculative hope alone. Yet, now that Science is herself becoming the substance of so many creeds, the lode-star of so many aspirations, it is important that she should not in any direction even appear to be either timid or cynical. Her humble missionaries at least need not show themselves too solicitous about possible failure, but should rather esteem it as dereliction of duty were some attempt not made to carry her illumination over the whole realm and mystery of man. Especially, indeed, is it to be desired that biology should show not indeed a moralising bias, but a moral care. There has been a natural tendency to insist with a certain disillusionising tenacity on the low beginnings of our race. When eminent but ill-instructed personages in Church or State have declared themselves, with many flourishes, "on the side of the Angel," there has been a grim satisfaction in proving that Science at any rate is "on the side of the Ape." But the victory of Science is won. She has dealt hard measure to man's tradition and his self-conceit; let her now show herself ready to sympathise with such of his aspirations as are still legitimate, to offer such prospects as the nature of things will allow. Nay, let her teach the world that the word evolution is the very formula and symbol of hope.

But here my paper must close. I will conclude it with a single reflection which may somewhat meet the fears of those who dislike any tamperings with our personality, who dread that this invading analysis may steal their very self away. All living things, it is said, strive towards their maximum of pleasure. In what hours, then, and under what conditions do we find that human beings have attained to their intensest joy? Do not our thoughts in answer turn instinctively to scenes and moments when all personal preoccupation, all care for individual interest, is lost in the sense of spiritual union, whether with one beloved soul, or with a mighty nation, or with "the whole world and creatures of God"? We think of Dante with Beatrice,[1] of Nelson at Trafalgar,[2] of St. Francis on the Umbrian hill.[3] And surely here, as in Galahad's cry of "If I lose myself I find myself,"[4] we have a hint that much, very much, of what we are wont to regard as an integral part of us may drop away, and yet leave us with a consciousness of our own being which is more vivid and purer than before. This web of habits and appetencies, of lusts and fears, is not, perhaps, the ultimate manifestation of what in truth we are. It is the cloak which our rude forefathers have woven themselves against the cosmic storm; but we are already learning to shift and refashion it as our gentler weather needs, and if perchance it slip from us in the sunshine then something more ancient and more glorious is for a moment guessed within.

4. From James Sully, "The Dream as Revelation," *Fortnightly* 59 (1893): 354–65

[James Sully (1842–1923) was an English psychologist. Like many early psychologists, he started out in a different area, being trained originally as a Nonconformist minister. In 1871 he decided to follow a literary and philosophical career and as a result of his publications was named Grote Professor of Mind and Logic at University College, London, in 1892. He studied psychology in the light of physiology, with special attention to art, education, and social order. He is credited with being one of the first British developmental psychologists; in *Studies of Childhood* (1895) and *Children's Ways* (1897) he compared

---

1 In Dante's *Vita Nuova*, the author's love for Beatrice becomes the vehicle for his own salvation.

2 Lord Horatio Nelson (1758–1805) was the Admiral in charge of the British fleet that defeated the French navy at Trafalgar (1805). Trafalgar Square in London is named after the battle and has a statue of Nelson at its centre.

3 St. Francis of Assisi decided to give up all worldly goods and devote his life to religion during a walk on the hills of Umbria.

4 A quotation from Tennyson's "The Holy Grail" (1869), line 30, in which Sir Galahad, alone of all the knights of Camelot, achieves a vision of the "holy grail," believed to be the cup from which Jesus drank at the Last Supper and which Joseph of Arimathea used to catch his blood as he hung on the cross.

the aesthetic senses of children and prehistoric civilizations, arguing that the tastes of children preserved the artistic sense of earlier generations. He applied a Darwinian model to child development. He is still widely cited for his *An Essay on Laughter* (1902) in which he attempted to create a taxonomy of laughter. In "James Sully, Evolutionist Psychology, and Late Victorian Gothic Fiction" (*Victorian Studies* 25:4 [Summer 1982]: 443–68), Ed Block, Jr. argues that both Sully's psychological texts and Stevenson's tale could be read in terms of "evolutionist psychology." Block also points out that Sully, like Stevenson, was interested in "dual" or "double" consciousness. In "The Dream as Revelation" (1893) Sully discusses contemporary psychological interest in "the double or alternating personality." The article is also interesting in the way in which it links the dream with both artistic creation and the unrepressed and wilder instincts of the psyche. Stevenson himself claims he saw the plot of "Jekyll and Hyde" in a dream and Sully's statements suggest that from his perspective Stevenson in doing so was tapping into some "primitive" area of his brain.]

In the history of human ideas we meet with two opposite views of the nature and significance of dreaming. The one attributes to it a degree of intelligence, of insight into things, vastly superior to that of waking cognition. The extreme form of this idea invested the vision of the night with the awful dignity of a supernatural revelation. The other view goes to the opposite extreme, and dismisses dream-experiences as so much intellectual fooling, as:

> "Children of an idle brain,
> Begot of nothing but vain phantasy."[1]

The modern scientific theory of dreaming may be said to combine and to reconcile these antagonistic ideas. It recognises and seeks to account for the irrational side of dream-life. At the same time it regards this life as an extension of human experience, as a revelation of what would otherwise have never been known....

It seems natural at first to think of this transition from waking to sleeping consciousness as a degradation, a reversion to a primitive infantile type of psychosis, in which sensation and its immediate offspring, sensuous imagination, are uncontrolled by the higher later-acquired functions—rational reflection, moral self-control. There is, no doubt, a certain appropriateness in this way of envisaging our

---

1   Shakespeare, *Romeo and Juliet* I.iv.98–99.

dreams. There is a good deal of the naiveté of the child in our ways of conceiving of things and of feeling about things during sleep. On entering dreamland we leave much of the later and maturer intelligence behind us, and survey the spectacle with the pristine directness, with the pure elemental emotions of little children.

Yet the change from waking to sleeping consciousness is less simple than the figure of retrogression from mature to infantile experience would suggest. Even the process of mental dissolution brought about by brain disease cannot, it is said, be accurately described as a mere removal of the higher and later acquired functions. And it is still less true of the reduction of consciousness during sleep. The dream may be a weakened mental activity but it is a weakened activity of a mature mind, of a mind that has been formed by complex human experience....

[Sully gives examples of dreams of his own and others.]

This simplification of the mature complex pattern of consciousness is at the same time a bringing to light of forces and tendencies which, under normal circumstances, are hidden under the superincumbent mass of the later and higher acquisitions. The newest conception of the brain is of a hierarchy of organs, the higher and later evolved seeming to control, and in a measure to repress, the functional activities of the lower and earlier. Translated into psychological language, this means that what is instinctive, primitive, elemental in our mental life, is being continually overborne by the fruit of experience, by the regulative process of reflection. By throwing the higher centres *hors de combat*:[1] you may bring back the earlier state of things in which sensation, instinct, and a rudimentary animal intelligence have it all their own way. Sleep is one means of stupefying the supreme controlling organs. Hence in sleep we have a reversion to a more primitive type of experience, an upwelling in vigorous pristine abundance of sensation and impulse.

And now, perhaps, the reader begins to see how the dream becomes a revelation. It strips the ego of its artificial wrappings and exposes it in its rude native nudity. It brings up from the dim depths of our subconscious life the primal, instinctive impulses, and discloses to us a side of ourselves which connects us with the great sentient world....

When asleep we may be said to go back to this primitive animal immersion in bodily sensation. The all-important groundwork of our life once more engages our thought. We hear the heart beat, and feel

---

1   Out of action (French).

the incoming and outgoing of the breath; we rejoice with the weary limb in its repose, with the chilled extremity warmed by an effusion of generous blood, or, on the other hand, suffer with the overladen stomach or with the cramp-seized muscle....

It is possible that this re-immersion during sleep in that primitive consciousness which grows out of the nutritive life may have its biological utility. When awake we are prevented, partly by the multiplex distractions of the situation, partly by the disturbing effect of imagination, from getting into close and accurate touch with our bodily condition. Hence the difficulty which most people experience when called upon in the physician's consulting room or elsewhere to give an account of their sensations. When asleep the curtain is withdrawn and we seem to have an immediate awareness of what is going on in our interior framework. It has been ingeniously suggested that, owing to this close rapport between spirit and body in sleep, the dream may take on a prophetic function by disclosing to the subject the slight initial stages of organic disturbance which would otherwise have been overlooked.

However this may be, our dreams, by restoring the bodily factor of consciousness to its primitive supremacy, may properly be described as revelations. By noting this aspect of our dreams, we may learn much concerning that organic substrate of our conscious personality which links us on to the animal series....

Here we find the dream touching analogically another and more distinctly abnormal region of human experience. Psychology has of late occupied itself much with the curious phenomenon of double or alternating personality. By this is meant the recurrent interruption of the normal state by the intrusion of a secondary state, in which the thoughts, feelings, and the whole person may become other than they were. This occasional substitution of a new for the old self is sometimes spontaneous, the result of brain-trouble; sometimes it is artificially brought about in specially susceptible persons by hypnotizing them. In the hypnotic trance it is possible to blot out from the subject's mind all that has occurred in his experience since a particular date and, in this way to restore the childish self. In the case of certain hysterical subjects, the hypnotic trance may disinter more than one abnormal personality which are buried and forgotten during the normal state.

The proposition that the soundest of men undergo changes of personality may well strike the reader as paradoxical; yet the paradox is only on the surface. Although we talk of ourselves as single personalities, as continuing to be the same as we were, a little thought suffices to show that this is not absolutely true. Just as our bodily framework undergoes material re-formation, so the pattern of our consciousness is ever being re-formed and transformed. As the years go by, old fancies, beliefs, emotions tend to drop out and new ones to take their place. I may dimly remember the fact that as a youth I felt about nature, music, religious subjects in a particular way, but I know I do not now feel in this way. Under the conditions of a happy development these changes are gradual, though most of us probably can refer a part of them to memorable crises, catastrophic shocks in our experience. However this be, where we sit down and quietly glance back over the succession of our years, we may see that by making the interval wide enough we confront what is, in a large part of its characteristic modes of consciousness, a new, foreign personality.

Now our dreams are a means of conserving these successive personalities. When asleep we go back to the old ways of looking at things and of feeling about them, to impulses and aesthetics which long ago dominated us, in a way which seems impossible in the waking hours, when the later self is in the ascendant. In this way the rhythmic change from wakefulness to sleep effects a recurrent reinstatement of our "dead selves," an overlapping of the successive personalities, the series of whose doings and transformations constitutes our history.

There is one other way in which dreams may become an unveiling of what is customarily hidden, viz., by giving freer play to individual characteristics and tendencies. It is a commonplace that our highly artificial form of social life tends greatly to restrict the sphere of individuality. Our peculiar tendencies get sadly crossed and driven back in the daily collision with our surroundings. Much that is deepest and most vital in us may in this way be repressed and atrophied. The particular personality which we have developed, which is all that our friends know of us, is a kind of selection from among many possible personalities, a selection effected by the peculiar conditions of our "environment."

Now these undeveloped, rudimentary selves belong to the hidden substrata of our mental being. Hence, according to what has been said above, they are very apt to disclose themselves when sleep has stupefied the dominant personality.

5. From Richard Krafft-Ebing, *Psychopathia Sexualis* (1886; Stuttgart: 1903)

[Richard Krafft-Ebing (1840–1902) was a German psychiatrist. He initially studied to be a doctor but later specialized in psychiatry. Like Maudsley, he worked in several asylums but became disillusioned with psychiatric institutions. He was appointed Professor of Psychiatry at Strasbourg at the age of 32 and wrote academic papers on a wide range of psychiatric conditions. In the mid-1860s he became interested in the origins of homoerotic desire and began to collect hundreds of medical and court reports that dealt with sexually-related crimes. His *Psychopathia Sexualis with Especial Reference to the Antipathic Sexual Instinct: A Medico-Forensic Study* (1886; translated into English 1892) contains 51 case histories examining a wide range of "deviant" sexual behaviours. He believed that some people were subject to "moral degeneracy" because of their own actions and the inheritance of the vices of their parents. He used terms such as "fetishism," "masochism," "sadism," and "sexual psychopath" that became key words in nineteenth- and twentieth-century psychiatry. By the time Krafft-Ebing died in 1902, *Psychopathia Sexualis* was in its twelfth edition and had grown tremendously in the number of cases cited. In "Psychopathia Sexualis: Stevenson's Strange Case" (*Critical Quarterly* 28 [1986]) Stephen Heath argues that in *Dr. Jekyll and Mr. Hyde* "random violence replaces the sexual drive" (93–94) and that Stevenson's story is actually about sexuality. Heath argues that the new field of sexology is akin to Stevenson's text because it "begins with and from *perversions*. What it studies is the *pathology* of the sexual, and a significant area of attention is then the *criminal*-sexual [italics Heath's]" (102). Heath cites Krafft-Ebing's section on "Lust-Murder" as the point at which *Dr. Jekyll and Mr. Hyde* and *Psychopathia Sexualis* approach each other most closely. In the edition (twelfth German edition) from which this extract is taken, Krafft-Ebing cites the "Jack the Ripper" case (see Appendix J) as an example of "lust-murder" and makes numerous references to the work of Lombroso. The translation is by Martin A. Danahay.]

(a) Lust-Murder (Lust Exhibited as Brutality, from Murderous Lust to Anthropophagy.)[1]

The most abominable example, but also one which most significantly shows the connection between lust and a desire to kill, is the case of Andreas Bichel, which Feuerbach published in his "Compendium of Descriptions of Unusual Crimes."

He killed and dissected the ravished girls. Referring to one of his victims, at his examination he gave the following testimony: "I opened her breast and with a knife cut through the fleshy parts of the body. Then I arranged the body as a butcher does beef, and hacked it with an axe into pieces of a size to fit the grave which I had dug in the mountains. I would like to say that while opening the body I was so greedy that I trembled, and could have cut out a piece and eaten it."

---

1 Anthropophagy is another term for cannibalism.

Lombroso also mentions cases falling in the same category. A certain Philippe indulged in strangling prostitutes, after the sex act, and said: "I love women, but it is sport for me to strangle them after having enjoyed them."

A certain Grassi was one night seized with sexual desire for a female relative. Provoked by her resistance, he stabbed her several times in the abdomen with a knife, and also murdered her father and uncle who attempted to restrain him. Immediately thereafter he rushed to visit a prostitute in order to cool in her embrace his sexual passion. But this was not sufficient, for he then murdered his own father and slaughtered several oxen in the stable.

It cannot be doubted, from the example above, that a great number of so-called lust murders depend upon a combination of excessive and perverted desire. As a result of this perverse state of mind, further acts of bestiality with the corpse may result—e.g., cutting it up and bur- rowing lustfully into the intestines. The case of Bichel points to this possibility....

CASE 16. An English clerk called Alton went for a walk out of town. He lured a child into the bushes and a short while later returned to his office and made this entry in his note-book: "Killed a young girl today; it was fine and hot." The child was missed, searched for, and found cut into pieces. Many parts, including the genitals, could not be found. A. did not show the slightest trace of emotion, and gave no explanation of the motive or circumstances of his horrible deed. He was a psycho- pathic individual, and occasionally subject to fits of depression and boredom. His father had had an attack of acute mania. A near relative suffered from mania with homicidal impulses. A. was executed.

CASE 17. Jack the Ripper.—On December 1, 1887, July 7, August 7, September 8, September 30, in October and on the 9th of November, 1888; on the 1st of June, the 17th of July and the 10th of September, 1889, the bodies of women were found in various lonely quarters of London ripped open and mutilated in a peculiar fashion, without the murderer ever being found. It is likely that in a bestial sacrifice he first cut the throats of his victims, then ripped open the abdomen and groped among the intestines. In some instances he cut off the genitals and carried them away, apparently so that he could arouse himself later by looking at them; in others he only tore them to pieces and left them behind. He does not seem to have had sexual intercourse with his victims, but very likely the murderous act and subsequent mutila- tion of the corpse were equivalents for the sexual act.

6. *Punch* Cartoon (12 August 1882)

[A cartoon from Cassell's *Popular Educator* (1852) entitled "The Influence of Morality or Immorality on the Countenance" showed a young boy taking a path that leads either to school, marriage, and the respectable position of aged "head of a family," or through juvenile prison, vice, and drinking to "beggar." The cartoon showed a direct physical correlation between morality and the face, with the "beggar" portrayed as a hideous, misshapen monster. This *Punch* cartoon from August 1882 takes this idea and applies it to an M.P. who will either become a respectable M.P. like Sir Danvers Carew[1] or a hideous, bespectacled reprobate; Stevenson's story undermines the easy assumption that the signs of vice can be "read" in somebody's face as easily as this cartoon would suggest.]

---

1   The fictional M.P. murdered by Mr. Hyde in *Dr. Jekyll and Mr. Hyde.*

Appendix L: The Victorian Gentleman: Body and Clothing

[The term "gentleman" is ambiguous in *Jekyll and Hyde*. Mr. Hyde is referred to several times as a gentleman, and his clothing is certainly that of a man of the upper classes. However, both his body and his behaviour belie his apparent social status, which leads to the cognitive dissonance experienced by those who meet him on the streets of London. In his actions toward both the young child and Sir Danvers Carew, he contradicts Newman's famous definition of the gentleman as "one who never inflicts pain" (in *The Idea of a University* below). One of the most extensive commentaries on the contrast between Mr. Hyde's body and his clothes comes from Mr. Lanyon, who describes his clothes as being "of rich and sober fabric" but much too large for his small stature (72-73). The disparity incites a "disgustful curiosity" in Lanyon to uncover the mystery of this contradictory character before him; the revelation of the secret, of course, brings about his death.

The category of the "gentleman" was under pressure from two forces in the Victorian period: the shift from inherited, land-based wealth to capital acquired through industry, and the mass production of relatively cheap, ready-to-wear clothing. While figures such as Josiah Bounderby, the self-made man in Charles Dickens's *Hard Times* (1854), were parodied for pretending to be from lower social origins than in reality they were, the opposite situation was more cause for anxiety. *The Gentleman's Art of Dressing with Economy* (1876) expressed in breezy tones the effect of cheaper, mass produced clothing on class distinctions:

The cheap tailor of the day, aided by the sewing machine, has been a great reformer and leveller of class, breaking down the social distinction which formerly separated men in dress. At present it is impossible to distinguish a gentleman by his raiment only; and whatever gradations of rank may exist in this country, I consider it an advantage that *prima facie* all should appear equal, and entitled to class themselves as a gentleman, so far as outward and visible signs may go. Even to be mistaken for a gentleman may often give noble aspirations and induce a man to try to "behave as such." (*The Gentleman's Art of Dressing with Economy*, "by a Lounger at the Clubs" [London: Frederick Warne & Co, 1876], ix)

This manual takes the approach that "clothes make the man" and assumes that expensive-looking clothes being made available to people of modest means will lead to an erosion of class distinctions; however, in a society where class distinctions were often seen as biological rather than socially constructed categories, the possibility of "passing" as a gentleman simply because of one's clothing would be deeply subversive. As Mr. Hyde's case shows, class was as much a question of the body as of clothing. While his clothing was that of a gentleman, his body belied a much lower social class.

Stevenson contributed two essays on the topic of gentlemen to *Scribner's Magazine* in May and June of 1888, the first entitled "Gentlemen," which was followed by "Some Gentlemen in Fiction" in the next issue. Stevenson's most relevant commentaries on the connections between class, clothing, and the body, however, come obliquely in two essays. In "The Philosophy of Umbrellas" he begins by asserting that umbrellas, in contrast to faces, reveal a great deal of information about the bearer and that a glance at the contents of the umbrella-stand will betray the social pretentions of the owner. Stevenson then complicates matters by asserting that there can be a "mendacious umbrella" signalling hypocrisy in the bearer. As is usual with his essays, he leaves much unresolved here about the class status of umbrellas.

In his "The Character of Dogs" Stevenson discusses class distinctions indirectly through animals. His dogs sound like those portrayed in such Landseer paintings as "Dignity and Impudence" and "Comical Dogs"; the dogs express as much about human social attitudes as they do about their ostensible animal subject. The dog, according to Stevenson, is a "gentleman of leisure" and "to follow for ten minutes in the street some swaggering, canine cavalier, is to receive a lesson in dramatic art and culture conduct of the body." The "conduct of the body" in dogs as well as humans is a class marker that betrays Mr. Hyde as somebody who should not be wearing the clothes of a gentleman.]

1. From Robert Louis Stevenson, "Gentlemen," *Scribner's Magazine* 3 (May 1888): 635–40

[In this extract from the longer essay, Stevenson initially asserts that everyone knows what the word "gentlemen" means, but then later suggests that it has become a hollow term.]

[...] And yet, for all this ambiguity, for all these imperfect examples, we know clearly what we mean by the word. When we meet a gentleman of another class, though all contrariety of habits, the essentials of the matter stand confessed: I never had a doubt of Jones. More than that, we recognize the type in books; the actors of history, the characters of fiction, bear the mark upon their brow; at a word, by a bare act, we discern and segregate the mass, this one a gentleman, the others not. [...]

More and more, as our knowledge widens, we have to reply to those who ask for a definition: "I can't give you that, but I will tell you a story." We cannot say what a thing will be, nor what it ought to be; but we can say what it has been, and how it came to be what it is: History instead of Definition. It is this which (if we continue teachable) will make short work of all political theories; it is on this we must fall back to explain our word, gentleman.

The life of our fathers was highly ceremonial; a man's steps were counted; his acts and gestures were prescribed; marriage, sale, adoption, and not only legal contracts, but the simplest necessary movements, must be all conventionally ordered and performed to rule. Life was a rehearsed piece; and only those who had been drilled in the rehearsals could appear with decency in the performance. A gentile man, one of a dominant race, hereditary priest, hereditary leader, was, by the circumstances of his birth and education, versed in this symbolic etiquette ... With the decay of the ceremonial element in life, the gentleman has lost some of his prestige, I had nearly said some of his importance; and yet his part is the more difficult to play. It is hard to preserve the figures of a dance when many of our partners dance at random. It is easy to be a gentleman in a very stiff society, where much of our action is prescribed; it is hard indeed in a very free society where (as it seems) almost any word or act must come by inspiration. The rehearsed piece is at an end; we are now floundering through an impromptu charade [...]

2. From Robert Louis Stevenson, "Some Gentlemen in Fiction," *Scribner's Magazine* 3 (June 1888): 764–68

[In this extract from his second essay for the magazine, Stevenson identifies gentlemen in stories by Charles Dickens.]

Just the other day, there were again two rival novelists in England: Thackeray and Dickens;[1] and the case of the last is, in this connection, full of interest. Here was a man and an artist, the most strenuous, one of the most endowed; and for how many years he labored in vain to create a gentleman! With all his watchfulness of men and manners, with all his fiery industry, with his exquisite native gift of characterization, with his clear knowledge of what he meant to do, there was yet

---

1   Two of the best-known novelists of the era, William Makepeace Thackeray (1811–63) and Charles Dickens (1812–70).

something lacking. In part after part, novel after novel, a whole menagerie of characters, the good, the bad, the droll and the tragic, came at his beck like slaves about an oriental despot; there was only one who stayed away: the gentleman. If this ill fortune had persisted it might have shaken man's belief in art and industry. But years were given and courage was continued to the indefatigable artist; and at length, after so many and such lamentable failures, success began to attend upon his arms. David Copperfield scrambled through on hands and knees; it was at least a negative success; and Dickens, keenly alive to all he did, must have heaved a sigh of infinite relief. Then came the evil days, the days of Dombey and Dorrit,[1] from which the lover of Dickens willingly averts his eyes; and when that temporary blight has passed away, and the artist began with a more resolute arm to reap the aftermath of his genius, we find him able to create a Carton, a Wrayburn, a Twemlow.[2] No mistake about these three; they are all gentlemen; the Scottish Carton, the effete Twemlow, the insolent Wrayburn, all have doubled the cape.[3]

3. From Robert Louis Stevenson, "The Philosophy of Umbrellas," in *Lay Morals and Other Papers* (London: Chatto and Windus, 1911), 139–45

It is wonderful to think what a turn has been given to our whole Society by the fact that we live under the sign of Aquarius—that our climate is essentially wet. A mere arbitrary distinction, like the walking-swords of yore, might have remained the symbol of foresight and respectability, had not the raw mists and dropping showers of our island pointed the inclination of Society to another exponent of those virtues. A ribbon of the Legion of Honour[4] or a string of medals may prove a person's courage; a title may prove his birth; a professorial chair his study and acquirement; but it is the habitual carriage of the umbrella that is the stamp of Respectability. The umbrella has become the acknowledged index of social position.

---

1 Dickens's novels *David Copperfield* (1850), *Dombey and Son* (1848), and *Little Dorrit* (1855–57).

2 Sydney Carton, the central character of *A Tale of Two Cities* (1859), Eugene Wrayburn, a character in *Our Mutual Friend* (1865), and Melvin Twemlow, also a character in *Our Mutual Friend*.

3 The Cape of Good Hope was notoriously dangerous for vessels, so "doubling" or successfully clearing the Cape means a noteworthy achievement.

4 The *Ordre national de la Légion d'honneur* is the highest decoration in France.

Robinson Crusoe[1] presents us with a touching instance of the hankering after them inherent in the civilised and educated mind. To the superficial, the hot suns of Juan Fernandez[2] may sufficiently account for his quaint choice of a luxury; but surely one who had borne the hard labour of a seaman under the tropics for all these years could have supported an excursion after goats or a peaceful *constitutional* arm in arm with the nude Friday.[3] No, it was not this: the memory of a vanished respectability called for some outward manifestation, and the result was—an umbrella. A pious castaway might have rigged up a belfry and solaced his Sunday mornings with the mimicry of church-bells; but Crusoe was rather a moralist than a pietist, and his leaf-umbrella is as fine an example of the civilised mind striving to express itself under adverse circumstances as we have ever met with.

It is not for nothing, either, that the umbrella has become the very foremost badge of modern civilisation—the Urim and Thummim[4] of respectability. Its pregnant symbolism has taken its rise in the most natural manner. Consider, for a moment, when umbrellas were first introduced into this country, what manner of men would use them, and what class would adhere to the useless but ornamental cane. The first, without doubt, would be the hypochondriacal, out of solicitude for their health, or the frugal, out of care for their raiment; the second, it is equally plain, would include the fop, the fool, and the Bobadil.[5] Any one acquainted with the growth of Society, and knowing out of what small seeds of cause are produced great revolutions, and wholly new conditions of intercourse, sees from this simple thought how the carriage of an umbrella came to indicate frugality, judicious regard for bodily welfare, and scorn for mere outward adornment, and, in one word, all those homely and solid virtues implied in the term RESPECTABIL-ITY. Not that the umbrella's costliness has nothing to do with its great influence. Its possession, besides symbolising (as we have already indicated) the change from wild Esau to plain Jacob dwelling in tents,[6] implies a certain comfortable provision of fortune. It is not every one that can expose twenty-six shillings' worth of property to so many

---

1 Daniel Defoe's *Robinson Crusoe* (1719), in which the castaway makes an umbrella for himself and declares that it makes him a gentleman.
2 The Juan Fernandez Islands are in the South Pacific Ocean.
3 Friday is the name Crusoe gives to his sole companion on the island, named for the day of the week in which they meet.
4 A device used in biblical accounts to distinguish the sinners from the just.
5 A cowardly and boastful person, named after Captain Bobadil, a character in Ben Jonson's *Every Man in His Humour* (1637).
6 In the Book of Genesis Jacob is forced to live in the wild when his brother Esau takes over his tents and livestock.

chances of loss and theft. So strongly do we feel on this point, indeed, that we are almost inclined to consider all who possess really well-conditioned umbrellas as worthy of the Franchise. They have a qualification standing in their lobbies; they carry a sufficient stake in the commonweal below their arm. One who bears with him an umbrella—such a complicated structure of whalebone, of silk, and of cane, that it becomes a very microcosm of modern industry—is necessarily a man of peace. A half-crown cane may be applied to an offender's head on a very moderate provocation; but a six-and-twenty shilling silk is a possession too precious to be adventured in the shock of war.

These are but a few glances at how umbrellas (in the general) came to their present high estate. But the true Umbrella-Philosopher meets with far stranger applications as he goes about the streets.

Umbrellas, like faces, acquire a certain sympathy with the individual who carries them: indeed, they are far more capable of betraying his trust; for whereas a face is given to us so far ready made, and all our power over it is in frowning, and laughing, and grimacing, during the first three or four decades of life, each umbrella is selected from a whole shopful, as being most consonant to the purchaser's disposition. An undoubted power of diagnosis rests with the practised Umbrella-Philosopher. O you who lisp, and amble, and change the fashion of your countenances—you who conceal all these, how little do you think that you left a proof of your weakness in our umbrella-stand—that even now, as you shake out the folds to meet the thickening snow, we read in its ivory handle the outward and visible sign of your snobbery, or from the exposed gingham of its cover detect, through coat and waistcoat, the hidden hypocrisy of the '*dickey*'![1] But alas! even the umbrella is no certain criterion. The falsity and the folly of the human race have degraded that graceful symbol to the ends of dishonesty; and while some umbrellas, from carelessness in selection, are not strikingly characteristic (for it is only in what a man loves that he displays his real nature), others, from certain prudential motives, are chosen directly opposite to the person's disposition. A mendacious umbrella is a sign of great moral degradation. Hypocrisy naturally shelters itself below a silk; while the fast youth goes to visit his religious friends armed with the decent and reputable gingham. May it not be said of the bearers of these inappropriate umbrellas that they go about the streets "with a lie in their right hand"?[2] [...]

---

1 A false, short shirt-front that looks like a full shirt but is made of cardboard or celluloid.
2 Isaiah 44:20: "He feedeth on ashes: a deceived heart hath turned him aside, that he cannot deliver his soul, nor say, 'Is there not a lie in my right hand?'"

4. From Robert Louis Stevenson, "The Character of Dogs," in *Memories and Portraits* (London: Chatto and Windus, 1887), 178–98

The civilisation, the manners, and the morals of dog-kind are to a great extent subordinated to those of his ancestral master, man. This animal, in many ways so superior, has accepted a position of inferiority, shares the domestic life, and humours the caprices of the tyrant. But the potentate, like the British in India, pays small regard to the character of his willing client, judges him with listless glances, and condemns him in a byword. Listless have been the looks of his admirers, who have exhausted idle terms of praise, and buried the poor soul below exaggerations. And yet more idle and, if possible, more unintelligent has been the attitude of his express detractors; those who are very fond of dogs "but in their proper place"; who say "poo' fellow, poo' fellow," and are themselves far poorer; who whet the knife of the vivisectionist or heat his oven; who are not ashamed to admire "the creature's instinct"; and flying far beyond folly, have dared to resuscitate the theory of animal machines.[1] The "dog's instinct" and the "automaton-dog," in this age of psychology and science, sound like strange anachronisms. An automaton he certainly is; a machine working independently of his control, the heart, like the mill-wheel, keeping all in motion, and the consciousness, like a person shut in the mill garret, enjoying the view out of the window and shaken by the thunder of the stones; an automaton in one corner of which a living spirit is confined: an automaton like man. Instinct again he certainly possesses. Inherited aptitudes are his, inherited frailties. Some things he at once views and understands, as though he were awakened from a sleep, as though he came "trailing clouds of glory."[2] But with him, as with man, the field of instinct is limited; its utterances are obscure and occasional; and about the far larger part of life both the dog and his master must conduct their steps by deduction and observation.

The leading distinction between dog and man, after and perhaps before the different duration of their lives, is that the one can speak and that the other cannot. The absence of the power of speech confines the dog in the development of his intellect. It hinders him from many speculations, for words are the beginning of metaphysic. At the same blow it saves him from many superstitions, and his silence has won for him

---

1 French philosopher René Descartes (1596–1650) posited that animals were machines, a theory that was revived in the nineteenth century.

2 "Trailing clouds of glory do we come / From God, who is our home": William Wordsworth, "Ode: Intimations of Immortality" 65-66 (1807).

a higher name for virtue than his conduct justifies. The faults of the dog are many. He is vainer than man, singularly greedy of notice, singularly intolerant of ridicule, suspicious like the deaf, jealous to the degree of frenzy, and radically devoid of truth. The day of an intelligent small dog is passed in the manufacture and the laborious communication of falsehood; he lies with his tail, he lies with his eye, he lies with his protesting paw; and when he rattles his dish or scratches at the door his purpose is other than appears. But he has some apology to offer for the vice. Many of the signs which form his dialect have come to bear an arbitrary meaning, clearly understood both by his master and himself; yet when a new want arises he must either invent a new vehicle of meaning or wrest an old one to a different purpose; and this necessity frequently recurring must tend to lessen his idea of the sanctity of symbols. Meanwhile the dog is clear in his own conscience, and draws, with a human nicety, the distinction between formal and essential truth. Of his punning perversions, his legitimate dexterity with symbols, he is even vain; but when he has told and been detected in a lie, there is not a hair upon his body but confesses guilt. To a dog of gentlemanly feeling, theft and falsehood are disgraceful vices. The canine, like the human gentleman, demands in his misdemeanours Montaigne's "*je ne sais quoi de genereux.*"[1] He is never more than half ashamed of having barked or bitten; and for those faults into which he has been led by the desire to shine before a lady of his race, he retains, even under physical correction, a share of pride. But to be caught lying, if he understands it, instantly uncurls his fleece.

Just as among dull observers he preserves a name for truth, the dog has been credited with modesty. It is amazing how the use of language blunts the faculties of man—that because vainglory finds no vent in words, creatures supplied with eyes have been unable to detect a fault so gross and obvious. If a small spoiled dog were suddenly to be endowed with speech, he would prate interminably, and still about himself; when we had friends, we should be forced to lock him in a garret; and what with his whining jealousies and his foible for false-hood, in a year's time he would have gone far to weary out our love. I was about to compare him to Sir Willoughby Patterne,[2] but the Pat-ternes have a manlier sense of their own merits; and the parallel, besides, is ready. Hans Christian Andersen,[3] as we behold him in his

---

1   Michel de Montaigne (1533–92), famous French essayist; the French could be glossed as "a certain generosity."

2   Sir Willoughby Patterne is the self-absorbed central character in George Meredith's *The Egoist* (1879).

3   Danish author (1805–75) best known in English for his children's stories. His *The Fairy Tale of My Life: An Autobiography* (1863) shows his belief in his own genius.

startling memoirs, thrilling from top to toe with an excruciating vanity, and scouting even along the street for shadows of offence—here was the talking dog.

It is just this rage for consideration that has betrayed the dog into his satellite position as the friend of man. The cat, an animal of franker appetites, preserves his independence. But the dog, with one eye ever on the audience, has been wheedled into slavery, and praised and patted into the renunciation of his nature. Once he ceased hunting and became man's plate-licker, the Rubicon was crossed.[1] Thenceforth he was a gentleman of leisure; and except the few whom we keep working, the whole race grew more and more self-conscious, mannered and affected. The number of things that a small dog does naturally is strangely small. Enjoying better spirits and not crushed under material cares, he is far more theatrical than average man. His whole life, if he be a dog of any pretension to gallantry, is spent in a vain show, and in the hot pursuit of admiration. Take out your puppy for a walk, and you will find the little ball of fur clumsy, stupid, bewildered, but natural. Let but a few months pass, and when you repeat the process you will find nature buried in convention. He will do nothing plainly; but the simplest processes of our material life will all be bent into the forms of an elaborate and mysterious etiquette. Instinct, says the fool, has awakened. But it is not so. Some dogs—some, at the very least—if they be kept separate from others, remain quite natural; and these, when at length they meet with a companion of experience, and have the game explained to them, distinguish themselves by the severity of their devotion to its rules. I wish I were allowed to tell a story which would radiantly illuminate the point; but men, like dogs, have an elaborate and mysterious etiquette. It is their bond of sympathy that both are the children of convention.

The person, man or dog, who has a conscience is eternally condemned to some degree of humbug; the sense of the law in their members fatally precipitates either towards a frozen and affected bearing. And the converse is true; and in the elaborate and conscious manners of the dog, moral opinions and the love of the ideal stand confessed. To follow for ten minutes in the street some swaggering, canine cavalier, is to receive a lesson in dramatic art and the cultured conduct of the body; in every act and gesture you see him true to a refined conception; and the dullest cur, beholding him, pricks up his ear and proceeds to imitate and parody that charming ease. For to be a high-mannered and high-minded gentleman, careless, affable, and gay, is the inborn pretension of the dog. The large dog, so much lazier, so much more weighed upon with matter, so majestic in repose, so

---

1 To "cross the Rubicon" means to reach a point of no return.

beautiful in effort, is born with the dramatic means to wholly represent the part. And it is more pathetic and perhaps more instructive to consider the small dog in his conscientious and imperfect efforts to outdo Sir Philip Sidney.[1] For the ideal of the dog is feudal and religious; the ever-present polytheism, the whip-bearing Olympus of mankind, rules them on the one hand; on the other, their singular difference of size and strength among themselves effectually prevents the appearance of the democratic notion. Or we might more exactly compare their society to the curious spectacle presented by a school— ushers, monitors, and big and little boys—qualified by one circumstance, the introduction of the other sex. In each, we should observe a somewhat similar tension of manner, and somewhat similar points of honour. In each the larger animal keeps a contemptuous good humour; in each the smaller annoys him with wasp-like impudence, certain of practical immunity; in each we shall find a double life producing double characters, and an excursive and noisy heroism combined with a fair amount of practical timidity. I have known dogs, and I have known school heroes that, set aside the fur, could hardly have been told apart; and if we desire to understand the chivalry of old, we must turn to the school playfields or the dungheap where the dogs are trooping.

Woman, with the dog, has been long enfranchised. Incessant massacre of female innocents has changed the proportions of the sexes and perverted their relations. Thus, when we regard the manners of the dog, we see a romantic and monogamous animal, once perhaps as delicate as the cat, at war with impossible conditions. Man has much to answer for; and the part he plays is yet more damnable and parlous than Corin's in the eyes of Touchstone.[2] But his intervention has at least created an imperial situation for the rare surviving ladies. In that society they reign without a rival: conscious queens; and in the only instance of a canine wife-beater that has ever fallen under my notice, the criminal was somewhat excused by the circumstances of his story. He is a little, very alert, well-bred, intelligent Skye,[3] as black as a hat, with a wet bramble for a nose and two cairngorms for eyes.[4] To the human observer, he is decidedly well-looking; but to the ladies of his

---

1 English poet, courtier, and soldier (1554–86).

2 Characters in Shakespeare's *As You Like It* (1623).

3 Skye terriers are short-legged with a long topcoat. The dog in the *Punch* cartoon below is a terrier, but of indeterminate breed.

4 The Cairngorms are Scottish mountains; the hair of a Skye terrier covers its eyes with a flowing coat, making them look like the slopes of mountains.

race he seems abhorrent. A thorough elaborate gentleman, of the plume and sword-knot order, he was born with a nice sense of gallantry to women. He took at their hands the most outrageous treatment; I have heard him bleating like a sheep, I have seen him streaming blood, and his ear tattered like a regimental banner; and yet he would scorn to make reprisals. Nay more, when a human lady upraised the contumelious[1] whip against the very dame who had been so cruelly misusing him, my little great-heart gave but one hoarse cry and fell upon the tyrant tooth and nail. This is the tale of a soul's tragedy. After three years of unavailing chivalry, he suddenly, in one hour, threw off the yoke of obligation; had he been Shakespeare he would then have written *Troilus and Cressida* to brand the offending sex; but being only a little dog, he began to bite them. The surprise of the ladies whom he attacked indicated the monstrosity of his offence; but he had fairly beaten off his better angel, fairly committed moral suicide; for almost in the same hour, throwing aside the last rags of decency, he proceeded to attack the aged also. The fact is worth remark, showing, as it does, that ethical laws are common both to dogs and men; and that with both a single deliberate violation of the conscience loosens all. "But while the lamp holds on to burn," says the paraphrase, "the greatest sinner may return."[2] I have been cheered to see symptoms of effectual penitence in my sweet ruffian; and by the handling that he accepted uncomplainingly the other day from an indignant fair one, I begin to hope the period of *Sturm und Drang*[3] is closed [...]

---

1 Scornful or insolent.
2 Isaac Watts (1674–1748), from *Hymns and Spiritual Songs* (1773): "And while the lamp holds out to burn, the vilest sinner may return."
3 The literal German means "storm and drive (or stress)," usually used in English to mean turmoil.

5. "The Grand Old Name of <u>Gentleman</u>," *Punch* (21 January 1888)[1]

"THE GRAND OLD NAME OF GENTLEMAN."

"Beg pardon, Mister, but what particklar *Breed* might yee be callin' this 'ere little Dawg o' yourn! You'll accuse me askin', Gov'ner'; but Me and *another Gentleman* 'ere 'as just been 'avin a small Bet about it!"

Disgust of Montmorency De Vere Snobly, who always described himself as a Gentleman.

---

1 Text courtesy of George P. Landow and the Victorian Web, the internet Archive and the University of Toronto Library.

6. From John Henry Newman, *The Idea of a University Defined and Illustrated: In Nine Discourses Delivered to the Catholics of Dublin* (1854; Project Gutenberg, 2008)

[In this classic definition of the "gentleman," noted essayist and theologian John Henry, Cardinal Newman (1801–90), describes the ideal in negative terms by what he does not do, rather than how he should act. A gentleman does not draw attention to himself and makes all around him comfortable in his presence. This presents a complete contrast to the effect of Mr. Hyde on the people he meets.]

Hence it is that it is almost a definition of a gentleman to say that he is one who never inflicts pain. This description is both refined and, as far as it goes, accurate. He is mainly occupied in merely removing the obstacles which hinder the free and unembarrassed action of those about him; and he concurs with their movements rather than takes the initiative himself. His benefits may be considered as parallel to what are called comforts or conveniences in arrangements of a personal nature; like an easy chair or a good fire, which do their part in dispelling cold and fatigue, though nature provides both means of rest and animal heat without them. The true gentleman in like manner carefully avoids whatever may cause a jar or a jolt in the minds of those with whom he is cast—all clashing of opinion, or collision of feeling, all restraint, or suspicion, or gloom, or resentment; his great concern being to make every one at his ease and at home. He has his eyes on all his company; he is tender towards the bashful, gentle towards the distant, and merciful towards the absurd; he can recollect to whom he is speaking; he guards against unseasonable allusions, or topics which may irritate; he is seldom prominent in conversation, and never wearisome. He makes light of favours while he does them, and seems to be receiving when he is conferring. He never speaks of himself except when compelled, never defends himself by a mere retort; he has no ears for slander or gossip, is scrupulous in imputing motives to those who interfere with him, and interprets everything for the best. He is never mean or little in his disputes, never takes unfair advantage, never mistakes personalities or sharp saying for arguments, or insinuates evil which he dare not say out. From a long-sighted prudence, he observes the maxim of the ancient sage, that we should ever conduct ourselves towards our enemy as if he were one day to be our friend. He has too much good sense to be affronted at insults, he is too well employed to remember injuries, and too indolent to bear malice. He is patient, forbearing, and resigned, on philosophical principles; he submits to pain, because it is inevitable, to bereavement, because it is irreparable, and to death, because it is his destiny.

If he engages in controversy of any kind, his disciplined intellect preserves him from the blundering discourtesy of better, perhaps, but less educated minds; who, like blunt weapons, tear and hack instead of cutting clean, who mistake the point in argument, waste their strength on trifles, misconceive their adversary, and leave the question more involved than they find it. He may be right or wrong in his opinion, but he is too clear-headed to be unjust; he is as simple as he is forcible, and as brief as he is decisive. Nowhere shall we find greater candour, consideration, indulgence: he throws himself into the minds of his opponents, he accounts for their mistakes. He knows the weakness of human reason as well as its strength, its province and its limits.

If he be an unbeliever, he will be too profound and large-minded to ridicule religion or to act against it; he is too wise to be a dogmatist or fanatic in his infidelity. He respects piety and devotion; he even supports institutions as venerable, beautiful, or useful, to which he does not assent; he honours the ministers of religion, and it contents him to decline its mysteries without assailing or denouncing them. He is a friend of religious toleration, and that, not only because his philosophy has taught him to look on all forms of faith with an impartial eye, but also from the gentleness and effeminacy of feeling, which is the attendant on civilization [...]

It is well to be a gentlemen, it is well to have a cultivated intellect, a delicate taste, a candid, equitable, dispassionate mind, a noble and courteous bearing in the conduct of life;—these are the connatural qualities of a large knowledge; they are the objects of a University; I am advocating, I shall illustrate and insist upon them; but still, I repeat, they are no guarantee for sanctity or even for conscientiousness, they may attach to the man of the world, to the profligate, to the heartless,—pleasant, alas, and attractive as he shows when decked out in them. Taken by themselves, they do but seem to be what they are not; they look like virtue at a distance, but they are detected by close observers, and on the long run; and hence it is that they are popularly accused of pretence and hypocrisy, not, I repeat, from their own fault, but because their professors and their admirers persist in taking them for what they are not, and are officious in arrogating for them a praise to which they have no claim. Quarry the granite rock with razors, or moor the vessel with a thread of silk; then may you hope with such keen and delicate instruments as human knowledge and human reason to contend against those giants, the passion and the pride of man.

7. **From John Ruskin, Letter to Miss Constance Oldham, 9 April 1876, in** *The Works of John Ruskin: Library Edition,* **vol. 37, ed. E.T. Cook and A. Wedderburn (London: George Allen, 1909), 197**

[Where Newman emphasizes the behaviour of the gentleman, John Ruskin (1819–1900), in this much quoted letter, initially emphasizes lineage and breeding, before moving on to how such a man should behave.]

... For C.'s debate with you, the *essence* is what the word says, that he comes of a pure *gens*, or is perfectly bred. After that, training in the accomplishments of his time, and to the highest point. A certain quality of self-restraint is generally a result of all this, but it is quite possible to be a passionate pilgrim and yet a gentleman. Ulysses is not more a gentleman than Achilles,[1] and Claverhouse[2] is only more of a gentleman than Fergus MacIvor,[3] not because his countenance never shows his emotion, but because all his emotions are unselfish and his principles honourable...... [ellipses in source text; emphases Ruskin's]

8. **From R.H. Hutton, "The Clothes of the Mind,"** *Spectator* **(2 March 1867): 237–38**

[Richard Holt Hutton (1826–97) was one of the best-known journalists and essayists of his day, although he is now infrequently studied. He was particularly noted for his discussions of both religion and contemporary philosophy in such publications as *Essays, Theological and Literary* (2 vols., 1871) and *Criticisms on Contemporary Thought and Thinkers* (2 vols., 1894). In this essay he uses a review of the German actor Ernst Schulz's performance, in which he changed his expression and outfits to portray 48 different characters in 96 minutes, to raise questions about how the body can be used as a disguise. Hutton's review voices concern over the possibility of a disjuncture between facial expression and emotion, which he finds unsettling. Mr. Utterson avoids the theatre for reasons that are not spelled out in the text; Victorians, because of their emphasis on sincerity and earnestness (parodied by Oscar Wilde in *The Importance of Being Earnest* [1895]), had a general distrust of playacting and it may be for this reason that Mr. Utterson avoided the stage. The images of Schulz reproduced

---

1 Achilles and Odysseus are Greek heroes in Homer's epic poem the *Iliad.*
2 John Graham of Claverhouse (1648–89) was a Scottish nobleman and soldier and the subject of a poem by Sir Walter Scott.
3 A character in Sir Walter Scott's novel *Waverley* (1814).

below come from Charles Darwin's notebooks for *The Expression of the Emotions in Man and Animals* (1872), where he drew on them as examples of different human emotions. The notebooks are now part of the Darwin Collection in Cambridge University Library, England.]

Ernst Schulz Studio Portraits

Anyone who has seen the forty eight utterly different transformations through which the young German's sensible, observant, slightly humorous, not otherwise very remarkable face passes in the course of the ninety six minutes or so during which the entertainment lasts—

just one transformation for every two minutes of time—will be dull if he does not begin asking himself a dozen different and not very easily answerable questions on the secret of mental clothes, the mode in which one and the same mind, in one and the same body, manages to assume and throw off this immense variety of widely separated moral costumes, ranging from the stupid, pudgy pride of the wealthy English Philistine, to the wild animal pride, deeply seamed with animal cares, of the Red Indian Chief. Of course in such a character as the Chief of the Fox Indians Mr. Schulz gives himself the help of a head-dress and costume but in several of the changes through which his face passes, there is absolutely no alteration even in the arrangement of his hair, the whole transformation being due to the alteration in the attitude and lines of his face, the altered curve of the eyebrows and the lips, the angle at which the head is held, or thrown back or forwards, and the lines, deep or shallow, into which he ploughs his pliant countenance [...]

It is curious to notice how much of our natural interpretation of the meaning of certain lines and attitudes of the face depends not so much on those lines and attitudes themselves, as on the context in which we find them, and which is made to suggest to us an interpretation of its own. In one part of his entertainment Mr. Schulz takes a framework of painted cardboard, or some substance of that nature, representing various head-dresses, such as a monthly nurse's, a scolding elderly female's in a bonnet with yellow strings, a fascinating spinster's "of a certain age," and so forth, and frames his own face in it, so as to give a new marginal gloss or commentary as it were to the very same attitudes of face which he has before presented to us under no such disguise. The same thing is done later in the evening by the use of real head-dresses—turbans, feathers, &c. In each case the observer, preoccupied and retained as it were in favour of a special interpretation by the associations connected with the headdress, whether painted or real, construes the very same lines and expressions of countenance which seemed to say one thing when they stood alone, into quite a different meaning when he is prejudiced by this external commentary. Thus two of Mr. Schulz's representations are really, if you compare the countenances alone—the mere lines and expressions of the face—precisely alike—the one which he calls, we think, "the genial man," and in which he is unaided by adventitious costume and framework, and the one in which he represents the amiable spinster whom he calls Miss Evelina Matilda Peablossom. Put your hand over the hair and neck-tie of the photograph of the one, and over the ringlets and lace of the photograph of the other, and precisely the same features in precisely the same posture, and lined with precisely the same lines, remain yet while the one picture seems to express a self-satisfied smirk of self-love overflowing into general approbation and good humour, the other seems to express a (rather vulgar) admiration felt for another, overflowing into a certain limited measure of humble-satis-faction with herself. The long ringlets are alone answerable for this dif-ference of impression. Long ringlets so uniformly plead for approba-tion, and are so expressive not of self-confidence, but of plaintive requests for admiration, that they put a new gloss on the smirk of the features, and turn it from the excess of self-esteem into the imploring hope of female vanity that it has not quite failed.

The least interesting and yet perhaps most popular part of the entertainment is the exhibition of the various kinds of beards and moustaches which Mr. Schulz manages to exhibit by means of an optical apparatus, which casts the appearance of a very black beard or moustache of any shape he chooses, on his face, from which it vanishes again at a touch like a shadow of a cloud on the appearance of the sun. The only intellectual interest this part of the exhibition has, is not in itself—for there is nothing but the novelty of the optical delusion which is its method to distinguish it from the disguising effect of false beards and moustaches in which none but children would take much interest—but in the illustration it gives us of the absolute externality of the whole machinery of expression. When you see the great, rough, black "democratic beard," as Mr. Schulz calls it, cloud the air for a moment with a shadowy flicker, and then settle in a solid grove on the face, and again at a touch dissipate into the air and leave it as white and pale as ever, we can scarcely help realizing not only that the special gleams of expression which Mr. Schulz brings and banishes at pleasure are equally shadows, and still more of intellectual shadows, but that the mind sits as loose to the mechanism of expression, worked through the movement of its own features, as it does to that worked by casting external shadows upon the face, or masking itself in actual cos-tumes. When Mr. Schulz, in imitating "the pious man," makes himself—no doubt without knowing it—look so absurdly like Lord Shaftesbury[1] in a moment of lugubrious devotion, or, in imitating "the melancholy man," makes himself the image of an acquaintance of ours who was once melancholy mad, it is impossible not to fancy that Mr. Schulz might, if he pleased, almost live one distinct life in his own mind, and quite a different apparent life in the external world that to himself he might be known, for instance, as a man never even for a moment content with his position, while to the world he might live as a man abounding in pride and self-elation or that to himself he might

---

1 Anthony Ashley-Cooper (1801–85), 7th Earl of Shaftesbury, British politician noted both for his campaigns for social reform and his religious beliefs; he had a rather severe and dour demeanour.

be known as an acute and vigilant observer, while he could seem to the world a model of absolute inanity. He makes us feel, at all events, that with him the expression assumed by the face is almost as voluntary as the costume assumed by the person, that he could as easily put on the one as the other, and become a Fox Indian to Fox Indians, or a monthly nurse to monthly nurses, as he can be a German physiognomist to his audience at the Egyptian Hall.[1] The most curious question which his entertainment suggests, is this: Has the character of each man a natural dress of its own beyond and over itself, as the body has? Is a certain costume of expression, which covers and conceals without properly disguising the true character, the natural clothing of a civilized mind, or is it the very character itself, the naked individual character, without dress of any sort, which should come out in the expression of sincere men? For our parts, we believe that just as it is natural with all civilized men to wear clothes, and clothes are not an insincerity, but a decency of the body—so that it is natural with all civilized minds to wear moral clothes—and that moral clothes, that is, moral lines of expression which express something more than mere individual man, moral lines of expression which, while they are individual enough to tell the intellectual stature, and the capacities, and the nature of the individual, still veil from the eye of others the inmost individuality—are not an insincerity or mask, but a decency of the mind. Mr. Schulz himself, while putting on all sorts of moral masks and dominoes[2] over his own personal moral costume, never took that off to show the absolute individual stripped of all moral conventions beneath. And the eras in any history or society when men are disposed to throw off all the national and conventional dress of character, as we may call it, and expose the naked individuality beneath, are usually eras of danger, revolution, and national shame.

---

1   An exhibition hall built in 1812 to house a collection of relics and curious objects.
2   A kind of hood worn during carnival in Venice, used here in the sense of a disguise.

Select Bibliography

Primary Texts

Dury, Richard. *The Annotated Dr. Jekyll and Mr. Hyde: Strange Case of Dr. Jekyll and Mr. Hyde*. Milan: A. Guerini, 1993.

——. *Strange Case of Dr. Jekyll and Mr. Hyde*. Edinburgh: Edinburgh UP, 2004.

Stevenson, Robert Louis. "The Character of Dogs." *The Works of Robert Louis Stevenson*. Vol. 9. Swanston Edition. London: Chatto and Windus, 1911. 105–15.

——. "Gentlemen." *Scribner's Magazine* 3 (May 1888): 635–40.

——. "The Philosophy of Umbrellas." *The Works of Robert Louis Stevenson*. Vol. 21. Edinburgh: Printed by T.A. Constable for Longmans Green & Co., 1896. 74–79.

——. "Some Gentlemen in Fiction." *Scribner's Magazine* 3 (June 1888): 764–68.

——. *Strange Case of Dr. Jekyll and Mr. Hyde*. London: Longmans, Green, and Co., 1886.

——. *Strange Case of Dr. Jekyll and Mr. Hyde*. New York: Scribner's, 1886.

——. *Strange Case of Dr. Jekyll and Mr. Hyde*. Ed. Sidney Colvin. New York: Scribner's, 1921.

——. *The Strange Case of Dr. Jekyll and Mr. Hyde and Other Stories*. Ed. Jenni Calder. Harmondsworth, UK: Penguin, 1979.

——. *Strange Case of Dr. Jekyll and Mr. Hyde*. Ed. Richard Drury. Edinburgh UP, 2004.

Veeder, William. "Collated Fractions of the Manuscript Drafts of *Strange Case of Dr. Jekyll and Mr. Hyde*." *Dr. Jekyll and Mr. Hyde after One Hundred Years*. Ed. William Veeder and Gordon Hirsch. Chicago: U of Chicago P, 1988. 14–58.

Wolf, Leonard. *The Essential Dr. Jekyll & Mr. Hyde: Including the Complete Novel*. New York: Plume, 1995.

Biographies

Balfour, Graham. *The Life of Robert Louis Stevenson*. 2 vols. New York: Scribner's, 1901.

Bell, Ian. *Dreams of Exile: Robert Louis Stevenson, A Biography*. New York: H. Holt, 1992.

Calder, Jenni. *RLS: A Life Study*. New York: Oxford UP, 1980.

Chesterton, G.K. *Robert Louis Stevenson*. New York: Dodd, Mead, & Co., 1928.

Daiches, David. *Robert Louis Stevenson*. Norfolk, CT: New Directions, 1947.

Daiches, Jenni. *Robert Louis Stevenson: A Life Study*. London: Hamish Hamilton, 1980.

Davies, Hunter. *The Teller of Tales: In Search of Robert Louis Stevenson*. London: Sinclair-Stevenson, 1994.

Furnas, J.C. *Voyage to Windward: The Life of Robert Louis Stevenson*. New York: William Sloane, 1951.

Gwynn, Stephen. *Robert Louis Stevenson*. London: Macmillan Publishing Co., 1939.

Hammerton, J.A. *Stevensoniana: An Anecdotal Life and Appreciation of Robert Louis Stevenson*. Edinburgh: John Grant, 1907.

Hammond, John R. *A Robert Louis Stevenson Chronology*. New York: St. Martin's Press, 1997.

Hellman, George S. *The True Stevenson: A Study in Clarification*. Boston: Little, Brown and Co., 1925.

Henley, W.E. "R.L.S." *Pall Mall Gazette* 25 (April 1901): 505–14.

Mackay, Margaret. *The Violent Friend: The Story of Mrs. Robert Louis Stevenson*. Garden City, NY: Doubleday and Co., 1968.

McLynn, Frank. J. *Robert Louis Stevenson: A Biography*. New York: Random House, 1993.

Osbourne, Lloyd. *An Intimate Portrait of R.L.S.* New York: Scribner's, 1924.

Sanchez, Nellie Van de Grift. *The Life of Mrs. Robert Louis Stevenson*. New York: Scribner's, 1920.

Terry, Reginald Charles. *Robert Louis Stevenson: Interviews and Recollections*. Iowa City: U of Iowa P, 1996.

Critical Studies

Abi-Ezzi, Nathalie. *The Double in the Fiction of R.L. Stevenson, Wilkie Collins, and Daphne du Maurier*. New York: Peter Lang, 2003.

Ambrosini, Richard, and Richard Dury, eds. *Robert Louis Stevenson: Writer of Boundaries*. Madison: U of Wisconsin P, 2006.

——. *European Stevenson*. Newcastle: Cambridge Scholars, 2009.

Arata, Stephen. *Fictions of Loss in the Victorian Fin de Siècle*. Cambridge: Cambridge UP, 1996.

Block, Ed, Jr. "James Sully, Evolutionary Psychology, and Late Victorian Gothic Fiction." *Victorian Studies* 25 (Summer 1982): 443–67.

Brantlinger, Patrick. *The Reading Lesson: The Threat of Mass Literacy in Nineteenth-Century British Fiction*. Bloomington, IN: Indiana UP, 1998.

Calder, Jenni, ed. *Stevenson and Victorian Scotland*. Edinburgh: Edinburgh UP, 1981.

——. *Robert Louis Stevenson: A Critical Celebration*. Totowa, NJ: Barnes & Noble Books, 1980.

——. *The Robert Louis Stevenson Companion*. Edinburgh: P. Harris, 1980.

Danahay, Martin A. *A Community of One: Masculine Autobiography and Autonomy in Nineteenth-Century Britain*. Albany, NY: State U of New York P, 1993.

Danahay, Martin A., and Alex Chisholm. *Jekyll and Hyde Dramatized*. Jefferson, NC: McFarland Press, 2004.

Dryden, Linda. *The Modern Gothic and Literary Doubles: Stevenson, Wilde, and Wells*. New York: Palgrave Macmillan, 2003.

Dryden, Linda, Stephen Arata, and Eric Massie, eds. *Robert Louis Stevenson and Joseph Conrad: Writers of Transition*. Lubbock, TX: Texas Tech UP, 2009.

Elwin, Malcolm. *The Strange Case of Robert Louis Stevenson*. London: Macdonald, 1950.

Geduld, Harry M., ed. *The Definitive Dr Jekyll and Mr Hyde Companion*. New York: Garland Publishing, 1983.

Halberstam, Judith. *Skin Shows: Gothic Horror and the Technology of Monsters*. Durham: Duke UP, 1995.

Heath, Stephen. "Psychopathia Sexualis: Stevenson's *Strange Case*." *Critical Quarterly* 28:1/2 (Spring/Summer 1986): 93–108.

Hennelly, Mark M., Jr. "Stevenson's 'Silent Symbols' of the 'Fatal Cross Roads' in *Dr. Jekyll and Mr. Hyde*." *Gothic* 1 (1979): 10–16.

Hubbard, Tom. *Seeking Mr. Hyde: Studies in Robert Louis Stevenson, Symbolism, Myth, and the Pre-Modern*. Frankfurt: Peter Lang, 1995.

Kanzer, Mark. "The Self-Analytic Literature of Robert Louis Stevenson." *Psychoanalysis and Culture*. Ed. George B. Wilbur and Warner Muensterberger. New York: International Universities Press, 1951. 425–35.

Keating, Peter. "The Fortunes of RLS." *Times Literary Supplement* (26 June 1981): 715–16.

Lang, Andrew. "Recollections of Robert Louis Stevenson." *Adventures Among Books*. London: Longmans, Green, and Co., 1903.

Maixner, Paul, ed. *Robert Louis Stevenson: The Critical Heritage*. London: Routledge and Kegan Paul, 1981.

McCracken-Fletcher, ed. *Approaches to Teaching the Works of Robert Louis Stevenson*. New York: Modern Language Association of America, 2013.

Miller, Karl. *Doubles: Studies in Literary History*. New York: Oxford UP, 1985.

Miyoshi, Masao. *The Divided Self*. New York: New York UP, 1969.

Moore, Grace. "Something to Hyde: The 'Strange Preference' of Henry Jekyll." *Victorian Crime, Madness and Sensation*. Ed. Andrew Maunder and Grace Moore. Aldershot: Ashgate, 2004.

Nabokov, Vladimir. "The Strange Case of Dr. Jekyll and Mr. Hyde." *Lectures on Literature*. Ed. Fredson Bowers. New York: Harcourt Brace Jovanovich, 1980. 179–206.

Noble, Andrew, ed. *Robert Louis Stevenson*. London: Vision P, 1983.

Nollen, Scott Allen. *Robert Louis Stevenson: Life, Literature, and the Silver Screen*. Jefferson, NC: McFarland & Co., 1994.

Pinkston, C. Alex, Jr. "The Stage Première of *Dr. Jekyll and Mr. Hyde*." *Nineteenth Century Theatre Research* 14:1/2 (1986): 21–44.

Reed, Thomas L., Jr. *The Transforming Draught: Jekyll and Hyde, Robert Louis Stevenson and the Victorian Alcohol Debate*. Jefferson, NC: McFarland, 2006.

Reid, Julia. *Robert Louis Stevenson, Science, and the Fin de Siècle*. London: Palgrave Macmillan, 2006.

Rogers, Robert. *Psychoanalytic Study of the Double in Literature*. Detroit: Wayne State UP, 1970.

Rose, Brian A. *Jekyll and Hyde Adapted: Dramatizations of Cultural Anxiety*. Westport, CT: Greenwood Press, 1996.

Saposnik, Irving S. *Robert Louis Stevenson*. New York: Twayne Publishers, 1974.

Schultz, Myron G. "The 'Strange Case' of Robert Louis Stevenson." *Journal of the American Medical Association* 216 (5 April 1971): 90–94.

Showalter, Elaine. *Sexual Anarchy: Gender and Culture at the Fin de Siècle*. Harmondsworth, UK: Penguin Books, 1990.

Swearingen, Roger G. *The Prose Writings of Robert Louis Stevenson*. Hamden, CT: Archon Books, 1980.

Swinnerton, Frank. *R.L. Stevenson: A Critical Study*. New York: George H. Doran, 1923.

Thomas, Ronald R. *Dreams of Authority: Freud and the Fictions of the Unconscious*. Ithaca, NY: Cornell UP, 1990.

Twitchell, James B. *Dreadful Pleasures*. New York: Oxford UP, 1985.

Tymms, Ralph. *Doubles in Literary Psychology*. Cambridge: Bowes and Bowes, 1949.

Veeder, William, and Gordon Hirsch, eds. *Dr. Jekyll and Mr. Hyde after One Hundred Years*. Chicago: U of Chicago P, 1988.

From the Publisher

A name never says it all, but the word "Broadview" expresses a good deal of the philosophy behind our company. We are open to a broad range of academic approaches and political viewpoints. We pay attention to the broad impact book publishing and book printing has in the wider world; for some years now we have used 100% recycled paper for most titles. Our publishing program is internationally oriented and broad-ranging. Our individual titles often appeal to a broad readership too; many are of interest as much to general readers as to academics and students.

Founded in 1985, Broadview remains a fully independent company owned by its shareholders—not an imprint or subsidiary of a larger multinational.

For the most accurate information on our books (including information on pricing, editions, and formats) please visit our website at www.broadviewpress.com. Our print books and ebooks are also available for sale on our site.

broadview press
www.broadviewpress.com

The interior of this book is printed on 100% recycled paper.